BIBLIOINTUITIVE

Bibliointuitive

Dear Ayse,
Books are magic!
Love, Amy Q Barker

AMY Q. BARKER

Bibliointuitive

Cover design by Charlie Alolkoy

www.amyqbarker.com

ISBN: 978-1-7353581-2-3
Library of Congress Control Number: 2021913302

Printed in the United States of America

For Sue Lynne

Biblio: When something happens in real life that's related to the current book you're reading

Bibliointuitive: When you have the sensory ability to receive a message in real life that's related to the current book you're reading

❧ PROLOGUE ❧
1983

TRACY DUMONT, THE BOSSIER OF THE TWINS, spoke into her walkie-talkie. "Breaker one-nine, breaker one-nine, can you hear me? Over."

A scratchy male voice replied, "Ten-four. I'm here. Is it time?"

"Yes, red rover, red rover, send number…eight over. Over."

"Over, over," he giggled. "That's two overs. Over."

Tracy rolled her eyes and said, "Steven! Pay attention. Are you ready? Over."

"Yes. Okay, I mean, ten-four. Sending number seven over. Over."

"Eight!" Tracy cried shrilly into the receiver.

"Ten-four! I mean eight!" Steven shouted back, then not knowing he still had his button pressed, said, "Dang, who cares? Seven, eight, ten, four, what does it matter? Jacob, pass me that remote control."

"Steven! I heard that!" Tracy hollered and then threw the walkie-talkie onto the couch.

Steven replied, "Sorry, babe. Here comes eight."

She shook her head and turned to the group in the shimmering darkness. "Okay, who has number eight?"

When no one replied, she grabbed a piece of paper out of her twin sister Tammy's hand. "Is it you?"

Tammy stammered, "No, I swear!"

Tracy sighed when she saw the number two and handed the paper back. She asked again, "Who has eight?"

I sat on the floor in the shadow of a Christmas tree, staring at the twinkle lights and brightly colored ornaments. I was trying to imagine being transported to another place and time. A mountain retreat, a log cabin in the woods, a snowy evening, a turkey dinner with all the fixings, a wall of books itching to be read by the light of the moon streaming through the frosted window, accompanied by a mug of hot chocolate with tiny white marshmallows floating languidly on the surface of the dark, swirling liquid.

The twins' parents insisted on a winter wonderland theme every year for their joint birthday. The house was a veritable North Pole, and the floorboards above our heads were shaking with the sounds of adult drinking, dancing, and laughter. As I sat in my secret bower, I scanned the cramped room and regarded fifteen giggling girls with turquoise makeup, teased hair, and sticky flavored lip gloss flanking an enchanted forest of Christmas trees. I heard the passel of boys in the room next door, where the Pac-Man and Asteroids arcade games were buzzing incessantly. I sighed, thinking the chances of me getting out of here before midnight were slim to none.

"Sarah?" Tracy asked, hunting down her next victim.

"Nope," Sarah answered, showing Tracy her number ten.

Tracy frowned. "Dina?"

Dina shook her head. Tracy looked around the room in the dim light, narrowing her eyes, finally landing on me. She walked over slowly and grabbed the piece of paper out of my hand. "Aha! Eight! Okay, Riley, you're up. Get in there."

I crouched down lower and gave her a pleading look. Tracy's response: "Oh no you don't. Come on." She grabbed me by the arm, forced me up, put a bandanna around my eyes, led me through the maze of trees, and pushed me into the closet, closing the door behind me. I stood inside the blackness, reaching around blindly, my hands landing on several shelves lined with plastic storage tubs and paint cans. I waited in the narrow space, my heart pounding and my palms sweating. After a minute or two, I heard a commotion outside. The door opened, and with a shove and a grunt, a boy was hurled into my arms, tall and broad-shouldered with the smell of ginger ale on his breath and snow on his coat. I gasped as he clamped onto my waist with both hands, his head falling against my shoulder.

He said to me with a smile in his voice, "Whoops, sorry. Hi there. Hang on."

He righted himself, let me go, turned toward the door, wrenching the door handle and hollering fruitlessly, "Hey! Unlock this door! You rats! Come on!"

The laughter outside rang in my ears. I could hear Tracy's voice above the din, "Seven minutes! And you know the rules: no taking off the blindfold, and no monkey business below the waist." I groaned as she cried one last sentiment over my thumping heart: "Have fun!"

I heard my co-captive turn to me and say, "Looks like we're stuck."

"I guess so," I whispered.

At first, we both stood apart quietly. Then he carefully placed his fingers around my arm. I didn't move. I felt the heat of his hand through my sweater. He laughed nervously, leaned in, and kissed the spot between my cheek and ear.

He said, "Sorry, missed. You okay?"

I nodded and then realized he couldn't see my nod, so I said softly, "Yes."

This time he tilted his head slightly and lowered his mouth to mine. It was a small touch, like the brush of a feather. I shivered as he took his hand off my arm and placed it on my back, pulling me to him. Then he kissed me again, but this kiss was soft and low and long and deep. It made my chest heave and my fingers tingle. I found myself sinking into him, wrapping my hands around his neck. After several moments, he pulled back, saying hoarsely, "One sec—let me get this coat off."

I let go and stood breathing hard as he feverishly detached himself from his coat and said with funny heated force, "That's better. Let's try that again." I laughed as he grabbed me in a strong embrace, covering my mouth with his. Suddenly it felt as if all external stimuli were banished and we were trapped on an island in the circle of an enchanted secret oasis. I had a sudden flash thought that saturated my mind and body: This is what it must feel like to be loved!

After a second to catch a wild, jagged breath of air, he continued until I felt my bones melting. Finally, with an unadulterated moan of joy, he quickly ripped off both of our bandannas, throwing them to the side with a flourish and lifting me off the ground in a tight embrace. The strength of this kiss was on the next level. I struggled to breathe, but I soon lost the urge to try, remaining suctioned to him in utter and complete abandon.

It was as if we were completely disconnected from reality. I was fifteen years old and had never been kissed before. I now thought with absolute shock and glory, this is what it is?! Like being engulfed by a boa constrictor and wanting more than anything to be consumed. I wanted Earth to stop turning on its axis. I wanted time to stop, hover, linger, and stay.

And then, too soon, out of our veritable dream state, "Gotcha!"

The light went on, and it was like a dagger to my skull. I never hated the light more. Tracy stood in the entryway, one hand on her hip, the other holding the egg timer, laughing, pointing, and saying, "Look at these two! Jeesh! Do I need to get you a room? Get outta there." She turned away, picked up the walkie-talkie, and relayed, "Breaker one-four, breaker one-four. Steven! Do you read me? Send number two over."

Steven responded, "Ten-four. Four, over. Oh wait...did you say four or two? Over."

I turned my exasperated and bemused face back to the boy still holding me tight and noticed in slow motion that he wasn't smiling. In fact, what I saw there was shock and horror, closely followed by anguish. Suddenly, he dropped me like a hot potato. A gasp escaped my lips, my hands covering my mouth as if my lips had been burned off. Without another word, I ran out of the closet, through the enchanted forest, up the stairs, out of the house, and all the way home.

PART I – 1980

CHAPTER I

THREE YEARS EARLIER, when I was twelve years old, I woke up in a hospital bed. There was an IV in my arm, a bandage on my forehead, and a cast on my leg. It was the middle of the night, and the only light was a sliver of white reflected off the wall opposite the bathroom. I looked to my left where Mom was asleep on a beige plastic chair. All was quiet except the sound of low murmurs in the hallway and the beeping of machines. After a few minutes, the nurse came in. She placed the blood pressure cuff on my arm and noticed my eyes on her. She said softly, "Why, hello there."

I asked her a few things, but she was counting and only responded with a pity-filled indulgence of a smile. I didn't understand.

Mom woke up and came to my side, saying, "Shhhh, sweetie, lie back down." My head felt heavy and swollen, like an overripe cantaloupe. I detected the caustic smell of dried blood in my hair.

"Mom," I croaked. My mouth was so dry. "Water." The nurse said she'd be right back. I nodded. I tried again with Mom, "What...happened? What... what am I doing here?"

Mom had a hold of my hand and said with reassurance, "You were in an accident. You were hurt, but you're going to be okay."

The nurse came back with the water. It felt like liquid silk down my sandpaper throat.

Mom continued, "I want you to rest now, and I'll explain later, okay?" I shook my head in protest, but she insisted, "Later."

I stared at the ceiling for a while and then slowly closed my eyes. I heard the nurse leave and Mom sit back down in her chair. A film reel started playing involuntarily in my mind. My best friend, Kathy, and I were in the back seat of her parents' Ford Escort, and her mom was driving us to the store. We had saved up our babysitting money for the latest pair of Kangaroos. Kathy wanted the pink sneaks with the zipper pocket. I wanted the multicolored high-tops with the Velcro.

Kathy was skeptical, "Why do you need high-tops?"

"Because I'm gonna try out for the basketball team this year."

"Come on, you? Pip-squeak?"

"I'm taller than *you*."

"Half an inch doesn't count."

"It does when it comes to layups."

"Please. I beat you at Horse five times last week."

"That was a fluke. The week before, you couldn't hold a candle to me."

"Whatever. Anyway, this is the pair I want, but I'm not sure what size. Mom thinks my feet have grown." Kathy flipped open the catalog and pointed to the page where the pink pair was displayed. Then she said, "Did you hear about Ted Walker? He has one foot an entire size larger than the other. His mother has to buy two sets of shoes and then swap the odds out and return them."

"Don't they notice that at the store?"

"Apparently not. He told my sister she's done it for years."

"Well, I know what size I wear. Seven and a half."

"Yeah, I know, Sasquatch. Next week I'm sending you to the Yukon with those snowshoes of yours."

"Very funny, nitwit, I'd rather have big feet than a big nose."

"Hey! That's not nice. I don't have a big nose! Like you should talk, Chompers."

"Shut up—my teeth are perfect." I bared my teeth in a fat grin.

"Uh-huh, if you eat a lot of carrots."

Our tongues were out, our laughter sweet and sour. I tried to grab the catalog from her hands, but she held firm until it ripped in half and fell to the floor. We both screamed and reached for it at the same time, nearly clunking heads, but then each coming up with a portion of it clutched in our grip, triumphantly shouting our victory in unison: "Got it!"

Before we could flip through the pages again, out of the blue I saw the reflection of a car coming like a bullet straight for Kathy's door. There was no time to scream a warning or take a breath or think. The sound of crushing metal and screeching brakes roared simultaneously toward us like a freight train. Kathy was slammed into me, then violently suctioned away and smashed with the force of a thousand rocket ships against the passenger-side door, shattering the window with her head.

Back in the hospital room, my eyes snapped open. I glanced over at Mom, who was now asleep, but her word *later* echoed off the sterile walls like a tribal drum keeping rhythm with my broken, traumatized heart.

When later came, I was walking into Kathy's funeral on crutches with a zigzag of stitches across my forehead. So many people. More than I had ever seen in one place. There were children and parents and friends and teachers and ministers and aunts and uncles and cousins. Throngs of mourners lined up to see that cold, translucent, made-up face in the casket. It was a macabre wax-doll recreation of a distant version of Kathy. So unlike her, with blush on her cheeks and a hideous brown lace dress and ribbon around her head covering her Frankenstein patched-up mess of a face and body. Kathy hated brown. Whispers, chatter, tears, sobs, coughing, sneezing, blowing of noses. I stood stock-still next to my dad and observed, detached and remote, like a video camera filming the proceedings.

After a while, which may have been minutes or hours, Mrs. Peters came up to my dad and started spouting, "I hope that boy fries. It's simply awful. Fourteen years old. Where were his parents? I think they should fry too. Or was it just the mom…? I'm confused about the whole family situation, but it doesn't matter—there's no excuse. As if you leave a fourteen-year-old boy home alone for a weekend. Idiocy! And you don't lock the liquor cabinet? And you leave the keys to the car, which is parked in the garage? What were they thinking? Simply tempting fate. Sure, we know most of the boys here start driving early—heck, my Jimmy was working the tractor out in the fields at age ten, and we gave him the keys to the F-150 at thirteen, but still, we had *rules*: no driving on the highway or in town. Yet, here comes this new family without a care in the world, apparently. Sure, just leave a teenager to his own devices. Barreled right through that red light. Despicable. Of course, not a scratch on him. Isn't that always the case? What is this town coming to? I hope he's put away for life. And the parents, if it comes to that. I for one plan to be there when they lock them all up. That's about the best we can hope for, isn't it? For justice to be served. That may be the only thing that would make any sense out of this terrible, terrible nightmare."

Dad stared at her mutely with tired eyes, so she turned to me with her oversized Coke-bottle glasses and said, "Justice for Kathy—right, dearie?"

I nodded slowly, wondering when the screaming in my head would stop.

Seeing my face, Dad jumped in. "Yes, Dolores, it's a tragedy all around. Excuse us." He led me down the corridor and out the door into the parking lot.

He put his hands in his pockets and stood looking off toward the trees. I watched him guardedly, wondering what he would say, but he was quiet. It was a chilly fall day and I shivered.

Finally, I said, "Dad?"

His eyes came back to me as he murmured, "Hmmh?"

"Is that what happened? Is that how Kathy died?"

He sighed and shook his head. "I don't know, Riley. I just don't know."

"So...they...they figured out it was some kid...some boy? He was... drinking or something? I don't understand."

He studied my face. "You don't remember?"

I shook my head slowly. "Nothing," I lied.

Of course I remembered. I remembered the car, the Kangaroos, the catalog. And I remembered teasing Kathy. And I remembered our joking around in the back seat, which probably distracted Kathy's mom. And I remembered the force of the suctioning—like a violent industrial vacuum, taking her away from me into a dark, remote tunnel. And I remembered the years preceding the accident. Hours spent up in her bedroom trying on clothes and playing checkers and eating Saltine crackers and writing notes about boys to share with each other and dancing to Donny and Marie, Shaun Cassidy, ABBA, KC and the Sunshine Band, and playing tape-recorder games and painting watercolors and talking about sports and laughing out loud at stupid things and running behind the dresser in her parents' bedroom during hide-and-seek. And I remembered ice-skating on the pond and sledding down Hawkins Hill and building igloos in the backyard and Christmas caroling with Mrs. Richter's choir group. And skateboarding and basketball and bicycling and swinging from the flagpole and hunting four-leaf clovers and playing Ding Dong Ditch and Marco Polo and Ghost in the Graveyard. I remembered.

Dad stood silently for a good minute regarding me. Then he said, "The police are still looking into it. They haven't told us what happened."

"Who is he? Do we know him?"

"No, it was the family that just moved into the Koehlers' house a few months ago. You don't know them."

"The Linders?"

He looked surprised. "You *do* know them?"

"Yes, Marc plays soccer with one of their boys."

His brow furrowed. "He does? I didn't realize..."

"Dad, was his name Adam?" I asked, praying with every fiber of my being that it was the other brother.

"Yes, that's it, I think. Adam Linder. Sorry, I didn't think you knew him... I'm sorry, Riley..."

I felt a sinking in my stomach, like a cold, dark cloth being draped over the sun. Adam Linder! The boy with the shaggy brown hair and kind brown eyes. The boy who said hi shyly when he bought a hot cider from me last week at the Booster Club booth. The boy I had followed from biology class, making me late for social studies. The boy whose name I had written in tiny, tiny letters on page sixty-five of my algebra textbook.

I asked, "Dad, what's going to happen to him?"

"I don't know."

"Will he go to jail?"

He shook his head slowly as I regarded him with something close to fearful yearning in my eyes. He waited to respond, thinking through his words carefully. He said, "I don't know. I hope and pray it just was a horrible accident, sweetie."

"Okay," I said.

Then this involuntary thought popped into my head: There are no accidents.

Chapter II

BACK AT SCHOOL A WEEK LATER, I began to think about tears. What were tears anyway? Drops of salty water involuntary released from your eyes. How were they different from water that came out of your nose or mouth or skin? Who decided that tears connoted sadness and these other bodily functions didn't? After all, weren't tears innate and often a reflex? Anyone who had seen a baby cry knew that tears were uncontrollable, instinctive, ingrained, like a river that must flow downstream. Tears of hunger, fatigue, anger, angst, boredom, loneliness. And conversely, why did tears sometimes mean pure, utter happiness, delight, joy? How could these water-filled buckets have two diametrically opposed meanings? Was that some type of trick or joke? How were we supposed to interpret them if they were so confusing? So many meanings with so few answers. Sad, sorrowful, happy, brave, empathetic, merciful, kind, caring, weak, broken.

And what did it mean to *not* cry?

What did it mean if I *couldn't* cry?

What did *that* make me?

A nonhuman?

A monster?

A monster.

Dad dropped me off at the front entrance, and I swung my backpack over both shoulders before gripping my crutches and taking a deep breath. I felt the curious eyes of bystanders on me as I navigated the busy hallway leading to my locker. I kept my face down, trying not to trip and wishing I were invisible. Jennifer Beatrice, who had the locker next to mine and had always been snotty and mean, said with fake cheer, "Hi, Riley. I'm glad you're back. Do you need help with your books?" When I looked at her, I noticed the pinched lips and pity-filled eyes. I replied with a gruff mumble, "No thanks—I've got it." I set my crutches aside to rifle through my backpack and rearrange the books in my locker until she got the hint and walked away.

That was the beginning. From that point forward, I realized I was being treated like a fragile piece of glass. No one quite knew how to approach or handle me. A few girls hugged me and told me how sorry they were and stood by awkwardly while I remained silent. The others avoided me. In every class, I kept my head down and transcribed paragraphs from my textbooks into my spiral notebook. Deflecting. The teachers gave me a break and let me be. To them, I was distant and unreachable. To me, I was numb.

After school, Mom picked me up and asked how my day was. I said good, meaning "Please don't ask me any more questions." Mercifully, she didn't. At home, I hobbled directly up to my room and lay down on my stomach on the bed. As I stared at the shards of light reflecting rainbow-colored orbs off my hair onto my hand, I tried to make myself cry. Why wouldn't the tears come? They were stuck, like glue, behind my eyes, in a locked cabinet where the sadness had flown to hide from the light. My forehead was aching, so I flipped over on my side and touched the yellow flowers on my wallpaper for a while. I must have fallen asleep because sometime later I woke to hear my brother Brent knocking on my door saying dinner was ready. I got up slowly and rubbed my eyes.

At dinner, Dad and Mom chatted with the boys about their schoolwork and soccer and other innocuous, miscellaneous drivel, simply to keep me from having to engage. It was kind of them but left me feeling nauseous. An hour later, I was studying Spanish at the desk in our den, next to Mom's potted plants and Marc's soccer schedule, when Dad leaned in and waited for me to look up.

I stared at him and said, "Hey."

He said slowly, "Hey." And then, with a furtive glance at his hands and back to me, "You know, Riley, it's okay to cry."

I sighed and frowned. Please, God, give me strength. Or in this case, please, God, give me weakness. Which apparently I didn't have. Not a single shred of weakness or feeling or empathy or normal decency.

I said, "I know. I know that."

"Then...?"

"Dad, I'm fine. Really."

His skeptical eyes stayed on me until I gave him a small smile and said, "I'm not sure...what..."

When I paused, his face lit up, but I only disappointed him with "...what to do about basketball. I guess I can't try out now."

He laughed despite himself and said, "Nope, guess not. Do they have a chess club?" Clearly, he had hoped I would open up to him, cry on his shoulder, make him feel less helpless, but instead I talked about basketball, which, after all, was easier, so there was some relief in that. He was trying to be funny, so I smiled. He added, "You know, you don't have to do anything for a while if you don't want to. You could just...coast...a bit..."

Instead of addressing the suggestion, I said quietly, "I gotta finish this homework."

He waited to see if I would say anything more. Then, with a curious opening and closing of his mouth, he said with finality, "Okay, well, then, I'll leave you to it."

I tried to memorize several more conjugations, but they didn't stick, so I went to my bedroom. As I put my pajamas on, I began to feel foolish and deflated. I thought no one knew. I thought I had a secret. I thought I had hidden it well. I thought everyone's embarrassment and uncomfortable awkwardness around me meant they hadn't really *looked* at me. I thought I had been doing so well, putting my head down and concentrating (very deeply) on other things. I had avoided looking into anyone's eyes so they wouldn't see me and I wouldn't see them. I thought it was working. And what's more, I thought about how they were all wrong anyway—I didn't want their attention, and I didn't want to coast either. I wanted it not to have happened. I wanted everyone to act as though it hadn't happened. Was that too much to ask? I was able to manage it. Why couldn't they? I went to bed.

The next day at school, I summed up all the courage in the universe and went to Ms. Tricky, the gym teacher (who also happened to be the basketball coach), and asked her if I could try out.

She looked at my crutches and my cast and laughed. "Sweetie, um, hello—you have a broken leg!"

"I know."

"For how long?"

"Three months."

"Well, that kind of puts a damper on the season, doesn't it?"

"I thought...I thought maybe I could do...something else."

"Oh! Well, let's see...that's a thought. Hmm, yeah, we could use a manager. Do you know how to keep score?"

"Um, yeah, I think so…anything I don't know, I could learn."

"Okay, okay, that's possible…you'll have to work the scoreboard and fill in the roster. You up for that?"

"Sure."

"Okay, two-thirty next Thursday. See you then."

Yes! She didn't pussyfoot around me. I was happier about that than getting the manager role. Although I was looking forward to that too. I needed something to keep me busy.

Later that night, while I was doing homework, I thought about how stupid algebra was. Mr. Jacobs insisted it was a useful tool. You never knew when someone might ask you to find the X over Y of life, right? Please. Now, if we were talking subtraction—that I understood: there were two, subtract one and you got one. But the way I saw subtraction, there were two, subtract one and you got zero. I was the leftover zero. And by myself, with no Kathy to anchor me, I was about as useful as algebra.

❧ Chapter III ❧

Several months passed like that—me in contemplation of the zero.

Then on a random Friday afternoon, Mom woke me up from my nap and said, "We're going to the library."

I rubbed my eyes and asked incredulously, "The library?"

That can't be right. Was I still asleep?

She repeated, "Yes, the library."

I protested but she insisted, and as I grabbed my coat out of the downstairs closet, I wondered what could possibly be going on. Our family, we weren't readers. We were *doers*. You know the type: fixers, cleaners, exercisers, talkers, travelers, shoppers, cookers, workers, socializers—essentially hyper productive masochists. I had never seen anyone in my family reading a book. Ever. Sometimes Mom leafed through *Better Homes and Gardens* or Dad referenced *Popular Mechanics*, but outside of that, nothing. Even with my brothers, I always wondered how they passed their classes because I never saw them doing homework. They were usually off playing sports or hanging out with friends.

As we drove the short distance to the library, I watched the tiny wisps of snow floating around outside the car window. They didn't provide any clarity about this trip or about anything, but I still stared.

"Mom?"

"Hmm?"

"Why are we going to the library? Do you need a book or something?"

"Nope."

"Then?"

"I just figured it might be...good for you."

"What? Why?"

"Oh, I don't know...lately, you seem different."

I groaned. Not this again. "Mom."

"Well, not different exactly," she corrected, "just less bubbly, less like my happy-go-lucky Raucous Riley, that's all."

She tweaked my nose and I stared at her. Raucous Riley. Her nickname for me when I was a child and used to wrestle with my brothers and do cartwheels in the yard and jump off the roof of the shed. I said, "Mom, I'm fine. And besides, what would be the point of going to the library? To send me into a coma?"

"Glad to see you still have your sense of humor. Actually, I was talking to Mrs. Randall the other day—"

"Mrs. Randall. No, Mom—please!"

"Oh, come on, she's not that bad. She's a very nice person."

I protested, "She's the biggest gossip. What did you tell her?!"

"She's not a gossip. And besides, she assured me all of her sessions are confidential."

"Uh-huh, right," I chided and laid my head back against the car seat.

Mom continued, "And she's a counselor, you know—a real certified doctor counselor."

I rolled my eyes.

I had been managing the basketball team for months, and I was getting great grades and had been doing all of my chores. The doctor said I could get my cast off in a week and a half. The zigzag scar on my forehead still looked like the front of Charlie Brown's shirt, but I had been using vitamin E on it every night, and the color had gone from ruby red to Barbie pink. It was nearly Christmas, so everyone was focused on shopping, putting up the tree, eating cookies, and making gingerbread houses. Everything was going great, stupendous, excellent! And now this.

I asked angrily, "So?"

"She thought it might be helpful…if you, well, if you were to write your thoughts down, so I got you this."

She handed me a book with the words "My Diary" written on the cover. I groaned and handed it back to her, but she refused with, "Take it. I'm not asking for much here. I'm only asking that you give it a try."

I pushed my lips together and shoved it roughly in my purse. I asked, "What does this have to do with the library?"

"I want you to devote some time to this, Riley. To focus. Dad and I agree, if this doesn't work—"

"Doesn't work? Doesn't work to do *what*?"

She paused and finally said, "Doesn't work to make you feel…better."

"Mom, what are you talking about? I feel *fine*."

"Okay, well, be that as it may, I still want you to make an *effort* at this. And if it doesn't work…I mean, if it doesn't *help*…then we're going to send you to Mrs. Randall for counseling."

"What?" I screeched. Holy crap, this was getting worse and worse. I pounded my fist on the car door.

We were at the library now, in the parking lot. She turned off the car. She sighed, turned to me, and said firmly, "Listen Riley, your dad and I, we haven't asked much of you these past few months because, well, you know why, but this is something we want you to do. If you won't talk to us and you won't meet with Mrs. Randall, we think it would be good if you wrote a few things down." She looked away, out the window at the snow. Then turning back to me, she said, "We're not sure if it'll work or change anything, but we want you to *try*, okay? And heck, you never know, you might like it!"

I thought about that for a minute and stared at the entrance to the library. Like a prison. Or purgatory. I shook my head. I asked, "What are you saying? I'm going to have to stay at the library tonight for like…what? An hour or something? Aren't you coming in with me?"

"No, Riley," she answered firmly, clarifying, "I want you to go in alone and stay a few hours. I'll pick you up at nine. And I want you to write or read or focus your attention on…whatever you want, but on *something*, okay?"

"Mom! It's like six fifteen. That's almost three hours!"

"You'll survive. Get yourself a library card too. You're gonna need it."

"No, I'm not, because I'm never coming back here again," I declared as I got out of the car and slammed the door, reaching in the back for my crutches and cursing under my breath. I gimped toward the entrance through a wall of snowflakes, wishing they were bullets.

Once inside, my crutches felt as if they were poured in concrete. The expression "like a fish out of water" came to mind. I shrunk down into my sweatshirt, zippering the zipper of my coat up to my chin, trying to disappear. Then I glanced to my left and my right. An old man in the corner was reading a newspaper, and a woman with a toddler was scrolling through a rack of children's books in the back. From this vantage point, I could see no one except of course the librarian, Mrs. Litchy, who was seated at the registration desk and whom everyone in town knew because she had been the librarian for about a hundred years.

Phew. I breathed a sigh of relief. At least there was no one here I knew. I made sure my tan suede purse with the turquoise beads was still wrapped cross-wise across my chest and headed slowly down the middle aisle, staring at the rows and rows of books—so foreign to me, numerous and mysterious. What was the big deal about books anyway? Words and words and words strung together to make sentences and paragraphs and pages and finally these square, squiggly inanimate objects that people associated with so much value. I mean, why? They didn't do anything, these books. They sat here in rows, not talking or eating or drinking or breathing or *feeling*. Come to think of it, God, I wish I were a book. They had it made. They could rest here in peace, in this cemetery of sorts, a place to go to be left *alone*. Well, until somebody came along out of the blue and picked you up and fiddled with you, scrolling through your pages as if exploring your kitchen cupboards, trying to disturb, decipher, absorb, and consume you. Maybe it wouldn't be so great to be a book.

I picked up a random big one, *The Forsythe Saga*. I fanned the pages using my thumb, like Kathy and I used to do with three-by-five cards, where we would draw a tiny stick figure on the edge of every page, each one slightly different, so when you flipped through them, it looked as though the stick figure was in motion. Mine were usually doing cartwheels or riding a bike; Kathy's were usually stabbing or shooting a gun at someone. Sometimes I think Kathy had a violent streak, but then I think no, she was just more interesting than me.

This book in my hands, it must have weighed three pounds. Why on earth would anyone read something so massive? It would take years—what a waste of time! I put it back on the shelf and kept going toward a table in the back of the library. I sat down, laying my crutches against the wall, and looked at my watch: six twenty-three. Two hours thirty-seven minutes left. I opened my purse and took the contents out, one at a time: Hubba Bubba bubble gum, cherry Chapstick, hairbrush, eight dollars and thirty-eight cents, a birthday party invite, bright blue sunglasses, three pig-shaped erasers, two pencils, a small plastic gorilla, "My Diary," and a pen. I sighed. Instead of opening the diary, I stared at the wall for a while. There was a poster with a cat hanging from a tree. It said: "Hang in there!" I laid my head down on my folded arms and tried to rest but couldn't. I rolled my closed eyes and inspected the insides of my eyelids. There was a foggy, pinkish quality to the image there, like TV static reflecting the sun. This felt like home. If only I could stay inside my eyelids forever, microscopically digesting the world through the literal lens of a blurry image of refracted, faded light. And emptiness.

Chapter IV

"Okay, tell me what happened from the beginning."

Adam Linder stared at the man for a brief instant before looking down again. The man had black hair and black eyes and a grim no-nonsense sneer. Adam didn't respond. The man had sent his mom to the waiting room, so Adam was left alone with him. Nowhere else to focus, nowhere to hide, nowhere to run in this cold, colorless, uninviting room.

"But...but I already told the cops—" Adam began.

"Yes, I know. This is different. Listen. Here's the deal: This can go fast or this can go slow. It's entirely up to you. But the only way I can help you is if you talk. I need to know everything. And I mean everything. No leaving important details out because you're scared or worried or don't want Mom and Dad to find out. This is not the time to be worried about punishment. Understand?"

Adam gave him a look of incredulity. "I'm not worried about that. I have nothing to hide." And yet he groaned inwardly. Didn't the man understand? Adam wanted to be punished! He pushed his rigid plastic chair back a smidge, and it made a loud scraping sound on the floor.

The man began by asking Adam his name, age, and address, and then said, "How about the morning of the seventh? Where were you? What were you doing? Start there and speak up so I can hear you."

Adam straightened up in his seat and began with a quiver in his voice, "I was home." He cleared his throat and repeated, "I was home." Then, slowly, quietly, still with that annoying vibration in his voice, "I got up, got dressed, and ate breakfast."

"Who was there?"

"At the house? No one. Just me and the dog."

"Where were your parents?"

"My mom," Adam corrected. "She left the night before with Jeremy."

"Jeremy?"

"My older brother."

"Where was your dad?"

"Not…not around," Adam answered vaguely, looking toward the door.

The man's eyes narrowed, and he said harshly, "No, really—where?"

Adam frowned and said more forcefully, "I don't know. I really don't know, okay? He's—he's no longer in the picture…" Adam exhaled as he watched the man write on his notepad, "Absentee father."

The man said, "Continue. Where did your mom and Jeremy go?"

"To Indy. Jeremy had a cross country meet. They rode up Friday night with the Thompsons."

"Why didn't you go?"

"Because I had a soccer game Saturday morning."

"Your mom left you home alone? Did she do that a lot?"

I thought about that for a minute. "No, not really."

"Why did she decide to leave you alone this time?"

"I don't know…I didn't ask. I guess because I'm older now…and she didn't have anyone to watch me, and I had a game."

"She trusted you?" he asked, almost as a challenge.

"Yes," I replied definitively.

"You've never been in trouble before? Given your mom grief by skipping school or getting caught smoking or shoplifting or cheating?"

Adam stared at him blankly and replied, "No. I've never given her a reason not to trust me."

"Okay, calm down," the man said as if Adam had been hysterical, even though he was perfectly calm—not to mention subdued and depressed. Clearly not defiant. Adam began to have a sinking suspicion that he was being baited. He didn't know why, but he stayed on his guard.

The man continued, "Did she leave you any instructions?"

"Instructions?"

"You know, turn off the TV, lock the door, feed the dog …"

"Yeah, I mean, she had something stuck on the fridge, but I didn't read it."

"Did the note say anything about the car?"

"I told you, I didn't read it."

The man's eyes narrowed, and he said, "What I mean is, did she say anything verbally about the car—you know, don't drive the car or stay away from the car…?"

"No."

"Okay, go on. What happened after you ate breakfast?"

"Darryl and his dad picked me up."

"What time was that?"

"Um, like, nine thirty. Darryl's on my soccer team. Mom made arrangements for me to hitch a ride with them to the game. Then we played our game and they drove me home."

"And you didn't stop anywhere on the way there or back?"

"Nope, nowhere."

"What time did you get home?"

"Um, I guess around eleven thirty or so."

"Did Darryl or his dad come into your house?"

"No, they just dropped me off."

"Okay, then what happened?"

"I went upstairs to take a shower, but I noticed my dog had puked on the floor of my bedroom. I tried to find him, called out his name, but he didn't come. Usually he greeted me at the door...so it was weird. Instead of taking a shower, I walked around the house looking for him. I found more places where he had been sick, on the floor in the kitchen and the living room, and some of it looked bloody." Adam's face wore a frown as he continued, "I kept calling and calling. Finally, I found him under Mom's bed, but his eyes were closed. He looked...dead. I pulled him out and tried to wake him, but he wouldn't wake up, so I scooped him up in my arms and put him in the car."

"Hold up." The black eyes shot at me. "Back it up. Okay, so in the house, your first thought was to put him in the car? You didn't, I don't know...check to see if he was bleeding or injured or having trouble breathing? You didn't call anyone?"

Adam shook his head. "I didn't see anything obvious. All I knew was that he was very sick and I needed to get him some help fast."

"You didn't read that note on the fridge? Look for emergency contact info? Go to the neighbor's house? Call a friend?"

"No, I mean, I wasn't thinking," Adam answered quickly and then repeated, "I wasn't thinking...clearly...or at all, really. I was in a panic. I thought Rocko was dead, honestly, but then I thought maybe he wasn't, and I didn't want him to die. I didn't know what to do, exactly, but I knew I needed to do *something*. I guess I could have gone to the neighbor's, but I didn't know them..."

"You didn't know your own neighbors?" Again with a challenge.

Adam shook his head. "We just moved here a couple of months ago. I don't really know anyone in our neighborhood yet."

"Okay...okay," he said, unsatisfied. "So, you put the dog in the car—in the front seat or back?"

"Um, front."

"What type of car?"

"Huh?"

"Two-seater, four-seater? Sedan? Standard? Automatic? Ford, Chevy, Dodge? Details are important here."

"It's a Buick LeSabre."

He wrote that down. "So, automatic, no gear shift in between the two of you, right? How big is the dog? What kind?"

"Right. A golden retriever."

"Okay. And what were you planning to do with him?"

"I guess I didn't really know...I think I thought I might try to find the vet's office."

"You knew where that was?"

"Yes, sort of. Mom and I had dropped Rocko off at the vet the month before to have a cyst removed from his leg."

"Okay. So, when you pulled out of the garage, the dog was over on the passenger seat, just lying there? Still? Not breathing? Or moving?"

"I could hear him breathing very slowly, with a sort of gurgle or something in his chest. He didn't sound right. I kind of pulled him up on my lap, or at least his head was on my lap."

More notes and then this statement, "You told me earlier that you're fourteen."

Adam nodded.

"But you somehow, at the age of fourteen, knew how to drive?"

"I didn't...I mean, I hadn't...ever," Adam stumbled, "not really, anyway... my grandpa let me drive his Lincoln Continental sometimes, just in the driveway and around the block...but that was years ago."

"So what made you think you could drive?" the man asked accusingly.

"I don't know," Adam answered lamely, putting his head in his hands. "I couldn't think of what else to do—I couldn't *think*."

When Adam finally looked up in the silence that followed, the man simply said, "Continue."

Adam wiped his nose with his hand and started again with a shaky voice, "I backed out of the driveway and headed down the street, trying to remember where the vet's office was. I mean, I remembered it was out in Paoli, but I wasn't sure how to get there. From our house, I drove down the hill and onto Broadway. I just kept going, heading toward where I thought the vet's office was. I knew it wasn't that close. A few minutes into the drive, Rocko woke up—"

"How fast were you going at this point?" the man interrupted.

"I don't know...maybe twenty or thirty."

He shuffled some papers and said, "This police report says you were going in excess of fifty miles an hour through the middle of town. We have several eyewitnesses who attest to the fact."

Adam sat there quietly and waited. His eyes wide, he finally said, "I don't remember...I really don't remember that..."

"And the red light?"

"There was a red light?" Adam asked blankly.

The man exhaled with irritation and said, "Yes. Apparently, you went through it."

"Oh," Adam said with shock.

Adam was still processing when the man picked up the thread, "The dog woke up and...?"

"Yes, he woke up and barked. He tried to sit up, but it was almost like he didn't have control over his legs or something because he slipped and fell down with a thud onto the floorboards." Adam took a deep breath, seeing something in his mind's eye that caused him to sob and say, "That was when...that was how...I—I must have reached for him or hit the gas instead of the brake...or both. I'm not sure...I don't...I don't really remember, but that was when I hit—I hit something and there was a loud noise, a crash."

The man sat there, letting Adam cry. Finally, he cleared his throat and said flatly, "And...then what happened?"

Adam rubbed his knuckles against his eyes. "The car...spun around and just sort of stopped. A few seconds later, I noticed the smell of burned rubber and saw a plume of smoke. I heard a horn blaring and people were screaming, but I didn't understand. I couldn't quite fit the pieces of the scene together. It was like watching a movie with no understanding of the plot. It was very chaotic. Rocko was whimpering on his side, and when I opened the door, he shot out and ran off without even limping or looking back. It was crazy. I got out of the car and stood up and screamed after him, but he just kept going, off into a field and then the woods. And that's when I...I noticed—" Adam burst into tears, laying his head on his crossed arms, shaking. After a long time, he asked weakly, "Can I have...a tissue?"

Without a word, the man went out of the room and came back, handing Adam a box of tissue.

Adam blew his nose and went on. "I first saw my car and how banged up it was, and I was thinking Mom was going to kill me, but suddenly I also saw this other car that was even more mangled. The back passenger-side door was half open, bent inward, and there was a head there...a horrible...crushed and bloody...head...with long, dark, straight hair, lying atop a set of blue jeans, which I guess was another girl's lap." Adam sobbed, trying to speak in between each sob, "The face...the face...wasn't right...wasn't quite there...it was like meat, it was like...red, ugly, battered meat...it was almost...not... not...human." Adam rocked back and forth, pushing on his temples, saying, "But the hair, the hair, was so perfect, so shiny and pretty. So—so—so long and straight...like a horse's tail or like water...like black water..."

The man waited a moment, then asked, "Were you hurt?"

"I wasn't sure...I wasn't sure...of anything...I didn't even look to see...I didn't even think to check myself. Before I had time to think or feel or look at anything else, a mob of people was coming out from the stores and buildings, rushing up to me and surrounding the other car. I remember one guy went and got his tire iron out of his trunk and came back to pry open the rest of the doors of the other car. He eventually got the front door open, and the mother came out, holding her bloody arm, and she was screaming so loud, just screaming over and over again until the guy pulled her away from the scene. Another guy was on the other side of the car, working over the girl with the hair and the girl with the blue jeans. At that point, I couldn't see them very well, and some woman was in my face, asking me if I was okay and telling me that help was on the way. I looked off toward the woods where Rocko had gone, wondering if I should try to find him. Then an ambulance guy came to look me over, and after a long time he cleared me and turned me over to a policeman who put me in the back of his car. The policeman went back out to check on the rest of the scene, and I watched as he drew a picture on his notepad—where my car was and where their car was and the cross streets and the bank and the shops and a few other things. At the same time, he went and talked to a few witnesses, showing them the picture and asking them questions."

Adam stopped and didn't say anything else for a while. As an afterthought, he finally said, "Later, at the police station, I noticed my finger was bandaged and my elbow hurt a lot. My mom was there and my brother."

"And what happened at the station?"

"The cop pulled us into a room and asked me a bunch of questions. After a few hours, the cop let us go. Mom asked the cop where the car was, and he gave her a card with a number to call, a tow place, I guess." Adam didn't mention that this was the point, right as they were about to leave the police station, when his mom broke down and cried. It was dawning on her then—the fundamental fact that Adam already knew in his gut—that this nightmare was just beginning, and none of their lives would ever be the same again. He realized, as he watched her and she pulled him in for a hug, that he had been crying too, probably for hours. Jeremy stood by them and watched, not sure what to do.

The black eyes stared, waiting for Adam to add more, but he remained silent. The man sorted through some papers on the desk, finally saying, "Okay, here's the statement from the police. It's seems to be consistent with your story. It says here...let's see, the accident occurred around noon, and you were brought into the police station for your interview at one forty-five and released at...um, six twenty. Sound about right?"

I shrugged. I didn't really remember. All sense of time that day was jumbled in my mind.

He continued, "How did you get home?"

"Mom called a friend to come get us."

"Okay," he said, winding down. "I guess we've accounted for the whole day now. Can you think of anything else?"

Adam shook his head.

The man thought of something, "Listen, do you have any proof about the dog? I mean, that the dog was hurt or that the dog was in the car?"

Adam stared at him. "What? No—I told you, he ran away."

He nodded, writing something in his notes. Then he said, "Yes, but there is some question about the dog, whether or not the dog was with you..."

Adam's defeated eyes sagged.

The man asked, "Where is the dog now? Would there be any way to tell that he had been sick that day? Would a vet be able to tell?

Adam mumbled, "I don't see how...I mean, he's gone. He never came back."

The man paused and then asked, "Okay, one last thing, you weren't drinking or smoking or doing anything else…you shouldn't have been doing, were you?"

"What? Of course not," Adam answered, his face awash with new grief and despair, the shock and realization of the implications hitting him.

"You're sure? You didn't explain how the soccer game ended or what you did after the game. You didn't smoke a joint with your buddies at the game? Or take a nip from your mom's liquor cabinet?"

Adam answered firmly and quietly, "No," then added, "I didn't do that…I wouldn't do that."

"You sure?" his face was skeptical, and Adam's nostrils flared in anger. The man added, "Would you tell me if you did?" He waited, pen posed in midair, but Adam remained silent and scowling. The man sighed and finally said, "Alright. That's it. You're free to go."

He stood up and followed Adam out to where his mom was sitting in a frayed orange chair by the entrance. She looked tired and tense. The man talked to her for a while as Adam stood off to the side, biting his nails, trying to swallow the sore, burning lump in his throat.

CHAPTER V

AFTER A FEW MINUTES, I opened my eyes reluctantly, placing everything carefully back in my purse except the diary. What was a diary anyway? Seemed strange to write words down on paper, words that went exactly where? Into the ether? And to whom? God? Heaven? Angels? To what? The past? The future? The present? Somewhere in time or space that was undefined? Or to nowhere and nothing and no one?

I stared at it for a while, then opened it.

I wrote:

Diary of Riley York Cartwright

Friday, December 18, 1980

Mom bought me this diary, and I'm supposed to write in it. I'm not sure what to say. I think she wants me to read books too. I'm at the library. It's very boring and quiet. This week I had basketball practice on Monday, Tuesday, and Thursday. We have a home game tomorrow at 10:15 a.m. Our record is 2 and 9. The team we're playing tomorrow sucks, so we might just win. Naomi's injured, so Shelly's going to play point guard. She's not as good as Naomi. Coach Tricky said I've been doing such a good job that she wants me to manage track in the spring. We'll see. I'd rather be running track than managing it, but I won't know if that's possible until this stupid cast is off.

Tomorrow night is the twins' annual birthday party. I'm not looking forward to it. Then Christmas break starts on Wednesday. I don't know why they don't just let us off all week. I have a social studies final on Monday and algebra on Tuesday. Mom wants me to help with the tree and cookies on Wednesday. We're celebrating Christmas at Grandma and Grandpa's this year, so we have to drive to Madison on Christmas Eve morning.

Hmmm, what else? There are so many books in this place! It takes me like fifteen minutes to read one page—why do people bother? You could just watch TV. Makes more sense.

Mom said I should write my feelings in this thing. Here goes: It's been 97 days since the accident. But who's counting, right? I mean, does it matter? Does anything really matter? What is "matter" anyway? Wait, I'll be right back. Very large dictionary. Definition of *matter*: "Something that occupies space." That would be me, for sure. I am something that occupies space. A very little, teensy-weensy bit of space. You know, I had a thought the other day: if I had been the one to die, would Kathy be crying and upset all the time? I doubt it. But then again, she was a lot nicer than me. Maybe she would. She cried when her cat Jumbo died, even though he was a fat, ugly, mean tyrant. She cried when we watched that *Boy in the Plastic Bubble* movie. I just ate more popcorn and felt uncomfortable sitting next to her on the couch as she cried. I don't know. Maybe I'm an awful person. Maybe I have no heart.

Another word in the dictionary is *morass*: "A marsh or a bog." Dad was watching a show the other night on PBS about the Bog of Allen in Ireland. I wanted to sink into the picture on the screen. It looked smooth and green and inviting. Another definition of *morass*: "Any confusing or troublesome situation, especially one from which it is difficult to free oneself."

I told Mom I didn't want to go to the twins' birthday party tomorrow night, but she said I had to. She said we were all going. When I frowned, she said, "Kathy would have wanted you to." I said okay, but I thought, would she? I wonder about that sometimes. Would she want me to go to parties, hang out with our mutual friends, have fun without her?

Kathy's mom was at our house on Tuesday. When I got home from basketball, I tripped over her shoes in the foyer, and Mom heard me and asked me to come into the living room and say hello. I hovered in the doorway, and Mrs. Metzger stood up and gave me a hug. She started to cry. I tried not to squirm. I tried to be limp like a rag doll. I tried to feel the way you're supposed to feel. When she pulled back, she was staring at me like she wanted me to say something, but I turned away and ran up the stairs to my bedroom.

I put the diary and pen away in my purse and sat staring at the poster. "Hang in there!" I felt like the poster was teasing me.

I went up to the librarian. She asked, "May I help you?" I was trying to figure out how to kill the rest of my time, so I stood there staring at her silently for a few minutes, trying to figure out what to say. She pressed, "Spit it out, sweetie. Cat got your tongue?"

Yes, I thought, cat has my tongue, and cat is dangling from a tree, telling me to "Hang in there!"

"Are there any…books…for girls?" I finally managed.

She smiled. "Of course—take your pick!"

I shrugged my shoulders helplessly and flew my hand across the great sweeping landscape. Something clicked. She said, "Oh, not sure what you want, eh? Okay, follow me, dear."

A few paces behind, I was reminded of that cartoon where the tall, dark butler says, "Walk this way" as he leads his victims to their death in a haunted castle. She caught me in a grin just as she turned suddenly and pointed to a kiosk—a turnstile of thin books with a sign that read "Children and Young Adult."

"Here you go." She pulled one out and handed it to me. "Try this."

I nodded with a faint smile, looking down at the book with two overly enthusiastic cheerleaders on the cover. She squeezed my arm encouragingly and said, "Good. All set. Hang in there, dearie. Come back to the circulation desk when you're ready to check out." She shuffled away and I stared after her incredulously. Did she just say, "Hang in there?"

I leafed through the book in my hands. On page fifty-two, there were these words:

> Jennifer stretched out her legs on the grass and asked Gidget if Frank had asked her to the dance yet. Gidget said, "Not yet, but I have a plan to get him alone after school, and I know for a fact he'll ask me then." "How do you know?" Jennifer wondered, and Gidget said, "Because Frank told Donald he would, and Rita overheard them and told me." Jennifer frowned. "Yes, but I heard Rita wanted to go with Frank herself, so I don't think I would trust her—she might have her own designs on him." Gidget shook her head and said, "No, Rita wouldn't do that to me and besides, I know Frank will ask me because I'm going to let him kiss me this time." Jennifer sat up and cried, "Gidget! You wouldn't!" Gidget laughed and screamed back, "Oh yes I would!"

I stuck my finger in my mouth and coughed out, "Gag me." After putting the cheerleaders away, I twirled the kiosk and plucked out several promising selections, including some under the "Nonfiction and Learning" section. After I had a fairly healthy stack piled up on the table, I sat down to go through them.

On page four of a book about Japan, there was a photo of two people in kimonos bowing to each other with speech bubbles over their heads: "Konnichiwa." Another page explained how Japanese people slept on something called a futon, which looked about as comfortable as a slab of marble. The entire book only took me fifteen minutes to finish. Then I picked up *Tales of a Fourth Grade Nothing*. I read the back cover and thought it sounded horrible, so I put it back down. *Frog and Toad Are Friends* looked too young for me. Same with *The Lorax*. I started *The Red Badge of Courage* but had to reread the same few paragraphs so many times that I gave up. More books about cheerleaders. Ugh. I read through a book about rocks: igneous, sedimentary, metamorphic. I liked the pictures with their informative captions. I began to think about that big sign on the way to Bedford that read "Limestone Capital of the World." Living in French Lick, we were only an hour or so from there. I guess I had never thought about all of the sedimentary rock in southern Indiana. I was probably sitting on thousands of layers of it right now. Whoa. A lot different from that bog in Ireland. If only life were like Bedford's limestone—solid and *predictable*.

After I finished the rock book, I picked up *The Shy Ones*. On the cover was a photo of a girl with glasses and a red dog, and it said, "A girl and her dog become champions." I liked the photo, and the book didn't seem too long or too old or too complicated or too young. Like Goldilocks. It was just right. This is the one I would take with me. I put all of the others back in the kiosk and used my crutches to hobble through the aisles some more. There was no one left in the library except the librarian, and she was absorbed in knitting an afghan behind her desk. I found the magazine rack and scrolled through two copies of *Teen Beat*, thinking why would anyone care what brand of toothpaste Chachi used or who he was dating?

I looked at my watch: eight thirty-two. I went to the table, sat, and began *The Shy Ones*.

> Saturday morning. Robin woke slowly, inch by inch, savoring the delicious no-school feeling. No need this morning to force her eyes open until they were ready to open. She rolled over to lie face down, toes hooked over the foot of the bed, hands dangling from either side, her nose pressed against the sheet. As usual, she had lost her pillow during the night. Someone, probably her father, was working in the yard under her open window. Through the hiss of the lawn sprinkler, Robin could hear the slow chunking of

a spade in the dirt. She couldn't hear anything from the kitchen under her room…

I stopped. Hmmm, seemed promising. Kathy would have loved this book. Anything about animals. She was a way better reader than me—she would have had this one finished in an afternoon. Sometimes she would get so excited about a particular book, she would spend an hour explaining the plot to me. And when she finished a book, sometimes she cried because she didn't want it to be over. Her enthusiasm was so catchy, it almost made me want to read. But then I never did. I wondered what she would think of me trying to read now. Maybe she would have been proud of me. I looked at my watch again—finally the time was nearly up.

At the circulation desk, I told Mrs. Litchy I needed a library card.

She handed me a form, which I filled out and handed back to her. She spent the next few minutes using the typewriter to imprint my information on a blank card, striking the keys one at a time with her index finger, stopping in between to inspect with her glasses. I stood and watched. When the proceedings were over, I stared at my new card. Wow, my first form of identification: Riley York Cartwright. 22 Summer Street. French Lick, Indiana. Library Card Number: 73856.

In writing. I must be real. I must be alive. I must not be a zero. Maybe *I* am matter. Maybe I matter.

She took the book from me, placed a stamped card into a slot on the inside back cover, and handed it back, saying, "Due in two weeks. Don't lose it, and don't be late or we charge."

I nodded. "Okay, thanks." I put the book and the library card in my purse just as I heard Mom's car horn out front. I looked back and saw the librarian putting her coat on—golly, I had closed the place down and survived my first visit to the library! Not too shabby.

Mom asked me how it went, and I said, "Slowly" and shrugged. She didn't pry any further, and that was just fine with me.

When we got home, I noticed Brent had listed himself as "Out" on Mom's "Where Are You?" bulletin board. I pointed and Mom said, "Brent's on a date with Maureen. He'll be back at eleven." I crinkled my nose. I hated that Maureen girl. She was such a know-it-all and talked over everybody at the dinner table. And she put ketchup on everything, including pizza! Who does that? A couple of weeks ago, right in front of me, she asked Brent, "What's the deal with your sister? She doesn't say a word. Is she a retard?" Brent laughed and said with a smirk, "Yes, yes she is." Nice. It wasn't enough to be hateful to me—they had to make it insulting to people with brain issues. I narrowed my eyes and scowled at them both, which made them smile all the more.

I went directly to my bedroom, changed into my nightgown, and flopped down on my pillow. I opened *The Shy Ones*, finished chapter one, and started chapter two. I wondered where that dog in the ditch had come from. Who had hurt it? What was Robin going to do about it? Was it going to be okay? After a few pages,

> He placed one of Robin's gloved hands on the good leg to keep it out of the way of the X-ray, her other hand on the dog's neck to quiet her feeble attempts to get up. Then he adjusted some knobs on the back of the machine and pressed a button. There was a buzz-click, and it was done.

Right around the "buzz-click," I felt a buzz-click in my brain telling me to go to sleep. I was tired. A huge yawn escaped my lips. I set the book aside and curled up under the covers, drifting off to sleep with a huge X-ray machine dancing in my head. What exactly was an X-ray machine anyway? A big camera? A cushioned vise? A flying operating table? Did it hurt? What did it do? Did it take photos of your internal organs? Your bones? Your skin? Your hair? Your *private* parts? Could it see through your clothes? Was it like Superman's X-ray vision? Could it read your mind?

The next morning, my alarm woke me at seven forty-five. Still thinking about the X-ray, I got ready for basketball and went downstairs. Dad, Marc, and Nate were already sitting at the dining room table eating eggs, pancakes, and bacon. I sat down right as Mom came in from the kitchen, placing a plate of pancakes on the table, saying, "Batch two. Get 'em while they're hot." The boys reached for them and Dad hollered, "Leave some for your sister!" As if that ever stopped them; they were like cadaver dogs scenting a fresh kill. I didn't want to lose a finger, so I waited until they were done snatching and then put what little remained on my plate: one scoop of eggs, one pancake, one piece of bacon.

Mom went around to the stairwell and screamed, "Brent! Time to get up—breakfast is ready."

Dad said casually to Mom, "Glad she got the X-ray."

I literally choked on my eggs and repeated with a cough, "X-ray?"

Mom looked at me funny, asked if I was okay, and then said to Dad, "Yes, thank goodness. What were they thinking? All of them. Going up there at night. You can't see your hand in front of your face."

"I think he's learned his lesson. Let him sleep."

Mom nodded. I stared wide-eyed at my brothers and then back at Mom and Dad. I finally asked, "What are you talking about?"

Dad regarded me with curiosity and answered, "Brent. He took Maureen out to the quarry pond last night. They were skating with the other kids, and Maureen fell and broke her wrist." After a minute, still staring at me, he added, "What's the matter with you? You don't even like Maureen."

I shut my gaping mouth and wiped the look off my face. I said dismissively, "Um, nothing. I thought you were talking about something else." I wolfed down the rest of my food and got up. "I'm gonna go get my gear—I'll be right back." I ran up the stairs to my room and sat on the bed breathing hard. I opened *The Shy Ones* and reread the section about the dog getting an X-ray. Such a random thing. There were coincidences in this world, right?

And then there was…*this*. Whatever *this* was. First the "Hang in there!" and now the X-ray.

Weird.

Chapter VI

My whole life, I have tried not to bother others with my presence. Even before Kathy died, I was a reserved child, leaving most of the wild gregariousness to my brothers. Yes, we were the family of doers, but for me that meant keeping busy and keeping quiet. After Kathy died, I became even more of an observer and less of a partaker. I think this was why Mom was trying the library thing with me. Sure, she saw me at basketball, but my manager job entailed me concentrating on the stats and scores, not so much on the human interaction aspect. Outside of that, I suppose I was spending a lot of time in my bedroom. As I was reading *The Shy Ones*, I began to ponder my solitary existence as if I were an orb floating on a separate plane from everyone and everything else. In the days that followed my trip to the library, I found myself absorbed in the book, striving to find a quiet, out-of-the-way corner so I wouldn't be interrupted. It was a pattern I would repeat throughout my life: hiding my face in a book, bending my head as if to brace against the wind, barring the view of my face with my hand or my hair as a shield. And yet, no matter how remote I made myself, someone would invariably ask, "What'cha reading?" or "Good book?" I often wondered if my reading and defensive posture were sending out an invitation of welcome. Entirely the opposite of my intention. Was it a way for others to snatch a piece of my peace? Or was it some type of reverse portal?

Even though I was a slow reader back then, to my utter amazement I finished *The Shy Ones* in three days. It was as if I couldn't put it down. As if I was *afraid* to put it down. I brought it with me to the game the next morning (which we won) and read it during the warm-up, breaks, and halftime. Saturday afternoon I went to my bedroom and read for a long while until Mom told me to "get moving—we're leaving in fifteen minutes." The first thing I noticed when the front door was opened for us at the twins' party was that they had a dog just like the one on the cover of *The Shy Ones*. I stared at it for a good minute until the twins' dad came up and took our coats. He said to me, "Her name is Shelby. She's the sweetest dog. You can pet her if you like. She doesn't bite." He smiled, and I laid my hand lightly on the top of her head as her big golden-brown eyes look up at me with happy affection. I ran my fingers over her silky velvet ears, and she wagged her tail so violently that it slapped up against my crutches. I laughed, laying one crutch down and pulling her to the side of my cast until Tracy came over with a pinched look, grabbed Shelby by the collar, and led her away, saying to her dad with annoyance, "Dad, I thought we were going to leave her locked upstairs." I stared after Shelby wistfully as she glanced back with a whimper.

The rest of the night was filled with the usual teenage chatter, especially on the part of the twins, who were all that you would expect of spoiled, selfish, overly indulged thirteen-year-olds. The staggering number of toys and gifts, and still, after each, there was a curt "thank you" and immediate storage in prearranged rubber totes to be sorted at a later date according to worthiness. On this perfect night, presents were not to be played with, nor shared.

I went hunting for a corner in which to hide. I noticed one of the girls from our class, Jane Parker, sitting on a flat black ottoman off to the side of the couch. She was a short brunette with a Dorothy Hamill haircut and a neat, tiny nose, and I realized with a jolt that she reminded me of the character in the book I was reading: she was shy. She always had her head in a book, barely spoke, and had the best grades in our class.

I asked her quietly, "Do you mind if I sit here with you?" She looked up from *The Red Pony* with surprise but nodded and scooched over on the ottoman. I couldn't remember a time when I had ever spoken to her before. I set my crutches against the wall and sat down beside her, taking *The Shy Ones* out of my purse and showing it to her with hopeful comradery. She smiled down at the title—was that a hint of respect, pretention, annoyance, acknowledgment, or indifference? I couldn't tell. As an excuse (in case it was pretention), I said, "I just started reading." She regarded me with interest. I dug in deeper with, "I really don't know *what* to read. I picked this book at the library because I liked the cover." Her brown eyes turned kind. Oh good, she hadn't been judging. I could see now that she had just been afraid of an interloper intruding on her private space. I could certainly understand that. I asked, "How do you pick?"

A range of emotions—curiosity, fear, excitement, caution—passed over her face. She finally answered slowly, "Um, well, I'm in the advanced reading class, and we were assigned this book, but normally when I'm able to pick, I usually read the classics—you know, Dickens, Austen, Twain, the Brontë's."

I thought, no, I don't know! I felt like a complete idiot. I didn't know what she meant by the "classics," and outside of Mark Twain, none of those names sounded familiar. I said with feigned confidence, "Oh, uh-huh, sure, sure."

I looked down at the floor, and she must have seen right through me because she added quickly, "But when I first started reading, I liked Judy Blume and Laura Ingalls Wilder and Louisa May Alcott. You may like these authors—they write timeless stories about young girls, and the words aren't too...too difficult." She smiled, and I wanted to hug her for that smile! "You should try them."

I watched her friendly face and thought, how have I never noticed this girl before? I said, "Right—we all have to start somewhere." She nodded. I then said, "But...but, I mean, doesn't it take you months to finish one?"

She tilted her head a little and admitted with a grin, "Sometimes, yes. Well, not months, but definitely weeks. Especially the classics that are written in the older English language. It takes some effort and practice to get used to. But you shouldn't have any trouble with the names I just gave you. The stories are rich and interesting, and they'll draw you right in. In fact, you'll probably speed right through them, and when you're done you'll wish they had never ended, and sometimes you'll want to start them all over again."

Wow—as she said this, she reminded me of Kathy and how Kathy used to cry at the end of a book. I stared into Jane's eyes and realized they were the same shade of dark amber as Kathy's. I must have been looking at her funny because Jane broke into my thoughts with, "You want a tip? Something I used to do?"

I snapped back to the present and said quietly, "Sure."

"Read out loud. Go to your room or somewhere where no one will hear you and read out loud to yourself. I don't know why, but when you're first getting started, it really helps. It'll be slow going, but then before you know it, it'll get faster and faster, and then eventually you can try the silent thing and you'll be a pro."

I smiled gratefully. "Okay, I will." I paused for a minute and then asked tentatively, "Do you ever have things in the book you're reading...sort of... like happen in real life?"

Her eyebrows furrowed and she said, "Huh? What do you mean?"

Now I was back to feeling like an idiot. I hid my embarrassment in a laugh and hedged, "Oh no, no, nothing. I just meant that sometimes, um, sometimes you get so attached to the story, you feel like you're living it, you know?"

"OH!" she said vehemently, "Yes! I *do* know what you mean! I get totally lost in a book, and then I forget where I am until whoops, my mom is calling me down to dinner." She laughed and I breathed again. "Yeah, that happens a lot. That's why I love to read."

"Right," I said with a nod.

❧ Chapter VII ❧

Adam begged his mom to let him transfer schools ("To where?" she asked) to his old school in Indy ("Where would you live?"), maybe live with one of his friends ("I would never allow you to impose on them in that way"), maybe do school from home ("How would that work? Who would teach you? I'm at work all day").

Anything not to have to go back with those kids who all looked at him like he was a murderer, which of course, in a way, he was.

"But Mom, how am I supposed to go back there?!" he cried.

"Adam, listen to me," she said, cupping his face softly. He was sitting on the edge of her bed, and she was standing over him. Jeremy was downstairs watching MTV. In the background, Adam could hear Alan Hunter's voice announcing the next video: Sailing by Christopher Cross. "Who cares what they think? You can't let people like that get to you. They don't know the truth, and they probably don't *want* to know the truth. They'd rather make rash judgments without knowing the facts because it's easier to sit in judgment than it is to be judged. But *you* know the truth."

"Yeah," said Adam, looking down, the guilt seeping like a poison into the cavernous well of his soul. "*I know.*"

"No, that's not what I mean. Sweetie, it was an *accident*. And accidents happen to everyone. And soon enough, once your legal case is heard, everyone else will know. Okay?" She let go of his face, and he lay back on her bed, defeated and defunct. "In the meantime, you just keep your chin up, your head high, and don't let those…gossipmongers and idle tongues bother you. You hear me? Yes, this is a big life lesson—you got knocked down, but you have to get back up again. You can't run away from your problems. You have to face them head-on in order to grow and move forward. It's the only way."

Adam sighed in resignation. His one consolation was that he knew those people couldn't hurt him anymore than he had already hurt himself. He was his *own* judge and jury. He knew the truth. He had killed that girl.

That first Monday back at school was awful. Adam tried to keep to himself, but the guys from soccer and even some of the girls in class were curious and asked questions. They wanted to know what happened. The guys asked a lot about the gory aspects of the accident—how bloody it was and if he had seen the dead body. Every word they said was like a knife to his heart. Why didn't they know enough not to ask? Why didn't they leave him alone? Adam simply shook his head and said, "I don't remember." That seemed to work, for the most part. The girls wanted to know more about the emotional toll, wondering if Adam had been crying a lot or was having nightmares. He didn't know how to respond, so he just shrugged.

After a few weeks, the curiosity factor died down and he was mostly left to himself. This was a blessing in a way, but also confusing. He felt oddly invisible and as though life would never get back to normal. Whatever *normal* looked like. Heck, he barely knew anyone at school *before* the accident, and now he was an outcast, a pariah, like a kid with the plague.

Mercifully, the one thing that didn't change was soccer. It was in full swing, and the guys didn't bring it up. They treated him as if nothing had happened. So, he spent much of his time practicing, running, training, perfecting his ball skills, mostly with the team but sometimes on his own for hours after everyone had gone home, staying out until the night sky was black and the moon had risen above the field. He would be so tired by the time he got home that he would crash in a heap on his bed, his latest goal of having a dreamless night of sleep finally achieved (or usually at least half-achieved).

One Saturday, in the middle of a game, Marc Cartwright was sitting next to him on the sidelines, waiting to sub in. He looked at Adam for a split second and said, "Hey, how's it going?"

Whoa. Riley's brother. Adam took a deep breath and answered cautiously, "Fine."

Marc nodded and looked away. Then after a few minutes, he turned back, searched Adam's face, and said, "No really, dude, are you okay?"

Adam realized with a shot of swift certainty that no one, not a single person, had asked him that, *really* asked him, since the accident. When he answered, he had to swallow down the sudden flame in his throat. "Not really." Marc nodded but didn't say anything. Finally, Adam inquired, "Is... is...is your sister okay?"

Marc shook his head slowly and answered, "Not really."

Adam looked down at his hands, hiding the tears that jumped up in his eyes and trickled down his face. Mercifully, at that moment, the coach called Marc's name and told him to sub in. Marc ran onto the field without looking back.

A few months went by. Adam didn't remember much from those months. When soccer season was over and it turned cold, he spent most of his time in the basement with his brother, Jeremy, playing Atari and listening to music on the record player. Sometimes they played their own music. Jeremy was pretty good at the drums, and Adam was starting to pick up the guitar. They both liked playing because it reminded them of their dad. He had been in a band with his buddies, and sometimes on a Friday night he would bring Mom and the boys to this local bar in Indianapolis. They would sit in the corner booth and watch the band play for hours or until Mom dragged them home to bed. His dad was so good, with a bluesy voice and a swift picking style. To Adam, those nights always felt like a magical escape into another world. He had loved it. He missed those carefree activities with his parents when they were still together. Sometimes Mom got on stage and sang with Dad. She had an amazing voice, soft and sultry, and when they sang together, it was like heaven.

Or not. Apparently. All of that was over now. It had been a year since their dad left. Just like that. Gone. He hadn't even taken his clothes. Or his instruments. Or said goodbye. Or given a reason. Not to the boys anyway. Adam wasn't sure what his mom knew. She never said. A few months after he left, Mom said they had to move because they couldn't afford the house in Indy anymore, and more importantly, they needed a new start. Adam and Jeremy thought it was odd that she insisted they move their dad's stuff with them (including his instruments). She said it was just for safekeeping, as if she thought he'd come back. But he hadn't.

As far back as Adam could remember, his mom had never worked. She had been a stay-at-home mom for all of their growing-up years. And a truly great, loving mother. But Adam knew she had several college degrees and had probably wanted a career. She said it hadn't been "in the cards" until the divorce, when she decided to "dust off" her resume and find a job. After that, everything happened really quickly. She put out "some feelers," had several interviews, and then, before they even had a moment to digest it all, she found a job and they moved from the big city to this tiny town in southern Indiana.

Her new job was as a professor at a place everyone called the Institute. The formal name was the Northwood Institute. A small college up in Michigan opened a satellite campus (for whatever reason) in the remains of this huge, amazing, historic building down the road that used to be called the West Baden Resort, known as the "Eighth Wonder of the World" back in the 1900s because of its massive freestanding dome construction. Kind of like a modern-day Stonehenge or Great Wall of China. Anyway, Mom loved her job there but said the building was starting to fall apart in some places and was barely usable in others. And oddly enough, the town was now less known for the Institute or the fantastical history of the "healing waters" provided at the resort and more known as the birthplace of Larry Bird. Apparently he worked at the Institute for a while and staged basketball clinics and practice games right in the middle of the atrium below the dome. Of course, Larry Bird also went to my high school, and some of the kids had even met him.

Spending all their free time in the basement, Adam and Jeremy began to think of themselves as the new Led Zeppelin or The Who or Aerosmith. Sometimes their mom would come down and play with them (on the tambourine or cymbals or triangle) and sing. Of course, she usually made them play Styx or Air Supply or some other soft rock, but they didn't mind because they loved hanging out with her, and she really did have a great voice.

Once she came down and had a letter from their dad in her hand. It had a postmark from Texas. For some reason, she didn't read it to them but relayed that "he missed them and sent his love." He had included three checks—one for each of them. Mom insisted that Adam and Jeremy each put theirs in a savings account. They weren't sure what she did with hers. Their mom never talked about money. She only mentioned that they all had to be careful with their spending now because finances were "tight." Mom didn't talk about much when it came to their dad or their old life. Sometimes Adam wished she would.

After their move last summer, when the boys started at the new school, they wore the same clothes as the prior year for the first time ever. She said they "mostly" still fit, and the brothers were going to have to "make do." Now that Mom had a check from Dad, Adam wondered if they would get some new clothes for Christmas. Adam's jeans were already "high waters," and he could hear the whispers at school when he walked by. Plus, under their new budget, there were things he missed, like new computer games and sneakers and having a bike. There were other, more subtle changes too. Like, they used to go out for dinner multiple times a week, but now they never did. And they used to take trips and go places, like Florida and Canada, but now they stayed home. Sometimes Adam wondered how they were making ends meet. And why didn't his dad call or send more money if he knew about the accident? He hadn't spoken to them, not even once, over the phone or otherwise, since he left. The letter was the first they'd heard about. But now Adam wondered if there had been more that Mom had been keeping secret from them, and if so, why.

Adam also thought about how much his lawyer was costing them. At least Jeremy was sixteen and old enough to get a job at the grocery store as a bagger. Adam was only fourteen, and there weren't many jobs open to kids his age. In between soccer, he had tried to help a local farmer with the harvest for $1.25 an hour, but less than a day into the job, he realized he had a horrible allergy to hay and wound up sick for days afterward.

Finally, in October, he found a job catching muskrats. It had all started with a hand-scrawled note pinned to the grocery store bulletin board. It read: "Need a kid to take over my trapping business. Contact Slipkey." There was no phone number, so Adam had to ask around to find where this mysterious note (and name) came from. He finally found him—a tall, scrawny nineteen-year-old with a big mop of black hair and a scratchy, gruff voice that belied his young age and pencil-thin body. Adam went and met him at his double-wide trailer in the mobile home park. His girlfriend was mega-pregnant (Slipkey's words, not Adam's), and he told Adam that he had gotten himself a better job at Aida's Diner bussing tables and dishwashing, so he didn't have time for trapping muskrats anymore. He walked Adam around to see his traps and told him how to set them and when to check them.

After Adam had all the instructions he needed, he became an official trapper. It involved walking for miles through crusty farm fields and into dark, cold streams and rivers, winding creeks, wide lakebeds, and murky ponds. When he found a trap full, he put the dead muskrat in a sack and carried it home to the freezer in the garage. Once a week, a guy came to the house and paid him fifteen dollars for each muskrat. The whole thing was a little disgusting, and it always made Adam feel bad for the little creatures, but the money was good. The first month, he gave half his earnings to Slipkey to pay for the traps and the other half to his mom to help with the lawyer bills.

Once the traps were paid off, he kept half for himself and gave the rest to his mom. After two months, he was able to buy himself two new pairs of jeans, a jacket, and a pair of boots.

In the beginning, Adam found the work tedious and exhausting, as though he was doing double duty—trapping during the wee hours of the morning before heading home to shower and off to a full day of school while still having soccer practice and games every afternoon and on Saturdays. When soccer season ended, it got a little better, but even then, sometimes he went to bed at seven o'clock because he was so tired. Toward mid-December, he started to feel as if he was in a rhythm. He was used to the early hours and the eerie, deafening quiet of the dusky mornings as he traipsed among bent corn-stalks and rushing river water. He actually began to enjoy the peaceful, quiet solitude of these mystical, foggy jaunts. Sometimes he stopped in the middle of his trek to take in the full moon or listen to a song sparrow welcoming the new day. There was a special kind of piercing beauty that touched his heart and made him wonder about his place in the world.

During these times, while staring into the depths of a stony creek or watching a bird dip its head into the edge of a pond for a drink, he would think about the downstream effect of that horrible day back in September. Downstream as in downhill, downtrodden, downed, drowned. He imagined a canoe drifting down a fast-rushing river and then crashing up against the rocks, shredding into a million tiny pieces, like his heart. No hope of being salvaged, no hope of being saved. He also thought about the muskrats and how they were downstream too—their necks snapped like toothpicks in traps they couldn't avoid or escape. Collateral damage. Isn't that what happened after an accident? It was to be expected and accepted.

The week before Christmas, Adam ran into Marc Cartwright. Soccer had been over for a while, and Adam hadn't talked to him. For some reason, on this day, Marc came into study hall and plopped down in the seat beside Adam.

Adam looked over and said, "Hey."

Marc smiled and said, "Hey."

"No volleyball?" Usually, Marc skipped study hall for volleyball practice.

"Nope. Coach Eckers is sick."

Adam nodded.

Marc opened a textbook and started taking notes on a handout. Adam buried his head in his geometry homework and remained silent. Then out of the blue, Marc said, "Hey, you wanna come over after school and hang out?"

"Really?" Adam asked, not hiding his shock.

"Yeah, really. We have a new video recorder—an early Christmas gift—and Dad wants me to figure out how to use it so I can film the family during the holiday. You know how to work one?"

Adam said, "Yeah, I think so."

"Okay, cool. You'll come then?"

"Uh-huh," Adam answered as evenly as he could. This was his first invitation from anyone, and he had to fight to pretend he didn't care.

"Okay," Marc said, turning back to his book.

Adam suddenly had a knot in his stomach and blurted out, "But...but...what about...your sister?"

Marc looked up, surprised. His forehead creased for a second, then quickly cleared as he said, "Oh, that. Eh, no biggie. She'll be at basketball anyway."

Adam nodded in relief. "You sure?"

"Yep, you're fine."

"Okay."

Two hours later, they were at his house, filming his dad's model train set in the basement, trying to figure out how to get the best angle for the shots. It was fun.

"This landscape is amazing," Adam said. "Your dad built this?"

"Uh-huh, took him four years. He made the mountains out of chicken wire and paper mâché and hand-painted the lake and the creek. I made the bridge with my erector set, and we spent an entire month putting the lighthouse together with my brother Nate. We used real cobblestones from out in the yard and real cement."

"Wow," Adam said, amazed. "It's super cool. The whole thing looks like something out of a museum." He had to admit it made him a little jealous, and not just about the train display.

Marc started the train running over the bridge and through the tunnel, and Adam filmed it coming out the other side of the mountain.

Marc asked Adam innocently, "Your dad like trains?"

"Um...no...I mean, I don't think so."

"Where is your dad anyway?" Marc asked bluntly. He stopped what he was doing and looked up and said, "Sorry. It's just, I've never seen him at our games or anything."

"No, it's okay. Thanks for asking. No one else ever does. So it, well, um, I mean, I think he's in Texas. I'm not really sure, though."

Marc nodded and started the train back up again. "But you guys used to be up in Indy, right?"

"Uh-huh. My dad worked at Rolls-Royce. He was an engineer there."

"How did you guys end up down here?" He glanced up again at Adam and added, "Do you mind me asking? You don't have to talk about it if you don't want to."

"I don't mind," Adam replied, wondering if he actually did mind and realizing that yes, it hurt, like a pinched nerve that was awakened when moved, but better to activate it and get it over with than to pretend it didn't exist. "Well, Dad quit his job and left—I'm not sure why. Then Mom decided we needed a new start, so she sold our house in Indy and got a job here, teaching over at the Institute in West Baden."

Marc nodded. He stopped the train in order to add more cars along with the caboose. He asked, "You like it here?"

Adam shrugged.

"What's your mom teach?"

"Accounting."

Adam pressed pause on the video camera and asked, "What about you? You live here your whole life?"

"Yup, born and raised. I've never even been to Indy. What was it like being up there in the big city?"

"Oh, I don't know, pretty much the same as here—there isn't much going on. We lived in a brick house up on Meridian Street in this neighborhood where we knew all the kids. Sometimes I wish we were still there. The guy who owned the house before us put a bowling alley in the basement, and we used to host parties down there all the time."

"What? A bowling alley? No way! That is *so* cool."

"Uh-huh."

Marc confessed, "The most excitement we get in French Lick is the annual Fourth of July parade, and it's really not that exciting. And sometimes Dad takes us to train shows in Louisville. Those are fun, but someday I want to go to Indy. Mom went with Riley a couple of years ago, to visit the L.S. Ayres Tea Room, but it was a 'girls-only' trip, obviously."

Adam nodded, trying not to jump at the mention of Riley's name.

Marc noticed. He asked, "You still weirded out about my sister?"

Adam took a minute to reply, putting the video recorder down on the table carefully. He simply said yes and looked down at his hands. "Do you think I should…talk to her? I mean, I'd really like to say I'm sorry. Do you think she would be…open to that?"

Marc shrugged. "Maybe."

Adam paused and then said cautiously, "Mom and I talked to Kathy's parents a few months ago."

Marc stared. "Whoa. How did that go?"

Adam swallowed the lump that had formed in his throat and said, "Hard."

Marc nodded. He waited a few minutes, fiddling with one of the train lights, then said, "Yeah, I mean, I think it would be good. With Riley. Do you want me to arrange it?"

"Um…okay," Adam answered softly.

"Okay." Marc nodded his reassurance, but he couldn't help but see the fear in Adam's eyes. He asked tentatively, "So, are you going to jail or juvie or something?"

"I don't know yet," Adam said, his voice shaking. "It's still being…discussed or worked on or whatever they do…with the lawyers and the police and the judge."

Marc nodded again. Finally, mercifully, after many minutes of silence, he said with a grin, "Wanna see how fast we can run the train backward?"

Adam smiled a little. "Sure."

Chapter VIII

BEFORE THE NIGHT WAS THROUGH, I had a reading list, written in Jane's neatly printed hand on a pink sheet of paper, folded up and stashed away in my purse. By the time I finished *The Shy Ones*, I was armed and ready for the next library visit. Imagine Mom's surprise when I asked to go to the library on Tuesday night instead of Friday.

"I want to pick up a few books before we head to Grandma and Grandpa's."

Mom tried to quickly rearrange the astonishment on her face before replying, "Um, sure, I need to go to the grocery store anyway. Be ready to go at six-thirty."

"Aye-aye, captain," I answered cheerfully, which set her face in a whole other trajectory of shock and awe. Riley. Smiling. And talking. Without being spoken to first.

Mom caught herself, cleared her throat, and pretended to focus on the mail, which she had just brought in, saying casually, "Well, okay then."

On the drive over, she asked tentatively, "So, um, you liked the book?"

"Yep, and I'm ready for more."

"No kidding? Wow, okay, great. Well, I'll probably be an hour or more running errands…"

"That's fine," I reassured her. Still with that look on her face. It actually made me chuckle as I looked out the window of the car at the snow-packed streets and Christmas lights on the houses.

First thing when I got to the library, I placed *The Shy Ones* in the return slot, pulled out the pink sheet, and went hunting. It was unwieldy trying to balance Jane's note in my hand and the books under my chin, so I laid my crutches down on the table under the "Hang in there!" poster and hopped around instead. Back and forth—to the aisle, the shelf, the book, the table, then repeat until I had a healthy stack of five waiting for me like a welcoming unexplored discovery zone. I wanted more than anything to crack one open and start reading right away, but I decided to pull out my diary first.

Tuesday, December 22, 1980

Three more days until Christmas. We're headed to Grandma and Grandpa's on Thursday. I asked for new running shoes in anticipation of the spring track season, but I doubt I'll get them because Dad said he thinks my leg might need more healing time before I jump into a sport. I get the cast off Monday, and I can't wait. At the twins' party, I met Jane Parker. She's super nice and a great reader. She gave me advice about books and reading. I'm here at the library picking up a few she recommended before our trip. I don't know if I'll be able to finish any of them before they're due, but I'm going to try.

Here is the list:
Freckles: Gene Stratton Porter
Anne of Green Gables: L. M. Montgomery
The Yearling: Marjorie Kinnan Rawlings
Little Women: Louisa May Alcott
Charlotte's Web: E. B. White

My finals were just okay. I don't know if I did well or not. Probably right down the middle. When I asked the boys how they did, they just mumbled "good." Brent's been doing varsity basketball and Marc's on JV volleyball, so I don't see how they have time to study. Nate's still around all the time, but he mostly stays up in his room playing Dungeons and Dragons with his friends. They're so loud! I had to knock on his door twice this weekend and tell them to shut up.

Now I'm going to tell you about something that happened at school today. But I also kind of don't want to tell you. It was right after I finished my algebra final. I was walking to my next class, but my head was still swimming in numbers and equations. I wasn't really paying attention. Then I saw Marc in the hallway outside the chemistry lab. He called my name and I went over to him, but I didn't notice until I was really close that Adam was right behind him. Yes, *that* Adam. Adam Linder. I felt my face get hot. I nearly stumbled on my crutches. Marc said, "Hey, Riley—this is Adam Linder. He wanted to say something to you." I could tell by Marc's voice that he was nervous about the whole thing and trying to cushion it for both of us. He started to step away, but I croaked out, "Marc! No, please stay." I grabbed his wrist and he sighed and stood there, looking down at the floor.

Up close, Adam looked so thin, like his cheeks were hollowed out or something, and his face was pinched as if he'd bitten into a lemon. I was tongue-tied by his expression, and I stood rocking on my crutches like a stunned animal. I noticed that his kind brown eyes had dark circles under them. He seemed like just a shadow of the boy I remembered from the Booster Club booth all those months ago. He had a strange sound in his voice, like he had a frog caught in there. "Riley, I wanted to let you know...how sorry I am about...about what happened." A tear escaped from one of his eyes and rolled down his cheek. I stared at it for a long minute. He said, "I'm sorry about...Kathy...I am so sorry. And about your leg. And about...about everything. It was a horrible accident...my dog, well, he was sick...and...I didn't know what I was doing or how to drive...and I'm just so sorry. If there was a way I could take it back, I would." I didn't know what to say. I kept watching the tear on his cheek. Eventually it fell onto his green T-shirt and left a dark spot there. I stared at the spot for a while. After a few minutes, Mr. Michaels came into the hall and told us to get to class because we were blocking the door to his chem lab. I went to the bathroom for half an hour and locked myself in one of the stalls. Then I went to Spanish class and told Mrs. Lopez I was sick. She sent me to the nurse's, and I stayed there the rest of the day.

I put the diary away and sat there at the "Hang in there!" table, staring at the dangling kitten, wondering what was still dangling in my life and about to fall.

I read *The Yearling* in the car on the way to Grandpa and Grandma's until I started to feel sick. I asked my dad, "Hey, Dad, are you not supposed to read in the car?"

"I don't see why not."

"I mean, is it bad for your eyes or something?"

"No, I don't think so—why?"

"I feel a little like I need to throw up."

Mom screamed from the passenger seat, "Pull over, David!!"

Dad pulled off the side of the road. I stuck my head out the window and tried to make something come out of my throat, but nothing did, so I took in a few big gulps of fresh air and slumped back into the car. Dad told me to hold off on reading until we got to Grandma and Grandpa's.

Brent said, "Good, I can't stand listening to her whisper the words anymore. Just because dingbat has suddenly decided to be even more of a geekoid nerd shouldn't mean we all have to be subjected to her annoying voice." I scowled and bared my teeth at him, to which he narrowed his eyes and pinched my thigh.

Dad eased back onto the road, and Mom hollered into the back seat, "Would you two stop? Just stop. Riley, why don't you lay your head back and rest. And Brent, please keep your thoughts and your hands to yourself."

An hour later, we pulled into town. I woke up and looked out the window. Madison, Indiana, was a cute village with a lot of old houses, cozy antique stores, and boutique gift shops. It was decorated to the hilt with Christmas lights, signs, candles, wreaths, garlands, and more. The Lanier Mansion Museum, off to the right, looked regal and stately, and Santa's village was tucked in behind the hardware store. You could see the hill where Hanover College stood overlooking the Ohio River. That was where Grandma and Grandpa had met. Once Grandma took me to campus, just me and her, and we sat on a wooden bench with a scenic view and ate a picnic lunch. I thought it was the prettiest place on earth. It was fall then, and the leaves were every shade of the autumn rainbow. Grandma said my hair was the same color as the foliage except that my hair had even more hues than a "kaleidoscope windmill" (whatever that was!). The sun was out and reflected off the river in bright beams of glitter, causing me to squint and smile at the same time. Grandma told me, "This is where your grandpa and I used to sit and spoon." I laughed and asked, "What do you mean, 'spoon,' Grandma?" She looked down at me and grinned, saying, "Where we fell in love." I nodded, ate my fried chicken, looked around, and thought, wow, I can see why!

Grandma and Grandpa's house was on the outskirts of town, up a hilly driveway, a two-story brick colonial with a huge yard and a barn out back. After we said our greetings and brought in our things, Grandpa and Dad took the boys to the barn to see Grandpa's latest toy. Grandpa used his barn as a workshop to assemble intricate remote-controlled airplanes, hand-painting the final products and machining the motors himself. Whenever we came to visit, the boys would spend hours out there helping him. In the summertime, we would come stay for a week, and every morning after breakfast we would pile into Grandpa's truck, drive out to a little runway that had been plowed in an old cornfield, and watch the airplane enthusiasts test out their creations. I found the level of detail and obsession for the sport, if that's what you called it, fascinating, like giants working with fairy-sized parts to create a mini-universe.

As the door closed behind the men leaving for the barn, Grandma sat Mom and me down in the breakfast nook and offered us hot chocolate and anisette pizzelles (my favorite!). Mom and Grandma chatted about various things while I watched the snow and wind whipping through the trees outside. At some point, Grandma glanced out the window toward the barn and said, "Those boys, they'll catch their death out there!"

Mom sipped her hot chocolate and said, "I thought Pa put a wood stove out there."

"Yes, he did, and he's liable to burn the whole thing down one of these days because of it. But yes, praise be, I'm sure he's out there filling the belly of the thing. He chopped up that dead beech last year from the north yard, and so far the cords of wood he got from it have been plenty, but I'm more worried about the boys. They aren't used to the outdoors, are they?"

"Eh," Mom answered with a wave of her hand. "They'll be fine. They were outside yesterday with their buddies making igloos in the front yard. They're tougher than you think."

Grandma nodded and smiled. She knocked her hand on my cast and asked, "When's this anvil come off your leg, sweetie?"

"Monday!" I said with a grin.

"I bet you can't wait."

"You have *no* idea."

"What will you do first?"

"Shower!" I cried, then added, "and scratch! I've been growing my nails out."

They both laughed. Grandma finally stopped chuckling and said, "Well, don't cause yourself to bleed. I've always used a good lathering of that Kiehl's lotion. That's the best—it'll soothe the driest skin."

I nodded and ate another cookie. After a while, I asked to be excused (to which they shooed me off airily) and went to the guest room to read. An hour or two went by and I had made it through several more chapters of *The Yearling* before I heard the boys come in, stomping the snow off their boots. I quickly wrote down a few words I didn't know on a piece of paper, to be looked up later in the dictionary at the library. Being new to reading, I hadn't realized that some sentences made no sense without knowing the full meaning of the words in their proper context. I would need to ask Mom or Dad for a pocket-sized dictionary or how else would I ever get through Jane's list?

I laid the book across my chest and waited a few minutes, anticipating Grandma's call to dinner. I felt myself breathing hard, thinking about the swamplands of Florida and how magical they were. So different from the frozen Indiana world outside the window. I had never been to Florida, but I imagined a state known for its sandy beaches and expansive ocean. But this book talked about dense moss-covered forests flanked by swampy wetlands, native Floridians, wild bears and boars, inland farms, dirt roads, and venomous snakes. I was intrigued and captivated. And I loved the story, anchored by a lonely boy finding a friend in an orphaned fawn. As I had this thought and put a bookmark in *The Yearling*, I lifted myself off the bed to grab my crutches by the window and, to my utter astonishment, saw a herd of deer just outside. The sun was low on the horizon, muted behind gray cumulus clouds, and there they were—six, no, seven of them—pushing their noses through the soft layer of snow to reach the stiff, grassy wheat stalks underneath. They looked so peaceful with the red barn in the background, like a painting of a winter scene. I studied them for a few minutes, watching their mouths chew side to side like cows and their deep, dark eyes flutter with long lashes. Their haunches twitched and their ears perked up several times, but they stayed put as I placed my head up against the cold windowpane until my breath fogged up the glass, staring at them in fascinated wonder.

"Riley!" Grandma's voice from the kitchen broke the spell. "Dinner's ready—come on down!"

I sighed and hobbled down the stairs. When I took my place at the table, I pointed out the window and said, "Look. Deer."

Grandpa, who had a huge bowl of green beans in his hands, steered away from the table and went to look out the bay window, saying, "Well, I'll be! We haven't seen them for ages. They used to come quite a bit, out of that patch of woods off to the left, but they haven't been around lately. Dolores, come here—check this out. Looks like those twin fawns have grown up. Their spots are gone now."

Grandma placed the mashed potatoes on the table and went to look for herself. "You don't say! Sure enough, yes, you're right. Of course, they all look alike, so it's hard to tell if those are the same ones. Well, aren't they sweet? Such pretty little things."

My brother Brent, anxious to get food in his never-satisfied gullet, leaned back in his chair and tapped on the window glass. As quick as a gunshot, the deer ran off, their tails popping up like white flags as they bounded away across the field.

Mom scolded, "Brent!" Then, as an apology to Grandma and Grandpa, she said, "Boys will be boys…"

Grandma replied, "Yes, and deer will be deer."

I didn't say a word as I watched them disappear into the woods.

PART II – 1985

CHAPTER IX

DO YOU EVER FEEL AS THOUGH YOU'RE A VESSEL for something bigger than yourself? I suppose that's what mothers feel when they have their first child. Or what actors feel when they're trying to embody the character they're portraying. Or what biographers feel when they write someone else's story. But what happens when you don't want to be the vessel? When you are an unwilling, involuntary host? When you push away all attempts to be inhabited?

I remember reading a book once that talked about brown-headed cowbirds. These dark, ugly birds with brown heads, about the size of a robin, lay their eggs in another bird's nest. Even though their eggs are bigger than the others, the host mother doesn't seem to notice, and when they hatch, she goes about feeding whatever mouth is crying and squawking the most. While Mom's away retrieving more food, that little usurper, who, by the way, hatches first, pushes the other eggs out of the nest like a sumo wrestler pushing boulders off the side of a flatbed truck. Mom comes back, thinks, "Hmm, something's different," but then she's distracted by the one remaining needy, gaping mouth, so she just keeps feeding it, none the wiser. Later, Momma is left to raise this alien monster twice her size.

Nature is so cruel! And confusing.

And so is humanity sometimes.

And life.

Five and a half years after I saw the deer frolicking in my grandparents' yard. I was sitting on the front porch of our house in French Lick, drinking a lemonade, thinking about that nature book, and watching this poor sucker momma song sparrow feeding one of those huge, nasty baby cowbirds. It was the summer after my junior year of high school, and I was thinking I was a lot like that momma bird—struggling to keep up with an invasive species that had taken over my unwilling body, mind, and spirit. I wasn't reconciled.

I was in trying-to-figure-it-out mode. For several years, I was plain confused, as though I was being probed by something that didn't talk or explain or provide reasons for *consuming* me. I was inert, inept, incapable of recourse. It was bigger than me, and I didn't know where it came from. Was it God? Was it Kathy? What if it was ghosts? Was it some strange influence of my surroundings? Was it all in my head? This last one scared me half to death, and it was the reason I ran from it, consciously avoided it, intentionally restricted myself from exploring, investigating, knowing it. In the beginning, I thought that if I ignored it, it would go away. For the first few years, when it would happen, I would shrug it off, telling myself it was all in my head, a coincidence, an aberration. But when it continued to happen, over and over again, I slowly began to acknowledge, explore, and investigate it, despite my doubts and fears and logical mind—despite myself.

That morning, I was in the middle of reading *The Thorn Birds* by Colleen McCullough when who comes walking down the street but a Catholic priest. He was dressed in black pants, a stiff black T-shirt, and a white collar, and walking straight toward our house. Now, maybe if we lived in Rome, Italy, or New York City, or just about anywhere else, this may not have been such a shocking thing, but in French Lick, Indiana, on a tiny street like ours where everybody knows everybody, and where I was completely unfamiliar with anything Catholic, this seemed to me like seeing a giraffe in a tutu tap-dancing up a mountain. I actually gasped! And threw my book down on the ground like a flaming hornet's nest.

I ran inside, the screen door slamming behind me, and screamed, "Dad! Dad! Come quick! There's a priest outside!"

Dad, who was faceup under the sink fixing a leaky pipe, said, "A what?"

"A priest! A priest!"

He popped his head out and regarded me with the strangest quizzical expression, saying with a laugh, "Sure—a priest, a rabbi, and a pastor walk into a bar..."

"No, Dad. I'm serious. He's probably here at the door *right now!*"

Sure enough, there was a knock. I pointed, my eyes big saucers. Still skeptical, Dad got up, wiping his hands on a dish towel, and headed toward the door.

"Good afternoon, sir. I'm Father Avery. May I come in?"

"Okay, why not?" Dad said sarcastically, looking back at me as if to say, "Is this really happening?" He shook the priest's outstretched hand. Dad introduced himself and led the priest into the living room, where they stood across from each other as I watched from the entryway, my mouth agape.

Dad started, "What can I do for you..." then cleared his throat and said (as if he wasn't sure of the right word), "Father?"

"Sorry to show up here on your doorstep unannounced like this on a Saturday, but I got your name from Tom Richards over at the hardware store, and he mentioned you're a handyman. Is that correct?"

Dad nodded, still assessing and wiping his hands on the towel. He answered simply, "Yes, that's my bread and butter. How can I help you?"

"Good. Well, I just moved down here from Indianapolis—I'm the new priest at Our Lady of the Springs—and I noticed that our beautiful 1887 building is getting, well, let's say, a little tired. And we have two other buildings on the property that also need some love. If you're not busy this week, I wondered if you wouldn't mind coming over and taking a look. It's just a few things here and there needing to be spruced up. I'd like to get everything in shipshape condition before we host the annual summer carnival. I'm not sure if this type of work is up your alley, though. Tom gave you quite the reference—said your work is the best in the county. Would you be interested?"

Throughout this speech, Dad was simply staring at the man. Like me, it was probably the first time he'd seen (let alone talked to) a priest in person. My mind flashed back to *The Thorn Birds*. The priest in the book was portrayed as handsome and confident, and here was a priest standing right in front of us, young (maybe in his mid-thirties), tall, good-looking, with bright blue eyes and thick brown hair. I began to wonder what he was doing here in French Lick. Maybe he had been sent down from Indy to stir things up, try something new at the church, maybe even to save it. We had a lot of churches in this small valley, and there were only so many people to go around. I honestly wondered how any of them stayed afloat. Regardless, something about his eyes, so intent and hopeful, made you want to be on his side, to help him in any way you could. He seemed calm, poised, and persuasive. I stood there, staring from one to the other, wondering what Dad would say.

Dad, being a thoughtful guy, didn't say a word for a minute or two. Like me, he was studying the priest's face, trying to take the measure of the man. Unlike me, he probably wasn't thinking, how does a guy this handsome take a vow of celibacy?

Dad finally held out his hand, and the priest obligingly took it. Dad said, "I'm free starting Tuesday. Will that do?"

The priest smiled—wow, those perfectly white teeth—and said, "Works for me. Morning prayers are over by ten. Come anytime after that."

"I'll be there."

They said their goodbyes, and the priest headed out the door and down the street. Dad went back under the sink with his wrench, and I stood in stunned silence for a few moments, then raced outside to catch the priest.

"Hey, mister, er, priest, sir, I mean, Father, stop, one sec, please—I have to talk to you."

He stopped, turned, and glanced at the house as if he had forgotten something, then seeing my hands were empty, back at my face with curiosity, waiting.

I said, a little out of breath, "Thanks. My name's Riley."

He smiled and held out his hand. "Hello, Riley—nice to meet you."

I began with a little stutter, "Can I—ca-can I walk with you for a bit?"

"Of course," he said naturally, as if people asked to walk with him every day.

I was suddenly nervous and tongue-tied. After all, it wasn't every day you approached a complete stranger, and a priest at that. I had run out to him on a whim, and now I was scared and stymied. I had thoughts, oh so many thoughts, but how to begin?

Finally, after a few minutes, I asked stupidly, "You like it here in French Lick?"

He smiled down at me and said, "Yes, very much." He scanned the neighborhood, smiling at the rows of houses, grassy yards, and front porch swings. "It's a quaint little town. Beautiful tree-lined streets, friendly people, rolling hills and farm fields, and of course, the history of the town is charming. I admit, I had no idea before I moved here...in fact, I'm still learning..."

"Oh yeah," I jumped in, "This place used to be super famous, you know. All the rich people would come down from Chicago and from all over the Midwest to bathe here. And to drink that stinky rotten-egg–smelling water, if you can believe it."

He nodded with a grin, "Yes, rather fascinating, I've tried it several times, and I must say, it's not bad." He laughed and said, "But what do I know? One thing is for sure, though—this was a wonderful town back then and still is. Mrs. Whitman, do you know her? She lives out on Brick Street. She's ninety years old, and she told me she remembered riding in horse-drawn carriages down Broadway and how you could barely get around during the summer season because it was so packed with people taking the waters, strolling along the avenue, riding the train, drinking directly from the wells at the West Baden Resort. Apparently, it was quite the sight."

"I bet," I replied, trying to picture it. "Hard to imagine now. My dad remembers hearing all the old stories. He moved here from Kentucky to work for Pluto Water in the sixties. That's how he met my mom—she was the receptionist there. He told me it used to be one of the top-selling bottled waters."

"Wow, I didn't know that." Then after a short silence, he asked, "So Riley, was there something else you wanted to talk about?"

I looked away, toward my neighbors' houses and then back at mine for a moment. Glancing quickly into his eyes, I said, "Yes..."

He smiled, raising his eyebrows in encouragement.

Cooking up my best shot at nerve, I finally spit out, "Have you ever, I mean, do you ever, do any exorcisms?"

He stopped in shock, a frown appearing on his face. Then, a second later, thinking I couldn't possibly be serious or that I was simply a curious, inquisitive girl, he began to walk again, his face placid as he asked, "Have you been watching too many movies?"

I rolled my eyes in frustration. "No, that's not it. In fact, I hate scary movies, and I've never seen that one."

"Okay," he nodded, validating my response with his penetrating eyes. He said lightly, "Well...in that case, the answer is no, I never have. Why do you ask?"

"I want to tell you something, but I don't...I don't know how."

He stared at me with vague amusement. "Of course. Keep in mind, I counsel people every day, from all walks of life. People with problems and histories and tragedies and life issues. All kinds of people." He smirked a little as he continued, "And so far, I haven't lost a one."

"Good. I have a mystery I'm trying to solve."

His face changed at that—he was curious, and more serious. He said, "Okay...go ahead...I'm all ears."

A car came down the street, so we walked onto the sidewalk, which gave me time to formulate my thoughts. I began, "When I was twelve...I...I was in a car accident...and...and...something happened, I'm not sure what, but I think my life sort of...shifted." I stopped. God, to go on was excruciating—for so many reasons! I exhaled and then talked as fast as I could, "And ever since then, something has been stuck inside me. Something I can't seem to *purge*, and I thought…I thought maybe you could perform an exorcism or a blessing or a conversion or…something to *get it out*. Do you do stuff like that?"

As I was talking, his brow was knit in deep thought, processing what I was saying. At the end, he stopped and stared at me. He said, "When you say 'something,' what do you mean exactly?"

I looked into those clear, bright blue eyes and cowered. I couldn't tell him! This stranger, this man of the cloth, this church person. He would think it came from me, from my imagination. Or worse, he would think it came from that *other* place—hell, evil, darkness. Not taking any chances, I asked, "Can't you tell me if you're able to help me first?"

"I'm afraid I would have to know what I'm dealing with…"

I suddenly realized I couldn't go through with it. I felt as though he would think me a stupid, screwed-up kid who was making up stories to impress him. Or like I was pulling a prank on him, and it was all just a cruel joke.

I stared wide-eyed at his face and spit out, "I'm sorry, I can't!" I turned and ran. He called after me, but I ignored him. When I stepped up onto my porch and peeked back, he was there on the sidewalk regarding me, stock-still and unwavering, as if to show me he would still listen, when I was ready. I ran inside as fast as I could, up to my room, and hid under my bed covers like a two-year-old afraid of the bogey man. And I was.

Chapter X

Someone died. In the accident. That girl Kathy Metzger. It had been five years, a lifetime ago, but Adam still thought about her. Maybe that was because he killed her. That wasn't something you forgot. Oh sure, the judge finally ruled that it was an accident, but did anyone really believe that? Least of all Adam? Yes, it was true that he hadn't meant to hurt anyone and that he hadn't known how to drive and that he had a sick dog distracting him, but those were just the circumstances of the case. Those facts left out certain critical factors, such as the absolute crushing of the spirit, the air being sucked out of life, the lack of light in the world. He had to face reality: she was gone, and he was the reason. He couldn't take it back. He couldn't remove that day from history. He couldn't be someone else. He couldn't pay retribution or sell his soul or trade in the memory for a new one. He couldn't do anything to make it go away. All he could do was live with it. And with her, in his thoughts.

To make matters worse, his dog, Rocko, never came back and was never found, so that weighed on him a lot too. Like fools, they had never updated his tags when they moved and had, in fact, removed the old ones with the old address and phone number. Why hadn't they gotten around to getting new tags? Sure, a dog wasn't a human, but that dog had been his friend, his buddy, his port in the storm when his parents divorced and his mom moved them to French Lick, away from all his friends and the only life he had ever known. He felt as though Rocko was a missing piece of his puzzle, and now when he looked at dogs or cats or horses or any animals, he wanted more than anything to commune with them on a spiritual level to see if there was a way to be forgiven, to get back in their good graces, to release the pain lingering there, to no longer be missing himself, to be found.

Adam was nineteen and still not reconciled, nor redeemed, nor released from these ruminations. He had even started working as a volunteer at the local animal clinic in Paoli, thinking maybe that was the way out of his personal purgatory. Thus far, the animals and their attention and unconditional love provided some distraction, satisfaction, and relief, but nowhere near the amount required. So, in addition to his volunteer job, he kept himself busy working at the local pizza place, striving to fill his hours so as not to think too much about his tragic past and to instead focus on the here and now.

It was a Friday night in June, and Adam was walking out the door just as Wayne was coming in.

Wayne asked, "Adam, what address?"

"Um…says twenty-one…Tulip Poplar Terrace. Why?"

"Oh, I might have another one for you in a sec, if you wanna wait, about a mile from there."

"Okay, sure," Adam said, then came back inside and waited by the counter.

Wayne, the owner of Pizza Shack, was just back from buying mushrooms at the grocery store. He quickly unpackaged, cut, and scattered them on a half-finished large pizza, and tossed it in the oven.

Adam asked, "Busy tonight?"

"God, yes. That's why I had to run out for mushrooms. As soon as the rush is over, I'm gonna give Gina a call and see if she can bring us more peppers and onions—we're getting low on those too. I guess I didn't plan our stock well enough this week. I'm not even sure why we're so busy. Is there something going on?"

"Beats the heck out of me," Adam answered with a shrug. "Probably the usual summer parties."

"I guess," Wayne said. He took the mushroom pizza order sheet off the board and smacked it down on the upward-facing nail where fifty other completed sheets had met their fateful end. Then he moved the other orders down a slot on the board, closer to his face, and started working on the next one, throwing the dough in the air with skilled hand-tossed precision.

Derek, the guy who handled the orders, was on the phone scribbling notes and asking directions. When he got off and tacked three more orders to the board, Wayne cursed under his breath. Then Derek used the paddle to take two pizzas out of the oven, landing each in an open box, cutting them into slices, and storing them on top of the oven.

Derek asked Adam, "You going to Matt's party tonight?"

"Party? Matt who?"

"Langford. Jennie's coming here at closing time to pick me up and head over there."

"Is it...open...to everyone?"

"Yeah, man, you can come. BYOB...or whatever you wanna bring..."

"Okay, cool," Adam said. It had been forever since he'd been to a party. His mom had just been saying that he needed to get out and socialize more.

When the mushroom pizza was done, Adam loaded up his insulated delivery bag and headed out the door. He looked at the addresses on the boxes. Wayne was right—the two customers' houses were close to one another. He was glad he had waited. Saved driving back and forth. Being the pizza delivery guy was mostly easy money, but there were times when it was the most irritating thing. Like when Derek got the address wrong or when Adam didn't know where the house was located and the dirty, beat-up, folded-up map in his car didn't show it either. Then he had to find a pay phone to call the people and ask where they lived. Worst of all was when people had angry dogs. If you had just ordered a pizza for delivery and you knew some stranger was showing up at your house, wouldn't you chain your dog? Sure, let the dog loose to run right at the guy with the food in his hand.

Adam had been home from college for over a month, having finished his freshman year at the University of Louisville with a 3.8 GPA. He was sharing a car with his brother, Jeremy, which was complicated at times but mostly worked out well. The 1977 Honda Civic had some rust under both side panels and around the trunk, but the engine and gas mileage were great. Jeremy used the car in the mornings (he was still working at the local grocery store, having been promoted to head of the produce department), and Adam had the car in the afternoons for the animal clinic and in the evenings for Pizza Shack.

It was a balmy summer night, so Adam had the windows down and the music cranked up—John Cougar's "Jack & Diane." As he drove through town, he noticed the smells of freshly mown grass and hot pavement. He wondered what Jeremy and his buddies were up to tonight. Were they going to Matt's party? After five years living in French Lick, Adam still didn't have a ton of friends. He was sort of a loner. Jeremy, on the other hand, made friends like a sponge soaks up water. Adam's theory was that Jeremy was more approachable—he was shorter, more outgoing, open and friendly to everyone. Adam was tall, six three, with shaggy brown hair, brown eyes, and a quiet, guarded personality. Even in college, he stuck to himself, focusing more on his studies and less on people. He hadn't dated—hadn't even gone on a single date yet. The closest he ever got was when he got up the nerve to say hello to a pretty girl in his geography class. She had simply smiled, said hi back, blushed, and looked away. Apparently, she was just as shy as he was, so that was the end of that.

As he drove down Broadway, his breath caught in his chest. It was that street. That intersection. Where the accident happened. Of course, he drove down it nearly every day, but once in a while it struck him again like a bolt of lightning. Probably because of the wooden cross there with her name on it, and the flowers and ribbons—a mini shrine to Kathy. To make matters worse, on this evening's delivery, he also had to pass her family's house. If the wooden cross was a stake in his heart, her house was a dagger. Sometimes his brain blocked it out, the whole accident and everything associated with it, only to have it come back to him in a wave, like a tsunami slamming against him. There it was: her house. Now, as he drove by, he wondered if her bedroom was preserved exactly as she left it, like a diorama set in glass, her shoes and clothes in the closet, her twelve-year-old's makeup on the dresser, her favorite stuffed animal sitting on the bed. Adam noticed that her older sister was sitting at the picnic table in the side yard, hanging out with some friends. That might have been Kathy, but it wasn't. Because she was gone.

Adam set his eyes straight forward and clenched his jaw so as not to go down that dark tunnel. Then a minute later, there was Riley Cartwright's house. The other girl he killed, in a different way. He still hung out with her brother Marc sometimes, but not as often anymore. Marc had gone to the University of Illinois, and Adam had gone to the University of Louisville, so they only saw each other during breaks. After Adam passed their house, he glanced back and there was Riley, on the front porch swing, reading a book, her red hair flowing behind her, her beautiful, freckled face concentrating on the pages, one leg straight out while the other dangled off the side, a flip-flop waving back and forth in the breeze. Adam wondered if she had seen him. Did she know his car? He hoped not. She was always reading. He remembered that from high school. Always with a book in her hand, everywhere she went. Sometimes the teachers actually scolded her about it, which seemed ridiculous. There were worse things to be doing in class than reading.

He had always been rather curious about Riley. She popped up in his mind a lot. In fact, sometimes he had to forcibly remove the image of her from his mind. Something about her stuck with him, like tree sap that you can't get off your fingers. Fascinating, intriguing, charming, sticky, wonderful sap. The way she could sit for hours concentrating on a book or simply staring off into space—so quiet and calm within herself, seemingly protected from external stimuli. She had the type of presence that drew you in like a moth to a flame. And those wide, sad blue-green eyes and that unruly auburn hair framing the perfect contours of her soft cheeks and freckled nose. Not to mention those full red lips. He remembered every single second with them in the closet at that birthday party all those years ago. How could he forget? It was like having a taste of paradise and then being told you must never partake again. Torture of the acutest kind. To be drawn to that which was the one thing on earth wholly forbidden. Granted, rightfully so. Unreasonable, untenable, unsustainable, unfathomable, not to mention unwise. No good could come of it. To think of her in *that* way. Not possible. That was for sure. That was for damned sure! Stupid, stupid, stupid, unhelpful thoughts of her absolute perfection in the form of something completely and inexorably unattainable!

Adam delivered both pizzas, trying to shake off the heavy weight that had descended on his soul. He headed back to Pizza Shack and forced his thoughts to the practical. He wondered how many deliveries he had left before he could head to the party. He wondered who would be there. Should he bring anything? Should he change into something different? He was wearing his Pizza Shack polo, but he had a green Mountain Dew T-shirt in his trunk. Maybe he would throw that on instead.

When he pulled into Pizza Shack, he saw that Slipkey was there, sitting on a barstool in the back, talking to Derek. After a couple of years, Adam had stopped trapping muskrats and sold the traps to another kid. But Adam kept in touch with Slipkey. He worked at Pizza Shack too, part-time, making the dough in the early-morning hours—mixing the ingredients in a huge metal mixer, weighing and cutting the dough into different sizes, and shelving it to rise before Wayne got there to prep the sauce and other ingredients. Sometimes Slipkey would come back at night too, stop by to chat and grab a pizza for his wife and kids. Adam wondered when he ever got any sleep because he came in around four in the morning to make the dough and then worked the breakfast and lunch shifts at Aida's Diner as a cook, and somehow still managed to come by Pizza Shack at night. He was a really good guy. Once, the summer before, he had come by the house to show Jeremy and Adam how to change the oil on their car and how to fix a few things around the house that were broken. Mom loved him after that and offered to pay him, but he refused. She asked him why everyone called him Slipkey, and he said, "I was so skinny with these long, dangly legs and arms that people said I looked like a Slinky, but in my child's mind I thought they were saying Slipkey. Somehow the name stuck."

That night, thankfully, the pizza delivery rush fizzled out as quickly as it began. Adam was pumped because he had made thirty-eight dollars in tips, which was the most he'd ever made. As the sun descended in the summer sky, he finished his last delivery and ate a few slices of a leftover pizza with the rest of the guys. After a few minutes, Jennie came by and picked up Derek. Adam called Jeremy and asked if he was going to the party. He said, yeah, but he needed a ride, so Adam said he'd come get him. Slipkey wolfed down the last slice, said bye to Wayne, and hitched a ride with Adam. At the house, Jeremy came out with his friend Mike, and they both jumped in the back seat.

Slipkey turned with a grin and asked, "What have you two derelicts been up to tonight?"

Jeremy responded, "The usual. No good."

"I figured."

"You bring us a pizza?"

"Negatory. Ate it."

"Bastards!" Jeremy cried and smacked Adam on the back of the head.

Adam cried, "Hey! What are you hitting *me* for?"

Jeremy didn't even bother to reply and instead turned to Mike and said, "You think Darlene'll be there? I heard she's working down at the DQ."

"Oh yeah, she'll be there," Mike replied with confidence. "I saw her brother the other day. He said she's not working at Dairy Queen anymore—she switched to Aida's Diner, where she can make more money."

Slipkey inserted, "Darlene? Oh yeah, I know her. Just started. She's great. You don't have a chance in hell, dude."

Jeremy scoffed, "What? Of course I do. Don't you know, the ladies love me."

"Ha! Sure they do," Slipkey responded.

When they turned onto the street, they saw cars lined up around the block. A massive bonfire in the backyard of the party house shot sparks and ash up into the darkening sky. Adam parked ten houses down and changed his shirt. Then they walked together toward the noise and crowd.

Groups of kids were standing and talking by the fire, and others were seated in chairs and lying on blankets around the yard. "Shout" by Tears for

Fears was blasting out of a speaker propped in an open window. The yard wasn't very wide but descended back into a tall, grassy field flanked by a meandering creek.

Slipkey said what they were all thinking. "Whoa, cool party."

Off to the side of the fire was a keg and a stack of red Solo cups, so they headed over there. Jeremy and Mike found a group of women by the food table, including (apparently, according to Slipkey) the infamous Darlene, and became immediately engrossed in conversation with them. Slipkey and Adam spotted Derek and Jennie already seated by the fire, so they filled their cups and sat down beside them. Adam sipped his beer and let his eyes adjust to the light of the fire. Derek was talking to a guy who was poking at the logs with a shovel.

Jennie turned and said, "Hey guys, how's it going? Can you believe this party?"

They nodded in response, held up their cups, and grinned. She had been dating Derek a while, so they knew her pretty well.

She asked Adam, "How's college going? Derek mentioned you were going to Louisville. You like it?"

He smiled and nodded. "Yeah, it's cool. It was kind of an adjustment when I first got there because it's, like, huge—bigger than our whole town and then some, you know?"

"How many?"

"I think like fifteen thousand."

"Oh wow, that is big. I can't even imagine. I mean, I'm working over at the salon now, you know—The Hair Hut—and we're lucky if we get ten people a day coming in, so I don't know what you do when you're surrounded by that many people in one place. Do you have to wait in line everywhere you go? Where do you eat? And study? And think?"

Adam laughed. "Yeah, it can be difficult at times. And I do hate the lines, especially at the bookstore at the beginning of the semester and definitely in the dining hall for most meals. But eventually you get used to it."

"You go to a lot of parties there? Meet a lot of girls?"

He answered with a nervous laugh, "No, not really. I guess I was too busy studying."

Slipkey jumped in at this point and said, "You realize that in order for Adam to meet a girl, he'd have to *talk* to one."

Adam turned, eyes wide, and slugged him in the arm, exclaiming, "Hey!"

Slipkey shrugged, not taking it back, and Jennie laughed. She said, "Well, you're talking to me right now, and we can certainly help your situation tonight. There are plenty of nice girls here. Look around. I know almost all of them, and I can introduce you."

Adam shook his head and started to say, "No-no—" when Slipkey cut him off and said, "Yes! That's exactly what he needs. Can't you get one of them to come over here?"

Before Adam had a chance to protest, Jennie was out of her seat and on the hunt. Adam gave a look of death to Slipkey, which prompted him to say, "What'cha gonna do? What better time than the present? You'll be fine. Drink."

Adam, instantly nervous, said, "Holy crap, Slipkey, why did you do that?"

"Because, dude, I've been friends with you for years now, and I've never once seen you even glance at anyone, and it's about time you did. I mean, look at Jeremy and Mike—they're over there whooping it up with at least five girls, and you're here, sitting and talking to me. What's wrong with this picture?"

"I didn't come here to pick someone up," Adam said lamely.

"Yeah, but it wouldn't hurt, would it?"

Adam tried to chug some liquid courage as Jennie headed back with three girls in tow, each carrying a chair. They sat down beside them and introduced themselves. Cindy, Susie, and Eve. Adam recognized Cindy and Susie from high school, but the other girl was new to him. Susie said she was her cousin from Indy who was visiting for part of the summer.

They immediately made a joke about their names (Adam and Eve), and Jennie squealed, "Whoa, totally biblical—you two have to sit next to each other and cuddle up. Eve, do you have an apple? Hardy-har-har, just kidding. Here, put your chair right here, and I'll bring you another beer." Jennie disappeared, and Slipkey started pulling pictures out of his wallet of his little girls, showing Cindy and Susie, who were as enthralled (and apparently knew his wife and kids) as Adam was tongue-tied next to the pretty blonde Eve, who was wearing a black and gold Vanderbilt T-shirt, black shorts, and black-and-white Converse sneaks.

She smiled and said, "Hi—you live around here?"

"Yes, well, a few miles from here, but yes."

"And what do you do?"

For some reason he was confused by this question. He said, "Not much, really."

She nodded and looked away.

He felt like a fool and added, "Well, I mean, I only just got home from college a few weeks ago, and I'm working."

"Oh?" she asked, her eyes perking up. "What college?"

"Louisville."

She smiled. "Nice. I'm at Vanderbilt. You like it there? What's your major?"

"Yeah, I like it...it's big, but...yeah...a good school. I'm a biology major."

"Cool. What are you gonna do with that?"

He laughed, thinking wow, she wasn't shy, was she? That was good. He answered thoughtfully, "I'm not totally sure, but I was thinking about maybe becoming a veterinarian one day. I'd really like to work with animals."

She said, "Awesome. That would be cool. I'm an art major, but I'm not sure if I'll stick with it."

"No? Why not? I mean, what kind of art do you do?"

"I love photography, but it's so competitive, the market is totally saturated, and to be honest, I don't know if I'm good enough to make it." She looked into the fire for a few minutes and continued, "I just finished my freshman year, and they made us take the prerequisites in all the media before declaring our concentration. You know, charcoal, ink, acrylic, sculpture, metal, watercolor, graphics, you name it. But I think that just confused me even more."

Adam nodded in empathy and said, "I get it. It's hard to figure it out when there are so many choices and you're not totally sure what you want to do." He had debated changing his major to math or finance, especially after a few exhausting weekends working in the lab on tricky research projects, but then he changed his mind, realizing if he really did want to become a vet, he'd better get used to long hours and missing out on things.

Jennie came back, handed over two fresh beers, and quickly disappeared again, a knowing smile on her face. Adam shook his head at Eve and laughed. A setup was a setup, but this wasn't bad so far. Eve smiled, her face soft and open. She waited a few minutes and then said, "Yeah, I'm not sure what to do about my parents, though."

"Oh?"

"Well, Vanderbilt's so expensive, and they were hoping I'd used my major to become a world-famous photojournalist, you know, like the next Dorothea Lange," she stopped to laugh self-consciously, "so clearly, that's not gonna happen. I have to start over again with a new major, and I don't even know what to switch to..."

He nodded, not knowing how to respond.

After a few minutes of silence, she asked, "Wanna go for a walk?"

"Sure," he said with a smile.

They headed down the sloping hill where a path was beaten down through the tall grasses. Adam told her where he used to live in Indianapolis and she said, "That's a nice part of town...those big old houses are amazing. I went to a slumber party at one of them a few years ago. They had a clawfoot tub in the bathroom and a four-poster bed that we all slept in. It was amazing. I felt like a princess."

When they found a bridge over the creek, they stopped to look up at the stars and moon, saying what a beautiful night it was. Eve talked about her family and her friends back home, and Adam mostly listened and smiled. At one point, much to Adam's surprise and pleasure, Eve took his hand and led him across a small bridge over the creek and off into a grove of trees on the other side of the bridge. After a few minutes, she stopped, still holding his hand, and leaned her back against a tree, facing him. They talked softly for a while and listened to the sound of the cicadas. Then she leaned in and kissed him on the cheek and said, "You're sweet."

Adam felt the blood rush to his head. Trying not to lose his nerve, he kissed her back, this time on the lips. It was a quick kiss, just a touching of their lips, after which she said (kindly, not as a rebuff), "We'd better get back."

Adam cleared his throat and said hoarsely, "Um, yeah, okay, sure."

As they walked back hand in hand, his mind was racing in a thousand different directions. He asked her how long she was staying in town ("A month"), which made his heart beat hard. Then he asked if maybe they could "hang out again sometime" ("Sure, that would be great"), which made him shine with a broad grin. His inhibitions loosened up, he rattled on, excited and talkative, asking her questions about her childhood and what high school she went to, what her favorite restaurant was. Within a few minutes, they had emerged out of the tall grasses and back into the party scene: the fire larger than ever, the music blasting, people buzzing around and huddling together in groups. He was telling her how there used to be an amazing buffet restaurant right off 86th Street, just a few miles from his old house, when he halted mid-sentence, the grin wiped from his face. There, standing not a foot away from them, was Riley Cartwright and her brother Marc, both staring in stunned recognition. Worse, he saw Riley's eyes flicker down to their interwoven hands, causing him to drop Eve's like a hot stone.

Chapter XI

DREAD IS A HORRIBLE THING. Prior to the accident, I never thought too much about the future or the past. I tended to focus on what I was doing *right now*. Eating, sleeping, showering, school, sports, homework, chores, errands, repeat. There wasn't a lot of introspection or deep thinking. I was simply a body completing the bodily functions. There was literally no time I could remember when I stopped to contemplate any theoretical questions, such as: Am I happy? Why am I here? What is the point of life? How do I fit into this world?

I was twelve years old at the time of the accident, so it was probably completely normal that these philosophical musings never crossed my mind before, let alone that I spent time brewing for deeper rumination. But after the accident, I began to think about things that weren't there. I don't mean ghosts or phantoms in the night—I mean the why behind things. Why had the accident happened? Why had Kathy died in the accident? Why had I lived? Why had my family moved to this street before I was born? Why did my parents become friends with Kathy's parents? Why did I become friends with Kathy? Why did we go shopping that day? Why not the day before or the day after? Why were we goofing around in the back seat at that exact moment?

And why did I now feel an overwhelming sense of dread a lot of the time?

At first, it was about going to school and facing life again after the accident. And then that got a little easier, especially after I started going to the library, writing in my diary, reading, and hanging out with Jane. But then the dread came back in waves, usually out of the blue, sometimes related to a special event or milestone in my life. At the age of thirteen, for instance, when I got my period, I walked around for months afterward in fear that it would appear out of nowhere in a gush, like the pool of blood that forms under someone's head when they are shot. I began to pack an extra pair of underwear and pants in my backpack every day, and I always kept a jacket in my locker that I could wrap around my waist if I needed to. Thankfully, my fears never came to fruition, but the dread was still there, like an irritating tagalong friend.

Birthdays were hard. Every year when one came around, I was anxious the whole week before, wondering if anyone knew about it or would acknowledge it. I would grit my teeth through the singing and cards and candles, hating to be the center of attention, hating to see them honor me, hating to acknowledge that I was a year older.

The season after my broken leg was fully healed, I started playing basketball again, but I kept having this irrational fear that my leg would be crushed in the middle of a game. Someone would trip me, or my foot would catch on the sticky floor, or I would get pushed or shoved or jostled, and boom! I would go down and my femur would be smashed in a thousand pieces, spiking up through the naked, vulnerable flesh of my thigh for all to see. For days before a game, I would feel the bile come up in my mouth every time I thought of it. Yet I went on to play fine, and no one was the wiser. Except me, of course, still wondering about the whys.

Final exams were the worst. I would study obsessively, to the point that the whites of my eyes turned red with broken capillaries and my sleep was reduced to a couple hours a night. On the day of an exam, I would get to the classroom early, close my eyes, and chant the study words or formulas under my breath for as long as I could until the test began. Then it was a race to purge the raging thoughts from mind and release them onto the paper.

I was living in this strange dichotomy. To all outward appearances, I was a strong, confident, quiet girl doing very well in life. Straight A's, excellent in sports, well-mannered, hard worker, organized, studious, punctual, kind. And I had to admit, part of my dread was keeping up this appearance. I made sure no one knew about my inner fears and anxieties. It was my own personal burden that I had to protect and keep hidden at all costs. Inwardly, I was struggling against the writhing, suffocating beast, the one that gripped me over matters big and small, lingering, stalking, waiting to pounce (never quite there all the time, but ready to appear at any time to catch me unaware or to sit in patient expectation of my inevitable failure).

The topmost danger that would trigger my dread was the thought, mention, sight, or presence of Adam Linder. So, when I saw him drive by delivering pizza that night as I was swinging on the front porch, I tried not to look, tried to keep my head in my book, but it didn't matter—the damage was done. I saw him and he saw me. Although he pretended not to, I knew his head turned back after he passed our house. Yes, I saw him, and I *felt* him.

It was always like that with him. Since the accident and then even more so after that night at the Dumont twins' birthday and the seven minutes in heaven with him in the closet. I never shared another word with him, or another kiss, or another anything. Although we went to the same high school and lived in the same tiny town, he was two years older than me and had a different crowd of friends, so mercifully we rarely encountered each other. But no matter how distant he was, physically or otherwise, I still felt him. It was as though we had this strange, cosmic, kismet connection that bonded us across the ether in an incongruous, unbreakable, sealed vortex of shared tragedy.

My dread that Friday evening was compounded on many fronts. Before the drive-by, Marc had mentioned Matt Langford's party and wanted to know if I was going. I said yes because Jane was out of town and I was bored. He was in the same boat, as his girlfriend was working all weekend. So, my first thought when contemplating any gathering like this was always, "Who will be there? Will anyone notice me? Where can I hide in a crowd of people?" and then the other layer related to Adam: "Will *he* be there? Will I have to talk to him? What should I say? How should I act?"

The last facet of my dread on that Friday night came from that strange encounter with the priest. Nearly a week had gone by, but I still lived in anxious anticipation of the continuation of our conversation, which I knew would come (regardless of my attempt to run from it). I was stuck between wanting desperately to get the whole thing off my chest and dreading the idea of saying another word about it to anyone—*ever*. When Dad headed out the door that Tuesday morning, I wondered if the priest would mention anything to him. That entire day, I could barely sit still. I went from the porch to my room to the kitchen to the basement until finally Mom said, "What, do you have ants in your pants? You're driving me crazy. Would you go outside and play?"

I went out to the driveway and shot a few hoops. Marc heard me, came out, and joined me, so we played several pickup games until I was hot, sweaty, and thirsty. I went in to get water and came back out just as Dad was pulling into the driveway, shooing us away so he could get the car in the garage. I anxiously watched his face as he got out and came to talk to us. He looked happy, carefree, nonchalant. Phew. He took the ball from Marc, dribbled around him handily, and executed a perfect layup. Marc retrieved the ball and challenged him to a one on one. Dad accepted with barely a glance my way. I sat down on the grass with a relieved grin, drank my water, and watched.

I had spent several days feeling the hairs on the back of my neck stand up. I always got this feeling when someone was thinking or talking about me. Not *to* me, mind you, but *about* me. I once asked my friend Jane about this. We were in English class—our favorite class (for obvious reasons)—and Mrs. Clarke had just asked an easy question about *The Scarlet Letter*, so I raised my hand and answered. Mrs. Clarke said, "Good, Riley" and moved on to another topic. This was about the time when I got the feeling.

I whispered to Jane, "There's someone talking about me."

She looked at me strangely and whispered back, "What?"

I said, "I feel it. Do you ever feel it? Like someone's thinking or talking about you?"

She said with a frown and a grunt, "Um, no, not unless I overhear them."

I waited and finally said again quietly, "Someone is…I know it…I can feel it."

Jane glanced around the room, and then her face came back to me with a start. Her eyes wide, she said, "My God, you're right!"

"Who?" I whispered.

She pointed to the back of the room. Two classmates, Sophia and Carrie, were hunkered down together, giggling and drawing a picture, which they promptly held up (when they noticed us watching). The drawing was of two wild-looking girls with unkempt hair, square dark-rimmed glasses, and hideous smiles facing each other, their noses touching, their bodies shaped liked octopuses, some of the eight arms wrapped around each other and the others wrapped around stacks of books. I stuck my tongue out at them. Jane rolled her eyes and turned in her chair to face Mrs. Clarke, her chin up, and stated disdainfully out of the side of her mouth, "Shrews. They can't even draw. We don't look like that at all!"

At the end of class when we were walking to our lockers, we heard their taunting singsong on the other side of the hall, "Riley and Jane, sitting in a tree, k-i-s-s-i-n-g, first comes love, then comes marriage, then come books in a baby carriage."

I said to Jane, "If only we could give birth to books, I would marry you."

Jane burst out laughing and confirmed, "Right?! Me too. Who needs boys?"

"Or bratty, stuck-up girls either."

"Totally."

As we swapped out our textbooks in our lockers, Jane asked me tentatively, "So, hey, that thing in there. Does that happen to you a lot?"

"What, the teasing? Of course. I'm a total book nerd. And I have three brothers, remember?"

"No, you ninny, not the teasing. I mean the thing where you can *feel* people talking about you."

I shrugged my shoulders and slammed my locker closed. "Sure. Can't you?"

She stared at me as if I had three heads. "What? No, of course not. It's not...," she paused, and I stiffened, figuring the next word was going to be *normal*, but instead she said, "...common." Then she asked with curiosity, "What does it feel like?"

I thought about it for a minute as we walked to the next class. I said slowly, "Hmmm, I don't know...it's hard to describe. It's like...remember that time we were down in my basement and we had just watched all of those late-night black-and-white horror movies with Vincent Price, and then we had to turn off the lamps down there and run up the stairs as fast as we could in the dark in order to get to my bedroom?"

She nodded.

"Well, it's like that. Sort of...where you almost feel the light touch of someone's fingers on the nape of your neck."

She shivered. "Whoa. So, it's scary?"

"Oh, no, hmmm, not like that exactly, more like unexpected and almost, I don't know, ticklish or something."

"Ticklish?" she asked, astonished.

We were sitting in chemistry class now, and Mr. Ryan was up front writing something on the blackboard, so I shook my head in defeat, saying, "Crud, I can't figure out how to describe it. Not scary and not ticklish, but it's like you *know* Mr. Ryan's about to start class in a minute, so you're anticipating it and you feel it coming, but until it's there, it's just some nebulous space in the universe that floats around you, hovering like a fuzzy orb, until he calls out, 'Class, sit down and take out your textbooks.' You see? It's the moment before that happens when time stands still in anticipation. Time and space are floating there and reaching out to the waiting minds in the room, but until he speaks, they're in a static state of freeze. Well, for me, during that brief instant, the static state is activated and shown to me as a *feeling*."

The furrow in Jane's brow had only gotten deeper as I talked, so I finally said, "Oh jeepers, just forget about it. I can't explain, and it's probably hocus-pocus anyway." And maybe it was. What the heck did I know? This sense or feeling I had, it had been part of me since the accident, which (as a given for me, but not for others) made it hard to articulate. On top of that, since it was not a concrete, tangible thing, I couldn't use the normal scientific, evidentiary, visual explanation and words that most humans craved in order to understand and believe in something. I struggled with the right words to describe these things to *myself*, let alone to others.

So, on that day with Jane, I threw in the towel, opting to pretend it was nothing and there was no need to discuss it further. But here I was on this day, watching Dad and Marc cut and duck around each other on the driveway with the basketball, thinking how I sensed with a strange, powerful force that the priest *was* thinking about me and our brief conversation the weekend before and wondering when I would come talk to him. I still wasn't sure why I had approached the priest in the first place. Probably just an impulse—religious people knew how to get to the heart of a thing, didn't they? Maybe this man could.

A few days passed without a hint of anything brewing. Dad spent his days working at the church and his nights home with us, and not a word about the priest. Then came Friday. Dad came home earlier than the other two days, at around three-thirty. I was upstairs working on an art project when he hollered to me. He was standing in the living room, reading the mail, in paint-covered overalls. When I came down, he looked up and smiled, saying rather absently, "Riley, hey, how's it going? How was the farm today?"

"Fine," I answered easily. "We've just about finished the strawberry harvest." I had been working most mornings at a local farm that was within walking distance, harvesting summer fruits and vegetables.

He looked up and lightly pinched one of my rosy cheeks, saying, "Oh, that explains the strawberry on your face."

"Dad!" I joked back. "Very funny. Yeah, I sort of forgot my sunscreen today."

"And your hat?"

"Yes, and my hat."

He shook his head and chided, "Your freckles have begun to merge, and I see patches of red underneath. Remember, we gingers have to be careful. Sun is not our friend."

"I know, I know—I put some aloe on it already. It's fine," I said and started to head back upstairs.

He was back reading the mail again, but he stopped me with, "Hey Riley, wait a sec."

"Uh-huh? Yeah? Is there mail for me?"

"No, no, that's not it." He set the mail down on the coffee table. He looked at me in a way that made me go a little cold, despite my sunburnt skin. He said flatly, "Father Avery asked about you today."

He was watching me closely now, and I tried not to react, even though my heart picked up a stuttering trot. I said casually, "Really? That's weird. He... he remembered me?"

"Yes, quite clearly, actually. Started by asking how long I had lived here, how many kids and what you were all like, and about Mom, how we met and if she was a stay-at-home mom or worked. But then he asked about you... wanted to know how old 'Riley' was and what grade she was in and what she was doing this summer. Wanted to know if she had any hobbies or friends or boyfriends."

"Oh?" I said weakly. His eyes were burrowing into mine. I felt my cheeks grow even redder.

His face curious, he continued, "See, it's kind of strange because, well, because I don't remember introducing you when he was here last Saturday. I mean, I don't remember telling him your name, so then I wondered, gee, how does he know my daughter's name? He didn't know the boys' names. And then to ask so many questions about you in particular...At first, I didn't think anything of it, but then he asked if you might want to come with me next time, which of course made me laugh out loud. Certainly, a seventeen-year-old girl would have no desire, and actually, no doubt, a complete *aversion*, to visiting a random Catholic priest." He chuckled a little, still watching me very closely.

I nodded, uncomfortable, and responded, "Right. Yeah, that would be *crazy*."

He waited, but I didn't say a word.

Finally, in that way he had of knowing things without them being expressed or explained, he said with a small smile, "You *can* come, though, if you like."

I paused, looked away, out the window for a minute, and then said quietly, looking down at my hands, "Okay."

When I hazarded a glance back up, he nodded inscrutably and said,

"Tomorrow then. I'll be leaving at eight. They have a wedding in the afternoon, so I told him I'd only come for a few hours in the morning."

What had I done?! Deep breath. "Alright, sounds good."

I went out to the porch swing and finished reading *The Thorn Birds*, setting it aside, all the while my thoughts full of the priest in the novel and the priest in my sights for a momentous meeting in the morning. Somewhere in the middle of my mixed-up, jumbled thoughts, I saw Adam Linder drive by just as Mom called us in for dinner. Brent was working and Nate was at a friend's house, so it was just Dad, Mom, Marc, and me. Mom had made burgers and hot dogs on the grill with a side of macaroni salad, which was my favorite. As we ate, Marc brought up the party. Dad wasn't too keen on us going, saying he didn't like these random parties where he didn't know the family, and I was almost relieved because it looked as though we wouldn't be going after all. But then Marc convinced Dad, saying he knew the Langfords and that Matt was cool and we would probably just be there for an hour or two. Dad relented and Mom simply said, "I want you both home by eleven. No later."

I went upstairs and got ready, putting on a black sleeveless cotton button-down shirt and beige shorts. I put on a new eyeliner I had just bought, one that brought out the green in my eyes more than the blue. I had been told (by several people throughout my life) that I had "amazing, changeable" eyes, like a kaleidoscope. I suppose this was true in the sense that the color changed daily based on what I was wearing or what makeup I used. Tonight was all about the green. My big auburn hair was even larger than normal because of the heat and humidity, so I tucked it up with a barrette. I looked quite pretty, I thought, as I took one last glance in the mirror.

In the car on the way over, Marc asked, "So where's your sidekick this weekend?"

"Jane? Oh, she's vacationing with her family in Canada."

"That's cool. I wish our family vacationed in Canada. That would be awesome. I've never even seen Niagara Falls. I mean, don't you ever wonder why we never take family trips? Everybody else does."

"I know—it sucks. I think Mom is too much of a homebody. Same with Dad. We'll have to wait until we're older and do the traveling on our own, I guess."

"Yep," he said, then went on to talk about the price of gas going up when mid-sentence, pulling onto the street full of cars, he exclaimed, "Wow!"

I felt an instant panic. So many people at the party already! This was the type of event that was my most dreaded, and I didn't even have a book to hide behind. Gulp.

Marc led the way, saying hi to a few people right as we got through the fence and were directed to the keg. I looked at him, not knowing how to react—I didn't know there was going to be beer. He laughed at my expression and said, "I won't tell if you won't."

"Um, okay…," I answered cautiously. I had never tasted beer before, but I thought, with a small smile, maybe it would help my nerves.

We stood in line, trying to get the lay of the land. The party was in full swing by that point, people everywhere, the night sky dark and humming with the sounds of happy voices and pop music. I was tapping my foot and swaying to the beat a little, surveying the scene, when, like a flash, I saw Adam Linder, right in front of us, holding hands with a girl I didn't know. I noticed his face instantly frown like a light switch being turned off. And he swiftly dropped the girl's hand. I tried to cover my confusion and shock by hiding behind Marc. Marc looked at each of us in turn, assessing the situation, and stepped forward casually with his hand out, saying, "Hey Adam, what's up? How's it going? Cool party, eh?"

Adam shook his hand and said absently, "Yep, uh-huh." Then Adam's eyes were on me with such intensity, I felt as if the sun had just broken free of a patch of black clouds. I blinked once, twice at him, then looked down, my cheeks flushing into my roots. After a long, awkward minute, Adam introduced the girl, saying her name was Eve. Marc took her extended hand, but I stayed back. I could see her looking me up and down while I stood as still and mute as a statue.

Marc covered my odd behavior with a nervous laugh and a nudge in my ribs, saying, "Come on, Riley, keg's free…let's go." As he grabbed two cups and handed me one, reaching for the keg spout, he turned to Adam briefly with, "Catch ya later, man."

"Sounds good." Adam nodded and they walked away, the girl staring back at me with a frown.

As Marc filled our cups, he regarded me and said in a low voice, "You know, you could just talk to him sometime. He doesn't bite. He's really a nice guy. If you would just give him a chance…"

I didn't respond and looked down into the foaming head of my beer, wishing I could sink down inside it like a heavy stone dropped into a bottomless lake.

CHAPTER XII

INTUITION IS A WORD THAT HAS TWO MEANINGS. Something is about to go horribly wrong or something is about to go horribly right. Option one: a sinking in the stomach, the hairs stand up on the back of your neck with fear or horror, an urge to stop, turn, run, fight. Option two: a listening, a paying attention, a leaning in, a looking deeper, an understanding, a giving, a communion. What if options one and two hit you at the same time, together, in one sweeping, all-encompassing swath of fear and joy? Then what do you do? What if the combined version starts as a whisper (easy to discount), meanders into a hint (question it), hits you right between the eyes (surely a once-and-done thing), and finally, causes an ongoing scream in the night, a slamming of forces into the very marrow of your being (this can no longer be ignored or discounted)?

The fear takes over, grips you, trains your inner compass to be cautious, to stay the course, to maintain the status quo, to remain still. But then the yearning calls you closer, draws you in to examine, absorb, and follow it. Yet you think, take warning, take heed, take it with a grain of salt. It's against your better judgment, it's against nature, it's against your beliefs, your rational mind, your *you*. Don't be paranoid, don't read into things, don't see something that isn't there. But then it happens over and over again. Then what do you do? You realize a portal has opened, one that didn't exist before. And you can't close it. It's there now, with you, a proof of sorts, and it isn't going away, so you must acknowledge, understand, explore, wrestle, tame, and embrace it. You must.

After Marc and I got home from the party, I tried to fall asleep but couldn't, so I sat up in bed half the night reading *Jane Eyre*. Several hours in, I hit on a certain passage that gave me a jolt, so I pulled out my diary and wrote for a while, trying to steady my overwrought nerves and my overburdened soul.

Saturday, June 29, 1985, the wee morning hours

    I saw Adam Linder a few hours ago. He was with a girl. I don't know why, but it hurt me, felt like I had to blink away some tears that popped up unexpectedly, without warning, pricking my eyes and my heart. He felt it too—dropped her hand and slunk away like a kid who'd been caught lying. I couldn't reconcile anything in my mind and spent the rest of the party struggling to pay attention to the people around me. Why did he affect me this way? This boy, or maybe now I suppose he was a man, who had taken my best friend from me, who had poked a hole in my heart that would never be filled, yet who watched me with such intensity and such tender, soul-filled eyes that I was left to wonder what he saw there that I was missing. Because, to be clear, there was something missing. In me. Especially when it came to Adam Linder. How could he still watch me that way when he knew (better than anyone) how my life, my "me" was irrevocably changed on that day, and what remained afterward was forever different? Forever questioning and wondering. Forever thinking death could happen at any time with no warning, no reason, no point, no discretion, no *decency.*

    So, I've been up half the night thinking about it. And about him. And wondering why I'm feeling jealous of that girl who was holding his hand and looking into his kind brown eyes while I pretended not to notice his furtive glances my way. I put on an act. And what's funny is he did too. I could tell. When I finally allowed myself to meet his eyes, they instantly changed, turned to the girl, and faked a casual smile that never quite reached his eyes.

    So I came home and read *Jane Eyre*, trying to distract and lose myself in that wild, unruly, far-off place that Brontë's prose always elicits. But that's the thing when you're trying to escape from something: it's always there lingering in the background, ready to reemerge like a hungry, stalking tiger just at the moment when you're feeling safe and secure.

    Bam! Pounce!

    Here's where it occurred in *Jane Eyre*:

> "Presentiments are strange things! And so are sympathies; And so are signs; And the three combined make one mystery to which humanity has not yet found the key. I never laughed at presentiments in my life; because I have had strange ones of my own. Sympathies, I believe, exist: (for instance, between far-distant, long-absent, wholly estranged relatives; asserting, notwithstanding their alienation, the unity of the source to which each traces his origin) whose workings baffle mortal comprehension. And

signs, for aught we know, may be but the sympathies of Nature with man."

I read the last sentence over and over again. Words written over 130 years ago that still pierce me to the quick today! What did Charlotte Brontë mean by "sympathies of Nature with man?" I wish she had said "sympathies of God with man." I would have felt more reassurance at that supposition. Or more concrete clarity anyway. She was a pious woman from a religious family, so I would have chalked it up to the usual attribution of life's mysteries to God and His ever-present desire to control the world in which we live. Why didn't she imply that those sympathies (with far-distant, long-absent relatives, etc.) were predestined by God, that He made those connections happen long before they were even seeds planted in our own small, innocuous, weakling minds? Why didn't she imply that man walks his every step under the power and guise of predestination orchestrated by the higher powerful being of God? Wouldn't that have made things more understandable for her? And for me? Why didn't she think about what she was saying to me, a future reader, wondering what she meant by *Nature*? Capital "N" *Nature*.

Now I know she didn't mean nature like leaves and trees and rivers and streams, although I'm sure she was akin to these things and found comfort in them (much as I do), not only for their great beauty and as a tribute to God's miraculous creation, but also for the restorative aspect of their wonders, a panacea for the human soul. You can sense that in her writing, and I get it because I feel that way about nature too. But I don't think she meant this kind of nature. I think she meant that signs might be the sympathies of "the other" with humanity. Not God. But something else. And when we see or sense or feel the signs, we are to take action. What action, though? That is the question.

I must have fallen asleep at this point because what seemed like minutes later, my alarm was going off and Dad was peeking his head in my bedroom, saying, "Up and at 'em, sweetie—leaving in twenty minutes."

I hit my hand on the alarm, groaned, covered my head with the pillow, and thought with dismay, did he just say, up and *Adam*?!

As we drove to the church, I was quiet and thoughtful. We pulled into the parking lot and Dad said, "Um, I'm not sure how busy Father Avery will be, and I didn't tell him you were coming, so why don't you just be my little assistant and we'll see how it goes."

I nodded.

The church was beautiful—very white wood with a tall steeple bell tower, a large stained-glass window set in a flower pattern above the front door, steps alongside a thick limestone wall leading to the main entrance, and a steeply pitched roof. As we walked inside, I took a deep breath and said a small prayer: "God, give me strength!" As we entered, I noticed the thick, dark wooden walls held beautifully framed tall windows, also stained-glass, these with geometric patterns. Father Avery was up front, standing below a massive statue of the crucifixion, talking with two women who were pointing at the rows of wooden seating, which I found out later were called *pews*. He waved Dad and me forward, saying good morning, and then said a few last words to the women, who promptly left and came back a few minutes later with several large displays of flowers and other decorations. Apparently, they were setting up for the wedding.

Father Avery, with a huge smile, shook hands with each of us and said, "Welcome. How are you two today? Nice weather out there, I see."

Dad nodded and said, "Certainly is. A fine day for a wedding."

"Yes, couldn't ask for anything better. I'm sure the photographs will be lovely. Come on, let's get out of their hair," he said with a nod of his head at the women.

He swept his hands up toward the pitched ceiling and tight wooden tongue-and-groove walls and asked me, "Well, Riley, what do you think of Our Lady of the Springs?"

His benevolent eyes glowed in a way that forced a smile out of me. He was so proud. I said, "It's beautiful." I pointed at the landing below the crucifix and asked, "Is this where you perform?"

Based on his laugh, I felt my face go hot. He said, "Well, yes, although I would say this is where the *Lord* performs with a little help from me. I conduct the liturgy, the communion, and other aspects of the Mass, but I leave it all in His hands. So, have you never been to Mass here?"

Dad replied, somewhat abashedly, "No, sorry, Father. We've never been much of a church family."

The priest nodded without judgment and said warmly, "You would be welcome here anytime, you know. Your whole family. And Riley, we have the most wonderful youth group, headed by the nicest young married couple, the Ingrams, who do all kinds of activities with the kids every week. Outings and scavenger hunts and volunteer projects. Just last week, they led a drive-through car wash right outside in the parking lot. They were having so much fun out there, I think they all got completely soaked, but you wouldn't have known it—they never stopped laughing the whole day. And they raised several hundred dollars. They're talking about going to Holiday World with the proceeds, and they intend to bring a group of local foster kids with them. Really inspirational stuff—I'm excited to see what they come up with next."

As he was talking, he led us out the entrance door and toward a detached building a few yards away. Inside was an open kitchen and dining area, and then through a side door we passed two rooms with chalkboards and desks facing forward like small schoolrooms. Then beyond those rooms were four closed doors, one of which he opened and waved us into, following behind. It was a rather ornate office filled with floor-to-ceiling bookshelves (which drew my eye immediately), white crown molding trimming the ceiling, a dark wooden desk flanked by a large brown leather chair and a six-paned window overlooking the grassy side yard. He motioned for us to sit, which we did, in matching brown wingback chairs. He immediately started rifling through a drawer in the desk, saying, "Hmmm, now where did I put that list? David, did I give it to you? I can't seem to remember. Forgive me. It's been a busy week. Three funerals and now this wedding, plus we had an extra service on Thursday, so I've let a few things slip my mind..."

Dad laughed, pulling a piece of paper out of the pocket of his overalls and holding it up, saying, "No worries, Father. I have it here."

The priest stopped his search and smiled gratefully. He said, "Perfect. So...?"

Dad brought the list around to him as he pulled a pen out of the desk, and they started marking through the repairs that had already been done and the ones that were still left. Dad asked a few questions, the priest replied, and I tried to remain as still and quiet as possible, looking at the titles of the books closest to me. They were all religious sounding and rather intimidating, including titles in other languages and bindings that looked to be a hundred years old or more. My urge in most libraries and bookstores was to touch the books (and smell them!), but I felt in awe and scared of these volumes—they were ancient and mysterious and godly, and I felt as though if I got too close to them, I would taint them in some way. I crossed my arms over my chest so as not to have the urge.

Father Avery was saying, "Great, so do you need anything else from me to get started in the CCD room? I think Mrs. Rutledge put the paint cans and brushes right in the corner by the windows, but let me know if we're missing anything."

Dad nodded and said, "Sounds good. I should be able to get the caulking and sanding done and get a head start on the primer today."

"Perfect. Okay then…," the priest stood up, so I stood up and started to follow Dad toward the door when Father Avery stopped me. "Riley, why… why don't you stay in here for a few minutes while your dad sets up? I can… um…I can tell you a little more about our youth group and some of the other activities we have for kids your age."

A flash of anxiety hit my belly, so I glanced at Dad, who regarded my face and said with assurance, "Sure, that would work. Riley, stay and then come find me when you're done."

I set my mouth and nodded. Now or never. Dad walked out and down the hall, leaving the door open to the priest's office. I turned around from his retreating form and faced Father Avery, who waved his hand toward the wingback chair again, his blue eyes warm and welcoming, his smile calm, ingratiating, inviting. I took a deep breath and sat down.

For the first few minutes, his chatter went something like this: "Now, let's see…I know I have some type of brochure or something about the youth group. Ah yes, here it is…take this…it has the Ingrams's phone number, if you're interested. It really is a great group. All the kids seem to love hanging out together, and the Ingrams are so creative with their activities. They love to have new members, kind of like an open-door policy—you're welcome to just show up…"

His voice drifted off, his smile fading slightly as he regarded my immobile face and tightly gripped hands. He stopped, exhaled, paused, and finally said, "Riley?"

"Uh-huh," I answered mechanically.

"Listen. Do you mind if we get down to brass tacks?"

I wasn't sure what that meant, but it sounded serious, and I was about to explode into a pile of nerves, so I said softly, "Yes, sir."

"Okay, good. When we met a week ago, you mentioned something about conducting an exorcism, correct? Well, I've been thinking about that ever since and wondering why you were interested in that…particular…topic. Is this in relation to you? Or someone else?"

"Me," I squeaked out.

He nodded, his brow furrowing. He said, "You feel…as if…what…? You are possessed?"

I nodded wordlessly.

"Um…okay…wha—what exactly is going on? Can you describe it for me?"

I shrugged. His eyes narrowed, trying to figure out a way in.

He said, "I mean, do you hear…voices? See visions? Feel as if your body is being manipulated by things outside of your control?"

I shook my head and said, "No."

"Okay…then…what?"

I sighed and stared out the window for a moment, trying to break free of that blue stare so I could think. How to begin? I asked with a challenge, "If I tell you my secret, do you promise not to tell anyone?"

He smiled at that and said, "Yes, of course. That is what I do, every day—I'm a secret keeper. It's part of my job. Go ahead."

"Even my dad?"

"Even your dad," he answered with assurance.

"Okay, and…and you won't laugh or…look at me like…like I'm crazy?"

"Riley," he replied with a kind look, "nothing you could say would make me do that."

"Okay," I said and sat there for a minute. Then I began, slowly at first, building up steam as I went, "Okay then. Well, I have this secret. I haven't told anyone, partly because I often don't believe it myself and partly because I've learned that it's not…*normal.*" I looked down at my hands and felt my face flush. I pressed on, "It began five years ago, and it's only gotten stronger since then."

I paused and regarded his face. He was listening intently, his eyes awash with curiosity. I pressed on, "I was in this accident. I was twelve years old, and that's when things started to happen."

He nodded encouragingly, questioningly, with reserve and confusion. "What things?"

It was so hard to say it out loud! I paused and he waited patiently, oh so patiently, with that attentive face and those penetrating eyes. I just needed to get it off my chest, and quick! I took another deep breath, exhaled, and rattled these words out as quickly and succinctly as I could: "After the accident, my mother thought it would be good for me to start a journal and start reading books…because…well, because I was hurt in the accident, broke my leg, and I couldn't play sports for a while, so I think she thought this was something I could do, you know, to help me heal, not just from the injury, but also from…the aftereffects of the accident. Before that, I don't think I had ever read a book—I mean, other than for school. So, I started to read books, real books, lots of books, like novels and biographies and mysteries and pretty much anything I could get my hands on. I checked out books from the library every week and wrote in my diary all the time, and it was great because, well, the books kept my mind off things I didn't want to think about, and the diary helped me write out my feelings."

His small smile was one of relief, as if he had just caught a child confessing to eating too many sweets. He waited.

This was where it got tough, so I plowed ahead, trying not to get swayed by his false sense of security or his knowing eyes—the eyes of a man who had heard it all, who knew people's innermost demons and was not about to be shaken by them, who could hear a human's deepest faults and could use the teachings of God to frame them, navigate them, purge them, provide a stage for forgiveness of them. Here was a man ready to receive whatever oyster I was about to hand him in order to hold it, process it, render it, and spit it back out, a perfectly clean, shiny pearl. Until I said the next words.

"Well, as soon as I started reading regularly, things started to happen. You asked about my body being manipulated without my control, and yes, it's sort of like that, but then again, it's not. Nothing happens to my body, but things around me seem to feel the force of the books, as if the energy of those words affects the space I am currently inhabiting."

He tried with difficulty to process what I was saying, the furrow deepening, the eyes narrowing.

I forged ahead recklessly, "I know…believe me, I *know* how this sounds, but I'm just gonna say it anyway. I can no longer deny that it's happening. In the beginning I did—I pretended it was all a big coincidence or something I generated by accident with my own thoughts or my own influence. But it's not that. I've tested it. When I read a book, no matter how I select it, no matter what the topic, no matter how much that book is or is not related to me, the book starts to take on a sort of life of its own. Somehow related to or connected to *my* life. My *real* life."

At this, he let out a fascinated exhale, then said, "Hmmm, okay, wow." He paused, stared, and asked tentatively, "Ca—can you provide an example? I'm not sure I understand."

"Sure, I can provide a hundred examples," I answered easily. "For instance, when you came up our street, I was reading *The Thorn Birds*, which is a book about a woman who falls in love with a priest." His eyes got big at that. "Yeah, there was that...actually, I've never in my entire life, not even once, seen a priest in person, ever, and the day I'm reading a book about a priest, there you are, looking very much like the protagonist in this novel, I might add."

"Huh," he said, still processing. "Do these...occurrences...always end up with an encounter?"

I shook my head. "No...no, not necessarily. It's all over the map, actually. From the most innocent, innocuous connections to more tightly related interactions. I might be reading a book about flowers and my mom will come home unexpectedly with a bouquet of flowers. Or there's a story set in Nebraska and all of a sudden, every movie or TV show I watch is set in Nebraska. I read a book about badgers—yes, badgers, those wild, nasty animals—and my dad comes home that night saying he's been invited to a Wisconsin Badgers game over the weekend. Do you see? Very arbitrary. Very random. Very closely linked to *me* for *no reason whatsoever.*"

He was nodding now, thinking. I could see it all over his face: this was new to him. In his vast experience of mining and minding people's problems and praying for the sins and sinners of the world, he had not encountered this. What to say? He asked, "So, it doesn't matter what type of book?"

"Nope. Nonfiction, fiction, biography, mystery, crime, classics, modern, you name it. Although, lately, I've been trying to come up with a system."

To that, he asked curiously, "Oh, a system? You try to control it, then...?"

"Sure, over the years I've tried everything. In the beginning, I would just brush it off, assuming everything was a coincidence and completely ridiculous. I mean, who wouldn't? I'm not crazy. As far as I know, anyway. Actually, I'm hoping you can help me clarify that. Yeah, the mind is an amazing thing, isn't it? Because I really did *try* to make it go away on my own. I thought, sure, where there's a will, there's a way. In fact, at one point, I almost convinced myself it *was* gone for a while. This was during the first phase of my plan to tackle it head-on, after months and months of it happening without any letup. I decided to *ignore* it. I would actively push it from my mind when I saw it or felt it or witnessed it happening. I wouldn't allow it near me, to touch me, or to get inside my head. Sadly, I realized that the more I ignored it, the more prevalent it became—like someone continuously knocking on my door saying, 'Hello, I'm here—notice me.'

"So, that failed and I tried a new tactic. I foolishly thought back then that I could *control* it. I decided to be more intentional with my choices—pick library books that were so obscure that there was *absolutely* no possibility of a connection to my real life. I'm talking books about dung beetles, fashion from the Victorian era, King Arthur and Camelot, biographies of black-and-white screen sirens, novels about the Old West and futuristic alien worlds and India. Yeah, you'd think this approach would work. Nope. Total failure. A new kid starts in our class whose family is from India, someone brings up Marlene Dietrich as their favorite actress, the dung beetle is our topic of study in science class, my cousin gets married and decides to replicate a Victorian walking dress as her bridal gown, my dad's favorite movie is playing on Channel 8, *Knights of Round Table*. Hopefully, you get the idea…!"

I took a breath and watched the priest smile and shake his head. I figured that was a good sign—at least he wasn't looking at me as if I needed a tonic and a straightjacket. I went on, "When that didn't work, I tried to trick the system, selecting books that were more stereotypical of my world— you know, those horrible, trashy teenage books about cheerleading and boy crushes, thinking well, if you can't beat 'em, join 'em. But that was the worst phase of all." I stopped to cringe. "I thought for sure that would kick it out of whack because I am so *not* like any of those stereotypes, but I *am* surrounded by them in my everyday life (at school, and so on), so maybe as they happened, I could chalk them up to normal occurrences. But no…! I was a stupid idiot, thinking I was going to make things *appear* to not really happen, or at least not truly be happening *to me*. I was wrong. Suddenly I had girls at school who had never spoken two words to me encouraging me to try out for the cheerleading squad, wondering who I was dating, and asking what makeup I used. Total nightmare."

Father Avery raised his eyebrows, and I gave him a no-nonsense look that caused him to grin. He had been so quiet throughout my whole barrage that I was now curious as to his thoughts about the whole thing. "Yeah, so after that phase failed, I stopped reading altogether."

His eyes got wide, and after a pause, I said seriously, "That was a sad time for me. I felt like a boat without a sail. I had no escape, no release, no way to get out of my head. I even stopped journaling. It was *not* a good time for me. And as surprising as it sounds, it didn't work anyway. In fact, it was actually much, much worse."

"How could that be?" he inquired.

I shook my head. "It is so much bigger than me. So much bigger than my own little measly powers. You know what happened then? There I was,

confident that I had finally come up with a solution that would work, regardless of its impact on my psyche. Guess what? It didn't. Books were everywhere! Every store I went to had a new display of books—and I'm not
talking bookstores, I'm talking the grocery store, the five-and-dime, the farm
store, the drugstore! Then every show I watched on TV, every radio program
I listened to, every place I went—books, books, books! Book drives, library
fundraisers, book fairs, billboards about books, miniseries on TV based on
best-selling books, movies in the theaters about books, friends riding down
the street with a basketful of books. You name it! I couldn't get away from
it. Finally, when the kids at school started to ask me incessantly (and almost
without realizing they were doing it) why I didn't have a book with me, where
my book was, how come my best friend (Book) wasn't with me, I gave in to
the monster and started reading again."

I paused for a minute and then, breathing hard, a few last words came to
mind, so I said, "Yeah, you know, I had to weigh it out, like which is worse—
to be reading and happy in my books knowing that it will trigger my 'disease'
again, or to be bombarded with images of what I can't do and be left alone.
I chose the former. And hey, as much as this sounds like a minuscule effort,
I still try to control it as best I can with a sort of system. I do a few tricks,
like I never read the back cover of a book before I pick it out (I only read the
title on the spine and look at the cover) so as not to influence what I know is
inevitably coming. And I try not to be shocked or surprised anymore when it
comes. I'm much more mature about it. I even have a pet name for it."

"You have?" he asked.

"Yeah, it's kind of stupid, but I had to come up with a name for it. Well,
you know how you hear about people who can talk to ghosts? Being in your
line of work, I'm sure you think it's witchcraft or sorcery or something from
the devil, which, hey, what do I know? It may be, and I hardly know anything
about it, but I do know that they call those people 'intuitive.' So, I figure I'm
some sort of intuitive like them, except instead of dead people, it's books. I'm
bibliointuitive. I realize this is a made-up word that only lives in my mind,
but it helps me cope, having a nickname for it. Makes it less scary and confusing. In fact, sometimes if I'm feeling rather silly about it, I think of it as
my friend, my constant companion, maybe even my place in this world. My
Biblio.'"

"You're bibliointuitive. Hmmm. Your Biblio," he repeated slowly, as if trying to feel the word on his tongue. My confession complete, he was rendered

mute, still regarding me with curiosity. I didn't move a muscle, and we sat there like that for a few minutes, staring at each other.

Of course, I didn't know then where my Biblio was headed. I could only lay my cards on the table in front of this godly man and hope he believed I was playing with a full deck and that between the two of us, maybe, just maybe, we could figure out what kind of game this was and how to play it.

Chapter XIII

THERE ARE SO MANY DIFFERENT TYPES OF HUGS. Isn't it fascinating that you can't tell which type of hug someone will give you until they're in your arms? Will it be soft and squishy and warm? Will it be cold and hard and standoff-ish? Will it be firm and strong and steadfast? Will it be hot and burning and lustful? Will it make your heart ache? Will it make your spirit soar? Will it make you feel safe? Or will it make you want to die?

Adam remembered that embrace in the twins' closet like it was yesterday. The feel of Riley's chest against his as he pulled her to him, his hand on the small of her back. His lips pressed to hers, a feverish, exploring kiss. The warmth of her body radiating through him. It was as if they had melted into each other, as if their bodies were formed by a sculptor specifically to be in-tertwined.

As one.

Forever.

Or for seven minutes. In heaven.

And then never again.

Fast-forward to the night of Matt Langford's party and he was kicking himself. Why had he not taken into account that she might be there? Why had he not prepared himself? He had simply stared, like a ravenous dog, into that spectacular sun-kissed face with those soul-crushing blue-green eyes. He was a fool. He had just spent a wonderful hour with this girl, Eve, who (by some miracle) seemed completely into him, and yet here he was transported into another space and time with Riley Cartwright filling out every single square inch of his mind, body, and soul.

Luckily (or unluckily?), this Eve girl wasn't put off. After the brief, awk-ward encounter by the keg with Riley and Marc, she had taken his hand again and brought him over to a fence post in the side yard. Adam followed like a lost puppy, not yet fully in control of his senses. After a minute of acute silence, she asked bluntly, "Ex-girlfriend?"

He laughed nervously in response and shook his head. She looked at him skeptically, so he said, "No. Really. I swear. It's...it's not like that. It's just, well, more complicated than that."

She pressed, "You like her, but she doesn't like you?"

"What? No," he said quickly, "It's not that either. Listen, I'm sorry, I...I can't explain. Let's just forget it. You want to go find the rest of the gang?"

She shrugged, a little disappointed, but agreed. They went back to where Derek, Jennie, Susie, Cindy, and Slipkey were sitting by the fire. The rest of the night was spent laughing, drinking, socializing. And pretending, with an Oscar-worthy performance, that this rocking party with its keen surroundings was the only thing on Adam's mind.

When the night drew to a close and they were all walking out to their cars, Eve paused to give Adam a hug. She whispered in his ear, "Give me a call."

Adam stuttered, "I—I will."

He got into the car and slammed his door shut, looking over at Slipkey as he slid into the passenger seat.

Slipkey asked, "You alright?"

Adam was mad, mostly at himself, about the whole Eve-Riley dichotomy and how to process it, so he said between his teeth, "Fine."

Slipkey frowned at him and asked again, this time with more inflection, "I mean, dude, *are you all right?*"

Adam gave him an irritated look and then realized what he was getting at. "Oh, you mean for driving? Yeah, I'm cool. I only had one beer, and that was hours ago."

Slipkey nodded. He was only trying to be helpful, after all, but this type of inquiry seemed to come at the worst possible time. Since Adam had gotten his driver's license three years ago, there had always been someone—his mom, his brother, his friends, Wayne at Pizza Shack—who put that pressure on him, the extra scrutiny. It wasn't as if he was surprised, but it still annoyed him, especially on nights like tonight when he had his mind on other things. He felt as though an enormous magnifying glass was hovering right over his car and on top of his head because of the accident. Of course, he was always vigilant and cautious, obeying the speed limit, buckling his seat belt, coming to a full stop at stop signs. Little things he thought would reduce even a hint of potential judgment, knowing that memories were long in this town and that he must always be on his guard. It was the reason he'd only had one beer and would never risk anything more. However, thinking about it now and with Slipkey questioning him, he realized he shouldn't have had any. Sure, he was underage, but almost everyone there had been, and at neighborhood parties it was common. That didn't excuse it for him. Nothing really ever did.

Adam exhaled between his teeth and countered, "You wanna drive?"

Slipkey snorted, "No, dude. That's not what I meant. You'll be fine. I just wanted to make sure, that was all. And actually," he stared out the window, then back at Adam, "I was also wondering what was going with *that*." He nodded his head toward the retreating Eve.

"Oh. Yeah, um, I'm not sure. She told me to call her."

"Uh-huh. And what did you say?"

"I told her I would."

Slipkey nodded, still staring out the window at her, then turned to Adam and challenged, "But will you?"

Adam thought he had been such a good actor, but somehow Slipkey had seen through his charade. He looked at Slipkey's face, trying to think of an honest answer without having to explain why he didn't know the answer himself. Thankfully, he was spared a response when Jeremy and Mike filed loudly into the back seat like a pair of wolves, wrestling with each other and growling. They'd definitely had more than one beer each. As Adam drove the car out of the neighborhood, he felt like a father scolding his children, hollering at them to shut up so he could drive. Honestly, though, in some ways he found the distraction helpful. Kept him from looking at Slipkey's knowing eyes and kept him from trying to figure out why he wouldn't be jumping at the chance to date a cute, smart college co-ed who seemed to like him.

After he dropped Slipkey off at his car, he drove the rest of the way home, shushing Mike and Jeremy and finally telling them not to wake up Mom as they bounded out of the car, up the front porch steps, and into the house. He followed, watching them head to the basement as he tiptoed up the stairs to his bedroom, listening at the landing and not hearing any movement. Good, she was still asleep. He got undressed and brushed his teeth, then lay faceup on his bed listening to the night sounds outside his bedroom window.

His thought process went something like this: *Eve is really nice. And pretty. And we have quite a bit in common. We're in the same year in college, both from Indy, both played soccer in high school. Even her dad is an engineer at Rolls Royce, just like my dad used to be. Probably if my parents had stayed together and we'd stayed in Indy, we would have met and dated. Maybe gone to prom together. Maybe we would still be dating now, totally in love and with the same group of friends. Maybe I would have come with her to visit her cousin down here in French Lick, a crazy adventure to see a small town together. Maybe we would be serious and talking about what we wanted to do with our lives after college. How many people would we have at our wedding? What would our careers be like? I'd be a vet, maybe up in Indy, and she'd be a photojournalist or a sculptor. We'd buy one of those big mansions up on Meridian Street and build a darkroom for her in the basement or maybe a kiln out in the backyard. We'd have three kids—two boys and a girl. They'd play soccer and be musicians. We'd do perfectly mundane things like going to the grocery store, watching our favorite TV shows, and eating watermelon out in the yard, spitting seeds at each other and the kids. Laughing together.*

Right out of a Norman Rockwell painting. Made total sense. Seemed so normal and completely plausible, right? Ert. Screech. Halt. Wake up. Earth to Adam: Come in, Adam. This is not *your life. This can never be your life. And trying to rewrite it will only bring you pain. But sometimes…still…it's nice to think…to wonder…to hope…if only…if only…*

Adam lay there in his little fantasy with his fake, happy past and future, trying with all his might not to let anything or any*one* else worm its way into his thoughts. That worked for at least twenty minutes, maybe thirty. The "if-only's" were starting to creep in, so he stopped. He tried to sleep. He tossed and turned. That didn't work. So, he let his thoughts meander over to a more realistic turn. One where he knew the self-awareness and self-flagellation began. And continued. And ended, as they should, with him, here and now, in the brutal *reality*. Fifty lashes and then some.

His thoughts started with a deeper analysis of that hug. The one Eve gave him before they parted. It was such a well-intentioned hug, with that little whisper in his ear about calling. If he'd had nothing to compare it to, he would have thought, wow, such a nice little hug, so well-meaning and so assertive. Really quite brave of her. But there was the rub. If he was being honest with himself, which he really, *really* didn't want to be, he would recognize that her hug (and their shared kiss in the grove of trees) was…how to say it? It was perfectly *adequate*. It was. To someone who's heart was wide open like the blue sky before a storm, it would have started an inviting spark. Honest. Pure. Unadulterated. Even *good*. Quite good, really.

But the problem was that the storm had already come in and replaced that blue sky with gray clouds and tumult. Many years ago. Before a thought even existed of Eve. It wasn't her fault. It wasn't anyone's fault. Funnily enough, Adam had fooled himself a little. That kiss felt pretty good in the sense that he hadn't kissed anyone since Riley, so he was overtaken by the sensation of being allowed to feel someone's lips on his, someone and something that set off the automatic sensors in his brain and his body like a skyrocket. But now, in the quiet, darkened stillness of his room, he knew the whole thing, laid out like an unfocused camera lens that finally comes into crisp, focused, magnifying clarity. And here is what he saw through that heartbreakingly crystal-clear lens: Despite his desperate, forceful best efforts to make the fantasy real, to make it feel right, it was *not* right, and he knew it. He knew it! And yet, he didn't want to face it. Because when it came down to it, nothing compared. No one could ever compare. It was like that expression (the one that he realized at this exact moment must have been written in the stars just for this situation, right here, right now): everything else *paled* in comparison. Eve was great, but she paled in comparison, as anyone would.

To her. To Riley. Seven minutes. The embrace. The kiss. The sensations—every synapse in his body going off, screaming, like a million volts of electricity. As though their lips were formed just for each other. The way her body melted into his. Now that was a hug! Perfection incarnate! It was as if everything else was black-and-white and Riley was color. Riley was the sun and the moon and the stars and *his* earth. His own personal planet that he revolved around and focused on and lived for. And she didn't even know. And she probably never would. He wanted all of his future fantasies to be with her.

And this was why some hugs made you want to die.

Chapter XIV

MY THOUGHTS ON *THE OTHER*: strange, mysterious, intangible, vague, separate, hovering. Usually comes in times of rest and quiet, almost never present in times of heavy traffic (chatter in the system), busyness, stress. Not all are blessed with it. Some psyches are too clouded by everyday earthly matters to be aware of it or to have the insight or fortitude or openness to let it in. Charlotte Brontë had it. Called it a sign, a sympathy, a presentiment. Something she never laughed at. Myself, I have it but struggle with it, and never laugh at it either. Well, that's not entirely true. Sometimes it is so insanely bizarre and ridiculous, and *accurate*, that I have to laugh. To keep from going crazy. I have tried not to acknowledge it, then to willfully ignore it, and now to see if I can conquer, control, and manipulate it. I have not succeeded. But I keep trying, like a dog with a bone. A nebulous, otherworldly, undefinable, ethereal bone.

After what seemed like an hour, Father Avery blinked three times in succession and broke our fixed stare, first looking at his books on the shelf, and rightfully distracted by that, eyes wide, then looking down at his hands, a crease forming between his brows. He cleared his throat, looked back at me, and said, "Um, I think we should meet again."

"Oh. Okay, sure," I answered. Honestly, I felt this overwhelming sense of relief, having confessed my secret and gotten the whole thing off my chest. I almost felt as though this little chat had cured me. Of course, not really—*it* was still there, I knew that much, but by virtue of talking it over with someone, it had shifted slightly in the universe, spread across a larger surface area, now to be explored, absorbed, examined by someone other than me. I felt a thousand times better already.

However, I could see he was still processing what I'd said, and the burden had been transferred from my chest to his shoulders. I felt kind of bad about that, but not so bad that I wanted to take it back. Here was a legitimate person. A man. And a religious one at that. For whatever reason, he felt like the *right man.* Don't get me wrong—before he walked down my street out of the blue, or rather out of the book I was reading, I would never have imagined coming within ten feet of a priest, let alone telling one my deepest, darkest secret, but then there he was. And I did. And it felt right. Maybe because I figured he had experience talking with people all day long and hearing their confessions and troubles and giving them guidance and advice. But also because he was a "man of the cloth," which I assumed meant he had inroads with God. Like a direct phone line to Him or some other telepathic way to make things happen with God, or *the other,* or whatever that nebulous thing was that humans were always trying to strive for, figure out, rely on, seek, understand, harness, be with. If anyone could decipher and fix my dilemma, he would be able to.

I certainly couldn't tell my parents or my brothers or even Jane Parker. They would have pooh-poohed everything and told me I was letting all of that reading affect my brain. My mom would have said, "Put that book down and get outside and play—all you need is a little fresh air and sunshine!" So instead I came to a complete stranger, talking about things that made no sense with a big, stupid grin on my face while he twiddled his thumbs in consternation, still unsure of what he was dealing with.

He said tentatively, think-talking out loud, "Hmm, let's see...I think that would be good. For you to come back, maybe somewhat regularly, for a while. I would like to think on what you have said for a bit, maybe even do some research, maybe see...um...if this...what—well, I don't know...I'm not sure, I would like to look into it, I guess. I'm not saying I can do anything...to help. I mean, I'm not even sure what—well, what to think, or what to tell you... but um, yes, I think, definitely, yes, you should come back."

"Okay, sure thing, Father, whatever you think is best. I appreciate it. I'll come back with Dad next week. I'll just have to check my work schedule, but it should be fine," I said breezily and stood up, reaching out my hand.

The priest took it, still foggy, focusing on my face once again and saying, "Yes, yes, good, good. See you then."

The next few days went by in a blur. I was still on a high from my talk with the priest, and Dad couldn't figure out my good mood. He kept asking me, "What did you talk about with Father Avery anyway? You look like the cat that swallowed the canary."

I laughed and said, "No canary, Dad. Just a nice talk with a nice man. I'm coming back with you next week, too, if that's alright."

"Sure—whatever floats your boat. I still have two more rooms to paint and some plumbing to fix in the kitchen, so I'll be there every day."

"Okey dokey, sounds good."

He shook his head, fluffed my hair, and smiled down in my face. He liked it when I was happy. Even Marc commented at dinner Sunday night that I was acting "mental" and had I "taken something"? I told him, "No, dingbat, I'm just happy. Is there anything wrong with that?" As a response, he rolled his eyes and dug into a huge plate of mashed potatoes, opening his mouth wide to show me the result. Brother Brent simply stuck his finger down his throat when I said the word *happy*, as if it were a horrid curse word. Brother Nate didn't even bother to look up from his Conan comic book long enough to comment. Mom said to the wind, "Leave your sister alone." And that was the end of that.

Meanwhile, I finished *Jane Eyre* and started *Out of Africa*. I had heard the movie was coming out, and that meant I had to read the book first so as not to ruin anything. One tenet of every book reader: the book is always better than the movie, and you must read the book first. Not to mention, with my Biblio, what often happened back then is I would randomly pick a book out of the library—per usual, with no prior reference or goading or relation to myself or recommendation from anyone or anything that might correlate or tie me to the book in any way. And then I would come to find out, midway through the book, that there was a movie in the works about the book! That happened with *The Outsiders*. I nearly choked on my Mexican pizza in the cafeteria when Jane saw me reading it and mentioned the movie coming out. Apparently, it was a big deal because Francis Ford Coppola was directing it. I had to admit, in that case, the movie did the book justice (it didn't hurt that it was cast with every available good-looking teenage actor at the time). But with *Out of Africa*, I thought I could bypass the Biblio altogether—another little trick of mine—which sometimes worked and sometimes didn't. It had worked with *Gremlins*; although that book was horrible—badly written—the movie was much better, but by reading the book first, it *did* keep me from having a Biblio occurrence. When I started reading it, I was a little worried that I might find a scary monster living under my bed, but nope, my trick worked, and I slept like a baby with no dreaded pop-out Mogwai gremlins coming to haunt me. Sometimes I looked back at that and thought, was it because the book was so bad? Why had the trick worked to squash my Biblio? It didn't happen often, and I wanted to see if I could recreate the magic (or lack of magic, in this case), but I had yet to figure out the formula. It wasn't the first time my Biblio had lain dormant, but it was rare. I still hadn't quite mastered it, that was for sure, thus my conversations with the priest.

Monday morning, I walked over to the farm, worked for a few hours harvesting, and came home around noon. I ate a sandwich, and Mom dropped me off at the church, saying as I got out of the car, "Don't distract Daddy too much from his work or Father Avery either, okay?" I nodded and waved. I wondered what Dad had told her. I hoped they didn't think anything weird was going on with the priest. I mean, something weird was going on, but nothing they needed to worry about.

As I walked into the church, it was quiet and dark coming in from the bright, sunlit street. When my eyes adjusted, there was Father Avery, up front, talking with an elderly lady. I walked up slowly, not wanting to disturb them. Father Avery called to me with a wave and a smile, "Riley—hi there. Hang on, let me just finish up here with Mrs. Campbell, and then I'll come find you. Your dad's in the Parish Hall," he pointed with a crook of his thumb.

"Okay, thanks," I said and headed out of the church and toward the building, catching Dad under the sink installing a new garbage disposal. Not wanting him to hit his head in surprise, I said softly, "Hey, Dad."

He hollered, "Hey, pumpkin'. How's it going? You see Father Avery yet?"

"Yep, he's up front talking with someone, but said he'd come find me in a minute."

"Great. Hey, can you hand me that wrench?"

"Sure, which one?"

"The biggest one," he pointed, "over on top of my toolbox."

As I handed it to him, he asked casually, "You looking forward to your talk...?"

"Uh-huh, yeah, I suppose," I answered evasively.

"You trying to...er...find some kind of...religion?" He cleared his throat, not wanting me to clam up. He knew his teenage daughter so well.

I said with a laugh, trying to keep it light, "Naw, it's nothing like that. Although you and Mom hardly gave me any foundation on that front, did you?"

"True enough," he said, satisfied with my answer and going back to his work. "Yeah, I don't know...I was raised Baptist by my parents back in

Kentucky, as you know, because you've had to endure Nana and Papa's all-day Sunday service on more than one occasion. Those never-ending days with the heat and flies and singing, and the prohibition on fishing, marbles, running, playing, or anything fun, turned me off religion for life. Your mom's not much better, having been taught to be prim and proper in those Madison Protestant establishments in her youth. She's like me and would rather spend her Sundays getting something done than listening to a swollen head talk about fire and brimstone, not to mention required tithing and offerings."

"Dad!" I cried in a short whisper, looking around to see if anyone could hear him in the hallway.

He chuckled and said, "Oh, I guess I should keep my voice down and my opinions to myself in this place. But anyway, Mom and I wanted to let you know that you're welcome to seek counsel from whatever source you want—a priest, a minister, a pastor, or if you're really desperate," he ducked his head out and winked at me, "your good ole D-A-D. Or M-O-M, if you prefer."

"Thanks," I said with a smile. I wasn't sure what to say because I didn't want them to think I was avoiding talking to them for the wrong reasons.

During Dad's minor harangue, I acknowledged in my mind that this was probably why I was having a bit of an existential crisis at the moment, knowing I didn't really have a place to turn when it came to discussions about the broader-themed, nontangible topics in life. I didn't blame my parents. I knew they were practical, action-oriented people and always had been. I knew it and I accepted it. Not everyone (including me, before the accident) thought about Life, with a capital "L," and what it really meant and what we're all doing here and why this person versus that person is the way they are and why and how it all ties together and how *we* all tie together. And how or if my Biblio was meant to tell me who I was or where I was going in my life. I knew I hadn't yet asked all the right questions, and I certainly didn't have all the answers. But Father Avery was a starting point, and at least I could count on him to look beyond what was right in front of his face, and that was exactly what I needed.

Somewhat conversely, though, I did have a strong sense that religion shoved down the throats of young children, especially with boredom and unendurable speeches, shuts off the waters early, and usually for good. Case in point, Dad. The jury was still out on me. I wasn't learned in the ways of God or religion, and certainly not expecting to get that from Father Avery, having come to him on an entirely different errand. I still suspected the theme might come up, though, being part of his duty, and I wasn't looking forward to it. I didn't want to be converted or convinced of anything from a structured religion standpoint or otherwise, but being able to talk about my issues with someone who might see to the beyond, to the other side, was my aim. Just then, Father Avery walked in the door, flashed a warm smile, and said, "Good afternoon."

I instantly thought, regardless, I like him. I simply like him, and more importantly, I trust him. I can't explain it. It certainly didn't happen this way normally, being an introvert and shy (a bookworm in the most explicit sense of the word, in that if I could worm my way into a cave and read for the rest of my life, I would), but for whatever reason, with this man, I no longer felt any fear, reticence, or bashfulness.

I said, "See ya later, Dad." He waved his foot in the air since his hands were occupied and replied, "Later, sweetie. Come find me when you're done."

Father Avery and I went into his office and sat in our usual spots. I waited for him to begin, which he did directly. "Let's begin with your original question, why don't we?"

I frowned. I couldn't remember my original question.

He laughed at my expression and filled me in, "You asked if I had ever performed an exorcism. Or if I knew how, anyway, I think—correct?"

My face cleared. "Oh yeah. That. Right. Yes."

"Well, I can say definitively that I have not had any experience with that. However, I have a question for you before we proceed down that route."

"Sure."

He began, his face open and probing, "This...um...thing...this Biblio, as you call it, do you really want to get rid of it? I mean, I can see why it would be, well, maybe bothersome at times, but it doesn't seem to be...harming you in any way or causing pain to others. I mean, it isn't keeping you up at night, is it?"

My mind flashed to the other night when I stayed up reading *Jane Eyre* and wondered if something written a hundred thirty years ago could be communicating with me today. Of course, I had been thinking about that encounter with Adam more than anything, but still...I reflected and answered, "For the most part, no."

"And if we're talking about an exorcism, we're usually talking about purging something rather...evil...out of a body. Is that what you feel would be needed in this case? Is that what you think this Biblio is? Something evil?"

I pondered that for a few minutes as I stared at his bookshelves. How could books and their aura (or whatever my Biblio was) be considered evil? I guess I had never considered it so bluntly, to put a name to the *source*. I loved books—they were my lifeblood. I finally said, "I'm not sure where it comes from. But I think that's why I'm…scared of it sometimes. I mean, don't get me wrong—it happens so often now that I'm rather used to it, but that doesn't mean it doesn't strike me right in the heart when it happens, like an electric shock. Wouldn't it you?"

He raised his eyebrows and snuffed a little, saying, "Yes, I suppose it would."

I went on, staring directly at him, trying to get the point across, "I don't know what exactly to compare it to, but I imagine it would be like meeting a long-lost child you didn't know you had and having that happen multiple times a week. How would you feel?"

At this, he laughed unexpectedly and said with a smile, "Well, I'm afraid that would be impossible," holding up his hands and pointing to his collar, to which I blushed. Duh! Stupid Riley! He continued, softer now, "But yes, I get the implication. It would be like being startled by a stranger in the dark."

"Yes!" I exclaimed.

He nodded. Then he asked, more soberly, "So, because we're not sure where it comes from, we don't know what its intent is, do we?"

At that, my eyes widened. First of all, he talked about my Biblio as an "it," which, on the one hand made my heart soar because it made me think he was taking it seriously, but on the other hand was strange to me. I had never thought about it as a physical thing, like a box or a ghost or an item. Of course, I didn't have any other good way to describe it and I suppose "it" was better than "nebulous pop-up visitor in my head that haunts me when I'm reading." And I was equally floored by the fact that he had used the word *we* as if he was on the hunt with me. An investigation we were going to solve together, like two private eyes! It wasn't until that moment that I realized, he believed me! He really believed me! He didn't think I was some dumb girl making up a story or trying to garner attention or be a show-off. I was telling the truth, and my Biblio was real and he believed it. Then I thought for a second, or he's just humoring me. Ugh. But when I looked into his clear blue eyes, focused solely on me, waiting patiently and eagerly for my response, I couldn't believe it was a put-on, just as my Biblio wasn't a put-on.

I answered him, "Yes, that's part of it. Certainly, coming to talk to you has made me very happy and humble—by the way, thank you for listening and for seeing me again—but there's also a part of me that's shaking in my boots, sir, as you might imagine, because I have now put this thing *out there*. And I believe that once something is out there in the universe, it gives it credence, you know? Makes a sort of icon or idol out of it, which is not my intention. What I mean is, now that the cat's out of the bag, so to speak, I still don't know where the cat came from or why it's here or where it will go. Will it stay with me? For how long? What is the reason for it? How will I manage it?"

He nodded, satisfied with my response, as if I had answered one of his unspoken questions. Then he said, "Let me ask you this: if we did solve it and it went away, would you miss it?"

Wow. I stopped to think about that one. I looked out the window. *Would* I? I was so *used* to it now, and it was, after all, a part of me. My frown turned to incredulity as I said, "Yes, I think I would." I paused and added, "Crazy, eh? Here I came to you to have it removed, like a festering boil or something, but now that I sit and think about it, I think I would miss it. I know I would probably go on a complete reading bender," I laughed, "trying to test whether it was really gone, that's for sure. But if it was truly gone, I guess I would miss it because it *does* add something to life—granted, a strange side gift that is unexpected and confusing, but still, something. Also, to be clear, I think it has shaped my life in the sense that I doubt I would have become such an avid reader without it. I guess I'll never know because I was never a reader before, but when I think about the joy books have given me over the years, I do think my Biblio is a small price to pay for the reward. My only qualm, really, comes when I question it and wonder why it appeared in the first place, and of course whether or not I have somehow unwittingly made the whole thing up in my head...as if I've been gaslighted."

"Gaslighted?" he asked.

"Oh yeah, have you ever seen that movie with Ingrid Bergman? *Gaslight*. Oh, it makes your heart break...and it makes you kind of angry too. This lovely young woman is drawn into this awful marriage with a man who slowly manipulates her into thinking she's going crazy." I stopped as he nodded, getting the reference. "I mean, I don't want to look back at my Biblio and think, holy crap, I lost my mind for a few years there, didn't I? Excuse my language, Father."

"You're okay," he said quickly, then mildly, "well, let's hope that doesn't happen. Besides, if it makes you feel any better, intuitive connections here on Earth may be more common than you think."

"Really?" I asked, a little too excited.

"Sure, my parishioners tell me about them all the time—how they feel departed loved ones with them in spirit, or how guardian angels have intervened in a tragic situation to save someone from something awful, or even minor things. The other evening, I was watching a show on PBS about playing the banjo, and lo and behold, the next morning we had a wedding, and the father of the bride played a banjo tune as part of the recessional. I couldn't have been more astonished." He paused as my eyebrows rose in unison with his. Then, softly, he said, "So, maybe—I'm not sure if you're up for this or not—but maybe we should try to understand your Biblio better before we make any rash decisions about purging it. What do you think?"

"Yeah, okay," I said, still processing the fact that maybe things like my Biblio weren't as uncommon as I thought, which meant that I definitely wasn't crazy.

Father Avery drew my attention back to him by saying, "You mentioned the other day that it started after an accident. Can you tell me more about that?"

I felt my stomach drop. He remembered that cast-off detail, and I had hoped that he wouldn't. Ugh. I said quietly, "Yes, there was a car accident. And my leg was broken…" I stopped.

He waited and then said, "And it started—the Biblio—right after that?"

I said, "No, not exactly. I mean, yes, I started reading around that time, but that was because my mom forced me to go to the library. I was having some trouble, I wasn't, I guess I wasn't…grieving the way people thought I should."

Now he was confused. "Grieving? The loss of…the use of your leg?"

I exhaled and gritted my teeth. Did we really have to *go there*? I finally said, "No, the loss of my best friend, Kathy. She died in the accident."

His eyes got big. "Oh," he said flatly. Then softly, "I am so sorry, Riley."

A minute passed. I noticed he had a clock on the wall behind his head, and it ticked out loud. It felt as though the tick had suddenly slowed down to a tick every twenty seconds instead of every second. Tick. Pause. Tick. Pause. Tick. Pause.

I broke the silence, "We were in the back seat together. The car that hit us rammed into her side of the car, and she died instantly." I said these words coldly, as I always did, because that was how my inner self processed them. I never knew why.

He nodded soberly. I could see the wheels turning in his head. His eyes never left my face, and he probably noticed (as I blushed) that I didn't cry or show any real emotion (other than slight mortification) when telling him.

I still hadn't cried. It had been five years.

He shifted the conversation then, in a way I hadn't expected, "So, if this Biblio started happening shortly after the accident, did you ever think that... I mean, it would have been logical, *natural*, for you to think, maybe it was coming from Kathy herself. Did you...see...Kathy during those episodes? Is that why you contemplated an exorcism?"

I think my look said it all, but to be on the safe side, I explained adamantly, "No, it's not like that."

"Okay, okay, I'm just checking...but the timing was definitely related, right? The Biblio came directly after the accident?"

"Yes, I think so, maybe a few months later. I can't remember exactly... things were hazy for a while after the accident."

He nodded.

"Hmmm, well, and did you hit your head during the accident?"

"What? No," I said, realizing he thought I had some traumatic brain injury that was causing my Biblio. "No, nothing like that."

"Okay...but you think it may be related to Kathy...?"

"I mean, I don't know...I don't think so. I can't tell where it comes from... but no, I never saw Kathy's face or image or anything associated with the books. I don't know if I really...believe in that. In ghosts or ghouls. Well, *believe* isn't the right word; I personally don't experience those types of anomalies, so it's difficult for me to judge or weigh in on them. However, I *do* believe in *energy* and what I like to call *the other*—things that aren't easily explained, like *this*, my Biblio. And the other things you mentioned earlier— people feeling things, sensing them, connections in this world." I raised both hands in a gesture of not knowing. "All I really remember is that it started the first moment my mom gave me a diary and took me to the local library."

"And this 'trouble' you were having with grieving, your mom thought this would help?"

"Yes...I suppose I wasn't talking very much back then, and everyone thought I should be, well, sad...and talking through my feelings, so I guess she figured I could write my feelings down instead."

"And did you? Did that help?"

"Yes, a little," I answered with a nod, "it did. I think so, I mean, it still does. I still have my diary and I still read, obviously."

He nodded with a smile.

I went on, "That first Friday in the library, my connection to this strange thing happened, and I simply dismissed it. I actually thought for a second that maybe I imagined it. I remembered seeing something on TV once where a guy was struck by lightning and afterward started speaking French. Did I have some type of delayed reaction like that? Who knows—maybe it was some strange misfiring of brain neurons. What did I know? But after that first time, there was another time, and another, and another until I couldn't dismiss it or ignore it or chalk it up to an overactive imagination or a misfiring."

He nodded and redirected with a new thought, "I wonder…now, I might be going out on a limb here, but I wonder, if this Biblio is a way to cope with your loss, just like the diary and the reading. Have you thought of that?"

"No, well, I don't know, not really…," I replied honestly.

Then he asked abruptly, "Have you ever been to a Catholic Mass?"

Oh no, was this the religious conversation I had feared? I said, "No."

He smiled at my expression and pressed on, "Don't worry, I'm not here to bring another sheep into the fold, although of course you are welcome to come anytime. We have Mass Tuesday mornings at eight and Sundays at eleven. Anyway, the reason I ask is that during every Mass, we have this ritual, a sort of shared activity with the congregants, where we ask them to turn to their neighbor in the pew, shake hands, and say, 'Peace be with you,' and the neighbor will say back, 'And also with you.' It's a way to offer a sort of mutual blessing or kindness to each other."

I was staring at him, trying to figure out where he was headed.

He continued, "The origin of this sign of peace goes all the way back to the New Testament, and it's one of my favorites traditions. You can see the congregants smiling at each other, greeting each other in such a hospitable, selfless way that you can't help but feel the warmth of union and connectedness. My theory, Riley, and here's my point, and I'm sorry it's taken me a few minutes to get to it: in this crazy, busy world we live in, with all of its hustle and bustle and tragedy, strife, and challenge, people want to feel *peace*. This simple gesture—a handshake and a few words—can actually suffuse people's hearts with a tiny bit of joy, maybe when it's needed most. They may not even realize they need it, but I believe people try with all their heart and soul to make sense out of chaos, out of difficult situations, out of this complex, tragedy-riddled world we live in because we crave stability and order. We wish to control the uncontrollable, but peace and calm are often so elusive. Sure, sometimes we can accomplish a sort of harmony through our own efforts and actions, but my belief is that true peace comes only from one place, and that is God. And in turn, I believe this is what God most wishes for us."

During Father Avery's speech, I listened to every inflection of his voice and observed every twinkle of his bright blue eyes, trying to see how what he was saying related to me. At first, I took it so literally that I thought it was just a ploy to bring me to church so I could receive the "sign of peace" from some random stranger, and that would somehow solve all of my troubles. But then toward the end, I could see something come into focus, and I wasn't sure I liked it (any more than I liked the thought of being dragged into church). I said accusingly, "You think my Biblio is coming from God? That it's some kind of peace offering? Because he took Kathy from me? To make it up to me or something?"

"What?" he seemed shocked and said, "No, Riley, that is not what I mean." He took a deep breath before continuing. His eyes softened as he went on, "Listen, I'm not sure why Kathy left us when she did, and your loss is like so many others, with no earthly rhyme or reason. Death is one of God's greatest mysteries. Why we leave this earth when we do—and why we come into it when we do, for that matter—is unknown. I don't think we're meant to know or understand fully. It's just something we must come to terms with—that death is part of life. I'm not sure why this death came to you at such a tender age, but I do know that you are not alone in your grief or in your attempt to understand its impact. All I can say, as I was trying to before, is that humans crave peace, predictability, structure, and order during traumatic periods in their lives, and maybe your Biblio is a way to bring you a form of peace to help you deal with the accident and its aftermath. I know it isn't actually a straight line or a direct correlation per se, and you've told me it isn't predictable either, but you also said you would miss it if it were gone, so it must be a sort of…friend to you, right? Maybe, just maybe, it's here to comfort you, to console you, to bring *you* peace. Not as a consolation for losing Kathy, but as something stable in the midst of the loss and the tragedy."

I had to think about that for a moment or two. I said, "Hmmm, maybe. I never thought about it that way. Reading books certainly gives me peace. I can escape into them and be part of a different world for a time, you know, be completely transported."

"Yes, exactly—I get that. Books are much the same for me. Books bring pleasure. In my case, especially the Good Book," he said with a laugh. I smiled. Then he asked, "So, would you...*could* you ever give up reading?"

"No, never!" I cried, rather forcefully.

He smiled at my outburst and replied calmly, "Right, that's what I thought, so although reading is a trigger for your Biblio, maybe you have to take the pain with the pleasure, if in fact it *is* pain. *Is* it truly painful?"

I wobbled my head, knowing now with conviction that it wasn't. I answered thoughtfully, "No, not pain—more like distraction, especially when it first pops up like it does, out of the blue. I try to willfully pretend it's not there as it's happening, but you can only keep something at bay for so long. I guess, well, I must acknowledge that even though I still don't understand it, I have to admit it's part of me now. I keep trying to make sense of it, trying to tie it to something *real*." I squeezed my hands into fists, wanting to break the code, to understand the riddle, the vague, untenable mysticism of it. "It's like I wonder if it's trying to *tell* me something, give me a message, or a sign or an action to take. Does it want me to *do* something? Why is it showing me this coincidence or connection right at this moment with this particular section of this particular book? And why me in general? Why *me*?!" I let a puff of frustrated air escape my lips and finally said, "I don't know...it's still such a mystery that I can't say it really does give me any peace right now. The reading does, but not the Biblio. In fact, when it first started, I had trouble concentrating on the reading, knowing what was coming. It almost frightened me, like watching a scary movie and waiting for something to jump out at me. But over time, when I realized it wasn't anything that was going to hurt me, I decided the reading was worth it, regardless of the outcome."

"Right. Much of life is a balance. Myself, I've never contemplated a world without books. I can't imagine what that would be like. Quite without color, I would say, wouldn't you?"

"No doubt," I agreed, "without color, without spark, without light."

"Yes," he agreed, rather solemnly.

"Without meaning."

❧ CHAPTER XV ❧

A WORLD WITHOUT BOOKS. Imagining it felt like death. And yet just five short years ago, before the accident, I never read. Not even a magazine. And certainly never a whole book. I barely skimmed textbooks, just enough to pass my tests. How much had changed! Father Avery's words made me think back—to that void I had lived in without knowing it, and where I was right now in relation to that void. Was it filled? Since that first day in the library, with *The Shy Ones*, the transformation had progressed so slowly and subtly that I hadn't taken time to acknowledge that there was a transformation or to contemplate what books were to me (apart from my Biblio). They were my lifeblood. My escape, my focus factor, my calming mechanism, my anxiety reliever. They entranced, intrigued, and consumed me. They fed my soul. A good book could turn a bad mood into a good one like the flick of a switch. I believed in the power of words. They were like living, palpable, three-dimensional beings to me, a lifeline exploding from the pages to grab me by the throat and draw me into their web. They turned me into a better person by making me smarter (yes, at the very least!) and also by enriching my life with a new field of vision, seeing things in a different way, from someone else's perspective, sending me off on a journey to another place and time that was new, intriguing, refreshing, entrancing, evocative, elucidating.

In the midst of my activity-driven world, reading was one of the few luxuries in which I actually longed to slow down. If a story was good, I purposely reread paragraphs and pages just to savor the words, to let them sink in like a savory soup lingering on the tongue before it is swallowed. I would sit back and let the words slowly, languidly be revealed to me, become part of my being, be analyzed, understood, absorbed, assimilated.

I wanted books to stay in my life forever, as my healers and my hearth and my heart. My header and my footer. And what fascinated me even more, as I stared into the eyes of this kind gentleman (a man who had turned his life over to God, much as I was now acknowledging I had turned my life over to the written word), was that both were formed at the beginning of time and would go on forever. There was no end to words (more than all the drops in the sea), and they could be manipulated, turned, twisted, formed and reformed, placed and placated, tied and tightened, mounted and mastered, dredged and dreaded, over and over again in every possible fashion, forever. Like God, they were infinite, all-knowing, all-seeing, omnipotent, never quite fully explored, never quite managed, never quite tamed, never quite complete.

In front of the priest, my eyes got wide because I had just thought something quite blasphemous: I had compared words to God. But then my next thought was: God gave us words. And I suppose He thought it was how we used them that mattered. He must have realized their power from the very beginning, or else why would His followers have written everything down? Words that millions were still talking about over two thousand years later.

Father Avery saw the emotions crossing my face as they twisted, turned, and projected, not knowing where I had gone in my mind or why. He broke the spell with, "So, out of curiosity, what is your latest Biblio?"

"Oh, that's easy," I answered, coming back into focus. "Right before coming to see you, I was reading *Jane Eyre*, and guess what it said?"

"What?"

"It talked about presentiments and signs and sympathies, which was basically Charlotte Brontë's way of screaming, 'Riley, I'm sending you a sign *right now* to go forth and tell someone!' And here I am confessing my deepest, darkest secret to you." I frowned for a moment and added, "And of course, I still question myself, every time. In fact, when I read that passage, I wondered, was that really meant to be a sign? Was that a premonition of me talking to you? Or was I just reading too much into it? Probably me looking for a Biblio, but it could have been nothing." I stopped and ventured, "What do you think?"

He exhaled and regarded me for a minute before answering cautiously, "You know, I'm not sure. You also might have skimmed right over that passage, right? Is it common for you to pause and reflect on one paragraph? Or was it two? Or twenty? Or five pages here and five pages there? Have you ever wondered *why* you've remembered something more vividly than something else? And then considered the Biblio in retrospect as it related to that memory?"

I looked away, a little deflated. I said reflectively, "I know what you're implying. And of course, I have considered this. A thousand times! Yes, I could be manipulating the situation and not even realizing it—forcing my *own* influence on a Biblio. I know how it looks, and believe me, I've wrestled with that possibility. But I will say this: I've done everything in my power to avoid that being the case, including flying through a book without allowing myself any introspection on individual words or sections, forcing myself to consume quickly and superficially, just to be done with it. And I've also tried to block the book from my mind when I'm not physically reading it, keeping myself busy just before and after, distracting myself with activity or sleep or just about anything else to keep my mind off the book. This, by the way, certainly reduces the pleasure quotient, and I wouldn't recommend it. But all of these tricks were…simply fruitless. Even if I avoid any possible influence or destiny over the inevitable Biblio, it's there, lingering and waiting to appear anyway. For instance, you probably think the example I gave from Jane Eyre is a stretch and maybe even completely farfetched, but that's because I haven't told you the other Biblio from *Jane Eyre*."

His curiosity piqued, he said, "Oh?"

"So, I don't know if you've read *Jane Eyre*, but the main protagonist is a man named Mr. Rochester. A rather uncommon name, I would imagine. Well, as Dad and I were walking out the door on the way to come see you, Mom mentioned that her cousin Linda had called the night before and invited all of us to come for a visit this summer."

I paused for effect and he waited, his face blank.

"Mom proceeds to say, 'Wouldn't that be great—we could stop on the way and see Niagara Falls.' Dad says, 'Sure, that sounds like fun. Wait, where are Linda and Tony moving to? I forgot. I thought they were in Cleveland.' And Mom replies, 'No, no, they moved last year. Just outside of Rochester, remember?' Dad said, 'Oh yeah, that's right.' During the car ride, that word—Rochester—kept reverberating in my mind, like a skipped record."

He said, "Wow."

"I know. Yes, a stupid, minor thing, but still…it happens like *that* sometimes. And after all this time, I shouldn't be shocked, but I almost always am. Especially when it isn't like a vague, barely there Biblio, but more like a spot-on bull's-eye. Then it's so hard to deny. Do you now see what I mean?"

He nodded slowly. I could see things from his perspective: as a priest, he wanted to help me, but that didn't necessarily mean he would fully acknowledge the forces that were at work in me, especially ones like these. It wasn't as though I was asking him to believe I saw a strange black cat run into my house. That could be explained with several rational theories. This was an entirely different animal.

He must have been thinking the same thing. He said, "Listen, I'm not exactly sure what to say or how to advise you at this point, but I think we've made some progress today, right? We've established that an exorcism is out of the question, if for no other reason than, quite frankly, I don't think it would help. Also, I don't necessarily believe in them. I've never actually performed or seen one, but I've always sort of wondered how something evil can fully possess a human outside of their will or intervention—"

"Wait," I interrupted, "does that mean you think my Biblio is something I've brought upon myself, of my own volition?"

He sighed and continued, "Let me finish. I'm a man of God, so of course I believe in things I cannot see. Faith. That is rather the main premise and tenet of this profession." He paused to chuckle, and I couldn't help but smile. "But that doesn't mean you throw away your human brain and all the wisdom and analytical thinking that go along with the gifts and skills God has given you. Descartes said, 'I think, therefore I am.' Maybe I'm being progressive, but I believe that, one, there are things here on Earth that are not understandable and that maybe God doesn't *want* us to understand, and two, yes—sometimes these things are being generated from the human brain and not from God nor from an otherworldly place, but does that make them any less *real* for the person experiencing them? Of course not. Regardless of the origin, maybe these unexplained phenomena are to be taken at face value, and the analysis of their derivation is not for us to adjudicate but rather to assimilate and handle as best we can as is. In other words, in their raw form. I personally believe that in the afterlife, many of these mysteries will be revealed and explained to us, but until then I will withhold judgment and instead accept them as they are and provide consult (and what little peace I can), based on the premise that I am only one lowly human and that I am not meant to *know* with certainty nor to unduly influence anything in the realm of possibility."

I stared, thoughtful and quiet. He was rather sanguine, wasn't he? This was a surprise to me, coming from a priest, whom I assumed had been indoctrinated in the ethos of judgment, disgust, disdain, and distance. A slow smile crept across my face, and he smiled back, observing my understanding graciously.

He said, almost as an aside, "You know, this Biblio of yours may just be something wonderful. Have you thought of that? No matter what its intent. Just think, you have a unique sort of hat trick, and who knows where it will lead?"

I nodded, contemplating things unknown and unseen with a newfound exhilaration. I liked that idea. Having a secret all these years made me taint my Biblio with a brush of ugliness, a forced exile into unacknowledged obscurity, an assumption of guilt. But maybe I was going at it with the wrong perspective. Maybe I should look at my Biblio as a friend, something to stay by my side, something to lean on, to signify that I was *alive*, I was human, I was meant to be here on Earth, in whatever capacity it gravitated toward me, as a portal, as something bigger than myself, a force for good, a safeguard, a coping mechanism. Maybe my Biblio was a companion to the lifeblood that was my reading. Or maybe it would show me the way (by some celestial miracle) to a meaningful purpose in my life. Or maybe it was present in place of Kathy or because of Kathy or simply as a way to deal with the loss of Kathy. Did it matter? It was here. With me. Was I ready to *embrace* it?

PART III – 1990

Chapter XVI

Did you ever wonder why God made our bodies the way he did? I think about it a lot, and I'm still confused. Why do we have to eat and drink and fuel ourselves, only to later purge it from our system as dirty waste? Why sleep? Why wake? Why talk, laugh, think, walk, run, shop, read, knit, horseback ride, hike, ski, play tennis, kayak, mountain climb, bungee jump, zipline? Why not be a self-fulfilling, self-actualizing, self-sufficient, mechanical android? Why not be powered by lithium batteries instead of food? Why not be pumped with a robotic heart that doesn't die? Why the stupid waste of time and space that is sleep? Why waste one-third of our lives lying inert like a slug, accomplishing absolutely nothing? Why are we all different? Wouldn't it have made more sense to make every fifth person (for instance) be the same? Then all the sames would hang out together, and the odds and ends would be off on their own. Instead, we're stuck with everyone being different. And to make matters more confusing, we have twins and triplets and other varieties of semi-sames. Is that some type of joke on us?

I remember watching a show once about people who were unable to see faces. They could detect one or two singular features (like the lips or nose), but not the sum of a whole face. It made me think, what are faces anyway? Why is it that one face, which anatomically has all the same parts, is somehow completely different from any other face? Same with bodies. So many variations.

Five years had gone by, and I was leafing through a *Playboy* magazine for the first time. I was a senior in college, and believe it or not, I had never seen breasts before (besides my own). Sure, there were the girls in the high school locker room and the women in the college dorm shower stalls who sashayed around in the nude, flaunting their bodacious curves, but I always averted my eyes, blushing and wondering how they had the balls (I know, wrong pun) to be so brazen and uninhibited.

As I sat on a bright orange beanbag in Ryan's room, turning one page slowly to the next, I thought, wow, I had no idea the multitude of breast sizes, shapes, and variations! It was a revelation to me. I could see why guys were so driven to the next pair and the next and the next—they were all so different, and each pair fascinating in its own right. Not to mention what was *down there*. Also highly intriguing. I would need to do some exploration of my own later—not only had I not seen anyone else's before, I hadn't made mine much of a study either. I was such a prude.

It reminded me of a trip to the mall with my mom when I was fourteen. It was a Saturday in the dead of winter, and I had just finished my weekend chores (dusting and vacuuming) when Mom said, "Riley, those jeans are two sizes too small for you. Let me get my purse. We need a shopping trip."

Crud. I was midway through Thompson's *Lark Rise to Candleford* and was hoping to finish it that weekend, but oh well. I sighed. I really did need clothes, and maybe we could be done in an hour or two.

On the way, my heart sank even further when my mom confessed, "Besides new jeans, Riley, what we really need to do is get you sized for a bra."

I choked and frowned. God, not *that*!

"Yes, I'm afraid so," she said, reading my face. "You can't keep wearing your brother's baggy old T-shirts to cover *them* up. You might be skinny as a rail and fast as a lightning bolt, but you're still a girl, and whether you like it or not, you have breasts!"

I rolled my eyes and turned as red as a beet. Mortification of all mortifications, it was true. How did that happen? The week before, I had spent fifteen minutes standing on the stepstool in our bathroom to get a better look at *them* in the medicine cabinet mirror. It was so strange to have these odd appendages staring back at me with their perfectly pink round half-dollar centers topped off with raspberry Dippin' Dots. In the beginning, they were such an anomaly that they scared me—as if someone else's torso had been attached to my body. But then I began to rather like them. They were perfectly symmetrical and soft as a baby's bottom. And the nipples stood at attention when I pinched them. But despite my growing sentimentality toward them, I most certainly did not want to have them examined by some strange saleswoman in a department store, or even worse, by my *mother*! Here I was thinking I had been hiding them so well, but Mom was like a bloodhound when it came to her children's secret biological needs. God forbid you should try to hide something from her. She always somehow sensed it or guessed it or simply, without any provocation, *knew* it. It was uncanny. The boys were always kept in ample supply of the most potent deodorant, athlete's foot spray, acne cream, mouthwash, and dandruff shampoo.

So there I was, an hour and a half later, trying to decode the cryptic mechanical nightmare known as the teenage training bra. Why did they call it that anyway? As if it were related to sports—your boobs were training to become breasts, and they needed to be exercised in order to make the Olympic team someday. Limber! Hike! Push! Pull! Squash! Stuff! But no matter what: FIT! It was worse than going to the dentist. I wanted to jump out the window, but there wasn't one in the tiny dressing room where my mother had cornered me to commandeer my body like a Barbie doll rugby match, along with two helpful saleswomen running back and forth to the lingerie racks to locate the perfectly sized, overly strappy, bumpy white cotton slingshot that was the beginning of the end of my careful and idyllic childhood. Mom bought three and made me wear one immediately.

Oddly enough, on the car ride home, although my skin chafed almost as much as my ego, I had the most confused and profound wave of gratitude and horror sweep over me when I realized with a smack that Kathy had never lived long enough to need a bra, and her mom was probably sitting home alone right now, reading a book or looking out the window, thinking about Kathy and wondering why she was excluded from this mother-daughter rite of passage. And I felt bad, almost guilty, for having breasts at all. After that, I stopped staring in the medicine cabinet mirror and tried to be gracious in my womanhood, knowing that although it was truly irritating to grow up, there was no denying that the alternative was worse.

And here I was, so many years later, gazing fixedly at so many naked breasts that my head was starting to spin. These women had no fear, no humiliation, no shame about their bodies, and I found it exhilarating. Why couldn't I be that way?

I suppose it didn't help that I hadn't *been* with anyone yet. There were a few snatched kisses and light groping explorations throughout the years, but I had always politely refused more and safely snuck back to the sanctity of my current cave, which was usually a proper lounging chair closely flanked by a shelf full of books. Even my Biblio had been somewhat of a hindrance in this regard, a secret that lived inside of me, and like all secrets, a barrier between me and intimacy with other humans on a deeper level. Of course, I was always outwardly friendly and kind, which was also part of my true self, but I had yet to let someone else see and experience the real me and all that came with me, including my body.

I looked up in wonder at Ryan and exclaimed, "Wow!"

He laughed out loud and said with a wicked grin, "You like? I have hundreds."

"Hundreds?!" I cried. "Wow, where did you get them?"

"My dad had a stash under his tool bench in the basement, and when he died, my brother Eddie and I grabbed them and hid them in the shed before Mom snatched them. Of course, I've only brought a few select favorites here to school, but there are plenty more at home."

"What if she goes in the shed?"

"She never goes out there. It's filled with lawn equipment and saws and drills and things."

I nodded.

Ryan smiled down at me from his desk chair and asked, "You wanna take that one?"

I blushed and said, "Naw, um, that's okay."

"Come on," he said with an encouraging, nonjudgmental smile, "take it—I promise I won't tell. Honestly, I'm thinking about tossing the ones I have here anyway."

"Really? Why?" I was surprised. They seemed like mementos of his dad, albeit twisted ones.

He exhaled and turned away, looking out the window for a second and then back at my face. "I don't know…they can be sort of addictive, you know. I've leafed through them so many times. Makes me feel a little skeevy, like I really ought to focus on a flesh-and-blood version instead."

"Oh," I said, embarrassed at his confession but appreciating his honesty.

He nodded at me for a few seconds, followed by a glint in his eye that included a small invitation. My eyes lowered as I slid off the beanbag and onto the floor. In my hurry to get away from that intense stare, I nearly tripped trying to stand up. I kept the magazine in my grip and scooted out the door with a quick, "Um, I better get going, catch you later, okay?"

"Uh-huh," he said with a knowing smile and a wave of his hand. In the safety of my bedroom, I hid the naughty glossy under my undies in the top drawer of my dresser.

My roommate, Christine, came in just as I slammed the drawer shut. She asked, "Hey, have you seen my blow-dryer?"

"Nope," I answered, picking up a book. I plopped down on my bed and started reading. I was halfway through *Tarzan of the Apes* and really enjoying it, wondering why I had never read it before.

Christine wandered out of the room and back in again, this time with the found blow-dryer in hand. She hung her head upside down and blew her hair dry, all the while chatting away.

"Are you going to Nick's with us tonight?" she asked.

I shrugged, not bothering to look up.

"Come on, you should!" she urged. "You haven't been out with us in weeks. All you do is stay inside and study. Oh, and read books, of course, Miss Goody Two-Shoes."

I raised one eyebrow at her. "You know, it wouldn't hurt you to crack a book once in a while yourself."

"I read," she said defiantly.

"CliffsNotes doesn't count."

"Yes, but it works. What do you want from me? I'm a *voice* major. As long as I can read music and read the conductor's direction, I don't need a book."

I rolled my eyes. Of course, she was probably right, but I suppose her way of learning seemed about as foreign to me as mine did to her.

She stood up straight, continuing to blow her hair out of her face, and said thoughtfully, "Besides, it's not like I'm illiterate. I just don't read."

I laughed at that. "I would argue there's very little distinction."

"Speak for yourself," she said with a toss of her head, shutting off the blow-dryer and sitting down on the bed beside me. "Listen, Riley. Next weekend is Little 500, so it'll be a complete shit show around town, which is why we're planning to make a big night of it tonight instead. You have to come. You might even enjoy yourself. Meet new people. Have a drink or two. It's our senior year and um, well…let's see…it's also *your birthday*."

I gasped as she pinched my cheek. I squealed and leaned away from her hand, crying, "Aarrrghh. No! You remembered?"

"Of course I remembered, you goober. April thirteenth, a day that will live in infamy!" She brandished her hand in the air with a flourish, which caused me to choke. "Yes, that's what I'm talking about! Come on—get dressed, and I'll do your hair and makeup. We have exactly, let's see…twenty-two minutes, so get a move on."

I sighed, reluctantly putting *Tarzan* aside, and went to my closet. What to wear? Maybe my new homemade tie-dye, tacked-up stonewashed jeans, bunched-up fluffy white socks with the white Keds? Perfect. Last Saturday, all of us spent the day out in the driveway of our seven-bedroom off-campus house making our own tie-dyes with five buckets of dye-filled water, six packages of men's undershirts, fifty industrial-sized rubber bands, and ten large spatulas. Sandy kept hers in the green too long, and it ended up looking like a compost heap, so that one had to be tossed, but the rest turned out awesome. Totally psychedelic, as the stoner dudes from high school would say. I loved that mine had hints of pale pink and blue and green in it, not too strong, muted and soft, to bring out the color in my cheeks and my eyes.

I came out of the closet and whispered to Christine, "Hey…I gotta tell you something."

She looked at me through the reflection in her makeup mirror, blush brush posed midair. "What?"

We had to be quiet because Ryan's room was right across from ours on the second floor. He shared his room with David, and I shared mine with Christine. Sandy, Erica, and Renee, our other roommates, each had a tiny single closet-sized room down on the first floor. And we had a huge unfinished attic, which came in handy during football season when we hosted postgame parties.

"Shhh, he'll hear us."

"Who'll hear us?"

I shushed her again and pointed across the way and said, "He will. Ryan. I think he made a pass at me."

She stared at me. "What? When? What did he say?"

"Just now. A few minutes ago. Well, he didn't say anything in particular—it was more the way he looked at me. That sort of come-hither look."

She thought my old-fashioned expression was hysterical. She went back to her face and dismissed me with a wave. "It was bound to happen. He's already tried with me and Sandy. Erica and Renee are taken, so it makes sense that you were next. I mean, you aren't considering it, are you?" She glanced at me and, by my look, said, "No, of course not. So, no biggie—hopefully that'll be the end of it, but if not, just tell him to buzz off. You might have to be blunt."

I sighed. "Right. Yeah. I will. If it ever comes to that. Which I hope it doesn't." Changing gears, I asked, "So, what do you think of my outfit?"

Christine turned around from her mirror and gave me the once-over, exclaiming, "Holy crap, Riley, totally awful! Go in my closet and put on my black pants, black ripped T-shirt, and Doc Martens. We're going to bring you into the 1990s, my friend, starting tonight. And man, what to do with that wild hair of yours…hmm…"

"Nothing too crazy," I warned, fear starting to fill my belly. Christine was going through a B52s phase where she wore onyx liquid eyeliner, which exaggerated her eyes into large black-cat almonds, and teased her hair into a huge black beehive, sometimes hiding the remains of a half-squashed empty can of Coke to raise the bouffant to a precarious and heightened state of skyrise architecture. It was like something out of a museum or a horror film.

Whereas I, nearly four years after high school, was still steeped in the Madonna–Debbie Gibson style guide glory days, my red hair left curly and unkempt (or sometimes pulled back with a cotton scrunchy), my skin piled with layers of beige foundation, my cheeks reddened with bright pink blush, my eyes graced with a quick stroke of baby blue eyeliner followed by thick green mascara, and my lips sealed with glossy orange lipstick.

In an amazing dash of speed and precision, Christine nixed all of that with five quickly coated makeup-removing pads and by French braiding my hair into one long train down my back, lining my eyes with a dark brown pencil and black mascara, leaving my freckled cheeks powder- and blush-free, and dressing me in black from head to toe. As I looked in the stand-up mirror, I thought I looked quite nice—Miss Goody Two-Shoes meets Joan Jett. I took note of my curves and thought for a second about those body parts so prominently displayed in the magazine earlier. I thought I had everything in all the right places, even if most of mine had never been touched.

Christine came up behind me, holding my shoulders, and said, "My masterpiece!"

I grinned and agreed, "Not bad."

"Good enough to eat. And on this, your birthday night, too. Let the games begin!"

I was afraid to guess what she meant by that, so I laughed as we grabbed our things and headed downstairs. Taking stock of her own impressive outfit, I couldn't help but notice our friends' loud gasps of delight, first at her and then, as a sort of shocked afterthought, at me. Christine's black hair was brushed up into two huge pigtails, each pointing directly perpendicular to her face, tied with large red ribbons. She was wearing a formfitting white crop top with white high-waisted Rizzo-style ankle-length pants and chunky white sandals with straps, topped off with a ruby red thickly lipsticked mouth.

She stopped on the bottom step and held one hand over her head with a queen wave for all to admire and fawn. Sandy, Renee, and Erica, who were used to Christine's shenanigans, simply shook their heads and laughed. But they came up to me with birthday hugs and said they "loved my new look" but wondered "what Christine had done with their friend Riley."

Before I could answer, a group of guys burst through the front door carrying two cases of beer. David led the pack and hollered at Ryan, who was coming down the stairs. "Hey, come help me put these in the fridge. They're for later. I've invited Darryl and Kent over and the rest of the gang. I told them no earlier than ten thirty. They said they'd probably see us beforehand at Nick's. Who else is coming?" As the guys headed toward the kitchen, David teased me, "Happy birthday, Riley! Love the Doc Martens. Where's your studded metal necklace?"

I grinned and said, "That'll come later. At the witching hour."

He raised his eyebrows and replied with a laugh, "Call me bewitched then."

I smiled and blushed a little. Neither David nor Ryan had ever noticed me at all, other than as the sisterly roommate sort, and now both of them had a strange twinkle for me on the same day. Were they just messing with me because it was my birthday? Living in a house with four other women and two men made for strange, suggestive energy. Everyone (besides me) had frequent "sleepovers" with the opposite sex, but none of us had ever hooked up with each other. It was like an unwritten rule. This house, which was originally built in the 1930s for a family of four, now housed seven grown co-eds and must remain neutral territory, meaning no inter-roommate sex or relationships.

A few minutes later, Christine placed a plastic bejeweled tiara on my head (to my stunned surprise) and insisted I wear it the whole night, no protesting. I couldn't help but smile as we headed out the door, walking and skipping the six blocks to Nick's, my crowned head in the clouds on this unusually warm spring night on my twenty-second birthday. Wow! It felt great to be outside in the newly fresh air after months of gray skies and cold, snowy afternoons. The daffodils and crocuses were blooming, and the student population was emerging from their apartments and dorms like butterflies escaping cocoons. We stopped along the way to pick up fellow revelers who got in step with us and exuded spring-has-sprung energy from their pores. I realized it had been...well, forever, it seemed, since I had felt this light and happy and free, knowing there were only a few short weeks left of my senior year at

Indiana University. We would all be moving on to bigger and better things (we hoped!) after years of toil and strife. My mood was a heady mix of nostalgia, pride, excitement, and anticipation for the next chapter. But for now, I was going to focus on tonight, this most perfect night with my closest friends on my birthday.

I caught up to Christine as she was saying to Sandy in a fake, haughty voice, "That is a very good question. I don't really know how I get the inspiration for my ensembles. I mean, how does the unicorn get its horn? How does the bird craft its song? How does the artist sculpt a bust? These are questions that will be pondered throughout the ages and cannot be answered with a simple explanation of human creativity or design."

Sandy countered, "How does the blind bear shit in the woods?"

I stifled a laugh and added, "How does the black dog make the yellow snow?"

Christine pursed her lips and said, "Hardy-har-har, you two. You're just jealous."

Sandy and I thought that was hysterical. Sandy was much like me and regarded her wardrobe as a simple function of necessity, certainly not as any type of statement, let alone a point of envy. Renee, along with her boyfriend, Jeff, came up behind us, hearing the tail end of our conversation, and added, "Do you think if Christine lived on a desert island, she would still dress up every day for the clubs?"

Jeff nudged Christine's side and said with a caveman grunt, "Me Tarzan, you Jane. We go to bar. Drink shots. Dance. Then you come. My tiki hut."

At this, Renee scooted in between them and fake-yelled, "Hey! That's my tiki hut. No women allowed."

Christine lifted her chin, shined her bright white teeth, and stated, "Me-Jane-no-need-Tarzan. Me-Jane-have-own-tiki-hut-with-no-man."

We all laughed. She really was that unique and independent, and I admired her for it. She added with a grin, "Besides, you know I'd be rocking the coconut husk bikini top and palm frond bottom. Eat your heart out, Brooke Shields!"

That set all the guys off on a tangent, screaming, "Oooo-ahhh!" while Renee grabbed Jeff's hand and led him away in a funny mock huff.

I chuckled with the rest of them, but my smile hid the usual shock of my Biblio, never far away from my reality or consciousness. I wondered quickly if Christine had noticed what I was reading earlier during our chat on my bed. Apparently not, since no sort of acknowledgment about the Tarzan reference flashed across her face. In all these years, I was still amazed that no one caught my Biblios. I certainly never hid what I was reading and always had a book in my hand. In this case, Jeff brought up the Biblio and could have no idea what I was reading. I shook my head, thinking of this fascinating aspect: it was like a bubble that frustratingly encased only me, never to be witnessed or acknowledged by others, never to be fully validated. And it was what, in its own secretive and metaphysical way, kept me separate from others, kept me straitlaced, structured, focused, studious, isolated, only partaking lightly, even at times superficially, of human interactions.

But then. This. All evidence to the contrary, I thought with a smirk, when I saw that Ryan and David had taken up the Tarzan mantra and were prancing around the ladies now, uttering all kinds of caveman grunts that made no sense whatsoever but were funny nonetheless. "Me-Tarzan-big-man-eat-stromboli-drink-beer." "Me-Tarzan-find-Jane-island." "Me-Tarzan-*explore*-Jane-island." "Me-Tarzan-live-on-island-as-king-with-large-harem." "Me-Tarzan-only-allow-young-hot-women-on-island." And so on and so forth. Somehow "Jane" was completely lost in this display, and Christine and I skipped along ahead of the guys, laughing and ignoring their beastly boasting and bragging.

Despite the Biblio island that I lived on (with no Tarzan!), sometimes I couldn't help but laugh at it. Yes, my Biblio was unnerving, on the one hand, but then also a staple of my existence on the other, and I had learned to take it in stride and even to recognize the ridiculousness of it at times. I still remembered (vividly) all those conversations with Father Avery and how he had taught me to stop questioning the source of it and the meaning behind it (still unanswered) and to simply take it for what it was. And I had, although I had never told another living soul about it (besides Father Avery), not even Dad or my best friend, Jane Parker.

When we got to Nick's, Christine pointed to the back of the bar and hollered above the noise, "Come on—Rick already has two booths."

We followed her and greeted our friends, who were (based on four half-empty pitchers on the table) already feeling pretty festive. A few stood up and hugged me, saying happy birthday, while the others made room in the booth for us to sit down.

Christine said, "First order of business: a shot for the birthday girl. What do you want?"

"I guess tequila, lord help me."

Ryan jumped up eagerly and said, "I'll get it. Be right back."

Christine raised her eyebrows at me and grinned. I rolled my eyes and shrugged. When he walked away, she said, "Why not? Make the most of it while you can."

The bar was packed and loud, and I felt an overwhelming sense of happiness and gratitude. To this great group of friends for taking me out on my birthday. To my university, which had opened my eyes to a new world of information and learning and had tested me, made me the strong, independent, smart, cultured, thoughtful woman I now was. To this moment, just a few weeks out from graduating magna cum laude and beginning a whole new life with a whole new future.

I gulped. A future unknown. A future filled with...what? I had no idea. Blank. We had all been attending IU's mandatory career preparation course with resume writing and interview simulations. In fact, Ryan, Sandy, David, and Renee were already squared away with real-life jobs lined up right after graduation, leaving school with the comfort of future fixed incomes in companies scattered all over the Midwest. I was jealous. My future lay like a wide-open bright white blank canvas waiting for something to be painted on it. I just didn't know what.

So far, I had only scored two phone interviews—one with an editor at the *Indianapolis Star* and the other with a consulting firm in New York City—both of which led to exactly nothing, as I'm sure they sensed my reservations. How could I—a shy, introverted, quiet, analytical book reader—be a fast-talking newspaper reporter or worse, a high-powered technical consultant at some big conglomerate in one of the noisiest, largest cities in the world?

Ryan broke into my thoughts, whispering in my ear, "Riley, your tequila, my dear. Let's get this birthday bash going."

I took it from his hand at the same time Christine snatched the others he was holding, saying dismissively (with a side wink to me), "Great—thanks, Ry. I'll take it from here. Can you do us a favor and fill these pitchers too?" Her saccharine-sweet smile caused him to frown and narrow his eyes at her, but he took the pitchers anyway and turned on his heel with a grunt.

I said, feeling a little bad, "Shouldn't we offer him money?"

"Um...nah...he's got that fancy job lined up in Chicago. And they gave him a pretty hefty sign-on bonus, so for tonight anyway, he's buying."

I nodded. She had brought up the topic I had just been thinking about, and now I found myself looking forlornly into my shot glass.

Christine noticed. "Oh no you don't. That face is *not* going to bleed into our party tonight. Listen: no great ponderings about the future. We're going to focus on the here and now. Got it?"

"Okay?" I said as a question, trying to smile.

"Hey, guys, everyone, grab a shot—it's time for a toast!"

Everyone posed dutifully, shots in hand, as Christine looked at me with her beautiful black doe eyes and her red-ribboned pigtails and said in all seriousness, "To Riley. Our petite redheaded bookworm who's never spoken out of turn, never raised her voice, never said no to a friend in need…and oh yeah, we have it on good authority, never been kissed! Happy birthday, Riley!"

"What?!" I screamed with a laugh as I protested, "That is *not* true! What authority are you talking about?" The gang all downed their shots and ignored me, so I finally followed suit with a scowl on my face.

Several helpful guys in the group offered, "Yeah, let's get Riley laid tonight! Do we have any volunteers?"

As I sucked the lime, I pulled it out of my mouth long enough to hiss at Christine, "You're dead." She grinned unapologetically.

Yowza. The night was starting off with a bang. Five minutes later, still feeling the burn in my throat from the first shot, another was placed in front of me, and I yelled across the table to Sandy, "Holy crap, I'm gonna need to pace myself."

She shrugged with a smile and said, "Why?"

I had this brief inner dialogue with myself: Did I want to get trashed tonight? On my birthday? Just a few short minutes ago, I had been letting my mind wander to those evil jitters and qualms about the future that kept plaguing me, so wasn't this moment in time possibly the best to unwind and let myself go a little? While I could, while it really was all still in the future?

I salted, slammed the shot, sucked on a lime wedge, and said with a giggle, "Why indeed."

Sandy said, "There you go. Right decision. Come on. Let's go change the music."

Chapter XVII

I NEEDED MY LIFE TO BE REAL. The good. The bad. The ugly. The everything. I knew that much was true. And if I was being real, I needed to admit to myself that I had come to this particular crossroads in my life by sailing. You know—skidding along the edge, doing the day-to-day activities and engagements and requirements, and flitting just above the surface of everything, never going deeper, never quite getting fully immersed in the water. Like a cat tapping the edge of her paw in the bathtub, but never her full foot, and certainly never her whole body. Because I knew what lay under the water, and that was the face of my own demons, my own memories, my own past. And beyond all else, I didn't want that. I didn't want to face it. I wanted to stay safety concealed and ensconced in the tight, gnarly cocoon I had constructed (along with my secret Biblio), maybe without meaning to, maybe unintentionally, but still, the cocoon was there, sheathing me so all the bad stuff was blurry and obscured, easy to dismiss, easy to make hazy, easy to forget. So I did. That strategy had kept me sane, content, calm, and blissfully oblivious in a way that left no time for pondering, no time for taking stock, no time to reengage with that which was gone and done and dead.

But just then, as Sandy took my hand and led me to the new music machine they had installed in the corner of Nick's to "request whatever my little heart desired," I had an overwhelming feeling sweep over me in a wave: someone was watching me. Someone was thinking of me. Someone was focusing all their attention on *me*. It was that odd tingle, my spidey sense, an awareness, a vibration in the energy. Or maybe it was the tequila, I thought with a nervous laugh, glancing around the bar. The alcohol may have loosened my inhibitions, dropped the shield of tangible, touchable things, and left this nebulous shot in its wake, right at the back of my neck, with goose bumps

and a shiver. It was crowded, and being short, my eyes only caught the backs
of people's heads and a sea of red-and-white IU jerseys. I cleared my throat
and tried again, on my tiptoes, but nothing, so I turned to Sandy, who had already put the money in the machine and was asking me what songs I wanted.
I said absently, muddled, "Anything. Um. I don't know. Whatever. What do
you think? The Clash? David Bowie. Duran Duran. Peter Gabriel."

"Okay, you got it!" she said cheerfully and scrolled through the selections.
When she was done, we headed back to the table, but she noticed my strange
obsession with looking around and asked, "You alright?"

"Uh-huh," I said, bringing my hurried, scanning eyes back to her face with
a strained smile. "Yeah, just buzzed, I guess. Thanks for the songs. I can't wait
'til they come on."

"Me either. Let's see who's buying the next round. My guess is David."

"Ha! Probably. Certainly not Ryan…he must be running out—" I stopped
mid-sentence. There it was. The reason. My mouth dropped open in shock.
Adam Linder. Standing not two feet from me. My heart suddenly started
pounding out of my chest. And I could tell his eyes had been tracking me the
whole time—before, during, and after our visit to the music machine. His
eyes flickered to my tiara and then back to my eyes and somehow also to my
mouth, quickly assessing my whole face.

Sandy was pushing Ryan out of the booth and motioning for me to slide
back in when she noticed me standing stock-still, staring directly at this man
who was a stranger to her. She touched my arm lightly and waited for me to respond, but I didn't. I didn't even blink. And yet, I drank in every inch of him,
as he had done with me—his warm brown eyes that had only gotten softer and
kinder looking, his feathered brown hair, his soft lips, his stature (which had
increased at least three or four inches since last I saw him), his broad shoulders,
his strong hands loosely holding a cup of beer. And the peculiar concoction
that was his expression: shock mixed with fear mixed with awe mixed with
admiration mixed with dread mixed with…what was it? Then I knew. Definitively. The final, most poignant emotion that lingered there: hope.

I drew in a gasp as if coming up for air after a deep dive. I felt all the blood
rush to my face, like a balloon filling with helium. I blinked several times in
succession and glanced at Sandy's worried face, saying to her, "Um, hey, it's
okay. I know him. I'll be right back."

"Okay," she said, watching me with a "you sure?" question mark on her
face, to which I nodded. She said loudly, I guess as a warning to Adam, which

I noticed made him smile, "Well, we'll be *right here* waiting. Don't go too far. We have a bunch of other stuff planned."

I nodded. Even in my abstraction, I thought she was sweet, trying to protect me, so I said again, "It's okay."

I turned to Adam as he simply said hi and held out his hand.

I shook it, echoing my own hi.

For what seemed like a full minute, we stood there, our hands clasped, staring into each other's eyes and not saying a word.

The lock finally broke. He leaned in and said, above the din of the crowd, "Can we talk?"

I felt the heat of his cheek graze mine as I answered, "Yes."

It was then that I noticed he was with a group of guys who were huddled in the booth a few feet from ours. He said something to them, and they waved him off as he led me toward the front of the bar, asking along the way if I needed a drink, to which I answered with a slight laugh, "Um...yeah."

Administered right into my jugular, please.

I realized with a start, as we pushed past the throng of hot, loud, sweaty co-eds, that I had never spoken a single solitary word directly to this shockingly handsome man despite the fact that I had known him for ten years. "Known" not in the way of a friend or a family member, but in the way of a tragic fate that caused two lives to collide inexorably and inevitably without warning and without end.

My stomach was in my throat. He claimed the only open spot up front, where one stool sat empty in the tight triangle between the wall, the window, and the bar. We squeezed in between a group of people. He offered me the stool, and I sat facing him as he motioned confidently to the bartender. He asked me what I wanted, and I shrugged, momentarily speechless at the brush of his hip against my knee. He ordered two beers, put a few dollars down on the bar, and turned to me. He smiled and I smiled back. He had a sort of crooked smile that caused me to stare unabashedly right at his mouth. His smile became even broader when he noticed me noticing him. In return, he was looking directly into the depths of my eyes. I felt as though he was a pirate trying to dig a treasure out from my very soul with that scouring glance.

At first we had no words, but when the beers came he said, "Cheers," and we clinked our glasses and drank. Then he pointed to my tiara and asked, "Special occasion?"

"My birthday."

"Oh, wow, happy birthday."

"Thanks. And what are you up to? I mean, um...what are you doing here?"

"It's my buddy's bachelor party tonight. He lives here in Bloomington, so we all came down and decided to make a weekend of it."

"Nice." I nodded, sipping more of my beer. He drank too, but his eyes never left my face. It was as if he was trying to count my freckles or memorize the specks in my irises. I couldn't help but feel self-conscious, but I wasn't sure how to react, so I kept myself in check, letting the tickles and tingles of his attention wash over me in a slow wave. All the while, I was wondering why the heat of him seemed to be tracing over me, permeating my body like a molten surge of liquid fire.

He said, "It's been a while."

"Uh-huh."

"Actually, we've never really talked, have we?"

"Nope."

His face was a show of earnestness as he asked, "Why is that?"

"I don't know." I kept hearing this strange thought in the back of my mind: I want my life to be real. I need my life to be real. Everything. Just as it is. Even when it feels uncomfortable, unknown, unpredictable. Even when it feels as if I'm on the edge of a cliff. Even though I feel everything up to this point has been a screen. One that hides me from the world. One that protects me from the unfamiliar. One that shields me from myself.

One that needs to be shattered.

He smiled again, with such warmth that I felt myself leaning toward him as the outside of his hand touched the side of my leg.

He said simply, "Let's change that."

"Let's," I agreed.

He laughed out loud then, a release of tension and a lifetime of worry, fear, and restraint. He said quickly, "You look...great."

My heart skipped a beat. I smiled and said, "Thank you" and "You look... different." *Like a man.*

Studying my face, he didn't press me to explain and instead asked lightly, "What have you been up to?"

I choked out a laugh. "That's a loaded question. Um, let's see...school." A wave of my hand toward campus. "I'm about to graduate. I'm still trying to figure out what's next, actually. What about you?"

"I'm getting my DVM, up at Purdue."

"DVM?"

"Vet school."

"No kidding? Wow, that's cool."

He grunted a little and responded, "Yes, it will be...someday. Right now, it's mostly a lot of studying and hard work." He grinned and then said, "For instance, I spent this morning trying to figure out what type of parasitic worms are most likely to feed on a horse's eyes and how best to treat them."

My face puckered as I said, "Ew. Sounds lovely."

He smirked. "Yep, loads of fun." He took another swig of his beer, still with his eyes piercing me. He asked, "Which birthday is it?"

"Twenty-second."

"Ah. I remember that one."

"Oh yeah? Was it a good one?"

"Hmm, let's see...I had just graduated Louisville and I was home again, living with Mom and Jeremy and trying to figure out if I had enough time for a summer job before heading to Purdue. Mom insisted yes, and I was thinking, what if I just lay around this summer and did nothing? After all, it would be the first time since I was fourteen that I had no school and no job and no commitments. I mean, why not loaf? Totally chill, right? Last chance."

In light of my own unknown future, I was curious. "So, what did you do?"

"What do you think? Mom gave me a birthday cake and shoved me out the door. I ended up back at Pizza Shack. Thankfully, the manager, Wayne, upgraded my job from deliveryman to co-manager. He ran the place four nights a week, and I was in charge the other three. It was a fun summer. The whole lot of us went out almost every night after closing. We'd drive over to the lake or hang out at someone's house or just stay there eating leftover pizza and wings."

I sighed and looked away for a minute. "Gosh, that sounds great. I wish I knew what I was going to do."

"Oh yeah?" he asked with such a kind, listening face that I wanted to confess all my thoughts and fears and hopes and dreams, but instead I redirected with, "Hey, speaking of home, when was the last time you were there?"

"Not since Christmas, believe it or not. Seems like forever. Mom isn't happy, says she misses feeding 'her boys.' Jeremy's working two or three jobs now, so he's not around a lot. I'm up at Purdue, so...yeah, I think Mom's a little lonely. How about you? Been home?"

"I went home about a month ago for spring break. A lot of my friends went to Daytona, but I…well, I sunburn so easily…and despite appearances tonight," I waved toward the bar with a grin, "I'm not a big partier. I'd rather be home with a stack of books."

He nodded. "Hey, how's your brother Marc doing? I haven't talked to him in ages." He chuckled and added, "God, I miss hanging out in your basement. Does your dad still have that huge train set down there? I remember we spent hours playing with that thing."

I remembered it too—I would hide up in my bedroom whenever Adam was in the house. Now I felt myself wanting to fall directly into those deep brown eyes, and maybe also into his lap. The war of feelings jostling around in my body and mind at that moment was utterly staggering. It was as if I was absorbing his being into my soul through some type of crazy, cosmic tether of osmosis. And yet, I used to wish with all my heart that Adam Linder didn't exist and that I could go about my daily life in our tiny town and never fear running into him again. And here I was, drinking him in like an intoxicating mirage in a desert.

Instead of expressing any of this, I said, "No, Dad finally took it apart and converted the basement into a bedroom. My brother Brent is living down there now. He's working at Pluto and trying to save enough money to buy a house. Anyway, Marc's doing well. He moved to Indianapolis about a year ago. Got a job at a big insurance company up there doing some type of actuarial work. I think he likes it. He's engaged to be married to a girl from Kokomo, but I haven't met her yet."

"No kidding? Engaged! Wow. Lucky dog. Well, good for him."

At this last statement, there was some sort of insinuation, a hint of something, fixed on me. I stared blankly, trying not to reveal my inner thoughts. As if to explain his own expression, he went on, "Yeah, my buddy in the back, the one we're having the bachelor party for, we were roommates at Louisville. He's getting married in a month, and I can still remember the day he met Katie at one of those campus block parties. It was as though he was starstruck or mesmerized—he couldn't keep his eyes off her and could barely get his words out." He paused, chuckling, as he remembered, and then stopped and blushed a little.

He glanced away for a moment in his confusion, and when he looked back, locking on my eyes, the space between us opened up. Not the physical space—in fact, that got much closer, his side resting easily against my knee, his hand grazing mine on the bar. It was the astral space that seemed to hover between us, to be recognized, processed, consumed. And I began to feel strange, almost like the word *heady* that people use. I felt heady or waif-like or light-headed. Something akin to *the other* was embodying us and yet, not knowing what to make of it or how to sort it out, we didn't say a word or move a muscle to acknowledge it. And I knew he was feeling it too. It was as if our eyes were attached to each other and we couldn't pull them apart because we had been transported into a separate, parallel existence together. The seconds became minutes.

Then, out of the blue, with a most unwelcome earthly, physical tug on my arm, Christine broke the spell. "Hey, where have you been? We've been looking all over for you!" She glanced at Adam, rather accusingly, to which he raised an eyebrow, then back at me with a frown. "Come on—there are about five more tequila shots waiting for you and two whole strombolis."

I stood up, my feet reluctantly and firmly planted back on Earth, and started to apologize to Adam, but he cut in politely. "It's okay—I need to head back as well."

As we trekked through the packed bar, Christine leading the way, someone knocked into me, and I felt Adam hold me steady and then grip my hand. My pulse quickened, and I turned to observe the huge smile on his face. When we were close to our respective booths, he spoke into my ear, "Come find me before you leave."

I nodded and snatched one last peek into his soul-crushing eyes before his hand released and he was gone.

Chapter XVIII

ADAM WONDERED IF HE WAS HAVING an out-of-body experience. He thought back to that miniseries he had watched a couple of years before about Shirley MacLaine—*Out on a Limb*—and how she sometimes left her body and drifted above it, watching herself below as if through a movie camera. At the time, he thought it was fascinating but also a load of hogwash. Now he was wondering if his skepticism was some kind of joke on him. He had just stood up from a booth at Nick's. His friends were behind him, laughing, teasing, reminiscing, drinking, having a rowdy, bang-up time, when it happened. It was Riley Cartwright. She was across the bar at the music machine with a friend. At that exact moment, he shivered (even though it was a hundred degrees in the hot, crowded bar) and felt himself detach from his body. Sure, he realized in his hyper-logical mind that Nick's was a very real, very loud, very substantial place—the kind of place you couldn't just dismiss from your mind, couldn't just pretend wasn't there. Couldn't just rise above like a phoenix rising from the ashes. And yet, without warning, he felt himself do just that: rise above the loud din, sweaty bodies, empty cups, spilled beer, and sticky counters to transport himself directly to her side as if through a fast-moving tunnel. He was separate and distinct from his body, a spectral being who left the world of Nick's in a foggy, forgotten haze and instead was laser-focused on every cell of the bright white, angelic form of Riley Cartwright. He was absorbed to the exclusion of all else—enveloped, encircled, wrapped in her aura.

Taking in the nearness of her, he saw the hair on the back of her neck stand up. She shivered (just as he had) and turned around, looking from one side of the bar to the other, trying to detect the origin of the tingle up her spine. She didn't see Adam (neither the bodily form nor the spectral form), but he realized with wonder, she *felt* him. He wanted to reach out to her. Feel the warmth of her skin on his fingertips. But of course, he couldn't. Instead, he took her in as if from a macro-focus camera lens: the red hair braided down her back with several loose tendrils spiraling down from her temples in a most becoming way, the blue-green widely set eyes with flecks of yellow and brown like a kaleidoscope of the ocean's deepest hues, the way her presence seemed to absorb into his soul with the warmth of the sun on a summer day. She was wearing all black, which was strange to him—it didn't seem to fit her personality, but then, he thought, how would he know what her personality was like? All these years, he had never once had a conversation with her or learned anything real or true about her. Yes, he had been a voyeur in high school, not the creepy kind, but the kind who can't keep from watching from afar to see what she would do, what she would say, how she would act, everything about how she was and who she was. But always so elusive because, for obvious reasons, he had never ventured to intrude, to scare her, to take up space in her world. And now he was balanced so close to her orbit, if only virtually. He lost all sense of reason, tangibility, presence. He hovered and drank her in, processing her every movement, pore, cell, breath, thought.

Meanwhile she distractedly rattled off some musicians and watched her friend enter them into the machine. Sensing the outside presence in the room that she knew was there but couldn't identify, couldn't quite put a finger on, she glanced around again and still didn't see him. As they finished and started walking back, just like a shot at the beginning of a footrace—bang—Adam was back in his body and facing her. Riley. She stopped, mid-stride, dumbfounded, her mouth agape, staring in stunned recognition. For the first time, he noticed the plastic crown on her head. Oh. It must have been a special occasion. God, he was at the wrong place at the wrong time, wasn't he? He felt his heartbeat drumming against his skull. He stepped forward and put out his hand, which she shook with as much enthusiasm as a startled baby deer. He smiled and said hi, noting with compassion that regardless of their mutual shock at meeting in this most unlikely place and time, he still had a head start on her, having just spent a period of strange, otherworldly time taking her in.

The next forty minutes were extraordinary. They talked. The former ice between them was shattered in a million pieces. More than an icebreaker—an ice obliterator. And miracle of miracles—Adam's nerves faded away, and they were normal, easy with each other. He couldn't take his eyes off her face because of her beauty, but also because to look at her was like watching a newly awakened piece of himself coming to life.

Eventually, her friend came and took her away, and Adam felt as though he had been left out in the icy tundra. He asked her to come see him before she left, and when she did, her cheeks were rosy from drinking, and he noted that she seemed less inhibited than she had been, putting her hand on his arm as she approached. He introduced her to his friends. They said hi and watched the two of them curiously for a few minutes, probably noticing how Adam's face lit up, but then they went back to their beers and banter, thankfully leaving Adam and Riley to themselves. He nodded toward a corner, where it was less crowded. The two of them walked over and stood facing each other.

She smiled apologetically and said briefly, "We're leaving—heading to the next place."

"Okay."

She leaned in so he could hear, her spectacular eyes awash in feeling, which caused Adam's heart to skip a beat. She said, "It was…really great…to see you, Adam. I'm glad we talked."

"Me too," Adam agreed, trying with all his might to restrain himself from screaming, "YES! Finally!" Instead, he asked, "Can I call you?"

Her smile broadened as she answered, "Yes, definitely."

She hugged him then, reaching her arms around his neck and crushing her body against him. He wrapped his arms around her back, holding her to his frame.

He closed his eyes, wishing time would stop.

But then she was gone, and he watched her retreating form with a wondrous perma-grin on his face. A split second later, he exhaled and ran after her, grabbing her hand as she looked back in surprise. He hollered above the noise, "Wait, I don't have your number."

"Oh yeah," she said with a laugh and grabbed a pen off a nearby table, writing her number on the palm of his hand. A hand that would need to be wrapped in plastic, sealed with an airtight rubber band, and preserved behind bulletproof glass in a museum.

She threw him one last smile, the crown on her head bobbing as she ran off toward her friends.

What happened over the next several hours, Adam couldn't say. The only thing certain was the fact that he was not going to touch anything with his right hand for the rest of the night, and when his friends asked him to play pool, he declined. He also waited to go to the bathroom for as long as he could, not wanting to wash his hands, until finally he asked to borrow a napkin and pen from the bartender, wrote the number down, shoved the napkin deep into his pocket, and ran as fast as he could to the urinal to relieve himself.

One thing he was not able to relieve was his state of shock, excitement, and hope. He barely partook of the ribbings and taunts that are part and parcel of any good bachelor party. He even grinned at the pokes and prods pointed at him when he refused to go to the strip club at the end of the night, saying he was tired and would walk back to the hotel alone. Their designated driver, Hector, tried to change his mind, saying, "Hey, if I'm able to endure these drunken assholes for another few hours, then you should be able to." Hector was seconded by a wavering Trent saying, "Yeah man, don't be a pussy!" followed by, "Instead, come and get some pussy!" to which several others added, "And don't forget boobs, lots and lots of boobs." Adam laughed and waved goodbye as he walked out onto the street, feeling the fresh air in his lungs and the neon signs glowing against his face. He weaved through gangs of students spilling out of the bars and restaurants onto the street in a rush of laughter, cigarette smoke, and sweaty bodies.

With his head down and his hands in his pockets, he walked steadily back to the hotel, which was about a mile away. He tried hard not to scan passing groups, seeking a plastic crown. He wondered if Riley and her friends had gone to other bars or had simply gone home to finish her birthday celebration. He hadn't even asked where she lived—was it a house or a dorm or an apartment? He really hadn't had a lot of time to ask her much of anything, but at least he had her number. There was promise in that. He was walking on air. He wondered if he could call her from the hotel room. That would be too soon, right?

Instead, back in the empty room, he lay faceup on the scratchy comforter and thought about her face, especially her eyes and lips, and the way they animated when she talked. And he thought about that hug and how he could still feel her presence in his arms, and how *right* that felt.

His mind hearkened back to the last time he had hugged a woman for the first time and how different that hug had been. It was Eve, the woman he had met at that fateful bonfire all those years ago. When they hugged that night, he knew immediately that she was a prim and proper sort of girl, but then she was also nice and pretty and smart and seemed really into him. When you're nineteen and trying to obliterate the one-in-a-million, unattainable, no-chance-in-hell only hope for love from your mind, you date the woman who's right in front of you. So he did. For four years. And received hundreds of cold, stiff hugs and more from her during that time.

It was almost as if they both knew it wouldn't work out from the beginning, but they started it up and kept at it anyway, not having any other prospects and not wanting to hurt each other's feelings. Or maybe not wanting to face the idea of starting over with someone new after the mechanics of this relationship had been established. It was quite easy to pretend with her. First of all, from day one, it was a long-distance relationship. That summer she was only in French Lick for a few shorts weeks and then went back to Indy. A month later, she was at Vanderbilt University in Tennessee, and he was at University of Louisville in Kentucky. They talked on the phone and met up during holidays. He stayed with her family for a week during Christmas, and she came down to her cousin's house in French Lick on and off during those years. He would take her out on dates after he closed up at Pizza Shack. Sometimes they would sneak out to the lake, watch the moon rise, and fool around in the back seat of his Honda. They said "I love you" to one another and seemed to really mean it at the time, but later he always wondered if he was playacting, trying to fit a square peg into a round hole with the force of a sledgehammer. Finally, when she graduated and got a job teaching art at an elementary school up in Indy and he was knee-deep in the intense first-year curriculum in Purdue's DVM program, he stopped calling her as much, blaming it on his classes, until one night over the phone, she stated, "Adam, we need to talk."

He made it easy on her, telling her he needed to focus all his attention on the next four years of school anyway and he "didn't want to hold her back" from anything or anyone, if that was what she wanted. She cried into the receiver and said she was sorry and wished they "had been able to make it work." They stayed on the phone for several more minutes before they said goodbye and hung up. The last Adam heard, a couple of years later, she was married and pregnant. He didn't regret a thing and actually felt very happy for her. She deserved more than his half-hearted love and his pathetic attempt to slot her into a space that was always meant to be filled by someone else.

And he hadn't lied when he said he had to focus on school. Lying on the bed in the hotel room, he thought about the fact that he was nearing the end of his second year of the four-year program at Purdue and how this weekend was a rare chance to get away in the midst of his coursework, which included pathology, bacteriology, virology, parasitology, pharmacology, epidemiology, and public health. Next year, he would be starting clinicals and would be even busier.

But for right now, all he wanted to think about was the way Riley's body had molded into his, like the way you might hug your pillow when trying to fall asleep after a long, hard day of physical labor. He knew with the certainly of a thousand sunrises that he wanted more of that and maybe *all* of that someday. Sooner rather than later. He took the napkin out of his pocket and stared at the number scrawled there, noting that the same number on his palm was fading fast. He wondered how to keep it from going away altogether. And not just the number.

CHAPTER XIX

DURING THE FIRST FEW MONTHS after Kathy died, before I had taken my first trip to the library, I had a recurring memory that replayed in my mind like a movie reel on autoloop. It was based on a conversation we had shortly before her death while we were lying faceup, head to toe, on the sectional couch in her basement and she told me she had nine lives and had already burned through seven of them.

"What?!" I exclaimed, laughing. "Only cats have nine lives. Plus, you're not old enough to have burned through seven!"

"Just call me Sylvester," she said with a giggle. After a pause, she muttered, "I'm serious, though."

"What do you mean?" I leaned up on my elbow to look at her face. Her eyes were thoughtful.

"You see, I've calculated it," she explained.

"Go on then," I said.

"Okay, so my first life was taken when I was born. I watched a documentary on TV where they showed the entire birthing process. Think about it: you're cooked like a stuffed pig inside a fishbowl for nine months, then shoved out of a canal the size of a hotdog and brought into this world with a red, matted, and crushed head, breathing air into totally unformed lungs, screaming bloody murder because you just went from the warmest, safest, most comfortable hotel into a cold, bright, harsh, loud heavy-metal concert on steroids."

"You make it sound so lovely," I said with a grunt.

"Exactly," Kathy stated flatly.

After a moment, I said, "Yeah, like how do we even breathe while we're in the womb? I mean, we don't have gills, so why is it that we don't drown? The stuff in there is some form of fluid, right? And why don't we come out all pruned up like we do when we've been playing Marco Polo in the pool for hours? The whole thing doesn't make sense."

"Ridiculous," she affirmed.

"Plus, I heard my mom say that sometimes you poop in the womb and swallow it, and they call it *plutonium*."

Kathy burst out laughing.

"What?" I asked. "It's not funny! Seriously, Mom said it can be pretty serious."

"Yes, I know," Kathy said, somehow managing to roll her eyes as she schooled me with dead seriousness, "it's called *meco*nium, not *plut*onium. We'd have much bigger problems if fetuses pooped out plutonium, believe me!"

For about the hundredth time, I felt like a total dolt around Kathy. She was always so much smarter than I was. I pouted and said, "Whatever. You knew what I meant."

She continued with a question, "Aren't you the least bit curious about the others?"

"Babies?" I responded in confusion.

"No, dingbat," she said, exasperated. "*My* other lives. That was number one—birth. Then I lost number two when I was holed up in that orphanage in Korea for the first year of my life. Who knows what I suffered?"

I thought about that for a minute. "Do you remember it?" I asked.

"No, of course not. I was only a baby. Do *you* remember anything from when you were one? But Mom and Dad told me it was a nasty, dirty, crowded kind of place."

"Really? Wow, I never knew that." I had been best friends with Kathy for as long as I could remember, but I guess there was still so much I didn't know about her. She didn't talk about her adoption. And as much as I realized (based on her appearance) that she was Korean, I still never thought about her being from a country thousands of miles away. She had always been the girl down the street. I looked at her now—her eyes were almond shaped and dark amber, and her skin was tawny, like butterscotch. But then, I thought, look at me—I'm freckled, redheaded, skinny, with a dimple in my chin. Honestly, in my mind, we *both* looked different from each other and from everyone else in our friend group.

I began to think that Kathy had definitely pondered way more about her existence here on Earth than I had. I mean, who cared about your "number of lives" at age twelve? Certainly not me. But apparently Kathy did. I had a quick thought: she was an *old soul.* I always wondered what that meant. Like a Buddhist with baggage from past lives? Or a young person who talked like an old person? Or someone who had deep thoughts before they even knew what they meant? She was like that—as if she knew things and said things that were beyond her years. She mentioned once or twice that she had been abandoned by her biological mother, tucked in a basket on the side of the road in Korea, and that was how she ended up in the orphanage. She talked about it in a matter-of-fact way, but I wondered if it affected her sense of herself—not knowing exactly from where or whom she came and whether her biological parents *had* to give her up or had *chosen* to give her up.

Did she stay up at night wondering if they were thinking about her at that very same moment, on the other side of world, and if so, what they were thinking? Did her biological father even know there had been a baby? And what about her biological mother? Had she ever visited the orphanage while Kathy was being cared for there? Had she waited for the orphanage staff to take the babies out in strollers and staged a drive-by to catch a glimpse of her daughter? Or was it too painful, so she simply wiped Kathy's existence from her mind after leaving her in that basket? Said a prayer over her, gave her little cheek a kiss, and walked away? Was it about money? Family issues? Having a girl instead of a boy? The awful thing for Kathy must have been: not ever knowing.

Meanwhile, Kathy moved on to the next one: "Uh-huh. Number three was being adopted. It was like a one in a million chance that I ended up with a normal, loving family. I mean, I could have been adopted by psychos or a cult or child abusers or who knows? Something even worse."

I said, "Worse, as in Daphne Reardon's parents."

She burst out laughing. "Exactly! Poor Daphne—like anal-retentive Nazis! Who makes their child clean her room every morning before school (make the bed, put away clothes, dust the surfaces, vacuum!) and also do a ton of afterschool chores (dishes, toilets, laundry!)? I feel so bad for her..."

"Me too. I can barely remember to put the cap on the toothpaste in the morning." I paused, then ventured, "But how do you figure your adoption was losing a life? I think that one should be counted as *gaining* a life, don't you? Your math is off, sister."

"And yet I just scored an A-plus on our algebra test on Tuesday."

"I know—stop rubbing it in. I'm horrible at math," I said woefully. She scored better than I did in every class but was especially proficient in math. "Yeah, well, this is a different kind of math."

She chuckled and agreed, "I suppose…sure, it ended up fine, but it was a total miracle. What if my parents had gotten me and then decided they didn't want me? Then what would have happened? I would have been plopped into some orphanage here in Indiana or given away to some other family."

"No way—they wouldn't have done that."

"Well, thank goodness! Like anyone would have wanted a baby who had been rejected by its birth mother *and* its adoptive parents."

It was hard to ignore the tinge of hurt in her voice. I wasn't sure how to react. Was that the conclusion she had drawn—about her mother? A rejection? In the absence of any other known reason, it must have been hard *not* to think that. That made me sad for her, so I countered with, "Well, it *didn't* happen, so there. I'll give you a life for the adoption, but remember, this is how you ultimately ended up with the coolest best friend ever."

She smiled at that, then asked suddenly, "Hey, do you wanna hear my Korean name?"

"Whoa…yes…totally!"

"Min Ji. Or rather, Minji. I've seen it spelled both ways. When the adoption agency called the first time, saying they had a match for my parents, for some reason (I don't know if it was the accent or what), my mom thought the woman said my name was 'Kathy' instead of 'Minji' and there you go—somehow it stuck. Years later, I told my mom that her logic made no sense—Kathy doesn't sound anything like Minji and why would a child in *Korea* be named Kathy?"

"Right?! Oh well. I like Kathy. It's funny, I always wondered why your full name wasn't Kathleen or Katherine."

"Now you know. Where did Riley come from?"

"After having three boys in succession, my parents hedged their bets and came up with a name that could be for a boy or a girl."

"I always thought it would be a good dog's name."

"Hey!" I cried, grabbing her foot and squeezing.

"Ouch!" She grabbed my ankle in return, and then we were writhing around until we both broke free, standing up and facing each other with a wrestler's stance and a giggle, our faces red, our hair tousled.

After a few seconds of mutual death stares, I gave in with "Truce" and she nodded as we both lay back down, breathing hard.

She continued as if the interlude hadn't happened. "Fourth life is my diabetes."

"Oh, okay, I'll give you that one."

I remembered one summer, many years before, when Kathy couldn't stop drinking water and was acting funny, like a drunkard, until one day she collapsed in the yard after doing a bunch of cartwheels. Her parents called the ambulance, and she was taken away, not returning for nearly a week. When they brought her home, I heard them explaining to my parents that she had this 'sugar' disease where she needed to be careful with her diet and to prick her finger for blood and stick a needle in her stomach a bunch of times a day. It sounded awful. And it was.

She continued, "So yeah, anyway, then there was the coma."

"Oh yeah, the coma," I echoed soberly. "Wait, what number are we up to?"

"Five."

"So, when was that? Two years ago? I can't remember."

"No, three. I was nine."

"God, that was horrible."

"Definitely not a walk in the park. It was the hardest on Mom and Dad. Honestly, for me, I don't remember much."

She had been having difficulty controlling her diabetes. At school one day, she had gone to the nurse's office to get her shot like normal, but then for some reason there was a delay opening the cafeteria for lunch, so we had to stand outside, waiting in line for about twenty minutes. When it finally opened, we still had to fill our trays and pay. Finally, we sat down across from each other, munching on our food and talking. That was when I noticed Kathy's face turn red, like a wave coming over her features, and a second later, it turned white in the same way the red had come and gone. Beads of sweat broke out on her forehead, and her words stopped making sense, as if she was trying to formulate a sentence and couldn't. Then, like a snap, the life went out of her eyes, and her head fell forward onto her tray. I stared in shock for a good five seconds before screaming and running to the lunch proctor, "Kathy's sick! She passed out!" By the time the ambulance came, she had already slipped into a coma and stayed that way for several weeks before coming out of it. By the time she came back to school, she had missed so much that her parents had to hire a tutor. She never talked about it, but I think the whole incident embarrassed her. There is nothing worse than a roomful of kids staring wide-eyed at the inert form of a classmate having CPR performed on them and then being taken away on a stretcher.

She went on, "So, six is when I fell skiing and got a concussion."

"Oh yeah…and we thought skiing in Michigan was going to be fun. No one told us about the ice, did they?"

"No."

"The agony of defeat."

We grunted.

"Seven?"

"Seven was my period. So much blood. It's really gross. By the way, you're next."

"Don't remind me. I'm hoping it'll be another few years."

"You should be so lucky."

"One can only hope." She was quiet for a minute, so I prodded, "And the eighth?"

"Hasn't happened yet."

"No? Well, good!" I said emphatically, "I was beginning to wonder if Sylvester wasn't going to land on his feet this time."

"Like I reminded you earlier, I'm good at math, so don't worry. Two lives ought to last me more than your long, slow, boring one.

"Hey!" I said and threw a pillow at her head.

She laughed and we both lay back, thinking our own thoughts. She really did have some intense stuff happen to her already, for only being twelve. And I figured she was right about my one life. I was so cautious in everything I did—definitely not a Sylvester but a true scaredy-cat—that I probably *would* only have one long life. And, I thought, what was so wrong with that?

In the quiet of the basement, I eventually fell asleep. I woke up to the sound of Kathy's mom hollering down to tell us it was dinnertime. Sitting up, I noticed that Kathy was already wide awake. She was staring at the wall, her face blank.

I rubbed the sleep out of my eyes and asked, "Hungry?"

She turned to me as if she hadn't realized I was there. I noticed she hadn't responded to her mom either. Ignoring my question, she said cryptically, "What do you think?"

"About what?"

"About the lives we have left."

She was still thinking about that? I had almost forgotten our conversation during my nap. I said with a small, uncomfortable laugh, "Um, all I'm thinking about is what's for dinner."

She stared at me then, her face suddenly stern. She said, "No, I mean it.

How long do you think I can stretch out those other two lives? The more I think about, the more I think not very long. I want to make sure I pack them full, make them worthy. Make it feel like I did them justice and it wasn't all a big mistake, you know?"

Her expression was so adamant that I could only take it in and try to understand, which I didn't. I nodded slowly, processing (in my inadequate twelve-year-old mind) the weight of her words and the intent behind them. A mistake? Did she feel her life was a *mistake*?

Finally, her eyes on me and not finding what they were seeking there, she looked away, stood up, smoothed out her clothes, and said abruptly, "Forget it. Come on, let's go."

Why didn't I say something? Why didn't I stop her from marching up the stairs, her mouth frowning, her shoulders slumped? Why didn't I tell her that even if she lived another thousand lives, she couldn't have been a better friend to me, and how could that ever be considered a mistake?

But I didn't.

And one month later, she was dead.

And I was alive.

And ten years later, I was up to twenty-two years in my one long life, and I still remembered that conversation and wished I had the right words, then and now.

CHAPTER XX

GOOD LORD, what was that obnoxious sound? I ventured to open one eyelid and quickly slammed it shut. It was bright. And loud. And something or some*one* was unnecessarily chipper. I waited. I groaned. Then I opened both eyes and squinted. It was Christine, sitting on the edge of her bed painting her toenails blood red and singing a Janet Jackson song that was playing (*way* too loud) on the college radio station.

"Tur'tha'don," I mumbled, my mouth not quite working, my teeth stuck together as if I had been chewing on a cotton candy spiderweb for several days.

She glanced up and said, "Oh good, you're awake. 'Bout time. You've missed two phone calls already." A sly, knowing grin. "From you-know-who. You gonna get up and tell me all about him or what?"

"Or what," I answered and sat up, chugging the glass of water on my nightstand, feeling as though I could drink all of Earth's water and still not be hydrated.

"Don't forget the aspirin. I put two there, see, next to the water. And you'll need to get some food in your stomach. Then you'll feel like a whole new person." She put her nail polish down and blew on her toes for a few seconds before adding, "Get in the shower, come downstairs, and I'll make you some toast and eggs. Okay, sweet'ums?" She leaned over me and pinched my cheek lightly.

I growled at her and rolled over to face the wall, feeling something crack and break in the bedsheets. I reached under my back, pulled out the tiara, now a mangled plastic mess, and whimpered. Christine grabbed it from me and said with a laugh, "Your day in the sun is over, my darling princess. Time to face the music. Come on, get up. I want you downstairs in ten minutes. Up!"

I figured I couldn't feel any worse, so I did as she said and got up, wondering absently what day of the week it was. Oh yeah, Saturday. Thank goodness, I had the whole weekend ahead of me. To recover. I would need it. My head hurt. And oddly, my right shin. I looked down and saw it had a large red welt with a purple bruise forming around the edges. How had that happened? I didn't remember. Had I run into something last night? Apparently. What else would come as a shock to me from last night? I jumped in the shower and blasted the hot water directly into my face, forehead, and temples. About thirty seconds in, I mumbled in vaguely acknowledged uncertainty, "Wow... Adam Linder..."

I got ready in a huff, throwing on some sweats, and nearly ran downstairs, where Christine, Sandy, and Ryan were all sitting around the kitchen table eating. A plate was waiting for me. I sat down, munched, and grunted, "How are you guys all bright-eyed and bushy-tailed? I feel like hell."

Ryan shrugged and said, "I never get hangovers."

"Me either," Sandy said, but added, "And I don't think any of us drank quite as much as you did, birthday girl, so that explains a lot."

Christine agreed with a quick nod. She waited until I'd had my second bite of toast before launching into, "So, what's with the guy, Riley?"

Ryan cut in before I could speak, "What guy? Is there a guy upstairs?"

I frowned at him and said, "Um, no, definitely not."

Christine looked at Ryan as though he was an idiot. "Don't you remember at Nick's last night when Riley disappeared on us for like an hour? She was talking to some tall, mysterious, hot guy."

Ryan's eyes narrowed, and he said, "Oh," and took a bite of his eggs, looking down.

Christine glanced back at me and pressed, "So? Who is he?"

I sloshed the eggs down (along with my dislodged heart) with a gulp of hot coffee.

Christine kept on, "Are you gonna call him? He said, and I quote, he 'wanted you to call him as *soon* as you woke up.'"

I sighed and said a bit defensively, "Listen. He's a guy from French Lick, that's all. And I *will* call him, but right now I'd really like to eat my breakfast in peace."

Christine shook her head back and forth in a mock snippy toss, saying, "Fine, be that way. Well, whatever. I'm headed to the auditorium for rehearsal in about ten minutes. Anyone else need a ride to campus?"

"Sure," Sandy replied, "Renee will come too, I think. She said she wanted to hit the gym and maybe the library today. Be right back."

Both Sandy and Ryan got up and left the kitchen, and I began to feel bad for snapping at Christine. I said, "Hey, thanks for making breakfast. And for last night. I really did have a great time. It was, like, totally tubular, dude. Best birthday ever."

She smiled, reconciled, and bragged, "Of course it was. I planned it. By the way, there are still several cupcakes in the tin over there, if you're interested."

"Thanks—not at the moment, but maybe later."

She said more softly now, "You don't want to talk about *him*?"

I shook my head slowly and answered, "Not yet. It's kind of…complicated."

Her huge eyes (still heavily eyelined from last night) regarded me thoughtfully as she said, "Okay. We can chat later. But let me just say this: I've watched you for four years now—your head in a book, studying constantly, with no thought toward any, let's say, *extracurricular* activities, and I've worried. I mean, I know you're not a lesbian because, well, I'm sure you would have been on me like stink on shit by now," she stopped to giggle at her own joke, which caused me to laugh in turn, "but I also know you've been…holding back…haven't you? I've never understood why. I'm not sure what this guy means to you, if anything, but if he is the antidote to your…restraint, then I think you should go for it. Remember how the Grinch's heart grew three sizes bigger in Whoville? That's what I want for you!" She formed her hands into the shape of a heart and beat it next to her chest.

I smiled. "Christine, you crack me up. But yes, I will take what you say to *heart*, haha, and think about it. I *am* going to call him back, as soon as y'all leave. One thing I don't need is an audience."

"Okey dokey," she said, zipping her thumb and finger across her mouth. "Mum's the word, and I'm gonna get gone right now."

She started stacking the plates in the sink, but I waved her away, telling her I would do the dishes. Within a few minutes, they had all packed up and left. I took my time finishing my coffee and cleaning up the kitchen, noticing that my headache had dissipated and my stomach had stabilized. Walking up the stairs to my bedroom, I started to feel something else in my stomach—butterflies. There it was: Adam's phone number, tacked to the bulletin board on our door. I took a deep breath, glancing at the clock (ten thirty) and thinking about one of my mom's mottos—"No better time than the present"—gulped, and dialed. When it started ringing, I felt my pulse pick up and the blood rush to my head. It rang only once before a deep male voice picked up. "Hello?"

There was a lot of noise in the background, guys talking and laughing. I asked, "Is Adam there?"

"Yes, I am, I mean, this is, I mean, this is Adam, hi, Riley?" he stumbled.

I laughed. Okay, I wasn't the only nervous one. After all, it was one thing to have a conversation while half-drunk in a crowded bar with someone who not only intimidates you but also *confuses* you. And an entirely different thing when you are stone-cold sober the morning after, standing in the blinding light of the spring sunshine blasting through your bedroom window like a spotlight. I hadn't had time to process the wall that had broken down between us, what that meant, and whether I was okay with it. I also hadn't been able to assimilate this quick-flash memory: the way he watched me, held my hand, hugged me, and sent a shiver down my spine. In a sense, it was like losing my footing, my bearings, and maybe a bit of myself as I fell into something new and unknown.

While I was thinking about the deep, warm tenor of his voice and how I hadn't noticed that above the noise in the bar last night, he was saying to his friends, "Hey! Guys, pipe down! I'm on the phone." To which I heard a mock singsong response, "Ohhheee, Adam's on the phone with his little lady friend. You guys saw her, right? The redhead with the Doc Martens? Oh yeah... nice—" Adam's hand over the mouthpiece wasn't enough to stifle his curse-laden reprimand, their responding laughter, and Adam's even more adamant words that were followed by a stifled murmur, and finally, a door shutting.

He came back on the line rather sheepishly, "Sorry about that."

I smiled to myself—poor guy. "No worries. You should have seen what *my* friends said."

"Ha! Really? Okay, phew." Then with a chuckle, "Anyhoo...how's it going?"

"Good. I'm mostly back to being somewhat human this morning."

"You had a good birthday then?"

"Yes, it was fun, but, well, tequila always seems like the right thing at the time, but less so the next day, if you know what I mean."

"Unfortunately, I do."

A few seconds of silence ensued before he launched into, "Um, well, yeah, sorry for calling you so early this morning (clearing his throat) *twice*, but I...

well, I'm only in town for another twenty-four hours, and I really wanted to see you again, if you're available." He paused, and I opened my mouth to speak but then shut it again as he went on, "I mean, if you can't, that's fine—I know this is last-minute and you might already have plans…it's just that we really didn't have enough time to talk last night, which is totally understandable given the circumstances, it being your birthday and Nick's being, well, Nick's, and all your friends, and all my friends, and the shock of seeing each other, and it being such a crazy coincidence that I was in town and in the same place at the same time as you, and on your birthday (wow!), but anyway, I just wondered…well, I wasn't sure…" He stopped and took a breath and with a little laugh said, "So, yeah, will you have lunch with me? I'll shut up now. I promise."

I was overcome with an odd mixture of empathy and surprise while he dragged out this meandering soliloquy because I kept thinking, for such a confident guy, I certainly have thrown him for a loop! I couldn't imagine why. As much as our shared past must have been a stumbling block up until now, mysteriously, I didn't feel this stuttering monologue he was spitting out was in any way related to that. His nerves seemed to be entirely related to me, the person I was *today*, and not how we met or what we were to each other. This dumbfounded me. In all my high school and college days thus far, I had been the girl in the corner with a book, hiding away so as not to be noticed, and certainly not to cause anyone a stitch of discomfort, fear, or nervousness. Sure, there had been guys like Ryan who lightly insinuated things to me, but my natural stance, state-of-mind, sense of being was an introvert fortified with a healthy wall of protection that functioned as a built-in rebuff to any and all casual advances. No one had ever pressed it. At least until now, if that's what this was. I wasn't sure, but I felt a strange thrill that it *could* be. Of course, the thrill was followed shortly thereafter by a slow, growing terror, which caused me to bite my lip. If this was (a what?) *date*, what did one say, think, do?

I put my jumbled-up mind on hold for the time being, though, and answered, "Sure." I smiled as he exhaled loudly into the phone. So funny—he had been holding his breath! I thought for a second and added, "Oh, but I just ate breakfast. When would you want to go?"

"Oh, well, we don't have to eat right away. We could walk around or do something else first."

"Do you have a car?"

"Yes."

"Why don't you come over here for a while? Our house is a few blocks off campus."

"Okay, that sounds great."

I gave him the address and told him to give me a few minutes to finish getting ready. I hung up and quickly got dressed, this time in the outfit I had intended for the night before—stonewashed jeans and a tie-dye T-shirt with white Keds minus the fluffy white socks. I left my hair big and curly and decided Christine's subdued makeup was actually better on my face than the pinks and blues I had been applying so conspicuously for years. As I looked in the mirror, I thought, sometimes small changes make all the difference… and maybe not just in makeup.

I looked at the clock and figured I had just enough time to make a quick phone call to Jane. She was going to Swarthmore College, in Pennsylvania, just finishing up her degree in women's studies. We still talked on the phone quite a bit, mostly about our classes and what books we were reading.

"Hello?"

"Hi, Jane."

"Riley? Is that you? So good to hear from you! Happy birthday, a day late. I'm so sorry I didn't call yesterday, I had a paper due, and I was up all night on Thursday and rushing around yesterday and—"

I cut her off. "Don't worry about that. It was fine." I paused for effect. "I have to tell you something."

"What? What's happened?" Her voice fell to a breathy whisper.

I laughed out loud at her tone, thinking, she's going to fall off her rocker when I tell her! "Guess who's on his way to my place *right now*? You'll never guess!"

"Um, I don't know…Patrick Swayze?"

"If only…! I wish. Come on, be serious."

"I mean, how do I know? Can't you give me a hint?"

"Let's see…he's *familiar* with French Lick."

"Familiar? I have no idea! Your dad? One of your brothers?"

"Nope."

"Riley!" she exclaimed frustrated and laughing. "Um…let's see…wait, I got it!"

"Yes…?"

"Jimmy Pierce," she answered with satisfaction.

"Good God, no! Ew! How could you say that?" Jimmy Pierce was a short, stocky wrestler in our calculus class. I always found him completely repulsive and obtuse.

"What? Didn't you have a crush on him in tenth grade? I just figured it had to be someone like that…"

"No, I did not! He was gross. Maybe *you* had a crush on him."

"Definitely not. Would you please just tell me? At this rate, *he'll* be able to get on the phone and tell me himself."

I took a deep breath, letting the laughter die out of my voice, and said as soberly as I could, "Adam Linder."

"Adam Linder! *The* Adam Linder?"

"One and the same."

"Wow," she said slowly, not excitedly and certainly not happily—more like a confused and concerned stretching out of her words. "Whoa. How?" Then another "Wow."

My voice dropped down to her level as I said, "Yeah, I know. Bu-but-but," I stuttered a little, trying to figure out how to explain, "I think, I really do think, it's…a *good* thing. I swear. My housemates took me out last night, and it was so crazy because he was just *there*, you know, at the bar with his friends, and before I had time to think about it, we got to talking and I realized he's such a nice guy and I felt like hey, we're not kids anymore and it's time to let bygones be bygones. And so yeah, we talked, and it was…nice, really nice."

"Wow."

"Would you stop with the 'wows,' please?" I asked with a laugh.

"Wow-ee?" she replied with a giggle. Then a pause and, "I'm sorry, I'm still processing. So, what did you talk about?"

"Oh, nothing special—just home and stuff."

"And he's coming over *now*…? To your house? What for? Did he leave his wallet at the bar or something?"

"Jane! No, he didn't leave his wallet." I think she could probably feel me rolling my eyes. "I mean, he's coming over to talk, you know, hang out. We…we…only had a few minutes together last night and well, at the end, we sort of…well, we hugged. And I don't know…it was…it was…" I was at a loss for words.

"Hold up—you hugged? What are you saying?" she exhaled into the phone and added with a small shriek, "Riley Cartwright! Are you telling me you *like* Adam Linder?"

I giggled like a schoolgirl and said, "Maaaaybe."

She was silent on the phone, probably looking for a defibrillator.

I kept talking, trying to process and articulate my thoughts at the same time, "Honestly, I don't *know* what to think. He's really cute, like, to be clear, totally grown up and filled out in all the right places. Plus, he's studying up at Purdue to be a veterinarian—how awesome is that? And the whole time we were talking, he was just…staring at me…like *really* staring at me, as if he couldn't keep his eyes off me. At first, it freaked me out a little, but then I kind of liked it, and anyway, I gave him my number and now he'll be here any minute, and Jane, oh my God—what do I do? This is brand-new territory for me. I have absolutely no experience with this kind of stuff."

She scoffed, "And I do?"

"Didn't you date that guy Gary your freshman year? What was it like? I mean, what did you talk about? What did you do?"

"Jeepers, I don't remember. That was kind of different anyway. I mean, you've known Adam for years—you should be fine, right? See if he knows what Jimmy Pierce has been up to."

"Funny…so helpful, Jane," I reprimanded sarcastically. Just then, the doorbell rang, and I nearly jumped out of my skin. I cried into the phone, "That's him, at the door. What do I do?"

"Um, go answer it, but first hang up with me. And Riley…?"

"Yes, yes, quick."

"Just be yourself and *let him take the lead.* Got it?"

Finally, some good advice. I said hurriedly before hanging up, "Right, right, makes sense. Will do. Okay, bye, thank you, please, please pray for me, bye."

"I will, but you don't need it, you'll be fine, relax, bye!"

I hung up and ran downstairs to the front door, opening it wide before I had time to think about my pounding heart and racing thoughts, and there he was, in a navy T-shirt and a pair of well-worn jeans, looking handsome, rugged, casual. He smiled as I said hey and let him in, closing the door behind us.

He looked around and said, "Cool house."

"Yeah, well, it better be for the rent we pay," I said with a grin. "I think most of my roommates are out. Although, actually, come to think of it, I haven't seen David or Erica today, so they might be hiding out in their bedrooms." I led him into the living room and quickly, embarrassed, scurried around the room, picking up empty beer bottles, half-eaten food wrappers, and a dirty ashtray, running them into the kitchen while I told him to make himself comfortable and take a seat.

When I came back, I sat down a few feet away from him on the couch, our bodies turned to face each other, his arm draped nonchalantly over the back. I couldn't help but notice how his broad chest was stretched against the fabric of his T-shirt. I forced my eyes back to his face and had a swift thought: even if his body had changed, his kind brown eyes were exactly the same as I remembered the first time I noticed him, when he bought a hot cider from me at the Booster Club Booth all those years ago.

He swept his hand toward my outfit and said with a laugh, "This makes more sense to me."

"Yeah, well, I was kind of Christine's dress-up Barbie last night. Or rather, her dress-up punk rocker. Not my normal gig."

"Hmm, I wondered...," he said, adding, "I like this better."

I smiled. "Me too." There was that spark again, the same as last night when I felt his eyes on me as if he was memorizing my face and maybe something more—trying to get inside my head to see how I ticked. It was strangely flattering but also disconcerting. I blushed a little and said, "How was the rest of the bachelor party?"

"Cool, although I cut out early and went back to the hotel to crash. I was beat. But I'm feeling a damn sight better than most of my friends this morning."

I grunted, thinking about how awful I had felt in the not-so-distant past. "I bet. That was smart."

"Yes," he agreed. "They're refueling at Denny's right now. We have a three o'clock tee time.

"Golf?"

"Yes, over at the IU course."

I nodded and asked tentatively, "And then you're headed back to Purdue?"

He frowned a little, but the glow in his eyes told a different story—he liked that I cared enough to ask. "Tomorrow morning."

"Oh," I said. I waited a second or two, but he didn't say anything else, and the silence started to feel like a living, breathing thing hovering between us in the room. I tore my eyes away from that intense stare, out the window, beginning to wonder if this whole thing had been a big mistake. After all, he had a busy day and then he was leaving...it was curious that he even wanted to come over in the first place.

"Riley," he said very softly, making me snap back to his face, "can I ask you a question?"

"Sure," I said, turning slightly more toward him.

A slow smile crossed his features, and I found myself watching his mouth as he said, "Will you do me a favor? I mean, I'm just going to go out on a limb because I realized something on the way over here—that I don't really know you. And you don't know me. And I think...I think it would be good if we got to know each other." His eyes traced across my face, a slight plea in them. "What do you think?"

I gulped and replied, "Um, yeah, I would like that."

His smile grew. "Maybe...you could...I don't know...tell me everything about yourself?"

My eyes got big, and I said with a little laugh, "Kind of a tall order."

"Yes, it is. But that's what I'm asking." His face didn't waver from that inviting smile, sending a shot of warmth down my spine.

So I smiled back. "Okay...um...okay." Goodness, how does that work? I giggled uncomfortably, saying, "But how? When you say everything, do you mean like *everything*? This could get awkward really quick!"

He laughed and amended, "Well, you can leave out the potty training, vomiting, and fainting stories. Does that help?"

"Darn, I was gonna lead with that," I teased.

"Oh really? Well, by all means...was one from last night?"

I grinned. "I wish. I mean, I would have felt a hell of a lot better this morning if I had vomited, but no such luck." I shrugged. "Did your friends have any problems with that last night?"

"Not as far as I know, although I was out like a light. Hopefully, there won't be any incidents on the golf course this afternoon."

"Right. Well, you know what they say, don't drink and *drive*."

"Ha! Good one," he said, shaking his head at my cheesy joke. Oh well, at least he didn't roll his eyes and scoff.

Then I sat there for a minute, not knowing what to say. I hadn't been put on the spot like this before, or at least not since high school when Mr. Crowley relished calling on a random student in French class to conjugate a verb in time with his stopwatch. Just like back then, I began to sweat a little. Finally, staring into Adam's face rather sheepishly, I said, "I really love mint chocolate chip ice cream." When his face broke into a smile, I added, "And chocolate-covered pretzels. And grape juice. And stuffed flounder, where the stuffing has little pieces of crab in it. Not together, mind you—I don't mean you would ever have any of these things together. That's disgusting. But separately, they're divine."

"Do you have a piece of paper and a pen? I need to write this down," he said jokingly. "Note: First dinner with Riley must consist of stuffed fish, followed separately by a glass of grape juice and then maybe an hour later chocolate-covered pretzels and a side of mint chocolate chip ice cream. I presume eating the pretzels and ice cream together is acceptable?"

I laughed. "I suppose." Then, very serious, "I would allow it."

"Okay, I promise not to tell anyone." He paused as they smiled at each other. After a minute, he said, "You know, in high school one time, I watched you eat an entire bag of chocolate-covered pretzels for lunch. You were in the cafeteria sitting across from Jane Parker, and here she was eating a sensible meal of congealed mush like the rest of us, and there you were, eating an entire one-pound bag of chocolate-covered pretzels. I guess now I understand why."

I blushed a little, thinking, how had he remembered that? But then I thought about how our shared past had always been such a deterrent, a torture of sorts, and how now, miraculously, it was a *bridge*. Granted, one founded loosely on the memory of me gorging myself. You'd think I'd be embarrassed, but I owned it outright. I said, "What can I say? They started selling them in the bulk section of the grocery store my sophomore year, and I was one hundred percent addicted after that." I held up my hands in happy capitulation. He nodded and smiled.

I waited a while and then said, "Now you. Play fair."

"Root beer, hot dogs, and Fritos. The trifecta."

"Together?"

"Oh yeah, as a meal."

"Uh-huh, I can see that…side of ketchup or mustard?"

"For the dog? Mustard all the way, of course."

"Oh no. Yuck. Ketchup."

"Well, we can agree to disagree." He paused, then said, "So…what else?"

"Um," I began, "come on…it's too hard to just…come up with stuff to talk about. I feel like I'm being examined by an archaeologist."

"And I'm digging it," he conceded with a wide grin.

Oh my God, he was just as cheesy as me! I laughed, thinking with astonishment, I'm sitting here joking with Adam Linder, my childhood fear factor, mind-boggler, and archnemesis! Life could not be any stranger…

He offered, "Want me to ask you questions instead?"

"Yes, phew, that would be great."

"Okay…hmm…let's see…," he peaked a brow before flooring me with this: "You knew I was in that bar last night before you saw me, didn't you?"

The smile was slashed from my face, my mouth agape as I stared into his flashing, too-deep, too-knowing eyes. I stuttered, "How—how did you know that?"

He leaned forward, a few inches from my face, suddenly very serious, and answered, "I can't explain it—in fact, nothing like this has ever happened to me before, but in some crazy way I sort of traveled to where you were in the bar, without leaving my chair, and I saw that *you sensed me there*."

I closed my mouth and gulped. "You—you *traveled* to me…?" Something in my carefully crafted wall just opened up—a slight chink in the mortar about to be hammered into a thousand stony shards.

"Yes," he said matter-of-factly, leaning back against the couch again. He looked away for a second, formulating his thoughts. He shook his head self-consciously, and coming back to me, in a heated rush, said, "Okay, I don't know if it's because we're, well, connected from what happened in our child-hood, but it was like I saw you there, across the room at that music machine, but then in an instant I was somehow transported right next to you, right around you, almost right *above* you. And I saw you looking around, I saw the hairs stand up on the back of your neck, I saw you sensing me. It was the craziest thing, Riley—I can't figure out how and what happened, but it was—was like I was *with* you, a part of you, for a few minutes before you were standing in front of me and we said hi."

As he said this, I felt the gooseflesh pop up on my arms, and I wondered if this is what it felt like to be standing naked on an exposed mountaintop with a line of strangers below training their binoculars up to the spot where you stood.

I didn't say a word.

A moment went by. Then two. He asked weakly, "Riley…?"

Still, no words.

"Are you…freaking out?" he wondered, "I know what it sounds like, and I can assure you, nothing like this has *ever* happened to me before."

I quickly thought, if only I could say the same!

He went on, "I had to tell you. I can't explain it. Do you think that maybe the universe or something wanted us to meet last night? Do you think that's what it was? What do you think? Please speak because I'm about to run out that door screaming in ten seconds." He laughed, but his worried eyes spoke volumes.

Finally, I forced my mind and my own weakened core back into my body. I slowly, cautiously put my arm on the back of the couch, next to his, and took his fingers in mine. His eyes lit up. I felt the strength of those fingers as I said in all deathly seriousness, "Yes, that's what I think."

The whoosh of air leaving his lips was like a pressure-cooker latch being released. He whispered, sounding shocked at his own admission, "Me too."

"Well," I said, more in control than before, and steady. "I'm glad we got that out of the way." I waited. He didn't say anything, so I added, "Well, what are we gonna do about it?"

His faced flashed with that expression from last night: Hope. "Maybe... lunch?"

I smiled. "Yes. Lunch."

He squeezed our intertwined hands, his eyes soft and glowing.

A spark ran through me. I said, "First, I need to know something."

"Anything."

"Will you be home this summer?"

He grinned. "Yes. You?"

"Yes."

At that, I stood up, pulling him up with me. "Okay. That'll work. Come on. For right now, for today, I know a good sub shop on Kirkwood."

He didn't flinch or add another word, following me out the door like a happy puppy being led out for a walk after a long rain shower.

CHAPTER XXI

"LINDER, GET YOUR HEAD IN THE GAME!"

Adam just laughed as he whacked yet another slice into the rough. He couldn't help it. He was never any good at golf in the first place, and this afternoon's go at it might as well have been him trying Krav Maga or hang gliding. His mind wasn't in it. Neither was his skill. Neither was his heart, which was now permanently lodged somewhere about three miles away in the blue-green eyes of a redhead whom he hoped at this very minute was thinking about him in the same wondrous, fascinated, desirous way as he was thinking about her.

Trent, the groom-to-be, came up behind Adam on the way to the golf cart, patting him on the shoulder, and said, "You're about as far as gone as I was when I met Katie, aren't you?"

Adam grinned sheepishly. "Maybe more."

Trent asked skeptically, "But didn't you just meet her last night?"

They got into the cart and drove down the fairway. "Met again, actually. She's from French Lick. We grew up together. Well, sort of. I mean, we were never friends, but we knew each other."

Trent raised one eyebrow. "Sounds like a good beginning."

Adam nodded in acknowledgment. "Yeah, well, we'll see. I hope it is."

Then Trent grinned and said, "And you know she goes to IU, right?"

Adam laughed as Trent stopped the cart and pulled out a five iron. Adam said, "I know. Hoosiers and Boilermakers. Never the two shall meet. Except at the Old Oaken Bucket. And this isn't that."

"Nope." He swung, his ball landing right on the green. "It isn't. What will you do?"

Trent hopped back in and drove them to the patch of tall grass where Adam's ball had gone, both searching fruitlessly. Adam said, "I guess we would have to sit in different sections of the stadium."

"Yep, I suppose," Trent said with a chuckle. "But seriously, are you interested in this girl?" He looked up at Adam.

Adam gave up the search for his ball and plopped another down on the fairway, hitting it with his three wood and groaning when it landed directly in the middle of a sand trap to the right of the green. In the cart, he thought about how to answer Trent's question. He finally said, "Let me ask you, how did you know Katie was the one?"

Trent looked over in surprise, saying, "The one? Shit, man, you think this new girl might be the one? But—but, correct me if I'm wrong, you haven't actually ever *dated* her, have you?"

Adam felt like a fool. Of course Trent wouldn't understand. Adam didn't understand it himself. "Listen, no…no, I mean, technically, until last night, we had barely ever spoken to each other, so yeah, it's like there's some crazy thing going on. All I know is that I…I feel a certain way about her that I can't even describe, and it's like nothing I've ever felt before."

Trent regarded him and nodded, his forehead creased. He said cautiously, "Yeah, okay, well, that happens…I suppose…sometimes. So, with Katie, I liked her from the very beginning—as you probably remember that day at the block party—but it took me, like, months to convince her to go out with me. She wasn't interested at all. Something about the chase, *me* having to pursue *her*, you know, was kind of a turn-on. I'd never had to do that before, and so when she finally agreed to go out with me, I had to pull out all the stops. I still feel that way now—like I have to be on my best game with her, you know? She makes me better. And I guess I can't imagine my life without her."

Adam nodded, thinking through Trent's words carefully. Was this how he felt about Riley? They both got out of the cart, Adam heading to the sand trap with his wedge and Trent heading to the green with his putter.

Sometime later, when Adam's arms and feet were tired from swinging and hunting balls and he wanted more than anything to be done with this ridiculous game, he thought back to Trent's comments. Trent had pursued Katie. Is that what Adam had been doing (from afar) with Riley? All these years thinking about her—granted, only in the back of his mind, like a nostalgic, fuzzy memory that lingered there and was only brought into focus with an uncomfortable, mixed-up shot of pain and anguish, coupled with captivating intrigue and remote longing. And now he finally had her right at his fingertips and was feeling giddy with anticipation and hope. Yet, had the dark cloud hanging over them truly dissipated?

He knew one thing for sure: he couldn't imagine a time when he wouldn't want to explore the depths of her thoughts and feelings, not to mention her aquamarine eyes and juicy red lips. Of course, their conversation this afternoon had been rather pedestrian, which was fine with him. He wanted to take it slow. He didn't want to screw anything up. He knew that underneath their surface conversation, a beast was waiting to pounce. And once that beast had awakened, there was no going back. It might just eat their relationship alive, but he hoped more than anything that it would cower and shrink away once they had time to face it, examine it, fight it.

At the end of their eighteen holes, Adam was brought back to reality fast when his friends saw his scorecard. It was fuel for a thousand taunts, and later, at dinner, gyro in hand, Adam had to sink in his booth chair at the Trojan Horse, trying to keep his head and self-esteem above water, firing back, "Hey, I challenge any of you to a game of darts at Kilroy's later." Shouts of "Twenty bucks and you're on" and "Better, thirty!" sent them into the wee hours of the night, with Adam gaining back a small semblance of pride, along with a laughing-so-hard-his-face-hurt night of drunken ribs, jokes, and comradery.

The next morning, with pats on the back and promises of seeing each at Trent's wedding in a couple of months, they parted ways. Adam felt a small sadness, knowing they were all leading separate lives now and their get-togethers would be few and far between. What was it about the friends you met during your isolating, fish-out-of-water years as an undergraduate that caused an instant connection and cemented lifelong friendships? Seems as though it has something to do with facing the same firsts: being away from home and away from parents, thrown into coursework way above the intellectual level tackled as a high school student, new teachers, new food, new activities, new girls, new everything.

During the two years since leaving Louisville and beginning his DVM at Purdue, he had met tons of great people—smart, inspiring animal lovers like himself—but somehow in the midst of their intense assignments and labs, when he stopped long enough to think about it, he was rather lonely and hadn't truly connected with anyone yet. His roommate, Brian, was stoic and quiet, spending most of his time away from the apartment or alone in his bedroom with the door closed. They would often go for days and sometimes weeks without setting eyes on each other. But Brian was neat and clean, and paid his half of the rent and utilities on time, and Adam figured that was more important at this stage in his life than having a close chum.

So, on the quiet car ride back to Purdue, listening to Depeche Mode on the cassette player, he felt a twinge of loss and oddly older, and wishing he could capture time in a bottle. The other half of his mind and body was wanting desperately to swing by Riley's one last time before leaving Bloomington to capture the sight of her in a bottle too. But then he didn't want to overwhelm her. After all, just because every synapse in his being went into overdrive every time he laid eyes on her, that didn't mean his presence had the same effect on her. He knew she was still a deer in the headlights—caught, stunned, processing, not knowing which way to turn. He steered onto State Road 37, feeling the ache in his chest. They had promised to talk on the phone, and they would, and that would have to be enough for now. Until summer came, when they could see each other again, and maybe, just maybe, sit *together* on that big front porch swing of hers and have a glass of lemonade or a Coke. He was so used to driving by and seeing her there by herself, absorbed in a book, her red hair blowing gently in the wind, the swing creaking on its chains.

This made him smile and filled his heart. He remembered a snippet of their conversation at lunch, one of the few times he felt she was holding something back. They had already talked fairly extensively about their families and what they were up to. They talked about when they would be home (three days apart from each other, in a few weeks). They talked about her graduation, whether she was nervous or excited (both), and what she planned to do with herself afterward ("Please don't ask—I have no idea!"). She talked about her housemates and where they were headed after graduation, and he talked about his crazy group of friends and what they were doing with their lives.

Then he asked her an innocuous question: "So, I guess being an English major, you're still reading a lot, eh? I remember in high school you always had your nose in a book." His face was open, thinking this seemed part and parcel of her personality—girl-with-book—as much as her quiet voice and reflective nature.

Instead of answering, she replied with an incongruous level of intensity, "Why, do you read?"

He frowned, not sure if this was some type of test and he was missing the cheat sheet. He hesitated with a frown, then replied with a sheepish laugh, "No, not if I can help it. Other than for my classes. I don't seem to have the time, really…or the inclination, for that matter. I've never really been much of a reader."

"Not even when you're on break from school…or on an airplane…waiting in line somewhere…?" she ventured.

He shrugged. "Nope, sorry. I'll read the occasional magazine, but that's about it."

Her face fell, and Adam felt a lurch in his stomach. Was he missing something? Why was this such a big deal? He obviously knew she was bookish, but did it really matter whether he was or wasn't? He didn't expect her to be familiar with the ways of animal husbandry or veterinarian skills. Surely they would have other things in common. It might take time to get to know each other on a personal, intimate level, but over time there would be more to hang their hat on. Certainly, something like reading shouldn't be an arbitrary showstopper, should it?

She looked down at her hands and said, "That's too bad."

Trying not to lose her, feeling he may have made an error in judgment, setting too little stock on this thing that maybe *wasn't* arbitrary for her, he said quietly, as a statement, "They mean a lot to you. Books."

"Yes," she whispered, not lifting her head.

He was still confused by her seriousness, so he tried to elucidate as best he could, putting himself in her shoes for a moment, "They're…more than a pastime for you…? They're an escape of sorts…?"

Her eyes shot up, and the flame that skidded across her cheeks caused him to gulp down a wave of desire that flashed like an unexpected bolt of lightning through him. He had never seen her more beautiful.

She exclaimed, "Exactly!"

He waited for her to say more but she didn't, and that was when he felt that she was hiding something from him, but he had no idea what. He waited and finally said, "I feel the same way about animals. It's why I wanted to become a vet. It's the unconditional love they give, but also that feeling of escape. And the fact that you can count on them. They won't let you down. They're steady…safe. When I'm with them, I think of nothing else."

Her beautiful, wide-set eyes hung on every word as if he was mining her inner thoughts for gold. When he stopped, her chest was heaving and she said, "That's exactly how I feel about books. And I guess…well…I hoped you were a reader too…because I wanted to share—"

She stopped and he watched her mutely. She seemed to change the sentence in mid-flight, finishing with, "…share the love of it with someone."

"Oh," Adam said with a smile, filled with relief. Was that all? "Well, maybe you can recommend some books to me, and I'd be happy to give it a go. Maybe you can teach an old dog new tricks."

She seemed relieved too, as if she had dodged a bullet, as if whatever the approached precipice had been, she had moved away from the edge. She said lightly, "Sure, I could do that. Or maybe I could read to you. What do you think of that?"

"I can't think of a better way to spend the summer."

During the rest of the drive to Purdue, Adam's mind lingered on the wide-open, giving smile she had flashed at him then, as if she had startled herself into realizing for the first time that this man sitting across from her might be a new, extraordinary puzzle piece she hadn't known was missing but who had shown up at the perfect time to fit into an open slot. Her wheels were turning—about what exactly, he didn't yet understand—but by acknowledging her need and really *seeing* her, maybe he was opening a door for her, as she was for him.

And he thought about her being like a buried treasure still waiting to be discovered and how he wanted more than anything to break the code, to uncover what was hidden underneath the quiet, tough, reticent exterior to get to the warmth of the rich, sweet soul he knew was waiting there to blossom.

Chapter XXII

I BEGAN TO THINK about the word *inertia*. Being stuck in a pattern or routine when it's so much easier and more manageable to keep the status quo, remain as is, unchanged. Don't make waves, don't rock the boat. Things in motion tend to stay in motion; things that are still tend to stay still. I also began to think about the word *catalyst*. Sometimes during our movement or stillness, without warning there is an unexpected trigger that causes a drastic change. Life can turn on a dime and go in an entirely new direction, a one-eighty, a fresh trajectory. There were scientific connotations behind these words, but I began to think about how they best described the human condition and actions equated with the stages of my life.

Take my Biblio. If I were to conduct a cause-and-effect scientific analysis, it would be: I read, I wait, there is a reaction (my Biblio). Much like my discussion with Father Avery: "I think, therefore I am." But despite that, I had to ask myself, what did my gut tell me about my Biblio? It certainly wasn't scientific, this feeling I got when I experienced my Biblio. It was more sensory, otherworldly, supernatural, clairvoyant, perceptive. I think that was why I was having so much trouble putting my finger on it, trying to pinpoint its meaning, trying to classify it and explain it to myself and to Father Avery. I began to think about other people with special "gifts," like mediums and other intuitives, and how coincidental it was that they called what they did a "reading." Was I doing a "reading" on my "reading" all along? Channeling a perception of a book into my consciousness so it would pop out in another form? Or, on the flip side, was I meant to read into these coincidences—take them as a trigger or challenge or invitation to do *something* with my life, something different from what I was doing? But *what*, though? I saw a show once about a woman who could speak to the dead, and she said she was afraid of her gift at first, but then she realized she could aid in the grieving process for so many by providing validation and closure through her ability to bridge the two worlds.

As time went on and I grew more comfortable with my Biblio, I began to wonder less what it meant to me and more if I could use it for some greater purpose outside of myself. Before long, like a wall coming down, I went in a completely different direction with my Biblio, allowing something to come into focus.

It started like this:

My inertia: surface-level, going through the motions, getting by with my action-oriented life; not letting myself dig deeper to understand the purpose of my actions, my past, my here and now, my future, my life. Accepting my Biblio as a given by virtue of me reading and reaping the outcome of the books; an uncontrollable, unforeseeable, unknowable reaction to a fusion between me and whatever book I was reading. And nothing more.

My catalyst: When I decided that I needed my life to be real, that I needed my gift to have a purpose.

My trigger: Adam Linder. My gut, my inner voice. Maybe Kathy too—something or someone was telling me to go toward a new version of my gift instead of staying with (or running from) the old.

My kickoff: Me, analyzing the way to get to the real, processing the newness that was my relationship with Adam, finding out more about my Biblio and the intent behind it. Finding out more about myself.

My fears: Where would this lead? How would I make it happen? How would I know what to follow, what was meant to be for me and for my Biblio?

My naivete: Should I have taken stock first? Paused and analyzed the risks versus the rewards before I took the leap? If I had known what was coming, would I have jumped anyway?

Yes. Yes, I would.

Saturday, June 9, 1990

I have started something new today. It's very scary, and I'm not sure where it will lead or how my life will change or how I will change because of it. Three things: (1) words are powerful, (2) words can be a blessing or a curse, (3) words should not be faked and should come from the heart. This is my new mantra. I will live and breathe the words.

I'll explain more later because I only have a few minutes right now to get some thoughts down.

Yesterday Mrs. Litchy said we had received an early-release copy of this new book about dinosaurs coming back from extinction (Michael Crichton's *Jurassic Park*). It's really good and hard to put down, but put it down I must because Adam's coming to get me in twenty minutes! I just wanted to take a moment to write down my current book choice because it will certainly be impossible to have a Biblio about dinosaurs! Yes, I am still testing my Biblio. Every time. I don't know why. After all these years, I still doubt it sometimes. And myself. But moving forward, I'm going to try to focus on my purpose, not my Biblio's.

Anyway, I worked thirty-three hours this week at the library, so I'm happy, happy, happy. The cash is nice, and working there is like an oasis, a sanctuary. I feel like I shouldn't get paid for it. I'm glad I do because Dad's still breathing down my neck about "figuring out what to do with my life," as if I don't already think about it nearly every second of every day, but at least I don't have to ask him for money.

Mrs. Litchy gave me a crazy idea. She had just finished her shift and was clocking out as I was clocking in, but she stayed behind a few minutes to talk with me. First of all, she mentioned for the tenth time that she was "very close" to retirement but was just "holding out" for the right person to fill her shoes. I can't blame her—she's been the librarian at the Melton for the past forty-three years! But mostly I was struck by the twinkle in her eye—essentially, her not-so-subtle hint (and words!) that I would be the perfect replacement. I asked her what would be required, and she said a master's degree in library science (an MLS). I don't know why I hadn't considered this before. After all, I've been working part-time at the Melton on and off for six years. But to go back to school, after having just graduated less than a month ago, seems too dreadful and daunting to consider. Plus, I don't have any money, and my student loans are about to start coming due. I told her I would think about it. And "do some research," to which she replied with a pat on my arm, "I wouldn't expect anything less from a future librarian."

By the way, one last thing: today a local girl came into the library with her mother. They brought in a school project the girl had created for her English class—a large, paneled triptych with images and a written history of the Limberlost. She wanted to leave it as a display in the library, which of course we were happy to accommodate. When I saw it, my heart swelled. Gene Stratton-Porter's *Freckles* was one of the first chapter books I ever read (thanks to Jane's recommended reading list). And here was a girl, probably about the same age I was back then, being so inspired by this book that she created an entire diorama about it. It included photos she'd taken of the author's house in Geneva, Indiana, and the writing desk where the author used to pen her novels. One of the captions read: "The feeling of a kindred spirit that lay hidden in the nature and magic of the Limberlost, swept up in a make-believe world that still rang true for our shared past and present." When I read that, I nearly cried because I felt (and still do) the same way about the transformative and transcendent, magical quality of books, especially to a young girl's impressionable heart. This arbitrary visit was like a helium balloon filling my soul in the wake of my earlier talk with Mrs. Litchy, as if I was being sent a sign. Did events like this, which affected me so profoundly, provide an answer to my future? As a librarian? Or something more?

I placed *Jurassic Park* and the diary on my dresser and thought about my Biblio for a moment. When and if I ever did find the reason, would all the world come into alignment, would I have the answers to life's mysteries, would I somehow see God? I mean, what exactly would happen? It felt almost sacrilegious to contemplate, as if by investigating it I risked angering it—or worse yet, popping its bubble, making it disappear without warning, gone before I ever figured out what it was all about.

Even now, I blocked any further probe, forcefully banishing it from my mind, jumping up, grabbing my purse, and checking myself in the mirror. Get gone—I was going to focus on my date with Adam and spend as many hours as I could Biblio-free. I fixed a few loose tendrils of curls poking out from my ponytail and applied some cherry Chapstick to my lips, thinking the slight tan on my skin highlighted the yellow flecks in my eyes and the rosy blush on my cheeks. Lately, it seemed as though no matter what I looked like, Adam always told me I looked "great" or "beautiful" or "pretty." I never knew how to respond to these compliments (other than the obvious blush and "thank you"). It was a bit disconcerting to go from a twenty-two-year existence trying to blend in with the furniture and hoping against hope not to be noticed (let alone be really *looked* at) to then suddenly be thrust under the microscope and be totally and completely *seen* (and, per Adam, to be "fascinating"). Not just the physical either. He was always prompting me to talk and share and be open with him, to tell him all of my thoughts, opinions, and feelings, the act of which was about as comfortable for me as a turtle wanting its underbelly rubbed.

As I looked out my bedroom window, I saw him pull into the driveway. He got out of the car, and I saw he was dressed in his blue scrubs, looking tall, confident, and casual. He started talking to my brother Nate, who was sitting on the porch going through a shoebox full of baseball trading cards.

I rushed downstairs to save him, but I needn't have bothered because Adam, being Adam, was fine chatting with Nate about the value of Ozzie Smith versus Don Mattingly.

I said as a greeting and a warning, "Hey, don't get started on that or we'll never get out of here."

Adam smiled at Nate and said, "Your sister doesn't have the collector's eye, does she?"

Nate replied, "Not for the good stuff."

I countered, "I have a roomful of books—doesn't that count?"

They both shook their heads and said at the same time, "No."

I rolled my eyes and laughed with a shrug, indicating to Adam, "Come on, let's go."

Adam said, "Later" to Nate, and we were off.

In the car, Adam turned to me as he drove, regarding my face in that piercing way, and said, "So, Red, it's Saturday night. And I have an idea."

"Would you stop calling me that?" I said with a laugh.

"Purple? Green? Orange?"

I groaned and looked out the window. "You're impossible," I said, and then, "What's your idea? By the way, I'm starving."

"Starving it is! So, Miss Starving, what would you like for dinner?"

I grinned. He was so silly sometimes. "I really like those new heated subs, don't you?"

"Yes—something about those rolls—I don't know where Wayne gets them, but they're perfect—crusty on the outside, warm and soft on the inside. Yum. Anyway, let me drop you off and I'll run home, wash up, change, and come back and get you. Sound good?"

"Sure. Why didn't you go home and get ready before you came and got me?"

He waited a second before replying, then said softly, "Because I wanted to see you sooner than that."

I blushed and said, "Oh." After a minute, I asked, "What's your idea?"

"It's something for tonight...a surprise. Are you up for it?"

"I guess it depends on 'it'. Can you be more specific?"

"Nope. You'll have to trust me."

"And if I don't?" I grinned.

"What? I'm crushed," he replied, clutching his heart. "Just take a chance, okay? I promise you'll like it. Or at least I think you will."

I smiled. "Well, alright. My future is in your hands."

"Yes," he said simply, with a look that said a lot more than just about tonight. My face turned a shade redder, and I was forced to look out the window.

Over the past two months, we had spoken countless times on the phone, sometimes for hours, and always with a sense of wanting more. He had been home from Purdue three weeks now, and although he was working every day for Dr. Gerard at the Orange County Animal Clinic in Paoli and I was working at the library, we managed to see each other nearly every night. I loved spending time with him, and we never ran out of things to talk about, but my only confusion-slash-hesitation was the fact that I never knew if we were truly *dating* or just hanging out or what exactly we were doing. Despite his barrage of innuendos, like the "future in your hands" one he had just thrown out so airily, he had yet to make a move on me, and the last time we had even touched was when I placed my fingers in his on the couch that Saturday at IU, and that was months ago. I knew he liked me by the way he looked at me and by his kind words, but I was beginning to wonder what that meant. I was so inexperienced with men that I questioned myself and kept my guard up, not knowing how this was supposed to work. I knew one thing, though—I wasn't going to be the fool who made the first move and realized after the fact that the feelings weren't reciprocated. I was bold (and lucky!) that day on the couch, knowing our connection was undeniable and needed to be acknowledged, and I had thought about our fingers touching a thousand times since. But now I was beginning to wonder if it was all in my head and if I was reading too much into things, as I was apt to do sometimes, with my strange intuitive nature. Maybe our connection was as friends, after all, and not meant for more. What did I know? It seemed implausible when I was with him—we fit together so well, how could it possibly be only platonic? But then again, where did we go from here? How did we break through the invisible barrier that seemed to sit between us?

He told me his food request and drove off, and I walked into Pizza Shack, saying hi to Jeremy, Derek, and Slipkey. It was funny how, over the course of the past three weeks, I had so quickly become friends (maybe only by association, but still) with Adam's brother and the guys at Pizza Shack. Apparently, Adam used to be the co-manager with Wayne, but when Adam moved to West Lafayette for his DVM, his brother, Jeremy, left his job at the grocery store to take over the co-manager role. Having grown up with three older brothers made this testosterone-filled environment not as intimidating as it might have otherwise been for me, but I always walked in the door a bit on edge, knowing I was in Adam's world now—new and uncharted territory that I was still figuring out how to navigate. I gathered that Derek was some type of jack-of-all-trades (taking orders, doing deliveries, buying ingredients, frying the wings, prepping boxes), and Slipkey came in the morning to make the dough and then came in the evening to "shoot the shit" (as he called it) and eat free pizza. Wayne was older and seemed more mature, letting the guys goof off while he held down the fort. He wasn't there tonight, though, so I guess that meant Jeremy was managing.

"Riley!" Slipkey hollered as I walked in. "How's it shaking?"

I laughed and said, "It's shaking just fine. How are you? Busy tonight?"

Jeremy answered, "Yes. Haven't had a break in two hours, and it's still early."

Derek was on the phone taking an order and waved briefly. I stood by the counter awkwardly. For a few minutes, I simply watched the hustle and bustle of their work: Jeremy tossing a large circle of dough in air, then adding the sauce, cheese, and pepperoni before placing it in the oven while Derek took three more calls, writing down each order on a pad of paper, ripping the sheet off, and hanging it in front of Jeremy's pizza-making station. Slipkey was bussing a table that had just been vacated by a family of four. I didn't want to disrupt their process, so I waited silently in the background, eventually sitting down on a barstool in the corner.

Finally, Derek was off the phone, and as he took a pizza out of the oven, placed it carefully in an open box, and cut it, he asked me where Adam was.

"He went to change out of his scrubs. He wanted me to place a to-go order."

"Sure, shoot."

I gave him the information, and he wrote it down and put it on Jeremy's board, asking, "Where you two going tonight?"

"I'm not sure."

He nodded abstractedly. Jeremy finished three more orders (including ours) and told Derek he was taking a break. I watched him walk into the back kitchen area and prop open the alley door with a brick, pulling something out of his shirt pocket and lighting it. As a plume of smoke drifted toward the front of the restaurant, the smell hit my nostrils—weed. I looked at Slipkey with an arched brow, and he just shrugged.

A minute or two later, Adam pulled up and came in, leaving the car running by the curb. He said hi to Slipkey and asked Derek if our subs were ready, to which he said, "Coming out right now." While Derek was getting them prepped in a to-go bag, Adam peeked around the edge of the counter, seeing Jeremy in back and, without another word, approached him.

I heard them talking in heated language, but I couldn't hear the exact words. The phone was ringing, and Slipkey was checking out a customer at the register, and as I stood back and watched, I wondered what was going on between Adam and Jeremy. After a few minutes, they both came up front, Jeremy going to his pizza station and beginning the next order while Adam paid for our subs and a couple of sodas and said curtly to me, "Let's go."

I said bye to everyone with a wave and got in the car.

As Adam pulled out of the parking lot, I noticed he gripped the steering wheel tightly, his knuckles turning white. I had never seen him angry before. I was afraid to speak, so I remained silent, waiting for him to broach the topic that was clearly troubling him.

Finally, after many minutes, I said quietly, "Adam…?"

He flinched a little at the sound of my voice, turning to me as if he had forgotten I was there.

I asked, "What's…what's going on?"

At that, he exhaled, releasing built-up tension, and said with a mirthless laugh, "Damned if I know."

This confused me, so I waited for him to explain, which he didn't. We rode like that for a while until he pulled up alongside the entrance to the old West Baden Resort. He turned off the car and said, "I thought we could stroll up the Avenue. What do you think?"

I nodded. Was this my surprise? He was so distracted now that he seemed not to make the connection, so I let it go and didn't ask. In addition, I was having a Biblio at this exact moment, which caused me to flinch, not because it came in the midst of something else, which of course, it always did, but because it was related to something new in my Biblio journey, which I had yet to reflect on or fully process.

He continued, "We'll bring our subs. I have a blanket in the back—we can picnic."

I said, "Okay," but before he got out of the car, I pushed the Biblio from my mind and touched his arm, saying softly, "And will you tell me what this whole thing with you and Jeremy is about?"

His face clouded and he exhaled in frustration. He answered, "Yes…no…I don't know. I guess I'm still trying to figure it."

As he looked into my eyes with something close to defeat, I said weakly, "Maybe I can help."

He looked away, saying, "If only you could. Come on."

It was a beautiful night, still a couple of hours from sunset, steamy with the smell of grass and flowering trees in the air. We got out and walked under the old chipped and decrepit stone archway titled "West Baden Springs • Carlsbad of America" and headed down the bumpy brick lane, quietly taking in the splendor of the evening and the mystical quality of the surroundings, our feet tapping along the stones, our eyes roving the vast field of trees on either side of us, the looming monstrosity of the hotel ahead of us in the distance, a beacon of a bygone era, lost to time. The grounds, although un-kempt, wild, and unruly, were expansive and felt like something out of a fairy tale or a long-lost zoo that had been abandoned. I breathed in the summer air, fresh and balmy.

When we got close to the building, which had fallen into disrepair and now sat like the broken hull of a ship left out to sea, its walls caved in, mosaic tile floors grown over with ivy, grand dining hall empty and barren, fireplace blackened, plaster Grecian columns peeling, wraparound porch moldy, I had a sad thought: this place is like going to visit a ghost. I shivered a little and tried to shake off the feeling as Adam led us to the left into what used to be an ornate sunken garden but was now an overgrown web of weeds and ivy surrounded by a rectangle-shaped stone and brick wall flanked by a private natural fence of evergreen trees and bushes. Despite its quality of abandon-ment, the remaining garden space felt oddly intimate and romantic.

Adam pointed to an old wooden bench and asked, "Do you want to sit here? Or we can spread the blanket on the grass…?"

"The grass is fine," I said, coming closer to the wooden bench and seeing that it was covered with spots of mold, then realizing with a start that those spots were actually the faded remains of a child's stickers. Dinosaur stickers. I exhaled and laughed to myself, peering down at the shiny little *T. rexes* fol-lowed by a *Triceratops* and a *Brontosaurus*. Of course, even out here, on the edge of a ghost town, another Biblio. I shook my head.

As he went to unfold and lay the blanket down, I noticed tucked inside was a bag of chocolate-covered pretzels tied in a white ribbon, which he handed over with a grin.

I said, "Aww, thank you! My favorite." This must have been the true surprise, along with the whole setup. He was so thoughtful. I added with a
smirk, "Do I still have to eat the sub?"

"Ha! That's entirely up to you. I won't judge."

I chuckled and put the pretzels down near my purse (safekeeping for later!). We sat on the blanket and started eating our subs in silence. I decided
not to bring up the Jeremy thing. I figured, when he was ready to talk, he
would, so after a while I asked him, "How was work today?"

"Good. Not too busy. We had a few sick dogs and a budgie with conjunc-
tivitis."

"A wha—?"

He laughed. "A pet bird thing. Anyway, this summer's already flying by. I
was trying to remember when I first started working for Dr. Gerard. I think
it was at least seven years ago when I began as a volunteer after school every
day, but now, as his assistant, I can really see the amount of stuff he has to
know and be an expert in. Every type of farm animal, pet, accident, injury,
disease, even truly hopeless cases…it's a lot some days. I'm just glad he's there
for my training—he's always so calm, straightforward, easy with the animals,
with the owners, and with me. I'm very grateful to have him as my mentor. I
can't imagine starting my career with anyone else."

I smiled. "That's nice. I feel the same way about Mrs. Litchy. In fact, she
was just asking me about my future. You know, that nebulous blob floating
over my head like the Hindenburg."

He chuckled. "Yeah, how's that going anyway? Any answers yet? I know
your dad's been on your case."

I frowned. "Yeah, he has. And Mom. And my brothers. I wish they would
all give me a break. I mean, it's not like I have a ton of options here in French
Lick, and where else am I gonna go?" I sighed and looked around the tangled
grounds, noting the empty ornamental water fountain, the grass-covered
bricks, the broken pieces of stone falling from the garden wall, and said, "I'm
like this place. All washed up and nowhere to go."

As I looked up at Adam, his eyes soft, his head shaking, he said, "You are
not. You're just trying to figure things out. Sometimes it takes time to make
a change, to know which direction to take."

I smiled—of course, he had read my mind. This was exactly what I had
been thinking about earlier. I continued, "I guess when I was growing up, I
figured going to college was the best way to learn what you were meant to do

with your life. You get exposure to a thousand different topics and a bunch of new people, all walks of life, stuff you've never encountered before, and somehow, by virtue of this opening up of doors, you should, at the end of the day, be able to say with some sort of clarity, yes, this is it—this is what I'm supposed to do with the rest of my life."

Adam shook his head and shrugged, then said thoughtfully, "You know, not everyone's life is meant to be a linear, perfect straight line to answers."

"I suppose," I agreed reluctantly, although I could tell he was thinking about something entirely different from my career when he spoke. I decided not to probe for now and instead said, "Well, Mrs. Litchy's been hinting at retiring soon, and I think she really wants me to take over as the librarian at the Melton."

His eyebrows raised. "Wow. Okay. What are your thoughts on that?"

"Well, of course, I would love that job. I mean, I think the pay is decent, and of course I would be surrounded by all my friends." I smirked.

He narrowed his eyes with a fake jealous scowl, "Ah, yes, your first love."

My heart skipped a beat at his words, and I found myself smiling, thinking about the meaning behind them in relation to him—was he implying there was a second love? I said, "Yes, books. They never let you down. Well, unless they suck, and then I don't finish them," I said with a grin. I paused for a second, redirecting with, "Anyway, the only thing is that I'd need a master's degree in library science if I do decide to go that route. I haven't looked into it yet, but I assume IU has a program. But at this point I've surely already missed the deadline for fall enrollment, and with my student loan payments starting next month..." I stared across the expansive lawn and groaned, "I just can't see a way to make it happen."

"Have you talked to your parents?"

"No, but they were very clear that with all of us kids, they would help with the first four years, and after that we were on our own. Plus, they don't have any money. It's not like Dad's got a 401(k) or anything, working for himself all these years. I don't think they have anything saved for retirement. Sure, Mom's working at the bank now, but I don't think that brings in very much."

He took a swig of his soda, thinking, then said, "If you really want to do this, you could at least apply and see if you get in. Maybe you wouldn't start until second semester, but who knows? You might get some financial aid in the meantime. That's how I'm able to be at Purdue—loans and grants and scholarships. Every little bit adds up. Plus, you're living at home right now, so you could sock away all your earnings. You could even ask Mrs. Litchy for more hours."

I nodded. Then my wheels started turning in a different direction. I wanted to tell him about my new venture, but I was loath to reveal it, knowing once the cat was out of the bag, there was no way to put it back in. I took a few bites of my sub, then said cautiously, "I have an idea. Something I want to tell you about, but I'm scared."

He frowned and said, "Okay, sure, what is it?"

"Well...hmmm...I'm not sure where to begin. Um, you know how much I love to read. Yes, haha, of course, we've already established that. So, lately, I've been thinking, what if...what if instead of reading a book, I try to *write* one." I stopped, breathless, my eyes wide, my heart in my throat. Saying it out loud was like setting it loose in the world—a raging caged tiger set free to roam the earth, not knowing where it will go or how it will navigate its new surroundings, its newly discovered freedom.

Luckily, mercifully, without hesitation, his frown turned into a broad smile. "Riley, that's a great idea! I'm sure you would be so good at that."

"You are?" I said with a nervous, relieved laugh.

"Of course! Why not? I mean, you were an English major, so you know all the writing and grammar stuff already. And then you love to read, so you probably know all about plots and settings and characters."

I nodded but tempered my enthusiasm with, "Yeah, that's all true, but I think it's kind of a leap to go from knowing the structure of a process to actually executing it."

"Well, sure, that's true of any vocation. You'll have to work hard, practice, get in a routine, learn all the steps, the ins and outs. Just like anything else. But Riley, if anyone can do it, it's you!"

My eyes could not have looked at him with more appreciation and gratitude than they did at that moment. He was so unabashedly confident in me, seemingly (in my timid, overly sensitive mind) without question, evidence, or reason, and it was exactly what I needed when I was at my most vulnerable and considering a life change with so many unknowns.

For a few moments, I couldn't do anything but grin at him. Finally, my heart still pounding in my chest, I asked, "I wonder...would you be...willing to help me?"

"Like you have to ask," he answered. "Of course, but how?"

"Well, remember at IU when you told me you weren't a reader, but I said instead maybe I could read *to* you? I thought maybe that's what I would do as I write—get some instant feedback as I went along."

"Sure, that's a great idea…although, I guess not being a reader myself means I'm probably not the ideal candidate to bounce this stuff off of, am I?"

"I was thinking the opposite—that maybe you'd be even better because if I can convince you to like it, then in theory I can convince anyone."

"Ha! Yeah, okay, makes sense. Well, call me your guinea pig then. I'm looking forward to it. So…so, do you have any idea what you'll write about? I mean, what kind of book?"

I took a deep breath and replied, "Yes, as a matter of fact, I do. I started outlining a story this morning and wrote the entire first chapter!" The last few words were accompanied by a squeal, my enthusiasm no longer contained.

"Holy crap! That's awesome. Wow. Good for you. Seems like you must have the aptitude for it. Already a first chapter! If I lived a thousand years, I probably couldn't string two pages of words together, let alone write a whole chapter in a day. Amazing!"

"Thanks," I said, my chest heaving with a newfound pride that came to me out of nowhere and warmed my insides.

He grinned at my glowing face, then wondered, looking over at my purse on the blanket, "You didn't bring your chapter here tonight, did you?"

"Oh no, not here. I'll need to go back through it, you know, proof it, and rethink a few things, but if I can get a head start on maybe two or three chapters this week, I'll let you know. We can set up an evening…maybe next weekend."

"Sounds perfect," he said with an encouraging smile.

"And, well, this will sound maybe too…ambitious, but what I'd really like to do with my writing is…help people, you know? I'm not exactly sure how yet, but I was thinking that if I come up with captivating fiction stories that also have a level of instruction or importance or meaning for others, wouldn't that be the best of both worlds? Maybe like walking a mile in my shoes, or encouraging people to take a risk, or analyzing the phases of grief, or even maybe…some of what you and I have learned, being survivors, and all the good and bad that came with that. I mean, I'm not totally sure how it will all work, but I want to give it a try—to see what I can make of it."

"Riley, that's awesome. I can't wait to see what you do with it."

We sat in silence for a while after that. He was probably thinking (with his kind heart) how he was happy I had found something new to pursue, something that would be a nice little hobby for me. And maybe he was even thinking (with his crazy confidence in me) that it would be a great side career (not my day job, but something to do during off-hours that could potentially lead to something more and that, if I reached my goal, would be fulfilling and purposeful). He was also probably thinking (as any logical person would), isn't writing a book a one-in-a-million shot? Heck, I was thinking that too, but on the other hand I was thinking about how crazy it was that my pen hit the paper at three o'clock in the morning when I woke up out of a dead sleep with an entire plot of a book flooding my mind like a tsunami and how this must be a sign. As in, maybe this was *it*. Capital "I." Capital "T." This was the sign I had been looking for, this was what I was meant to do, this was my be-all and end-all. This was the purpose of my Biblio. This was *me*.

It hit me just like that. Like a bolt of lightning. Here I had been reading, reading, reading, like a rabid dog given a thousand books as a bone, since I was twelve years old when my mom left me in that library as part of my recovery from the accident, and these books had seeped into my pores and bled over as Biblios into my real life. I had become one with the books, and they had become one with me.

But then as my pen flew across the pages of my notebook during the wee morning hours, the world outside dark and still, my bedroom lamp a beacon of light, I came to feel as though *I was the book*. I was the one meant to make the book, be the creator, the thinker, the wrestler, the artist, the originator, the speaker, the conveyor, the sage, the wordsmith.

I was meant to be the Biblio.

My epiphany: I was the Biblio. *My* writing was meant to be the Biblio. Not someone else's. My words, my pen, my stories, my Biblio. I was meant to trigger the Biblio, not someone else's book—*my book*. My Biblio was no longer meant to rule my world—I was meant to rule my Biblio with my own direction, my own meaning, my own purpose-filled path.

My proof: when Adam pulled up to the West Baden arch and said we were going to walk down the Avenue and picnic on the lawn. The flinch came from the immediate Biblio—not from the book I was reading, but from the book I was *writing*!

Chapter one summary: The year is 1909, the setting is West Baden, the characters (Charlotte Beauford and Charles Eckhart) are strolling down the Avenue toward the West Baden Inn, dressed in their Edwardian finery, speaking softly to one another about the beauty of the evening, the manicured grounds, the quality of the springs compared to Saratoga's, when suddenly they are approached by a young woman in distress. She is with an elderly woman who has stumbled on one of the paving bricks and twisted her ankle. As Charles rushes to the elderly woman's side to assist, he looks up and notices with a shock that the young woman's face is one of the most beautiful he has ever seen. He finds himself staring deep into her eyes, which are such a vibrant dark blue that they are nearly purple, like the petals of an iris, and he blushes, something he almost never does. Charles and the young lady cradle the elderly woman between them, holding her weight, as they gingerly lead her toward the inn. Charlotte follows behind with a frown on her face, detecting an aberrant disruption in her perfectly ordered world, something amiss. She regards the exchange of glances above the injured woman's head between her fiancé and this young woman with a note of suspicion drawn less from their words or actions and more from a tightening in the pit of her stomach. The young woman, on the other hand, is thinking about her frail heart and how it started pounding so hard when she noticed the man's cheeks turn red at the sight of her. And now she's worried she may stumble herself.

Thus, it all began. The catalyst that shattered the inertia and sent my Biblio in an entirely new direction—where I made it *mine.*

On the Avenue in 1909, swished through time to the Avenue in 1990.

Chapter XXIII

Meanwhile, Adam was eating his sub contentedly, listening to the birds and cicadas chirping and watching the evening sun flicker through the trees. Riley was lost in thought for a while, but when she returned, she asked softly, "What's going on with Jeremy?"

Adam looked away for a moment, his face suddenly tighter, more constrained. He answered, "He's pissing me off lately—that's what's going on." He sighed, exasperated, and continued, "I swear, he's my older brother, but half the time I'm the one who has to watch out for *him*."

"Yeah, I...um...I noticed what he was doing at Pizza Shack. I didn't... didn't know he did that."

Adam acknowledged the words she wasn't saying with a grunt. "Me either. Well, I mean, I knew he tried some things back in high school, but lately he's just taken it to a whole new level. And as cool as Wayne is about everything, he told me that he chatted with Jeremy the other day and told him he can't be smoking it in the open alley like that anymore. Wayne's worried about the cops busting him and then holding the Shack responsible. And who knows what else."

"So...did you talk to Jeremy about it?"

"Yes, I've tried to about a dozen times, but he won't listen, says it doesn't affect him and thinks he'll never get caught. I brought it up to Mom too— well, not in so many words—just asked her what she thought about Jeremy lately. She acknowledged that he's going through some stuff these days. She tried to get him to open up and tried to reason with him too, told him to get off the drugs and figure out what he wants to do with his life, but he won't let her in or listen to her. She guessed that he's probably missing a father figure and going about filling that hole in all the wrong places."

"Hmm, yeah...she may be right."

"I know it…" He frowned and sat there quietly for a few minutes. "Back when we were younger, we used to pretend we were in a band together. Did I ever tell you that? Jeremy's amazing on guitar and drums, and he has a great voice. I could never hold a candle to him. I always thought he should pursue a career in music. But I think he's always lacked the confidence to make something happen. Then when he tried college, he couldn't get into the schoolwork and ended up dropping out after only one semester. Ever since then, he's been sort of aimless, without any clear direction in his life. I don't know, I have this feeling like he's kind of stuck, you know? Then the other day, he brought up something…I wasn't sure how to react."

He pulled up some blades of grass and began shredding them, looking away. Finally, minutes later, he stared at Riley and said, "He said he wanted to go visit Dad."

"Whoa," Riley responded. In all of their conversations over the phone and in person, this was the first time Adam had mentioned his dad. "Is that… even an option? I didn't realize you guys kept in touch with him."

Adam scoffed, "Oh no, we don't. Let me be clear—when he left my mom, he left us too. I haven't set eyes on him since I was thirteen. He used to send us cards and letters once in a while, with a little bit of money, but after a while even that stopped. I've always figured he must be just about the shittiest, most selfish prick there is, or at least it's always been easier for me to think of him that way. I mean, what kind of man does that?" Adam exhaled in frustration and disbelief, but then regarded Riley with a separate, resolved thought. "But the truth is, if I'm being fair, which I don't want to be, I simply don't know the man."

"And…do you want to?"

He shook his head. "I don't know. I mean, what if he is what I imagine— what would be the point in going? He'd probably kick us out, or worse. Then where would Jeremy be? Where would I be? Certainly not better off, that's for sure. And on the opposite side, let's say Dad's secretly some type of great guy, well then why did he leave us, and what the heck has he been doing for the past ten years? Does he have a whole new family down there? A whole new life? Why didn't he ever call us or explain anything to us? Was it because he wanted to forget we ever existed? How is that gonna go when we show up on his doorstep in Texas out of the blue?"

He finished the last bite of his sub, crinkling up the paper wrapper, fisting it tightly in his hands. While he had been talking, Riley had wrapped the remaining half of her sub in the paper bag and set it aside. She stretched out on her side on the blanket, her elbow propped under her, her eyes staring up at Adam with kindness and caring. He went on, "I mean, I remember so many good times with him when we were younger—he was such a hands-on dad, came to our games, taught us to play different instruments, goofed around with us. I just can't figure out what could have happened to make him leave. And Mom doesn't say a word either. The whole thing is a mystery, which makes it even worse. It's like on the one hand, I would love to see him and get some answers, but on the other hand, I want to run away, put it out of my mind, maybe just let bygones be bygones and accept that my life has this one component missing."

Suddenly, on a different tack, he stretched out, facing her and tossed the balled paper wrapper into the empty bag. His eyes were aglow with something new and fierce as he said, "Riley. Here's the thing: Jeremy talked about taking a road trip to Texas. Like soon. This summer. And guess what my first thought was?"

Riley regarded him with a blank stare.

He took her free hand in his and said, "All I could think about was, there is no way I'm going to Texas right now because there is no way I'm going to take a single second away from being with you."

Riley sat in stunned silence.

He waited for a reaction, and not getting one, went on, "I know…I've been…holding out on you lately, but that's because I wanted to go slow, for you to feel comfortable with me, and I wanted you to take the lead. I need you to know, though, that ever since I saw you standing in Nick's that night, Riley, *you* are all I think about." He lifted himself up on his arm, his piercing eyes trained on her. "I don't want to freak you out, but I don't think I can take it anymore. I don't think I can hold myself back anymore. I know we have some…*stuff*…to talk about…our shared past, the accident…" his voice was soft then, nearly a whisper, and he glanced down at the blanket, finding it hard to look into her eyes. "I'm afraid to bring it up, but if it helps us move forward, helps us get comfortable with the *idea of us*, then that's what I want to do, even if—" His face suddenly turned dark and brooding, "even if that means we ultimately decide to say…goodbye."

Adam waited, not breathing, trying to measure the weight of the world in her blue-green eyes as he forced himself to stare directly into their probing depths. She regarded him with no expression whatsoever, and he began to squirm, wondering if he should have kept his mouth shut. Was he a fool to bring it up? They might have enjoyed an entire summer of superficial, lighthearted outings. Wouldn't that have been better than a swift severing of everything? Wouldn't that have been better than looking back on this picnic as a trip down Asinine Alley, the moment when he took his life in his hands and threw it all away? He swallowed.

Finally, her eyes began to melt, like a slow sunrise warming frozen icicles suspended from a mountain cliff. Adam let out a long exhale at the sight of this and felt himself dizzy with relief when she did something that sent him to the moon. She sat up, crossed her legs underneath her, and faced him. He watched in awe as she cupped his face in her hands and kissed him full on the mouth. At first, it was light and tentative. Then, pulling back for just a moment to look into his flabbergasted eyes, she smiled and turned her face to get a better press on his lips. When she did, Adam felt an explosion inside his body, every pulse in his veins accelerated into overdrive. He didn't move or try to touch her; he simply tilted his head to allow it, welcome it, drink it in, deeper, longer, with meaning and feeling. She stayed there, like that, for so many minutes that he felt himself transported onto a separate plane with her, wishing the moment would never end.

When she finally pulled away, breathless and grinning, inches from his face, she said, "I've been dreaming about this since that damned closet seven years ago!"

He laughed out loud, feeling an anvil lift off his chest. He burst out airily, "Well?"

"Even better than I remember!" she exclaimed and clamped her lips on his again as they tumbled down on the blanket, her body half atop his as he held her crazy red curls off her face to get at her mouth unencumbered.

After five minutes, which was really an eternity, she drew away and placed her head on his chest so he couldn't see her face. He wondered if she could hear his wildly beating heart. He noticed she was breathing hard and that she waited until that had died down before she spoke. She said, "I think you should go to Texas. I think it would be good for both of you. And I was also thinking about something else…"

Her voice drifted off, and when she didn't say another word, he sat up a little so she was forced to lift her face to him. She asked cryptically, "Do you have to work tomorrow?"

He frowned. "Farm visits in the morning, but I'll be done by noon. Why?"

"I was thinking…," again she paused, and he felt a slight tremor of worry sneak up his spine, "maybe we could go…I mean, it's just a thought…we don't have to…but I thought maybe…maybe we could visit Kathy's grave together."

At these last words, her eyes flickered, and she nuzzled into the crook of his arm as if she couldn't face him or the words she had just released into the universe. And there it was—the elephant in their shared room that he had touched on and she had thrown down, that was now sitting like a crying baby waiting to be picked up.

He sighed and touched his finger under the dimple in her chin until she looked up. He said, "Okay. Let's do that."

"Okay," she echoed and hid her face again.

He kissed the top of her head and asked, "Can I ask you something?"

"Yes."

"What did your family think about us…hanging out…?"

She chuckled a little and said, "Oddly enough, Dad wasn't even surprised. He said he sensed something between us years ago, which is kind of crazy since I certainly never let on—I mean, not that there was anything to let on about back then, but he must have sensed how I was…somehow different when you were around, visiting with Marc or at soccer or school. Anyway, Mom just said, 'Don't break that boy's heart, Riley' as if it was all a one-sided thing and my aim was to hurt you. Well, and you know what Marc said—"

Adam cut her off and said, "Wait a minute. What did your mom mean?"

She sat up and shrugged, "I don't know…I guess she wondered if we were more than friends and didn't want me to do anything stupid, you know, do anything I couldn't handle."

"Oh," he said, realizing that was probably a fair warning. He said thoughtfully, "We can take this as slow as you want, Riley. I'm in no rush."

She kissed him then and said, "I know. I'm not worried about that—I'm really not. I'm more worried about that thing they always say: *falling hard*. I mean, why do they put it that way anyway? Like you've just jumped out of a fifty-story building and you're about to smash onto the pavement in a bloody heap."

"Ouch," he said with a grimace. "Well, when you put it that way…"

She smirked. "Okay, sorry to get graphic, but that's what I'm worried about—this, I mean, these feelings…I have for you…they're all new to me, and I don't want to plunge right into them, not knowing where they'll lead.

I don't really want to fall at all but instead maybe sink slowly, like when you have to suck on a Tootsie Pop for half an hour before you get to the Tootsie middle."

He raised an eyebrow and chuckled before responding, "Well, I hope you'll like what you find when you get to the Tootsie middle."

She pecked his lips and smiled. "Oh, I'm sure I will. In fact, I know it'll take *all* my willpower to not chomp right down on it after two licks."

With a broad grin, he took her in his arms and kissed her. The feel of her wrapped in his cocoon was something he had never felt before, soft and wonderful, and he began to think how lucky he was to hold her and that she wanted him to hold her, as though it was the most natural thing in the world for both of them.

After a few minutes, they rested their lips, lying back against the blanket, both lost in their own thoughts. She finally said, "It was kind of funny seeing Marc's face when you showed up on our doorstep last weekend."

"Yeah, you could have given me a warning that he was home, you know…"

"I didn't know he was supposed to be. I guess Mom insisted he come with his fiancée so they could get some wedding planning done. The guest list and dresses and all that. Anyway, I think at first he thought you were there to see him, but then when I came crashing down the stairs and we headed to your car together, I'll never forget that look—his jaw slack…he could've caught a net full of flies."

They both laughed. Adam said, "Yeah, I need to give him a call…"

"Eventually," she agreed. Then, "You might have more to tell him now."

He replied with a grin, "Oh, do I?"

"Definitely," was her easy response.

When the sun started to set and the bugs started to descend, they stood up, gathered their things, and walked back to the car along the Avenue. Riley seemed to drift off into another space, quiet and thoughtful. Out of the dusky quietude, she asked suddenly, "What were you doing there anyway?"

He traced back in his mind to their recent conversations and drew a blank. "Where?"

"The twins' party. The Dumont girls were in my grade, not yours, and I remember afterward wondering if it had all been a dream. I couldn't reconcile it in my mind that *you* were the one in that closet with me. I mean, I knew it was true, but I think it brought up such mixed emotions at the time that I almost wanted to deny it to myself."

He answered her, wondering if realizing the circumstances would make it any easier for her to reconcile. "Steven, Tammy Dumont's boyfriend, was on the soccer team with me and Marc. He insisted we come. Apparently, Tammy was worried they would have too many girls at her special quote 'boy-girl' party. Of course, if I had known what we were getting ourselves into…" His voice drifted off.

She said, "Oh yeah, Marc was there with me, wasn't he? And my parents. I'd forgotten all about that. I think they drove and then were upset because at the end of the night, they couldn't find me. Of course, I had run all the way home hours before…"

"Yeah, I know. Tammy kept asking me what I'd done to you, and I kept saying nothing, but I got quite a few dirty looks from the girls after that."

Riley looked at Adam and put her hand on his arm to slow his walking. "Oh Adam, I didn't know that. I'm sorry."

He brushed off her concern with, "It's okay…not like I won a bunch of popularity contests or had any prospects before that. Actually, I don't think I noticed any particular difference in my already rather dismal high school existence." She blinked a few times and he added, "Besides, Riley, after that kiss, I didn't care what anyone thought of me—all I really cared about was you."

She leaned in and kissed him then. She said, "Me too. I guess I kept think-ing it was wrong of me to think about you in that way, though, so I would shove the thought to the back of my mind when it popped up, which was often. Always with a strange wash of guilt—for thinking about you and then for not allowing myself to think about you." She paused as he processed that. She said with a bit of surprise in her voice, "It's kind of how I think about Kathy, even now—a strange mixture of guilt, fear, sadness, wonder, joy, an-ger, confusion, frustration."

He nodded. "I know" was all he could get out without his voice showing the emotion he was feeling.

Chapter XXIV

I set my alarm for six but woke up at four-thirty, overflowing with visions of Charlotte, Charles, Gwendolyn (the young woman), and Mrs. Frontenac (the elderly woman). My notebook pages were filling up quickly as I scrawled away, barely taking time to breathe. It felt like a blissful and fully baked compulsion, one that had come out of nowhere and that now I couldn't slow, let alone squelch. And I didn't want to. It felt freeing, alive, *right*.

When I finally paused, due to a knock on my door from Mom telling me breakfast was ready, I blinked several times in succession, coming back with a shock to the year 1990 in my Minnie Mouse pj's and the birds singing outside my window. I got up, shaking off the otherworldliness of my words, got ready, and went downstairs.

By then, everyone else had finished and gone off to start their day, so as I sat alone, eating my pancakes, I let the words drift out of my mind and began to think about Kathy. I had only visited her grave one other time, a few months after the accident. It was a sort of test. What would I feel? Anything? I had walked over there and stared down at her gravestone. I remember the weather was harsh and raw, and the freshly mounded earth was frozen, hard, and crunchy beneath my feet. I wondered if she was cold in that deep, dark grave. Was she frozen? Could I dig down and hold her head in my hands and feel her hair break off in my fingers? She'd always had such pretty hair—thick, dark, straight—and she'd always made fun of my wiry, curly red mass, so different from hers. Then, as I stood above her, I began to think maybe her hair wasn't there anymore. Did hair decompose? I supposed it must be gone by now. In fact, I thought there must be very little left of her besides her bones. Where did her brain go and her heart? Why didn't anyone explain this to me?

Where do people go? Where did Kathy go?

It was ten years later now, and I still didn't know.

I got up just as my brother Brent came into the kitchen to refill his coffee. Apparently, he hadn't quite started his day. He said noncommittally, "Hey."

"Hey," I said.

Then he walked out of the room. I shook my head. It was funny because now that Marc, who had always been my closest brother, was living in Indy, I felt as though I had no real connection to my two other brothers, although they were the ones still living at home. While I was finishing up high school and going to IU, Brent had gone right into the workforce with his job at Pluto Bottling Company, and even though he was living in our basement, I rarely saw or talked to him. Nate was a math teacher at our old high school (and, in my opinion, still looked like a fifteen-year-old kid), and much like when we were younger, I never had anything in common with either of them.

Just then, Mom appeared and said, "Morning, sweetie. You working at the library today?"

"No, not today," I answered curtly. I didn't know why, but I couldn't share with anyone that Adam and I were going to visit Kathy's grave. It was enough that we were going; I couldn't also be expected to explain it or answer any questions about it. I added, "Um, Adam's coming by."

"Oh, okay, well, I'm headed to the grocery store. You need anything?"

Mom was so great. Now that I was older, she rarely pried, and I so appreciated that. She was always there to listen when I needed advice, but she let me live my life on my own terms and in my own time. And she had (very reluctantly) agreed not to have a graduation party for me (based on my request). "But we only want to celebrate you and everything you've accomplished."

"But I don't want that. I dread being the center of attention. And I certainly don't want people giving me gifts and money. It seems so weird."

"Honey, it's not weird—it's expected. It's what everyone does. We could have cake and games and keep everyone occupied. Your grandparents would come—it would only be a small gathering."

"No, please."

Finally, "Oh, all right. I don't get it, but if that's what you want, we won't have it."

"Thank you." My grandparents still sent checks and cards, which was sweet of them. I suspect Mom explained the situation. Their words of pride and congratulations were all I needed and meant more to me than ginger ale, party favors, and red-and-white streamers.

"We're out of milk and cereal."

"Yep, got it. Hey, by the way, Jane called you the other day. Did you return her call?"

"Yeah, I saw that on the whiteboard. I haven't. I will, though. I need to set up some time to see her."

"You do. She's such a sweet girl. You're welcome to have her over here for supper sometime if you like."

"Okay, maybe I will. I'll let you know."

She slung her purse over her shoulder, keys in hand, and said, "Okay, see ya later then."

"Bye."

At the mention of Jane, I started to feel a little guilty. I had only seen her once this summer. I had to admit that most of my free hours were spent with Adam, and as a result I had neglected Jane. I finished my pancakes and looked at the clock—ten forty-five. I picked up the phone and called her.

"Hi, Jane."

"Hi, stranger."

"Ouch. Guess I deserve that. How've you been?"

"Good. Still looking for a job. What have you been up to?"

"Working at the library and hanging out. That's about it," I answered with a twinge of guilt—about being with Adam so much but also thinking, if only she knew about my writing! She would die! But it was way too early to talk about it with her. She would want to read it, and she was a super bibliophile, and I couldn't quite face the thought of that yet.

"And by 'hanging out,' you mean…?"

"Yes, with Adam. I'm sorry, I know I've been rather…absent lately. And I always hated those girls in college who started dating and you never saw them again. Please don't tell me I'm becoming one of them!" I laughed. When she didn't respond, I cleared my throat. "I'm sorry. I know. I suck. Not that I have an excuse, but he's only home for about six more weeks, and I'm trying to take advantage of our time together while I can. Anyway, enough about that. Listen, are you available for dinner some night this week?"

Jane graciously replied, "Sure, that would be great." Then a pause and, "So you and Adam…you're officially dating now?"

"Um…yeah, I guess so. I mean, we haven't used the b word or the g word yet, but I think that's kind of assumed at this point."

"Wow."

"Yeah, sometimes I think about it and I have to pinch myself."

She made a sort of questioning noise, and before she could ask me more, I diverted with, "How's John doing? You two still going strong?"

"Yep, he's coming to visit next week for a few days. Did I tell you he got a job in Chicago?"

"No kidding, that's awesome. But what does that mean for you...?"

"Yeah, we're still trying to figure that out. I applied for a few jobs up there too, and actually, I have three phone interviews this week. We'll see."

"So, you would move to Chicago? That's a big city!"

"Yeah, I know...but it would be kind of cool too. Have you ever been? You should see their library!"

I laughed. "No doubt. Speaking of that, what are you reading right now?"

The rest of the conversation went down the much-beloved reading rabbit hole and lasted until I heard Adam coming through the door with a "Hey Riley, you ready?"

"Whoops—hey, Jane, sorry to interrupt, but I gotta go. Adam's here. Let me know when you can come for dinner. We can catch up. Talk soon."

As I hung the phone up and grabbed my purse, I glanced at Adam with his white T-shirt and khaki shorts and thought, damn, he's good looking—how did I get so lucky? I noticed his eyes did a quick once-over on my black shorts and chocolate brown button-down sleeveless top, and if his eyebrows were any indication, he liked what he saw as much as I did.

On the car ride to the cemetery, we were both quiet, and I felt the space between us growing like a cavern that had opened up in the middle of the front seat. Finally, when he pulled onto the gravel drive, he shut the car off and turned to me. His eyes, hooded and cautious, took mine in like a deep-sea diver digging for a precious cache. I waited and didn't move a muscle.

Slowly, he took my hand and asked, "Scared?"

I let out a puff of air, realizing I hadn't been breathing, and said, "Yes." Then I looked away from his probing eyes because they were killing me softly with their exploration. He was wanting me to set the tone for the visit, he was wanting me to work it out for both of us, and I was floundering under the weight of it. I stared out the window at the rows of granite, plastic flowers, and flags, trying to draw strength from their numbers and their solidity in the midst of my shaky emotions and jumbled thoughts.

After a while, I looked back at his haunted eyes and said with a sort of stable, logical footing, "I recently read this book by Albert Camus called *The Stranger*. It was such an odd little book about a man who murders another man for no apparent reason. It was set during that period right after World War II when young men had witnessed so much death and destruction first-hand that they were questioning the point of life, the point of human existence. The main character had no understanding of the reason for his actions, and therefore no true conscience or feeling of guilt. People died and people lived. In this case, he lived but the man he shot died. Ironically, he is eventually sentenced to death for the murder. The prosecutor utters something about the emptiness of a man's soul and how it can be an abyss threatening to swallow up society. The murderer wonders what God or the lives left above-ground matter when we are all elected to the same fate. And yet, the author never uses the word *death* to describe this—he calls it *fate* instead of death because without using the word *death*, one can always surmise what is meant by fate as the ultimate end result for all of us."

Adam's brow furrowed as if he wasn't quite processing this.

I pressed on, trying to articulate, "I've been wondering…if you and I… well, haven't you wondered about the fate that brought us together? The *death* that brought us together?"

At this, his face looked crestfallen, which made me stop short. I couldn't go on. He answered softly, "Of course, I think about it all the time, Riley. I wish…I wish…well, I wish a lot of things. But wishing doesn't change anything, does it?"

"No—no, it doesn't," I answered quickly. Then slowly, gently, I lifted his hand to my lips, never letting my eyes leave his. I kissed the strong, tanned skin there and said, "I wouldn't change *this*. I wouldn't wish *this* away."

Oh, his eyes at that moment! If only I could bottle that concoction of love, sorrow, gratitude, and tender solicitude. His voice had left him. I took his palm and placed it against my cheek and leaned into it, and we sat there like that for a few moments.

Then putting our hands down on my lap, I said, "I've been thinking about things lately, about you, about me, about Kathy. And how I need my life to be real. I need my life to be about the past and the present and the future. In my logical mind, I know we all die—just like the book said, our fate is the same for all—but then that begs the question: *How do we live in the mean-time?* How do we *live?* Not just waking up every day like robotic zombies and performing daily tasks and activities without awareness or thought of what is *real*. Pretending that everything is an easy, pretty package of perfection, or worse, knowing the fallacy of that misconception but never acknowledging

it or absorbing it and working through it. That's where I think I've been for
these many years, floating by on the surface of things, and in fact, actually
sometimes blatantly ignoring the signs of those deeper meanings that are
staring me right in the face! I mean, heck, just think about my writing—how
did I not ever think about it before? Now it's like I'm on a mission, and I
can't stop."

My chest was heaving with the fervor of my conviction—to state these
thoughts out loud—that which had been simmering in me for so long and
was now set afire. It was as if the momentum of the words was pulling me
forward, almost of its own accord, bubbling up my innermost thoughts and
feelings, and spewing them out involuntarily. I kept on, watching his eyes
track my mouth, my eyes, my red cheeks, the burning rubbing off on him
like a cathartic stain. "So…so, I want to be real. Can I just get *real* for one
moment, please?"

He whispered with a force that set my heart beating even more wildly,
"*Yes.*"

I took in a deep breath and exhaled my words out in a quick, steady statement: "Kathy died. And we lived. I don't know why. You don't know why.
Yes, you hit us with your car, and she died." At this, he pulled back as if I had
slapped him, which caused me to pause, but then I pressed on because it had
to be said. "I'm sorry. Stay with me. Please. Yes, that is the way it happened.
Even though it was an accident and you didn't mean it. But the outcome was
that you lived. And I lived. And Kathy died. And in the grand scheme of
things, I should probably never want to see you again. I should probably hate
you. I should probably want *you* to die."

He pulled his hand away and swallowed. The sobering, withered look he
trained on me at that moment nearly caused me to buckle, and I could see
the tears prick his eyes, but I bowled right through that. "Here's where everything goes haywire, though. I haven't wanted that. Because what good would
that do? And on the same note, when I used to think about the fact that I'm
here and she's not, I used to think, that makes no sense whatsoever. Why
couldn't *I* have gone away, and she have stayed? Wouldn't it have been better
that way? Why didn't I die? There have been so many times when I've wished
for it, prayed for it, since that day: I wanted to die."

Again, the brutal honestly being ravaged from my bones and out of my
mouth was causing him to recoil, and similarly, every synapse in my own
body was screaming to stop and to run and to never come back and to never

think these thoughts again, let alone speak them. But I was done with that—I was done with the avoidance, the innocuous stone skimming along the water's surface that was my life. I was *done* with that!

"Yes, I admit it. I wanted to die. Every day. For a long time. Don't you get it? Nothing made sense in this world and especially not Kathy dying. Kathy, who was good and smart and strong and *worthy*. And what am *I* to *that*? Nothing. What do *I* matter? Not a bit. Not one single solitary iota in this stinking godforsaken world. Nothing. Just plain nothing."

He tilted his head at me and shook it so slowly as a tear fell down his cheek that I nearly let my stoic walls crumble down in an explosive avalanche, but I couldn't yet—I must forge ahead before all was lost. Just then, I had a flash, a blip of a memory of a tear falling down a cheek and staining the fabric of a green T-shirt, oh so many years ago, from a boy who was broken, just like I was feeling now. I took in a jagged breath and pressed on. "I was so mad. So mad! Why? Why, why, why? There's no logic. None. But somehow, we're supposed to keep going. Because that's what people do. And so that's what I did. But I didn't understand it. I wondered what the point was. I thought it was some kind of awful, evil joke—on me, on you, on our families, on this world. She's gone and I'm here, and how could that be something that was meant to be? I couldn't understand it, couldn't reconcile it.

"But then, somehow, somewhere along the way, just recently, I began to think about how I need my life to be real. And I need to *own* it all. Even if there's no logical reason for the way it is. Even if it hurts. Even if it opens up a cavern in my soul that can never be filled. Even if there's no forgiveness." At this, his eyes got big. I gripped his hand again and said with forcefulness, "Oh, I'm not talking about forgiving you. That I did in my mind and in my heart long ago. In fact, I don't remember ever blaming you, *ever*. I'm talking about forgiving God. And forgiving Kathy, for leaving me. She left me without saying goodbye, without letting *me* say goodbye, without letting me tell her how much she meant to me, that I admired her, that I loved her, that she was a piece of my puzzle that I can never fill again. She left me to pick up the pieces and to figure this all out on my own. I don't know how to forgive that."

I stopped and sighed for a minute, building my way to the next plateau in my journey, a courage and conviction overtaking me as I said, "But forgive I must. And reconcile I must. Because otherwise, what's the point? To keep taking a poison that will never kill me but will continue to make me sick? I can't do it anymore. I can't. And I won't. What do you say? Will you stand with me and let it all go? Will you create a new path with me—the survivor's path, where we will commit to be *here*, fully present, with no guilt, with no shame, facing it all, with the will to *live*?"

The tears were still streaming down his face, and when I stopped, without a word, he put his hand behind my head and pulled me to him, softening my tightly wound lips and my tightly wound heart with a kiss that shattered me. I fell into a pile of tiny pieces in his arms. After many moments when our lips were reliving every connection forged and broken in both our young lives, he drew away with the slightest, tenderest movement in order to place my head against the crook of his shoulder and neck, cradling me there as I sobbed, and sobbed, and sobbed. I wanted to die in a different way than I ever had before. Not in the way of trading my worthless life for Kathy's or anyone else's, but in the way that I was brought here to this exact moment for a reason, and I must stay in it and stay alive and be who I am now and who I'm meant to be, and that was not a worthless venture.

❧ Chapter XXV ❧

Adam's heart burst a hundred times during Riley's speech, and it took every fiber of his being not to cut her off and scream, "Stop! I can't take it! Please stop! You're breaking my heart and you're breaking me!"

But instead, he listened and absorbed every flagellating word, knowing it was the only way to the other side. Knowing that to climb a mountain, you had to start in the depths of the valley of despair.

When the release came at the end, with the eternal wails from the bottom of her heart, he could do nothing but hold her and comfort her, realizing with gratitude the gift she had given him, even with its spiky, jagged exterior wrapping.

A long time went by, and she quieted. He kissed her hair and held her tight to let her know he was there and he wasn't going anywhere. Eventually he reached around her into the glove box to hand her a napkin, which she used to blow her nose and wipe her eyes. Then she sat up and away from him, saying with shaky resolve, "I'm okay now. You ready?"

He nodded and they got out of the car soundlessly, walking to Kathy's grave. The rustling trees, sunny skies, and chirping birds belied the unearthly silence shrouding the palpably somber mood of their mission.

They looked down at the inscription, which read:

Kathy Metzger, Beloved Daughter and Sister, 1967–1980
May you rest in peace on angel's wings.

Standing separately side by side, trapped in hushed reverence, they stayed that way for many minutes, ruminating on their own internal thoughts.

Finally, Riley broke the silence. She pointed at the faded plastic flowers poking crookedly out of the ground on either side of the grave and said, "You know, they moved."

Adam looked up to Riley's face and asked, "The flowers?"

A curt shake of her head. "No, her parents and sister. They moved. Last year. To Ohio. My dad told me. That's probably why the flowers are so faded and trampled down like that."

"Oh," Adam said lamely, looking back down with a frown. After a minute, he added, "We can bring fresh ones next time, if you like."

She nodded. He noted that she was all cried out now, her eyes dry, red, and swollen. She was still the most beautiful girl he had ever seen—her red hair spilling down her back in soft curls, her freckles popping out in the sun, her lips oddly full and red from crying. What was more, her eyes were ablaze with something new he had never witnessed before. Yes, the sadness and weariness lingered, but at the same time her eyes seemed infused with a brand-new glowing, stalwart purpose. He knew it was the words she had spoken and how she was determined to make her life real, and his too.

Thinking about it now, he knew it was the right thing to do. But *so* hard. He thought about the last month and how many of his hometown friends raised their eyebrows when he brought up Riley's name, as if it went against the laws of nature that he should be allowed in her space, let alone be her friend, and now so much more. No one said anything to his face, but he felt their questioning, confused, and sometimes judgmental thoughts. And who was he to deny or defend? He didn't deserve her. He loved her. God, he really loved her! He hadn't told her yet, and wouldn't, until she was ready. But in the meantime, he still knew with a fierce, healthy sense of justice that he didn't deserve her or her forgiveness, which she so casually threw down at him minutes ago. He was in absolute awe of her now. The feelings he had forced himself to bury deep down in his gut for years in order to survive and get from one day to the next she had unearthed like a raging volcano erupting and spewing its lava far and wide, and now the remaining heat was left to simmer in his lap. Guilt. Horror. Fear. Yearning. Hope.

She turned to face him just then and said with a strange challenge in her voice, "You know, that there," she pointed to the car they had left on the gravel drive, "that was the first time I cried. Did you know that?"

He covered a flash of astonishment as swiftly as he could from his face, but not before she saw it and smiled a mirthless little tight-lipped smirk, saying, "Now you know what a monster I am."

"Riley…no…," he said, shaking his head slowly and trying to put his hand on her shoulder.

She shrugged it away and cut him off when he tried to continue. "No, stop, let me get this out. Even that—that crying, I'm not sure it wasn't more for me than her." Her eyes were piercing him, angry, fueled, intense, as if she needed to unburden her heart, confessing everything that had been smoldering there for years, releasing the colossal wave of the tsunami in one fell swoop. He couldn't help but think, how brave she is! Especially as he was keeping his own newly sprung feelings under wraps, swirling erratically in multiple directions like unfettered buoys on an ocean's swell.

She declared, "Resilient. That's what my mom used to say to people about me, back then, when Kathy died. As if it was a compliment. I knew she was just making excuses for me. I'm sure she was embarrassed by me, ashamed of me. Why didn't I cry? *Oh, she's just very resilient. Oh yes, she's back at school now, doing fine, thanks for asking, but she's really very resilient, you know.* She might as well have said, *She's part robot, she has no heart, she could care less, but isn't that a marvel, isn't that something to see...! So resilient.* Meanwhile, I was *mortified.* Why couldn't I cry? You see people in movies cry all the time, about the silliest and most ridiculous things, yet I couldn't cry when my best friend died in my arms in the back seat of a car, her head a mashed-up piece of bloody pulp in my lap as I stared down into what was left of her dead brown eyes! *What is wrong with me?!*"

Adam's heart broke for her. He grabbed her by both shoulders this time and forced her to listen. "Riley, there is *nothing* wrong with you. You were in shock. You were just a kid. And you had just been through a horrible accident. It makes sense that you couldn't cry. The brain and the body aren't always in sync during trauma or its aftereffects. Clearly, without *you* having *any* control over it, your body went into survival mode. Maybe that meant not being able to feel what had just happened—maybe it meant not allowing yourself to absorb the trauma, the loss, the grief. And you know what? That's okay. It's okay, Riley, it's okay."

Her face, skeptical and resistant, watched him talk as if she was humoring a foolish, uneducated child. When he finished, she said, "For ten years, Adam. Really? You're going to say it was perfectly normal for me not to be able to process this for *ten years?*"

"What I'm saying is that there is no *normal* when it comes to trauma and grief. No perfect timeline, no perfect reaction, no perfect way to cope. It doesn't mean that she meant any less to you. In fact, it may actually mean that she meant quite a bit more. And *resilient* isn't a dirty word. Maybe being resilient and moving on with your life as best you could was your way of grieving, your way of making your life move on and move forward when you knew that was no longer an option for Kathy." He paused, breathing hard and holding her arms tighter than he should. "Have you thought of that? Maybe Kathy would have wanted it that way. Maybe Kathy was up there, looking down on you, and thinking, go, Riley, go! Just keep going, get on with your life, because no amount of sinking down into a puddle is going to bring me back anyway."

At this, her eyes scouring his face, she began to crumble, sinking into his arms, and allowing him to hold her close. She mumbled into his chest a short admission, barely above a whisper, "Maybe."

CHAPTER XXVI

TWO WEEKS LATER, I walked into Our Lady of the Springs and scanned the inside of the church for Father Avery. Not seeing him, I walked up to the front to ask a nun, who indicated that he was seeing someone in the confessional at the moment and I could wait for him, if I liked, or be next in line if I preferred. I answered, okay, not entirely sure what that meant. She pointed to the back of the church, where a wooden room was built into the corner of the building, looking almost like a large coat closet with a cross hanging over the door.

I sat down on a pew and waited. After a few minutes, a woman came out, rosary in hand, and went directly to a pew several rows away to kneel in prayer. Building up my nerve, since I had never done this before, I went into the confessional and took over her vacated seat, closing the door behind me. I could see Father Avery on the other side of a grated wooden panel, sitting in prayer, his head bent, his hand to his forehead. I waited quietly until I heard him speak, saying a prayer and then encouraging me to unburden myself. At this, I wondered if I had bitten off more than I could chew. My heart started pounding.

I whispered a few words of greeting, realizing I may have unintentionally created a sort of subterfuge, "Hi Father Avery—it's me, Riley Cartwright. They said you were here, in this closet...um, confessional...so I thought I'd just come in...to talk to you...but now that I'm here, I'm not sure what to do." A small laugh escaped my lips.

I could just make out his murmur of shock through the grate as he said, "Riley, well, this is a pleasant surprise. It's been such a long time. How are you?"

"Yeah, sorry about that. I've been rather neglectful, haven't I?"

"No bother—I know you've been busy," he answered, adding with a chuckle, "and I suspect this time you're not here to ask me about our youth group, CCD classes, or Masses, are you?"

"Um, nope. Sorry again."

"Eh…you win some, you lose some," he said magnanimously. "Well, it's a standing invitation. What brings you in today? How's your dad? And the rest of the family? Shall we come out of here and take a walk?"

"Wait," I said, a little more forcefully than I intended. "I do…have a sort of confession…"

"Ah, okay, that's fine. However, we do have a few rules that apply to confessional…namely, that you must be Catholic, intending to become Catholic, or on your deathbed. I don't believe any of those are true of you today, are they?"

"No," I said, not hiding the disappointment from my voice. When I first came into the narrow closet I was intimidated, but now, the ice broken, I could see the appeal of it—telling your deepest, darkest secrets without having to see the facial expressions of any potential judgment, plus the closet-like aspect (nowhere to hide), the disembodied voice through the grate that seemed like a ventriloquist of God—it was rather inviting.

Sadly, the spell broken, he stood up and opened the door, and I came out and shook his hand. His warm blue eyes upon me, I remembered back to that first meeting with him all those years ago as a shy and confused teenager, and I knew I had nothing to fear about coming into the light of a summer's day with him. He said simply, "Riley."

"Good to see you, Father."

"Let's head to my office, what do you say?"

"Okay."

There we were, as if time stood still, back in the place where it all began—my journey of investigation and discovery into my strange gift-slash-curse-slash-squishy-unknown-thing. I had been back several times over the years, mostly to say hi and give him an update on my life and studies, but also as a safe haven—the one and only place where I could talk freely about my Biblio. He had always been so gracious, letting me go on and on about it, continuing to try to explain it, expand on it, understand it, harness it. And never quite doing so, thus the necessity of coming back now, when I had a better handle on it than ever. Or at least it seemed so. I was curious to hear his reaction and whether he also felt I was onto something.

Today, being older and maybe a touch wiser and more mature, I remembered that the world did not revolve around Riley and asked, "How are you doing, Father? How have you been?"

He smiled, an acknowledgment of the unexpected question, and said, "My dear, I am fine. In fact, later today, we have two back-to-back baptisms, always a blessing from God. The sun is shining, the birds are singing, and what more could a servant of God ask for?"

"Indeed," I agreed. After all, it was a beautiful day out, and I imagine having two adorable babies coming into the fold was one of those happy occasions that priests could rejoice over, as opposed to the drudgery of many of their other obligations. Such a self-sacrificing job! You had to hand it to anyone taking on such a role—not just priests, but also pastors and rabbis and other men and women of God. Granted, despite my friendship with Father Avery and the fact that I had in no way been converted or even begun to understand what the world of religious service entailed, I could definitely note the amazing courage, stability, and perseverance it took to do a job where you must almost always think of yourself last.

"So, your family is well?"

"Yep, everyone's good, thanks for asking. I told Dad I was coming to see you, and he said to say hi and to ask if you need anything fixed, haha."

"That was kind of him to ask, but alas, God has been good to our little church in the valley—our buildings are sound and solid. Tell him I said hello and thank him in return." He paused as we smiled at each other and then broached, "And so, you have a confession for me? Something you want to tell me?"

I took a gulp. Wow, jumping right in. "Yes, well, I suppose. I'm not sure how to begin," I struggled. He folded his hands calmly, patiently on his lap and waited with that inviting smile of his. I took a deep breath and started, "I've…recently started to date someone…new…but he's not really new, actually." His brow furrowed at this, forcing me to press on, "I don't know if you remember this, but when I first came to you to talk about my…well, my intuition, my Biblio, I told you how it started after I was involved in a car accident." He nodded mutely. "Well, the boy who was driving the car that ran into us—his name is Adam Linder—he's the one…the one I'm dating now."

His eyes got big as he said, "Oh. Hm. I see."

I felt my face go red, which I hated, but it couldn't be helped. "Believe me, it came as a surprise to me too. I always felt a sort of connection to him, from afar of course, but then I ran into him a couple of months ago, and it was as if I was seeing him in a different light for the first time. I struggled with my feelings, wondering if this was a…I don't know…a *betrayal* of some kind, you know? Of Kathy. Of her memory. Of the shattering of my old life after that day. But then, I started talking to him and realized that the blight of this tragedy had as much of an impact on his life as it did mine—in fact, maybe more so on his. I know he still struggles with guilt and grief, even today, though it truly was an accident. I can't remove that any more than I can remove the memory or pain from my own life."

When I paused, he said, "Of course not" and waited, knowing there was more.

"I can't explain it fully, but we've both gained a sort of healing peace, being together, as if…as if it was always supposed to end up this way. I mean, don't get me wrong, there have been some deep, gut-wrenching conversations, and we don't have everything worked out yet. In fact, we haven't even officially declared ourselves boyfriend-girlfriend or shared our true feelings for each other, but it's like when I'm with him, I feel safe. And I feel like I can tell him anything. And I feel like we're…*home* to each other, we're meant to be together." I found myself breathing hard with the force of my strange urge to provide convincing evidence. To pile on, I asked, "Is it crazy?"

"Riley," he began, mercifully all reassurance and kindness in his eyes, "no, it's not crazy. I actually think there is something poignantly beautiful about it, like the closing up of a festering wound with a healing balm. Yes, it is least expected, but certainly most needed, perfectly tailored, and well deserved."

I nodded, feeling relief and a spark of joy. I was excited that he understood implicitly, without my having to explain further or to rationalize, which made me sick inside when I felt the need to do so. I conceded, "It *is* like that! I just keep saying to Adam that I want my life to be *real*, you know, and the only way I know how to do that right now is to be with him and to let all of the feelings in, even when they hurt or confuse or make us both want to run and hide, because that's the only way to release them."

He nodded and said, "I have found, in my counsel with others, that yes, this is the only way—to face it all and get to the other side."

"It won't be easy."

"No."

"But I'm going to try. We're going to try."

"Yes."

"On that note," I redirected, "So, here is my other confession: I haven't told him about my Biblio."

He gave me a small smile. "Ah, yes, your Biblio. How is *that* going?"

"Wow, well, I have an interesting update for you. It came out of the blue, but now that I'm in the thick of it, I must admit that it seems almost *natural* the way it happened, much like me and Adam, and somehow, without me guessing it beforehand or seeing it coming, it's here and oddly *meant to be.* Crazy. Serendipitous—isn't that the word? Anyway, what I'm getting at is this: Instead of just reading, I've started to write. And not just a little. Like a lot and all the time. Actually, like an obsessed person on speed—forgive me, Father!—like my fingers have been taken over by a very fast writing squirrel running on a hamster wheel, haha. I can't seem to stop. I get up in the middle of the night and write for hours, and I take my notebook with me everywhere. I'm writing at the library in between work and as soon as I get home. I think my family's beginning to think I have a bug or something because I'm locked up in my room so much. I mean, they're used to me hiding out, but this is extreme. Of course, I haven't told them yet what's really going on. I'm waiting to see what becomes of it. But I did tell Adam, and now, poor guy, our dates consist mostly of me reading my story to him. It's kind of funny because prior to this, he was never into books, but he says he really likes what I've written so far. It's actually brought us closer together. After all, as much as my story is fiction, every single word and every single character came from me, so I guess it's like opening myself up to him more than I ever have before."

"Well, that's wonderful, Riley."

"Thanks. I love it. And what's even more amazing is how my writing and my choice to be more real in my life have cracked open this wall of emotion I never thought I possessed. I never used to cry, you know—like I *couldn't* cry. After the accident, all my tears were stuck inside me, like a sealed vault, but then lately, they've just started to pour out. At first I thought it was a selfish indulgence—me feeling sorry for myself—but then when it started to happen more and more, I realized maybe this is finally my way of allowing myself to *feel* things again. I mean, for example, while writing my story, I find myself crying all the time, as if *I'm* the one experiencing the things that my characters are going through. My story, it's set here in West Baden, and it's about a poor young woman who had rheumatic fever as a child, and her heart was affected, so she's come here as a companion to an elderly woman because it was the only way she could afford to take the healing waters. Well, in the course of the story, she meets and falls in love with a handsome young man who unfortunately is already engaged to a haughty, pretentious young heiress who definitely isn't going to take this budding romance lying down. Anyway, as I put the innocent young woman, Gwendolyn, through so many hateful, awful situations, I find my throat getting sore and before I know it, tears are flowing down my face and I'm heaving in sobs that I never knew existed before!"

I paused, completely mystified by my emotions. Even talking about it was making me tear up.

Father Avery blinked a few times and cleared his throat, his blue eyes aglow with this amazing new development. He said after a moment, "Riley, dare I say it? I think this is quite a breakthrough. It's wonderful, really. I think God gives us only what we can handle, and then only when the timing is right and with the right tools to take on our demons. Maybe this writing is His way of saying now is the time and that you can handle it, you can let go now, you can be free. Yes, you are crying for your character, but really I believe you are crying for *you*, for the twelve-year-old Riley who had to go through what you went through, for the Riley today who hasn't been able to face it but maybe wants to try now."

I nodded, unable to talk, allowing the tears to flow.

Father Avery reached behind his desk for a box of tissues and handed them to me. I pulled out a few and put them to my face, dropping my head into my hands. Outside of Adam, I hadn't cried in front of anyone, but it was as if I had turned on a faucet. The tears kept coming and I let them, resisting the urge to make excuses or say I'm sorry because despite how uncomfortable they made me feel (being so foreign to me), these tears, they were me being real, making my life real, right here, right now, and I wasn't going to make any excuses for that or for them.

He sat with his reassuring small smile, waiting patiently for me to begin again, which I eventually did, wiping my eyes, raising my chin, and saying, "So, in answer to your question, it's still going—my Biblio. Except now, it's from the books and from my writing. And I'm trying to make my writing be meaningful, you know? Yes, the story is fiction, but I've woven in some thought-provoking situations. Not to get into too many details, but because Gwendolyn has faced death due to her childhood illness, she's more mature than other women her age, and she's used to tackling the deeper meanings of life head-on, which is one of the reasons Charles falls in love with her so quickly—because in this way, she's very different from the superficial Charlotte. I guess what I'm saying is that this version of my Biblio, the writing version, seems more profound to me than the reading version. I can take it to another level because I'm the one who controls it. Sure, I don't know how it will manifest, just like before, but at least I feel it is driving to an ultimate purpose, which I never felt before."

"Hmpf, interesting! So, is that a bit disconcerting...?"

"Yes, to say the least!" I confirmed. "In fact, the other day, I had a two-fer. Nearly blew my mind. I had just finished reading Nevil Shute's *On The Beach*, which is a rather sad rendering of the end of days, a book from the fifties about a nuclear holocaust. The radiation is slowly heading south toward Australia, where the book is set, and the people know it's coming and are doing all kinds of crazy things knowing they're about to die, and this one American Navy guy stationed in Australia keeps trying to buy a pogo stick for his daughter, even though his whole family is back in the States and probably long since dead because the bomb hit the Northern Hemisphere first. So, of course, what did I see over the past week? Kids on pogo sticks. Down the street, over in the parking lot, in front of the grocery store, in the yard, a plague of pogo sticks!"

As I sighed, he laughed and said, "Well, at least you weren't reading *The Death of Ivan Ilyich*."

"Oh!" I laughed and replied, "Can you imagine? Pogo sticks are definitely better than dead bodies. Although that's a great story too—I love Tolstoy."

Our own little twisted quip caused us both to chuckle. I continued, "So on the same day, I was writing about my main character having rheumatic fever, and then I hear on the news that Bobby Darin, who apparently had rheumatic fever as a child and was rather frail the rest of his life because of it, was just inducted into the Rock & Roll Hall of Fame. I don't know, it just seemed so coincidental—it's not like you hear about rheumatic fever every day, and the fact that the news story talked about how he had overcome so much, including his health, to become a world-famous singer, all before the age of thirty-seven when he died, made me think about my Charlotte and how much she has had to overcome in her short life thus far in order to get where she is."

"Wow."

"Yep."

He nodded for a minute or so, then brought it around again to "Okay, so you haven't told Adam yet, eh? Why not?"

"I'm not sure, to be honest. You're still the only one who knows. I can't bring myself to tell anyone else. It's almost like admitting I've been abducted by aliens or that I've got a sixth toe on my left foot. Who wants to open yourself up to that kind of ridicule? Not that Adam would ever ridicule me—it's more the potential picture of confusion that would be plastered on his face. I'm not sure how I would react to that. I mean, it's such an abstract thing to articulate, let alone have someone accept and understand."

"Well, okay, so maybe you don't tell him. There's nothing that says you have to, right?"

"Only that I keep saying I want my life to be real. How can I say that and not talk about this most intimate and integral part of me? I don't want to be a hypocrite."

"So, maybe take out an ad? Post a billboard?" He grinned.

I smiled. "Funny. Okay, so I didn't say that. I'm just not sure what to do..."

His blue eyes crinkled in his calm, accepting way as he shared, "Listen, every relationship unfolds differently. We're not on a timeline where all must be revealed the instant we meet someone. In fact, even God tends to reveal Himself to us slowly, often building trust, knowledge, and understanding over many years. I often feel myself a novice when it comes to truly knowing Him, despite my daily endeavors to do just that. And I think our human relationships are much the same—they must be peeled back slowly, like the layers of an onion."

I nodded. "True. I guess if I hold this one thing close to the vest, it doesn't necessarily mean I'm a hypocrite...it may only mean I'm not ready to share it yet."

"Right. Now, if you were holding something back that might harm Adam or you or your relationship, I would advise you to be open and honest about it sooner rather than later, but I don't see this as the case. I feel like this is something that can come later, and maybe even as part of your own continued discovery of the origin and impetus behind it, for which I presume nothing has changed?"

I sighed again. "Yeah, I'm still always trying to figure it out."

"No answers yet?"

"Nope. I mean, I think I know the what and a little bit of the why now, but not the how or where from."

"Maybe God is providing you with your own onion with many layers left to be revealed."

I nodded and said, "I suppose."

After that, we talked for a few minutes about my graduation and future plans and Dad's current construction projects and other miscellaneous topics until I took my leave.

As I drove away, I rolled down the windows and let the hot air hit my face, thinking about what he said. My Biblio was like an onion! It revealed something new to me every day. And yet, before a few weeks ago, it had provided no real answers. Sure, it intrigued me every time, wondering about the meaning and purpose behind it. Such a strange, nebulous, inexplicable thing! But never with anything concrete to tie it to. Then, whack, like a sledgehammer on my head, it was shown in a new light—with my writing leading it, not the other way around, and with my thoughts, words, and feelings generating it. With my heart and my head planting a bulb in the ground to see what would grow there—to see if an onion, in all of its glorious layers, would be revealed.

Chapter XXVII

A FEW MINUTES LATER, I pulled into Adam's driveway and knocked on the door. He opened it and greeted me with a kiss. His kisses never got old, and I sunk into his arms with a smile.

"How's it goin'?" he asked.

"Good. Better now."

He let go of me and said, "Come upstairs with me. I need your help packing."

"I can't believe you're leaving me for two weeks," I pouted as he took my hand and led me to his bedroom.

"I know—it's going to suck being apart from you for that long," he said, lifting my hand to his lips. "But it's now or never. With my clinicals starting in a few weeks, this is the last chance I'll get to do a trip like this."

I sat down on his bed as he pulled his suitcase out of the closet and started opening drawers and placing items in it.

"Yeah, it'll be good for you and Jeremy. Do you think your dad's freaking out?"

"Hard to say. Probably not as much as we are, and certainly not as much as Mom is," he said with consternation. "She's still on the fence about us going at all. Keeps making excuses about it being such a long drive and what if the car breaks down or we run out of gas in the middle of nowhere. And she keeps saying we don't know what we're getting ourselves into."

"Why would she say that?"

He stopped in the middle of tossing a T-shirt in his suitcase and said with a frown, "Honestly, I don't know. I think she's happy for us to see him again, but then I can't tell if she's worried we'll get our hearts broken or if it's just her own resentment built up...after all, he did leave her, and us, without any real explanation, and he hasn't exactly been in touch over the years."

"Yeah, I get that. Aren't you worried about that too?"

"Of course. I think that's why we *have* to go. Lately, Jeremy's been filled with rage. Always in a bad mood. He's smoking too much dope and getting in fights. I'm worried he'll end up in jail. He doesn't seem to have any direction in his life. He's twenty-six years old, working at Pizza Shack, and kind of stuck in a rut. I keep wondering if his angst about Dad is causing him to make the wrong decisions. It's not like we had a great role model to help guide us. Half the time the only reason I feel like I'm able to stick to the straight and narrow is because of Dr. Gerard. He's been such a great mentor and has kept me focused on the animals and my dream of becoming a vet. Without his help, I don't think I would have known what steps to take or even where to begin. I have to remember that Jeremy didn't have that. He's always loved music, but there was no one there to say, hey, here's how to make a career out of it. I mean, sure, back in the day, I used Pizza Shack as a way to make money since I didn't make anything volunteering at the animal clinic, but that was different. Jeremy's job at Pizza Shack is kind of a dead end and isn't at all what he wants to be doing with his life, as far as I can tell. I feel like he's kind of given up. He doesn't have that ambition moving him toward something new. And he doesn't see a way out of this town or a way forward to make a different life for himself."

"So, what do you think he'll do when you get to your dad's?"

Adam scoffed a little and said, "Hopefully not punch him in the face."

"Well, could you blame him?" I said sarcastically but with some truth, which Adam didn't miss.

He gave a sideways smirk and said, "No, not really. Heck, it's not like I can justify my dad's actions—I don't understand them myself." He continued his packing with a thoughtful look on his face and added, "I can't figure out how someone can be living a perfectly happy life, or at least that's what it seemed like to me, with a great wife and kids and house and friends and family, and poof! Gone. Just like that! *Who does that?* It's really messed up. And then not even call us or try to keep any kind of relationship with us, his own kids? It doesn't make any sense to me. It actually pisses me off when I think about it too much, which I try not to. You should have heard his voice when we called him. It wasn't like, wow, great to hear from you, I've missed you, I would love to see you. No, it was like complete shock and confusion, trying to figure out how to not be rude while also being uninviting."

"Yikes."

"Yeah. I know. I have no idea what we'll find when we get there. Believe me, I'm already thinking, am I really giving up two weeks at the clinic for this? Dr. Gerard was nice enough to give me the time off because he gets that this is important, but I just keep second-guessing the whole thing."

He finished filling his suitcase and came and sat on the bed with me.

I put my hand on his knee and said, "Well, I'm proud of you. Both of you. It won't be easy, but hopefully you'll look back and be glad you did it. If nothing else, maybe you'll get some answers."

He lay back on the bed, staring up at the ceiling, and said, "I hope so."

Waiting a few minutes, I decided to shift gears, leaning back beside him, I asked with what little bit of coy I possessed, "Speaking of Jeremy…where is he?"

Adam's face changed as he grinned at me with a raised eyebrow and said, "Working."

"And your mom?"

"Out with a friend."

"Hmmm, what shall we do with ourselves?"

He put his arm around me and pulled me into a kiss. He murmured softly into my neck, "So many options, so little time…"

For these past several months, he had been so careful with me, maybe recognizing we were teetering on the brink of something important, life-changing, and long-term. I could tell he was holding himself back from the physical aspect of our relationship, choosing instead to focus on building trust, friendship, and openness between us. And I had to admit it was one of the many reasons I felt so safe with him. But then, after those first kisses in the sunken garden, there had been a few times, when he dropped me off after a date or when we were alone out by the lake or at the park or on a walk, he had let the tightly controlled mask down, and there, bursting forth out of his eyes, was the unmistakable flame of desire. It was always squelched a second later as he would draw away from me, suddenly tense and distant. I wouldn't know how to react, so I would follow his lead, choosing to stop and quickly change course, redirecting his attention (and mine) with some sort of small talk or short goodbye. Afterward, I always wondered what he was waiting for and why he was holding off. Was it me? After all, what did I know? I had only been kissed a few other times in my life and by guys I didn't care about. Otherwise, I was completely inexperienced. Yet I knew he had dated before, so surely he knew what he was doing. Why didn't he ever try anything more with me? Was he being protective, or was he worried about that aspect of our relationship not being what he'd expected, hoped, and yearned for? And maybe I made it worse by not talking about it or not being more assertive with my own desires. I felt so confused about how to proceed. His kisses always sent me to the moon, and I certainly wanted more of them, but I didn't want to ruin anything by bringing the wrong tone and action to our time together.

As my mind was racing with these thoughts, he repositioned us so our heads were on the pillow and we were facing each other. We kissed and he placed his hand on my hip. After a few minutes, he stopped and stared into my eyes with that intense, watchful heat of his.

I said cautiously, "Can I ask you a question?"

He pulled away with a surprised smile. "Of course."

I murmured, my cheeks suddenly on fire, "Why don't you ever...try anything?"

His face was confused. "Try anything?"

I wanted to crawl in a hole, but I bucked up and said with big eyes, "You know...try anything...else with me? Do you not like me in *that* way?"

Oh, the recognition that flashed across his face! A red light that had just turned green. The biggest grin. Then tempered, very difficult, slow restraint. "Riley, you silly girl, I like you in *every* way. And it has taken every ounce of strength and focus to keep from ravaging you every time I see you." At this, he laughed, and I felt a huge wave of relief wash over me. He put his hand on my cheek and slowly let his fingers trace down my neck and along my collarbone, landing softly on my shoulder. I felt a chill that was followed closely by a warmth that spread down my spine and into my core. He said, "But I've tried to go slow on purpose. To let you catch up, to let *us* catch up, to whatever speed makes sense. I don't want anything to feel rushed, especially not that. I want to savor every moment of discovery between us. And I don't want to make mistakes."

He took a few strands of my hair and brushed them off my shoulder. I watched his eyes shift from mine to the skin he was grazing on my upper arm and then back again. There was that lick of desire behind the cloak of his restraint. My sudden intake of breath caused his eyes to flicker to my mouth and stay there, staring with something close to an animal's mesmerized gaze.

I was starting to melt under his touch and the heat of his watchful eye as I asked weakly, "Mistakes?"

Not looking away from my mouth, he answered absently but still somehow in possession of his words, "I know a little something about when things aren't quite right. I've been…a fool…in the past. And I can't let that happen here. I *won't* let that happen. For you. For me. I don't want either of us to doubt or worry or question in any way. I want us to both feel safe and sure."

I smiled and said, "Okay. I do." I began concentrating my attention on his waist, where I had my hand, slowly tracing back and forth along his side, lifting his T-shirt so I could feel the skin there. I continued thoughtfully, "But I *am* worried about one thing."

He was distracted, but his eyes swiftly came back to mine. "You are? About what?"

"My lack of experience. I don't know what I'm doing. Will you…will you teach me?" I flashed him a demure smile, which caused whatever tenuous remains of a wall between us to come crashing down. His mouth was on mine in an instant, and it was as if we were back in that closet again where we couldn't get enough of each other. He pulled me to him so there wasn't an ounce of space between us. I felt the full length of him molded into my frame. His hand reached underneath my T-shirt and up my back so that the exposed skin of our midsections was touching, and I wanted nothing more than to feel the rest of his nakedness against me.

Our mouths united under the overwhelming force of our passion. Suddenly with a jolt, I felt the sun was blotted out for a second when he pulled away with a groan and said, "Hang on." He jumped off the bed, standing before me, his clothes disheveled, breathing hard. "Just hang on. One second." I let him catch his breath and waited. When he didn't say anything, I reached for his hand, confused. His jaw set, he stepped away from me, my hand finding air instead.

"Adam!" I cried, wondering what was going on. "Are you teasing me?!"

"Riley," he said, rolling his eyes. "No! Not that. But before we go further, I need to know you're okay…with this. And I need to know something else."

"What?" All I could think was, what could possibly be *that* important?

Instead of answering me, he went over to the window and pulled down the shade. Then he closed his bedroom door and grabbed something small out of his dresser drawer, setting it on his nightstand. I didn't look because I thought I knew what it was, and despite my eager anticipation, it sent a twinge of fear down my spine. In the semi-dark room, he came back, sitting beside me on the bed and taking my hand.

His heart in his eyes, he said softly, "Riley, I want you to know that I love you."

"You do?" I whispered, suddenly taking in the seriousness of him and marveling at that willpower he mentioned earlier. I knew he was just as hot and bothered as I was, and yet he (the guy, no less!) was pausing to talk about his feelings.

He leaned forward and kissed me lightly on the lips. "Yes, I do. I love those lips and your curiously changeable eyes and your wild and unruly red hair. And I love it when you're quiet and concentrating on your reading as if the world didn't exist outside of those words. And when you're being kind and thoughtful, making me talk about myself and my life. And when we go to the record store and talk for hours about music. And the day you told me your favorite food was chocolate-covered pretzels, as if that was some kind of staple of the American diet." We both laughed. He paused and added quietly, "And I love that you don't have everything figured out. That you're still trying to understand this crazy, mixed-up world we live in and your place in it. And I love that you have a heart for forgiveness and understanding, maybe because you *don't* have all the answers, maybe because you're willing to walk a mile in someone else's shoes, maybe because of your compassion and caring and honesty. You are simply *so brave*, Riley."

I sat in stunned silence, tears pricking my eyes. I had a flash memory of the words I wrote in my diary all those years ago about "matter" and what did *I* matter to this world, and here was a gorgeous, considerate, sweet hunk of a man telling me I mattered to him and that he loved me not despite my confused, muddled stab at life but *because* of it. This was someone who took me exactly as I was and still loved me! And I realized with even more unexpected insight that it wasn't just him—I knew now that *I* mattered to *me*! I had been drifting through life for so many years, a stranger to self-reflection, and now that I had turned inward, no longer running away, I found myself liking the person I saw in the mirror. My escapist life (into books, into surface-level activities, even at times into my Biblio) had been replaced by deeper relationships and a more intimate understanding of my place in this world (with my writing, my visit to Kathy's grave, my chat with Father Avery, my time with Adam, my potential future endeavors). And I could only hope it would develop and grow even more over time.

In the ensuing quiet, he watched my reaction carefully, his dark eyes glowing in a strange, fixed way against the low light peeking out from the sides of the shade.

Finally, I said with the warmth of a thousand suns, "Adam, I love you too. How could I not? You're the best kind of person—kind, thoughtful, warm, smart, sexy…"

We kissed and he said with a wicked grin, two inches from my face, "Okay, now that we got that out of the way, are you ready?"

I laughed and said, "Gosh, you make it sound like we're about to plunge down a ten-story roller coaster."

"Somewhat…similar," he replied with a laugh.

Thinking back to the condom he placed on the dresser, I felt stupid but had to ask anyway, "Will it hurt?"

"Not if I'm doing my job," he said, placing his hand on my exposed flat stomach, spreading a shot of heat into my lower depths.

"Oh, it's a job, is it?" I prompted playfully.

"Put it this way," he answered with a grin, "I'm going to keep practicing until I get it right. How does that sound?"

My only answer was to reach for him. His mouth found mine in a rush of passion, and his hands explored my body in ways I never thought possible, sending an overwhelming sense of anticipation and longing pulsing through my core as I clutched and cradled his head and body to me. Our fascination with each other was fostered further by Adam's expert ministrations and by his openness to instruction, for me, for him, and when we at last launched into our exploding bliss, I was struck with wondrous awe at the physical manifestation of our love, now coupled with our spiritual and emotional link, and together forming a new kind of perfect destiny. In the end, both sated and smiling, we lay back and envisioned years stretching out before us in an endless expanse of joyful unions, shared among equals, our love the antidote to our painful past, our connection forged as a loving bonded alchemy.

PART IV – 1992

❧ Chapter XXVIII ❧

What do you do when you are full to bursting? Oh, I'm not talking about food—I'm talking about life. Something had shifted in me, and now I was harnessing life and riding it like a trusted and true stallion. Did it mean I had everything worked out? Heck, no. But the days of me waking up with a dark cloud over my head and those wretched insidious thoughts that would seep into my psyche and pull me down in the mire were now tempered and in their rightful place as I allowed myself to feel the pain of my past and made peace with it. I wanted my life to be real, and it *was*. Gone were the days of hiding behind the superficial, the secrets, the self-doubt, the questioning, the wondering about my purpose and reason for being. These fundamentals from my past were still there, within me, but now they were integrated into a more complete, emotionally accessible, complex version of myself. I was working with a new rule book that let each day unfold new and clean and pure, an unblemished space just as it was, just as I was, just as I *am*.

This didn't happen overnight, and as I accepted myself as an ongoing work in progress, I allowed the light in, reflecting that whatever was meant to be would be, which may even include a stroke of unadulterated (and yes, unexpected, but still real) happiness. It was like that scene from the movie *White Christmas* where Rosemary Clooney encourages people to go to sleep counting their blessing—I did this now, daily!

And on *this* day especially. It was two years after Adam and I took that first trip down lovers' lane in his tiny bedroom in the heat of a summer afternoon. Today, standing in my own bedroom, glancing out the window, I noticed that the spring flowers were beginning to wane and be replaced by more permanent perennial blooms, arching their bright faces toward the tulip poplar tree blossoms as they fell, accepting the offerings like tossed candy at a parade, and I smiled with anticipated glee. I inspected my kelly-green dress and bejeweled sandals with a satisfied grin, as I knew Adam would love the ensemble and would probably note how well it went with my eyes. I heard a car horn, so I grabbed my purse and rushed downstairs, hollering goodbye to Mom and Dad, who were sitting at the dining room table eating breakfast. How much had changed! To think, just a few short years ago that table had been full of four raucous and ravenous teenagers fighting over the last strip of bacon, and now Mom and Dad were sitting there alone, a shared newspaper lying between them in the quiet morning sunshine. They were nearly empty nesters and perfectly silent and content with this status upgrade.

My brothers were all on their own now. Brent finally saved up enough money working at Pluto and living in our basement to afford a small house down the road, where he lived with his girlfriend, Stephanie. For years, he had dated that unpleasant Maureen, whom we all found mean and controlling, but eventually he saw the light and dumped her, thus opening the door for Stephanie, who was an angel in comparison. Marc was happily married and living in Indianapolis, and his wife was expecting their first child, about which Mom was over the moon and used as an excuse to buy a plethora of baby-related clothing, toys, and accessories. Last week, I heard Dad ask when he would be getting his den back because it now looked as though a cotton-candy grenade had exploded in there. Brother Nate was still teaching math at the high school, living in an apartment, and had just begun dating the new school nurse, a shy, petite brunette who had recently moved here from Ohio. In all these years, none of us had known Nate to go on a single date, and at the age of twenty-five we had given up hope that he ever would, and here he was finally getting his head out of the Dungeons and Dragons world and dating a real live human female. Mom and Dad were so worried about jinxing it that they barely breathed a word, and when she came to the house for the first time, they did everything short of cutting her steak for her so as not to scare her off.

And here I was, about to begin the next phase of my life, getting into a car with Adam's mom and brother for the three-hour drive to Adam's commencement ceremony at Purdue, where he would finally be declared a doctor of veterinary medicine. All the hard work, studying, clinicals, labs, and two years spent apart from each other had finally paid off, and he would start his career in a week, shadowing Dr. Gerard for the summer as head vet at the Orange County Animal Clinic, with a full transition to replacing Dr. Gerard on October first. More than anything (I hadn't seen him in two months), I was aching to hold him, knowing he was finally packing up and coming home to me. Now we would be together in the same location for the first time since we started dating. I couldn't contain my anticipation and excitement over our long-awaited reunion. I wasn't quite done with my master of library science at IU, so it would be tough during weekdays while I still commuted back and forth two hours a day for another semester, but after that we would be free and clear. And to be able to see him and spend time with him every weekend would be a luxury compared to our brief visits and drawn-out phone calls.

I exchanged pleasantries with Adam's mom and Jeremy. They were just as excited as I was for Adam and his accomplishment—eight years is a long time to be in college! Mrs. Linder told me I looked very pretty, which made me smile. She was so nice. Jeremy said hi, and I noticed a marked change in him since the last time I saw him, which was over a year ago. His hair was long now but tied back, and his tattoos were just peeking out from under his black T-shirt. But it wasn't his appearance that had changed—it was the calm, thoughtful way in which he asked me about my family and my degree. He seemed more mature and less angry, somehow more self-assured, more comfortable in his own skin.

I asked him, "When'd you get in?"

"Late last night, around midnight. It was a long drive, but I made it."

Adam's mom jumped in, saying to Jeremy, "It's so good to have you home for a few weeks. I know Adam appreciates it."

"Yeah, I think his exact words to me were, 'If you don't get your butt home for my graduation, I'm going to take a golf club to your drum set.'"

Mrs. Linder laughed. "He certainly knows how to motivate you, doesn't he?"

"Threat. Motivate. You pick. But anyway, here I am. And actually, he's got a point—one of my goals is to clean out that basement while I'm here—get all of the instruments, and anything else, packed into my truck before I head back."

"Sounds good to me. While you're at it, can you clean out your bedroom? I've left it like a shrine, not a single thing moved, but now that you're a grown man, I can't see you wanting to wake up to a choo-choo train lamp like you used to."

She winked and he grinned back. "Hey, don't mock the choo-choo train lamp—it's a classic. As is the choo-choo train border hung over the chair rail."

"Well, I'm glad you like it because you're going to help me remove it while you're home—you can frame a commemorative strip of it for posterity. I'm planning to make your bedroom into an office, so everything's got to go."

"What? Dang!" he scoffed. "Where will I sleep when I come visit next year?"

"There's always the pull-out couch in the living room. Or maybe Adam's room can be a rotating shared bedroom. Come to think of it, Adam hasn't explained exactly what his long-term living situation is going to be." She looked in the rearview mirror and asked me, "Do you know, Riley?"

I shrugged. It was funny because we had both been so busy lately and so excited to finally be living within a few miles of each other that we hadn't pondered anything beyond that. "Not sure. I mean, I think he intends to stay with you for a while at least."

She nodded and asked, "You're still at your parents' house?"

"Yes, for now."

"And when are you done with your schooling?"

"Hopefully December."

She nodded. After a few minutes of silence, she asked Jeremy, "And how is the band?"

"Good. Although they're not too happy with me for ditching them for two weeks. We had a gig set up every night."

"Wow, it's great that you guys are really in demand now. So, what does it mean with you not there—did they have to cancel?"

"Naw, it just means Paul will have to sing and Reggie will back him up. They'll be okay." He added with a smirk, "Of course they won't sound as good or have as many groupies."

He winked back at me in the back seat and I smiled. He said, "You and Adam should really come visit sometime. Austin is such a cool town—you would not believe the amazing music scene there. And the food—Texas barbeque and Tex-Mex everything—so good. Plus, everyone is very chill. It's not just cowboys, ranchers, and oil in Texas—there's also this up-and-coming cultural thing going on. I can't do it justice with my descriptions. You two just need to come and stay a while."

"I'd love that," I said readily. "Maybe next spring."

Mrs. Linder put her hand on his knee, smiled, and said, "I'm glad you're doing so well."

I asked, "You planning to hang out with Wayne and Slipkey and the old gang while you're home?"

"Sure thing. Tomorrow night at the Shack. Didn't Adam mention it?"

"No, but we haven't talked in a couple of days."

"Well, I think we're going out to the lake afterward—you're welcome to come."

"Sounds good."

We were quiet for a while after that, all lost in our own thoughts, when Mrs. Linder broke the silence with, "So...how is...how is your father doing?" She glanced at Jeremy with a begrudging look, as though she didn't want to have to ask but couldn't stop herself.

"Fine, I think."

"You think? You don't know?"

"Well, I mean, I went out with him and Darrin last Friday night before I left to come here, and they were both doing fine."

"Hmm," was her only response.

Nothing more was said after that. Both of them looked away out the window.

My thoughts turned to a memorable phone call two summers earlier when Adam and Jeremy traveled to their dad's place for the first time and I heard Adam's breathless voice on the other end of the line, "Riley, holy—I'm—like—I'm not sure—stunned."

"What? What's going on? Everything alright? Where are you?"

"We're here. We made it. We arrived about five last night. I got up early this morning to find this pay phone and call you. I don't even know where the heck I am. And oh man, Riley, I don't know where to begin!" I heard his voice rise over the sound of car traffic in the background.

"What is it? Is something wrong with Jeremy? Your Dad?"

"Yes...well, no, not exactly. I—I still—can't believe it," he stuttered.

"What? Would you just spit it out! You're starting to frighten me."

"Riley...my dad...he's...well, he's *gay*."

"He's *gay*?!" I exclaimed.

"Yes."

"Whoa!"

"Yeah, exactly."

"How do you know?" I asked.

"Well, because when we got there, he gave us each a big hug and told us how happy he was to see us, and then *he introduced us to his partner, Darrin.* Darrin and him, they...they live together. I mean, really *live* together. As in one big master bedroom suite and matching blue monogrammed towels in the bathroom and two Adirondack chairs out on the back porch, and they—they cooked for us last night, *together*, buzzing around the kitchen in sync, like it was all second nature and part of their nightly routine. I don't know... it's not like they sat us down and explained it or anything, but it was just completely obvious."

"Holy crap, wow...," I said, still processing.

"Yeah."

"So, what do you think? What did Jeremy say?"

"That was the strangest part. After dinner, we were all sitting outside with our drinks, and Jeremy got up, excused himself, and went to the bedroom, and by the time I came in an hour or so later, he was asleep. Then, when I got up this morning, he was gone."

"Huh? Gone where?"

"I don't know...I mean, he couldn't have gone far because he left the car in the driveway. But Dad's place, it's on a bunch of acres of land and kind of down a long dirt road, out in the middle of nowhere, super rural. Jeremy must be out walking. Hopefully not jumping down a well or anything. I'll go back in a few minutes and find him."

"So...did your dad say anything? About *anything*?"

I heard a big sigh over the phone, and he put a few more quarters in before saying, "Yeah, after Jeremy went to bed, Darrin got up discreetly, saying he was going inside to wash the dishes, and Dad looked over at me and began talking. He said he was so sorry and how he hated having to leave us boys and that it was biggest regret of his life and that if he had it to do all over again, he would have done it differently, but that one thing he'd learned in his life was that you can't change the past and that he was going to try to make it up to us starting right now."

"Wow, that was a lot!"

"Yeah. I was kind of glad he copped to everything right away. But then I wished Jeremy had been there because I think with both of us sitting there absorbing this news together, it would have defused the bomb a little. I have no idea how things will go down today. Anyway, then Dad kept going, saying that the reason he left the way he did was partly because he was still so confused about the feelings he was having at the time, but that he knew no matter what, he couldn't be married to our mom anymore because that wasn't fair to her or to him. Apparently, he had met Darrin at a work conference, but they both were married at the time, so they had to come to terms with the pain and hurt they would be causing their respective families before moving forward. He said they decided to make a clean break. Of course, in retrospect, he said this was probably the worst move for both them and their families. I asked him if Darrin talked to his family now, and he said yes, he had reconciled with his twin daughters a few years ago, but that he still didn't talk to his parents or his ex."

"I know I keep saying it, but wow!"

"Yeah. Right. Hey, listen, I have to go because I'm almost out of quarters, and I want to drive around and see if I can find Jeremy, but I'll call you later, okay?"

"Okay, sure. Love you, sweetie. I hope it all works out...and that you get more answers."

"Me too. Love you."

As I watched the flat farm fields rolling by on the way to Purdue, I looked at the back of Mrs. Linder's head and marveled at how brave she was. She raised those boys on her own and did a good job too, and then to hear years later the reason for her ex's abandonment...it must have been a shock, not to mention a betrayal. I couldn't imagine how that must feel. I wondered when Mrs. Linder found out. Had she always suspected it, or was she completely blindsided? To know it was the result of an affair, and then to find out the person you thought you knew was somehow entirely different must have been heart-wrenching. Yet I also understood that Adam's dad, just like me, needed his life to be real, and I marveled at his bravery in being his authentic self, despite the unknown consequences.

Adam said he asked his mother once about it, but she didn't want to talk about it and that it was better as water under the bridge. Adam never found out the full story about Jeremy either. They drove there together two years ago and spent hours getting to know their father and his partner, and at the end of the trip, Jeremy simply said he was going to stay, so Adam drove back to Indiana by himself. Adam thinks Jeremy finally came to terms with their dad's decisions and eventually realized how much he had in common with him—they looked alike and were both obsessed with music and had crazy chops when it came to playing guitar and drums and every other rock instrument. Ultimately, it was their dad who hooked Jeremy up with his band members, a local Austin group that needed a new singer and guitarist. Jeremy came along right at the perfect time.

As for Adam, the relationship with his dad was different, more considerate and less intimate. They had their time together in Texas, where Adam said his dad was an open book, answering his questions and also encouraging Adam to speak about himself, which he appreciated. Since then, they had spoken on the phone every month or so, but Adam, who was more like his mom in looks and sentiments, was often left feeling a sort of cautious distance between them. He said they were perfectly civil with each other and he didn't harbor any bad feelings toward his dad, but he also didn't have a close relationship with him and didn't think he ever would. Too much time and distance had gone by.

Thinking about my own great relationship with my dad, this made me sad for Adam. But I knew that at least he had an amazing mentor in Dr. Gerard, who had served as a father figure to him through the years. It was crazy to think that in a week, Adam would be taking over his practice. Of course, there was going to be a transition period over the summer so Dr. Gerard could make sure Adam was able to stand on his own two feet before he officially retired. It would be a busy summer, but at least it meant Adam would be home. I smiled as I thought about it—Adam was coming home!

❦ Chapter XXIX ❦

We drove by a horse farm, and I thought about my last diary entry:

Wednesday, May 6, 1992

I'm sorry I've been so neglectful lately. I never seem to find time to write in you anymore, what with all of my other writing and schoolwork. But today, I'm going to fill you in and catch you up.

Can you believe it's been two years since Adam and I started dating? Seems like a lifetime ago, and also somehow like the blink of an eye. Time is funny like that. All I know is that I can't wait to look at his face and hold his hand and feel his arms around me and his lips on mine. Those few brief moments we've had alone together—snatches of stolen kisses here and there, and speedy built-up lovemaking in his apartment when his roommate left for an hour or two to give us privacy—were few and far between, and only just barely filled the void left in the interim. It was enough to drive us both mad. Thank goodness we were too busy with the daily grind to have time to dwell on it too much.

My drive back and forth to Bloomington during the week and working thirty-plus hours at the Melton at night and on weekends, not to mention writing every morning, has been insane, but after my summer classes are over, I only have two classes left in the fall, so that's a relief and then I'll finally have my MLS. And I must admit, as difficult as it's been, nothing can hold a candle to the countless euphoric hours I've spent in IU's Lilly Library, surrounded by (and even sometimes getting my hands on!) the rare jewels contained there. I mean, who else can say they've held the original handwritten poetry of Sylvia Plath and felt every last breath of her intensity, authenticity, and intrigue coursing from the pages into their fingertips and landing directly like a piercing arrow into their soul? I wouldn't trade it for anything!

Granted, there were days when my Biblio felt as though it would swallow me whole. Between steeping myself in the research and cataloging methodology of voluminous words and pages and bindings, and writing for hours every morning, there were days when my Biblio was triggered on an almost hourly basis. My senses overloaded, I wondered if this was what it felt like when a medium went to visit a cemetery. How did they handle it? All those voices, feelings, sensations inundating, pestering, prodding to be noticed, recognized, acknowledged, understood. For me, I found it exhausting at times. In addition to my Biblios, many of my other sensory gifts that had been mostly dormant in recent years began to reappear. It was like my spirit was more "open" to *the other* and (much to my surprise) to people who also had the ability to see or connect with *the other*. For example, this woman (Lucy) in my children's literature class, whom I had only spoken to a handful of times before this, leaned over one day before class to ask me if I was writing a book. I nearly choked! Keep in mind, I had only told Adam and Father Avery about my writing. Well, my face must have given it away that she had guessed correctly, so I didn't deny it. I asked her how she knew, and she said she had a dream about it and that in the dream, she was supposed to offer her services to me in any way she could with the book. I swear, I had to lift my jaw off the floor! We began to talk after that, and now I consider her one of my closest friends and biggest champions.

By the way, speaking of assistance, you know what I've learned over these past two years? Writing can't be done in a vacuum. In fact, it requires a whole community of helpers. It started with Adam listening to me read my early chapters. Even though he wasn't a reader, he gave me a lot of great advice on dialogue that didn't ring true and sentences that seemed out of place. Then that shot of adrenaline from Lucy was just what I needed at the time, when I was hitting a critical juncture in the story structure and wasn't sure which way to turn. An avid reader herself, she knew exactly how to instruct me on how to flesh out my characters more and to direct the story line toward a more realistic turn. She was helpful without being pushy, and her delivery was kind and constructive. Being a new writer and overly sensitive to criticism, I couldn't have asked for a better guide (especially when her advice was direct and accurate but always couched in a softly cushioned pillow). And we talked a lot about the fact that there was some "supernatural" connection between us, like we were meant to meet each other when we did. She "felt" things and connections just like I did, and after a few months of being with her and trusting her, I told her about my Biblio. She was amazed and thought it was the reason she was placed in my life the way she was—to help with my purpose-driven Biblio.

The other part of the "community" came just a few months ago, after I finished my draft. I started by asking Mrs. Litchy to read it (much to her astonishment that

I had been writing and had finished an entire book without her knowing!). Then Father Avery (he was so excited!). Then my collection development professor, who not only read it and provided great feedback, but also loaned me her word processor so I could type it up and print it. Finally, I called Jane (as you know, married and living in Chicago now) to see if I could mail her a copy. Her squeal over the phone was deafening, but I appreciated the enthusiasm. In the meantime, I began reading every "how to publish" book in the library and began crafting the perfect knockout (or so I hoped) query letter to send out to agents when the manuscript was ready. Anyway, these next few weeks are crazy busy with the end of the semester, Adam's graduation, and work at the Melton, plus I'm waiting for my three alpha readers to finish their copies and let me know their thoughts, so I'm thinking I won't get the final version out until this fall. We'll see.

In the meantime, though, Lucy gave me a great suggestion to reduce my Biblio stress (she said she does this to clear her mind when she gets too many "messages" or "connections" flowing in). She suggested I get out in nature, commune with the outdoors and the elements of God's green earth that are physical, tangible, recognizable as beautiful and fortifying in and of themselves, with no additional adornment needed. Sure enough, she was right! Something about a quiet walk in the woods, a quick jog through the park, watching the birds through binoculars out by the lake. I wasn't sure why, but this turned down the volume and allowed my overwhelmed circuitry to reset. It was such a great trick! The other thing I do sometimes now, especially if I can't sleep, is to hum. Yes, you heard me. I hum. I read this book by an Indian author, and there was a mention of meditation and how the quintessential "ohmm" can clear your head and create focus, calm, and clarity. So, whenever my mind is racing or full, I make myself hum. If I concentrate on the humming, it eventually pushes everything else out, and I can rest, reset, and rejuvenate.

And finally—the other part of my "community" is Kathy. I've started visiting her grave more regularly, often as part of my nature walks. To talk to her, to hum to her, to tell her my hopes and dreams. I feel like she hears me. I also feel like she's up there cheering me on with my writing, every day. I *feel* her. Last week when I went to visit her, I confessed how sorry I was that I didn't cry for her back then and, oddly enough, how I had trouble *not* crying lately—about my book and about her, about just about anything (even a sentimental commercial on TV sets me off!). I told her that when I was twelve (and all those years after), it wasn't that I didn't miss her or that I didn't wish the accident hadn't happened. Or that my staying here aboveground made any sense to me whatsoever while she was gone, but regardless, I couldn't process it, I couldn't allow myself to absorb it back then. It was as though my soul was too crushed by the weight of it, and one last stone placed on top of it would sink me forever. I asked her forgiveness.

I brought the latest book I was reading: Cormac McCarthy's *All the Pretty Horses*. I read this to her:

> "If there is a pattern there it will not shape itself to anything these eyes can recognize. Because the question for me was always whether that shape we see in our lives was there from the beginning or whether these random events are only called a pattern after the fact. Because otherwise we are nothing. Do you believe in fate? Yes mam. I guess I do. My father had a great sense of the connectedness of things. I'm not sure I share it. He claimed that the responsibility for a decision could never be abandoned to a blind agency but could only be relegated to human decision more and more remote from the consequences."

I said to Kathy, "This gives me comfort. To know that not only did Charlotte Brontë realize the crazy futility of questioning or trying to define presentiments 145 years ago, but Cormac McCarthy in 1992 is essentially saying the same thing. The connectedness of things, the relation of random acts, the ties that bind in a pattern, the known quantity of relationships unknown prior to discovery are all the makings of fate and a calling of sorts, aren't they? And I'm just going to say it, Kathy: I thank you. With all my heart because I know you had a hand in bringing me Adam and my Biblio (in all of its miscellaneous forms). I know this was your way to save me. To feed my soul and my mind and my heart. To bring me purpose. To bring me love (which I didn't know was possible or deserved). And because of this truth, my friend, my guardian angel, I thank you. Even when it's confusing, even when I don't understand it, even when it hurts. I'm still grateful. And will be. Forever. Or until I see you again."

CHAPTER XXX

It was a hot July evening, and Adam was nervous. He felt the sweat building up under his collar and dripping down his back, and he had no way to stop it or to even consider it, as his brain was swimming with anxiety and anticipation over the magnificent feat in which he was about to partake.

He was walking with Riley down the Avenue leading to the old West Baden Hotel. Portions of the neglected landmark had collapsed from ice over the winter, and now the big news in town was that some organization called Indiana Landmarks was pouring money into the structure to keep it from falling to the ground and disappearing. The poor old building and grounds had fallen into disrepair and were tangled up in litigation for years, but there was a seed of hope that they could return to their former glory and someday come back to life as the "Eighth Wonder of the World."

But these things were not top of mind for Adam either. Instead, as he carried a grocery sack filled with picnic food, two fold-up chairs, and his heart on his sleeve, and Riley carried a tiny fold-up table, he concentrated (to the best of his ability under the circumstances) on Riley's innocuous chatter about her day at the library and how her friend Jane, who was in town, planned an outing for them, a "book shopping" trip to Louisville.

Adam answered "Uh-huh, that's nice," and other platitudes at the proper times, but when they arrived at the sunken garden where they had first kissed two years ago, his mind left him completely. He didn't realize he had stopped all intelligent conversation until the food was set up on the table and they were seated in their chairs eating the cheese, crackers, and grapes, and drinking a bottle of wine, and Riley said abruptly, "Hey! Earth to Adam. Come in, Adam. What's *with* you tonight?"

He exhaled his first breath of air in what seemed like the last twenty minutes and turned to her. He stopped and smiled, his heart in his throat, taking a piece of cheese out of her hand and placing it on the table (to which she looked confused and slightly annoyed) and said, "Riley, forgive me. I can't wait any longer. I need to ask you something." He dropped to one knee in front of her, and as her amazing, changeable eyes bugged out of her head and her hand flew to her mouth in surprise, he said with as much gusto and aplomb as he could muster, "Riley Cartwright, I love you. And I want to be with you. You are my best friend. You are my life. Would you do me the honor of being my wife?"

He pulled the ring box out of his shorts pocket and opened it, but instead of the instant answer he was expecting, she sat there in stunned silence, her hand wobbling against her mouth as her face fell.

Not knowing how to react, Adam stayed put, his mouth pulling down into a confused frown. A minute went by. Then two. Finally, almost in a whisper, his voice shaky and strained, he said, "Well?"

Without a word, she knelt down across from him, carefully taking the ring box from his hand and placing it beside the cheese on the table. Turning back to him, she kissed him and pulled him into a brief hug. As she drew away, she said quickly, "Adam, I'm so sorry, you surprised me. I guess I thought you would wait until I was done with school. And I...I didn't expect this tonight. You see, I thought I had more time..."

"More time?" he asked, leaning back on his heels, beginning to get angry as a way to hide the hurt that flashed like a wave of dread through his body. "What do you mean? We've been together for *two years*, Riley, and I thought this was what you wanted. Don't you—what do you—I thought—what do you mean, *more time?*"

She sighed and said, "Here, let's sit back down and I'll explain. Please don't be mad at me. You just caught me off guard, that's all."

He got off the ground and sat back in his chair as she did the same. He waited, crossing his arms, breathing hard, wondering what she could possibly say to justify this strange interlude that he would not have seen coming in a million years. They had always been so connected and in love—there had never been a moment of doubt in his mind about her, even during those harsh (and needed) conversations in the beginning of their relationship and the long months of living apart ever since. What could this possibly be about?

He watched her face—the one he had memorized, in every subtle nuanced inflection and movement, the one he studied in order to feel her beauty and not just to see it. Her eyes shifted to the ground and back to him and then to her hands, clearly wrestling with some form of internal struggle. No matter how he scoured the length and breadth of their interactions over the years, he could not identify or fathom what it could be.

At this point, she picked up her chair and set it in front of him and then took both of his hands in hers. Looking directly at his face with her loving eyes, obviously trying to put him at ease while also hiding something behind a veil that he detected but could not decipher. She said, "Adam. Sweetie. What I meant about more time was not about you and me being together. Nothing like that. I love you and I will always love you. Forever. Period. End of story. Okay?"

"Okay...?" he answered as a question, not understanding.

"But there's something I have to tell you. Before I can agree to marry you. It's something about me. A sort of secret. Something I'm a little afraid to tell you. Something I've wanted to tell you for a long time, but I haven't known how. Truth be told, I'm not sure how you'll react."

"My God, Riley, what is it?" He was starting to freak out.

She stood up abruptly and started pacing back and forth on the grass. Wringing her hands, she asked, "Do you remember once, right when we got together, I asked you if you liked to read books?"

Adam's brow furrowed. Where was she going with this? "Um...yeah... vaguely. I told you I didn't, but then you started writing your story and reading it to me. Riley, is this about your book?"

She exhaled and said, "No, not exactly, but kind of."

"Riley!" he exclaimed, exasperated. "Would you *please* tell me what you're talking about?"

"Okay. So—so—so it started with Father Avery—"

He cut her off, "What?! What is it with that priest anyway? You're not even Catholic!"

She stopped her pacing and regarded him levelly, saying, "I know. He's a *friend*. And he was kind to me when I needed help and there was no one else to turn to. Please...please, I don't mean to be rude, but can you not interrupt? Can you just listen? I want...I *need* to get this off my chest, and it's not going to work if you keep interrupting."

Adam unfolded his hands in an upward, frustrated gesture and nodded without a word.

"Thank you," she said with a tight smile and a curt nod, continued her pacing, looking anywhere but at him. "Actually, it didn't *start* with Father

Avery. He was just the only one I told. It started with the accident. After the accident and Kathy's death, I wasn't…coping well…I mean, at least in my parents' eyes. I wasn't really grieving—I wasn't allowing myself to *feel* anything. I guess I was stuck, and I didn't know it. I was just going about my life as I had before, outside of the fact that I had this big cast on my leg, and I was going to school and doing homework and hanging out at home, the usual. To this day, I'm not exactly sure what was expected of me, but apparently I wasn't displaying whatever emotions I should have, so my mom bought me a diary and sent me to the library and wanted me to…I don't know…*express* myself, get my feelings out, write everything down, and maybe read books to help me deal with the trauma of the accident. Actually, come to think of it, I've never asked her what her exact motives were, but regardless, there I was, the kid who had never read before, let alone written in a diary, stuck in the library for hours every Friday night."

Adam listened patiently, as he had been instructed, still wondering what this had to do with his proposal but also fascinated by the fact that Riley hadn't always been a prolific reader. This was news to him. With how she was now, he figured she must have been born with a book in her hand and had been consuming books like candy ever since.

"Anyway, I noticed from that first Friday night that something weird happened every time I went to the library…well, and every time I read a book. At first, I thought it was my imagination. Or maybe there really was something wrong with me after the accident. Maybe the accident had messed with my head. But…but this…this *thing*…started to happen. So—so, here it is." She paused to watch his reaction, a look of abject fear on her face. "Whenever I read a book, something in the book would happen or appear or be connected to my real life, to the real world, to me in my everyday life. Back then and even now, it's part of my life, part of who I am, but it's taken me so long to tell you because I guess I worried that it made me some sort of freak or like I couldn't lead a normal life. I had this secret that no one could see or detect except me, and telling you, telling anyone, was so scary for me in the beginning. Even now, although I've learned to accept it and embrace it as a gift, I fear others' reactions. Especially because sometimes it's just a little snippet or a coincidence that seems out of place or a feeling or a sentiment that relates to the book, which makes it all the more difficult to explain and define. When it happens and it's highly palpable, I can point to it and say, see, that's what I'm talking about! But more often than not, it's totally nebulous, like a vague apparition that leaves me questioning it. All I can say is that it is *real.* Oddly enough, now that I'm writing, I get it with my writing too." Breathing hard, she watched Adam then, her eyes flashing in the fervor to confess her secret. She added quickly, with finality, "So, for better or worse, it's part of me and I wanted you to know. I call it my Biblio."

Adam was sitting there, taking it all in, his face scrunched up in confusion and in a state of "Wait. What?" He opened his mouth to speak several times but quickly closed it again. Instead of trying to ask a bunch of questions, he decided on a different tact in the interest of time and in the interest of calming them both down. He said reassuringly, "I'm not sure I understand completely, and I think I'll need a bit of a tutorial on what you're talking about, but putting that aside for now, hey, listen—no matter what, I take you just as you are, always, and you never have to keep anything from me. Especially not something as big as this. Were you worried that I...I wouldn't want to *be* with you if you told me this?"

She glanced off toward the massive decrepit hotel building and back again at Adam before replying, "No, it wasn't that, exactly. It's been such a strange secret of mine for so long, and it's the one thing I've kept from you and from almost everyone, and I guess I just didn't want to freak you out or make you think I'm fibbing or trying to make something up for attention or to make myself special or different. And on the flip side, I didn't want you to think worse of me because I have this very unmanageable, undefinable, bizarre intuitive gift, and I guess I wanted to make sure you were okay with it and okay with it being a part of me before we agreed to get married."

At that, he stood up and took her into his arms, kissing the top of her head and rocking her back and forth as she melted into him.

He waited a while, both of them silent, and then finally said thoughtfully, "You know, Riley, look around this place with its faded, overgrown garden and its dilapidated, falling-down building." She pulled away from his chest and stared at their surroundings with curiosity. He continued, "Despite its state of disrepair, do you know what I've always thought about this town— where moguls of industry used to vacation and gamble, where history was made, where dreams came true, where you decided to set your first novel, *where you first kissed me?*"

She looked up at him, her eyes aflame with something fierce. Was he cutting through the mire to get to the essence? She waited with bated breath. He ventured, "I think there is something *magical* about this place, this town, this spot. Something magical and mystical and otherworldly. And you know what, Riley? That's what I think about *you* too. It's what I've always thought about you. You make connections, and sense things, and bring what is blurry into focus, into the light. I think you even gave me a piece of your magic that night we met at Nick's when I felt myself hovering over you and knowing you sensed me there. And just like that night, I'll always happily partake of whatever magic you possess, believing it, relishing it, wanting it, just as much as I want you. In fact, I can't think of a better, more adept, more perfectly positioned vessel to embody it than you, Riley Cartwright."

With sheer relief and joy, she began to cry, throwing herself into his arms as he stroked her hair and held her close. When she was able, she stated these words with definitive force, which would cut him to the quick and make him cleave to her all the more, "My Biblio, my magic (as you say), my reading, my writing, *you*—these are my ways to be real, to be present, to be tethered to this world, and a way to honor Kathy's life by living my own life to the fullest because she can't be here to live *her* life at all. And living my life to the fullest includes pursuing my dream for this book and for future books, a pursuit that will have a life of its own and will be formed from—and forged by—a piece of Kathy, a piece of me, and a piece of you. Something that will live on long after we're gone. I can't think of anything more magical and worthy of pursuit than that."

As tears filled his eyes, now mirroring hers, he murmured, "I agree." Then, clearing his throat, he asked softly with a tiny smile in his voice, "Does this mean you *will* marry me?"

"Yes," she answered simply, her mouth finding his, a kiss sealed by fate and trust, and by things unknown and unseen, but felt, always *felt*.

The End

About the Author

Amy Q. Barker is the author of the women's fiction novels *Rue*, *Punk*, and *Bibliointuitive*. Her books focus on the feel-good place where romance and drama meet.

Amy can usually be found reading the classics, walking the beaches of Siesta Key, or hiking in the woods near her home in Indiana, where she lives with her husband and several nearly tame wild birds. Amy holds a BA from Syracuse University and an MBA from Rensselaer Polytechnic Institute. She grew up in Spencerport, New York.

To connect with Amy, check out her Instagram @amyqbarker_author.

Thank you for reading Amy Q. Barker's imaginings set to words. If you enjoyed this book, please consider leaving an honest review on your favorite site.

Made in the USA
Columbia, SC
12 February 2022

56058409R00146